RUN TO GROUND

KATIE RUGGLE

sourcebooks
casablanca

Published by Sourcebooks Casablanca, an imprint of Sourcebooks, Inc.
P.O. Box 4410, Naperville, Illinois 60567-4410
(630) 961-3900
Fax: (630) 961-2168
www.sourcebooks.com

Printed and bound in the United States of America.
LSC 10 9 8 7 6 5 4 3

"Romantic suspense fans will enjoy the unusual setting, and Ruggle's ice-rescue certification adds an element of authenticity to the rescue descriptions."

—*Publishers Weekly* for *Hold Your Breath*

"*Hold Your Breath* will appeal to both readers of romance as well as mystery/suspense novels. [It is] a fantastic read. You do not want to miss it."

—*Book Briefs Book Review Blog*
for *Hold Your Breath*

"Katie Ruggle, you amaze me! What a perfectly clever plot, with smoking-hot characters and an arresting environment that begs to be the scene of the crime."

—*It's About the Book Blog* for *Hold Your Breath*

"If you like your romance with a lot of suspense, or your suspense with a bit of romance, like heroes that are sexy and a little dangerous, and heroines who are strong and can easily take care of themselves, then give this a try."

—*Book Gannet Reviews* for *Fan the Flames*

"Author Katie Ruggle has created an exciting, tension-filled series."

—**Heroesandheartbreakers.com** for *Fan the Flames*

"This series just keeps getting better! For outstanding romantic suspense, strong characters, and a fabulous plot that keeps thickening, read Katie Ruggle...and prepare to get burned by an amazing story."

—*Romance Junkies* for *Fan the Flames*

"I cannot read these books fast enough. Waiting for the next book to see what happens is going to be pure torture."
—*Fresh Fiction* for *Gone Too Deep*

"As this series draws to a close, the most fascinating of the heroines is introduced. Her story is both heartbreaking and uplifting at the same time. She's a sympathetic sweetheart who carries the reader along on her journey to emotional healing."
—*RT Book Reviews*, 4 Stars for *In Safe Hands*

Thank you to Lieutenant Mike Drees with the Rochester (MN) Police Department for patiently answering my thousand and one K9-related questions.

CHAPTER 1

THE NEW WAITRESS WAS HOT. SQUIRRELLY, BUT HOT.

Theo always got to the diner early for the K9 unit's breakfast and informal roll call. Those fifteen minutes before Otto and Hugh showed up usually were, if not exactly peaceful, at least a break from having to hide the mess he'd become. This morning, though, he was distracted by the way the dark-haired stranger kept trying not to stare at him. Since she didn't seem to be bothered by anyone else in the diner, Theo assumed his uniform was making her nervous—and her nerves were putting him on edge. He'd caught himself watching her four times already, and he'd only been in the diner for five minutes.

A mug thumped on the table in front of him, and Theo turned his frown toward Megan. They had a morning ritual: He scowled. She aggressively delivered his food and coffee. Neither said a word.

This morning, as Megan was turning away, Theo was almost tempted to break the silence. He caught himself before a question about the new server popped out of his mouth. Stopping the words just in time, he snatched up his coffee and took a drink, burning his tongue in the process. He set down the mug with enough force to make the coffee almost slosh over the rim. *Shit*.

Before Theo could stop himself, his gaze searched

out the new waitress again. She was delivering two plates of food to a table across the diner. By the look of concentration on her face and the exaggerated care she was taking, Theo assumed she was new to waiting tables. She was definitely new to Monroe, Colorado. If she'd been around, he would've noticed her. There was no doubt about that.

As she turned away from the table, smiling, their gazes caught for a second before she ducked her head and hurried toward the kitchen. He knew he shouldn't take it personally. Theo had the feeling she would have had the same response to any cop.

"Who's that?" Otto dropped onto the bench next to him.

Tearing away his gaze, Theo gave his fellow K9 officer a flat stare. "Move."

"No." Otto stretched out his legs until his lumberjack-sized boots bumped the opposite bench. "I always sit here."

Just for the past two months. Theo didn't want to say that, though. That might've led to talking about what had happened two months ago, and he *really* didn't want to discuss it. Still, he couldn't let it drop. "I'm not one of your wounded strays."

Otto made a noncommittal sound that heated Theo's simmering anger another few degrees. Before he could rip into Otto, Hugh slid into the opposite side of the booth.

"Hey." Hugh greeted them with his standard, easygoing grin. "Who's the new waitress?"

"You're not going to squeeze onto this bench, too?" Theo asked with thick sarcasm.

Hugh gave Theo an earnest look. "Did you want me to sit with you two? Because I can. It'll be cozy."

Several smart-assed retorts hovered on Theo's tongue, but he swallowed them down. All that would do was convince Hugh to move to Theo's and Otto's side of the table, and they'd be uncomfortable and awkward all through breakfast. Behind Hugh's placid exterior was a mile-high wall of stubbornness.

Theo stayed silent.

With a slight smirk, Hugh settled back on his side of the table. "Anything fun and exciting happen last night?"

"Eh," Otto said with a lift of one shoulder. "Carson Byers got picked up again."

Hugh frowned. "That's not fun. Or exciting. In fact, that's something that happens almost every shift. What was it this time?"

"Trespass."

"He was drunk and thought the Andersons' house was his again?"

"The Daggs' place this time."

"Wait. Isn't that on the other side of town?"

"Yep."

"Dumbass."

"Yep."

Only half listening, Theo let the other men's conversation wash over him. His gaze wandered to find the new server again. She was topping off the coffee mugs of the customers sitting at the counter as she listened to something Megan was telling her.

"I ran into Sherry at the gas station last night."

Otto's too-casual statement jerked Theo's attention back to their conversation.

Rubbing the back of his head, Hugh asked, "How's she doing?"

"Not good. But what do you expect when her dad—"

"Let me out." Theo cut off the rest of Otto's words, glaring at him until the other man slid out of the booth. As Theo stalked from the table, there was only silence behind him—a heavy, suffocating silence. He didn't have a destination in mind except *away*, but his feet carried him toward the new server as if they had a mind of their own.

The woman watched him, her blue eyes getting wider and wider, until he stopped in front of her. They stared at each other for several moments. She was even prettier and looked even more scared up close. There were dark shadows smudged beneath her eyes, and her face had a drawn, tight look. Her throat moved as she swallowed, and her eyes darted to the side. Theo tensed, his cop instincts urging him to chase her if she ran.

When she ran.

"Theo," Megan barked as she passed, "go sit down. You're being creepy."

He shot her a frown, but most of his attention was still on the new server. "What's your name?"

She swallowed again and tried to force a smile, but it quickly fell away. "Jules. Um…for Julie." Even in those few words, her Southern drawl was obvious.

"Last name?"

"Uh…Jackson." Her gaze jumped toward the door.

"Where are you from?" He couldn't stop asking questions. It was partly his ingrained curiosity, and partly a personal interest he couldn't seem to smother.

"Arkansas."

Theo called bullshit on that. While she'd said her last name too slowly, this had come quickly, as if she'd practiced her answer. He could see the tension vibrating through her, her body projecting the urge to flee. What was she running from? An abusive husband? The consequences of a crime she'd committed? "What brings you to Colorado?"

"It's…a nice state?" Her eyes squeezed closed for a second, as if she was mentally reprimanding herself.

Every glance at the door, every stifled flinch, every half-assed response made Theo more suspicious. "You move here by yourself?"

"I…um…" Her hunted gaze fixed on Megan's back, but the other server was occupied helping a little boy get ketchup out of a recalcitrant bottle and didn't see her silent plea. "I should get back to work."

"Wait." Without thinking, he reached for her arm.

"Theo." Hugh stood right behind him, and Theo's jaw tightened as his hand dropped to his side. Why did they feel a need to watch him like he was a ticking bomb? "Food'll be here soon."

Theo didn't want to return to the table, didn't want to eat, didn't want to talk about Sherry or anything else. What he did want was to find out more about the new, pretty, squirrelly waitress whose name may—but more likely may *not*—be Julie Jackson.

Jules.

He was tempted to send Hugh back to the table without him, but what was the point? All she would do was keep lying…badly. Later, in the squad car, he'd run her name, although "Julie Jackson" from Arkansas would produce enough hits to keep him busy for months.

He'd give it time. They were at the diner every morning. He'd have plenty of opportunities to try to get information.

Assuming she didn't skip town first.

Ignoring his screaming instincts—his curiosity—his *interest*—he gave a short, reluctant nod and returned to the table. He could wait.

Still, it was hard not looking back.

CHAPTER 2

One Week Earlier

"MR. ESPINA..." JULES'S VOICE CRACKED ON THE LAST syllable. Clearing her throat, she forced her fist to release the crumpled handful of skirt and tried again. "Mr. Espina, I need your help."

Mateo Espina didn't say a word. In fact, he didn't even twitch a muscle. It was a struggle not to stare at him. He was just so *different* than his brother that it was hard to believe the two were related. For over three years, Jules had worked for Luis Espina, and she'd never, ever been this nervous. Luis was a chatterbox who wore a constant, beaming, contagious smile on his round face. His brother, on the other hand, was all hard lines and angles, glaring eyes, and stubble. Even the tattoos peeking from his shirt collar and rolled-up cuffs looked angry.

Jules realized she'd been silent for much too long, and she had to hide her cringe. It had been almost impossible to set up this meeting with Mr. Espina, and she was crashing and burning not even five minutes and ten words in. As she opened her mouth to say who knew what, a bored voice interrupted.

"What can I get you two?"

Although Mr. Espina ordered a beer from the server, Jules stuck to water. The meeting would be hard enough with all of her wits about her. Besides, the sad fact was that she was broke. Drinks were the last thing on her stuff-I-need-to-buy list. Lawyers were number one. *Good* lawyers. *Miracle-working* lawyers.

"I was hoping," she said, "that you could give me a reference."

There was a reaction to that. It wasn't much of one—just the slightest lift of his eyebrow and twitch of a small muscle in his cheek.

"Although I wasn't charged with anything, I lost my CPA license and all my clients when Luis was investigated." The remembered terror and humiliation of being questioned by the FBI made her hands shake, and she clutched them together to keep them still. "I didn't give them any information about Luis's finances, though, even after they told me I'd be able to keep my license and my business if I did. My clients' confidentiality is sacred."

Instead of looking pleased by that, Mr. Espina's entire face drew tight, stiffening into a hard mask. His voice was smooth, deep, and as cold as ice. "Are you *threatening* me, Ms. Young?"

Horror flushed through her, turning her blood cold and then hot enough to burn. "No! No, God, no! I'm not an idiot! I mean, it was probably dumb of me to work as Luis's accountant when I knew he wasn't great at...well, coloring inside the lines, but I'm not trying to threaten you! I just wanted..."

The sheer futility of what she was attempting flooded her, and she started to stand. "Never mind. I'm sorry to have wasted your time. I'll figure something out."

"Sit." Something about his clipped tone made her obey before she realized what she was doing. "What do you want?"

"A job." Once again, the command in his voice had her answering before she considered whether it was wise to be so blunt. "I know Luis would give me a reference and, well, new employer contact information, if he wasn't..." She paused, trying to think of a polite term. "Dealing with more serious concerns right now."

Those dark, dark eyes regarded her over his raised beer for a long time. Jules let him stare, determined not to break again. "You want me to hire you?" he finally asked.

"Oh, not *you*!" she blurted, and then cringed. "Sorry. That came out wrong. I'd be happy to work with you, of course. It's just...I have expenses, so I need to have more than one client—unless I find a single client with extensive accounting needs. I was thinking I could work for some of Luis's colleagues, since they'd probably not care about the whole FBI thing, as long as I know what I'm doing and can keep my mouth shut."

Mr. Espina didn't hurry to answer her. Instead, he eyed her for another painfully long time before finally speaking. "Anyone specific in mind?"

"The Blanchetts?" she suggested tentatively. Most of Luis's business associates had been names on a computer screen to her. At best, she'd met a few in passing. "Maybe the Jovanovics?"

He choked—actually *choked*—on his beer when she said the second name. Carefully placing the bottle on the table, he sat back and closed his eyes for several seconds.

"So that's a no on the Jovanovics?" Disappointment flooded her. They'd been her best prospect. With their hands in what seemed like every not-quite-legal pie, their empire was huge. She'd imagined that the Jovanovics needed a good accountant—and a discreet one.

"It's a no. On the Blanchetts, too."

"Oh." Her disappointment was quickly heading toward despair. "Is there anyone you *could* recommend?"

"No."

That single bald word made Jules's eyes burn with threatening tears. She wasn't a crier. Even as a little girl, she'd rarely cried. It was just that Mr. Espina had been her only hope of getting the kind of job she needed to afford the kind of *lawyers* she needed. Her tough, sixteen-year-old brother had actually *cried* on the phone with her the night before—cried and begged to live with her. If Sam was breaking, God only knew how bad it was getting for him and the younger kids. This had been her one clear chance to get the money she needed to help them. Staring at Mr. Espina's expressionless face, she felt the last of her dwindling optimism being sucked out of her, leaving Jules hopeless and planless and heartbroken.

She bit the inside of her cheek hard enough to shock herself out of self-pity. This wasn't the end of her dream. This couldn't be the end. She'd keep fighting for her brothers and her sister until the youngest, Dee, turned eighteen. Even if Jules was broke and lawyerless, she'd still do whatever it took to get her siblings out of that house.

Jules stood as well as she could on shaking legs and said, "Okay. Thank you, Mr. Espina."

"Sit."

This time, she managed to resist the compulsion to obey and moved until she was standing next to the table.

Digging in her purse, she pulled out a crumpled ten and laid it next to her untouched water. Even though Mr. Espina hadn't been much—or any—help, he had met with her. Also, he hadn't killed her. The least she could do was buy his beer.

"Thank you for your help, but I need to go now." She tried and failed to force a smile. "Job hunting to do." She turned to leave.

"Ms. Young." Automatic courtesy made her stop and look over her shoulder. "No matter what lawyer you hire, you will never get legal custody of your brothers and sister."

Her entire body jerked as if he'd stabbed her. It wasn't only the shock of realizing that Mr. Espina—a stranger, and a terrifying one at that—was aware of her family's situation. She'd never allowed herself to consider that she might fail to get custody. Hearing the words out loud was more horrible than she'd ever imagined.

"How did you... *What?*" she wheezed, her hand pressed to her chest.

Mr. Espina gestured toward her recently vacated seat, and she managed the few steps back to the table and plopped down on the bench. Her knees had gone even more wobbly, and she knew she had to sit before she fell.

"As you said, you could've made it worse for my brother. I appreciate that you didn't."

Her stunned brain didn't register the words for a minute. Confused, Jules stared at him. "Then why aren't you helping me?"

"I am helping you." He pulled out his cell phone and tapped at his screen. Even the way he did that screamed aggression. Jules's cell chirped from her purse. Instead of checking the text, she kept her gaze fixed on Mr. Espina. "Call Dennis Lee. I just sent you his number. He'll get you what you need to take your family...elsewhere."

"Take?" she repeated, knowing she sounded dazed. The conversation felt surreal.

"Ms. Young." His gaze sharpened as he leaned forward slightly. It was the most engagement he'd shown for the entire meeting, and she mimicked his posture before she realized what she was doing. "Your father's Alzheimer's is getting worse. Your stepmother is not a good person. Your brothers and sister are in a bad situation. You need to get them out."

"But..." Her voice lowered until barely any sound escaped. "Kidnapping?"

"Sometimes you have to trust what you feel in your gut to be right, even if others are telling you it's wrong."

The idea was overwhelming, terrifying, and wonderful, all at the same time. For years, through countless frustrating, futile, expensive custody battles, Jules had followed the rules. It had gotten her nowhere. Her siblings were still stuck in hell, and Jules was broke and desperate enough to work for criminals. Maybe it was time to change the rules. Maybe, if she started playing dirty, her family could win for once.

Maybe instead of working for criminals, she should become one.

"It'd never work." The tempting dream of just stealing her brothers and sister away crumbled. "There'd be an Amber Alert. Their pictures—my picture—would be everywhere. We wouldn't even make it out of the state before someone would recognize us. My stepmother would paint me as a monster. No one would believe that she…" Jules couldn't finish the thought. It was too awful. "I'd go to prison, and the kids would lose their last hope of escape."

Mr. Espina didn't look bothered. "I'll have a talk with your father's wife. After that, she won't report the children's disappearance."

"Uh…what kind of talk?"

"Nothing violent." He seemed amused by her wary tone. "I'll just make her aware that I have information she won't want getting out."

Jules clenched her hands into fists. "That won't work. She won't care. I've been trying to get people to believe me for years, but Courtney has the perfect-mother act down."

His unruffled expression did not waver. "It will work. I have video."

"Video?" Her stomach lurched. "You can't make that public. Sam…"

He raised a hand, and her objection trailed off. "The threat will be enough. She won't go to the police."

Jules studied his face as she chewed the inside of her lip. "She won't just let them go. She'll hire private investigators if she has to."

"If that happens, you'll deal with it."

"I… Yes." His calm certainty brought a trickle of optimism. She *could* deal with a PI, just one person searching for them, rather than every member of law enforcement, every concerned person who saw their pictures on TV or the Internet. Mr. Espina's threat just made kidnapping—as crazy as it seemed—a viable possibility.

"Ms. Young." She was jerked out of her thoughts as Mr. Espina pushed a laptop case across the table toward her. Jules's gaze bounced from the bag to his face and back again as she tried to figure out what he was doing. "As thanks for what you did for Luis. He's a pain in the ass, but he's my brother, and I love him."

"But…"

"Consider it a bonus that Luis never got around to giving you." After dropping a few bills on the table, Mr. Espina picked up her crumpled ten and held it out to Jules. With numb fingers, she automatically accepted it. He slid from his seat and moved toward the exit. Jules stared at his back, too bewildered by the entire meeting to call after him. Instead, she watched as he walked out the door.

Refocusing on the laptop bag, she cautiously pulled it to her. It was lighter than she'd expected, and she lowered it to her lap before tugging open the heavy zipper. Inside was a bulky envelope.

Her teeth closing on the sore spot where she'd bitten the inside of her cheek earlier, Jules unfastened the clasp without taking the envelope out of the bag. The unsealed flap opened easily, and she tilted the envelope so she could see inside.

Catching a glimpse of the contents, she restrained a gasp that would've carried through the bar and down the street. Instead, she made a small sound, part squeak and part sigh, touching the stacks of twenty-dollar bills with a disbelieving brush of her fingers.

Her heart was racing as thoughts ran through her mind, too quickly for her to make sense of any of them. The first thing she was able to grab hold of was the idea that she'd just been given a whole lot of money—most likely *dirty* money. Jules thought she'd accepted her decision to dive into a life of crime, but the sight of all that cash shocked her.

I can't keep the money, one part of her brain kept telling her. She barely knew Mr. Espina. For goodness' sake, she still called him *Mr. Espina*. Who handed off stacks of cash like that to a near stranger?

Apparently, Mr. Espina did. She supposed that was one more thing she knew about Mr. Espina, then.

A hysterical giggle bubbled into her throat, threatening to escape. She swallowed, holding down the laughter that would only draw curious stares. Jules did not want any stares, curious or otherwise—not when she was toting a bag full of dirty money.

Should she keep it? *Could* she keep it?

For her family? *Yes.* Yes, she could.

Mr. Espina's words rang in her brain, cementing her resolve. She'd wasted enough time, left her siblings in that hellhole for too long. It was time to do what she had to, no matter how badly it scared her.

She resealed the clasp and zipped the bag with hands that trembled even more than before. Jules was surprised her entire body wasn't vibrating with nerves. Gathering the precious bag and her purse, Jules stood and hurried for the door as fast as she could without looking like she was rushing to leave the bar with a bagful of money.

Once she was in her elderly Camry with the air conditioner running, the windows up, and the doors locked, she called the number Mr. Espina had texted her. *Dennis Lee*. Jules knew that if she didn't contact him immediately, she might talk herself out of it.

As the line rang, Jules tapped a still-shaking finger against the steering wheel.

"This is Dennis."

The smooth tone took her off guard. Maybe she'd been watching too many movies, but she'd expected a "disappearance expert" to answer the phone with a barked "*What?!*" or even just a surly grunt. Dennis sounded like a college professor answering calls in his office.

"Hello?"

Jules jumped. "Oh. Sorry. Yes. I...um. I got your number from Mr. Espina. He thought you might be able to help me...plan a trip." She winced. Her attempt at code made her sound like an idiot.

"Plan a trip?" Apparently, Dennis agreed with her; his words carried more than a hint of amusement. "I'm a travel agent now?"

"Well, I..." She trailed off, flustered. Did he really want her to tell him flat out what she needed? Shouldn't they be on a secure line or something? Although Jules wasn't positive what a secure line entailed, she was fairly sure it didn't involve cell phones in a parking lot at five thirty in the evening. "Could we meet somewhere to talk about this?"

He was silent for a long, long time. As she waited for him to respond, she felt a trickle of sweat follow the line of her spine until it met the waistband of her skirt.

"Let's take a walk," he finally said, and her head fell back against the seat in relief. "Are you familiar with Collins Park?"

"Yes." Glancing at the digital clock, she did some mental math. Taking the rush-hour traffic into account, she'd be able to make it there in about an hour.

"I'll meet you by the dinosaurs at six."

"Oh, but…" Her protests fell into empty air. He'd already ended the call. Jules let out a puff of breath and tossed her phone into the passenger's seat. Reversing out of the parking spot, she set her jaw.

She was going to do this. All her efforts to follow the rules had gotten her nowhere. She'd never get legal custody, and her brothers and sister *needed* to get out of that house. If she had to become a kidnapper to make that happen, so be it.

This is it. Jules, former lifelong rule follower, was jumping across the line into felon-hood.

As she flew out of the parking lot, Jules was a bit disappointed that her tires didn't squeal.

CHAPTER 3

Present Day

THE COP WAS BACK.

Jules fumbled with the sugar packets she was refilling as she tried to watch without him noticing. She had to admit that he was gorgeous. In her old life—her other life—she might have flirted with him. Now, she looked at the uniform and all she could see was the prison time it represented. She wanted to hide—almost enough to duck into the walk-in cooler in back and not come out until he was gone. Jules's fear of the cooler, however—with its heavy, safe-like door and exterior light switch and horribly claustrophobic feel—was just slightly greater than her fear of facing the hot police officer.

"Seriously?" Megan muttered, making Jules jump and scatter sugar packets across the counter. "He's here again? Why can't he just keep his cranky ass at home and stop ruining everyone else's day?"

Her laugh came out as more of a gasp, drawing a sharp look from Megan.

"You all right? Don't you let him bother you, okay? He's surly to everyone, so it's nothing you did. He didn't used to be this bad, at least not until... Well, let's not talk about that. Want to do rock-paper-scissors to see who has to take table four?"

Jules's laugh came easier that time. She was relieved that Megan thought Jules's nerves were because of Theo's crabbiness, rather than the fact that he was a cop. The last thing she needed was for Megan to be suspicious of her too. "Sure."

Under the cover of the counter, they held their fists out and chanted quietly, "One, two, three!"

Jules sighed at her smothered rock. "Shoot. Well, thanks for the offer."

"If I were a nice person, I'd take the pissy cop's table anyway." When Jules looked at her hopefully, Megan smirked. "I said 'if.' I'm truly not a nice person."

Jules watched Megan walk toward one of her tables. Her shoulders lifting and dropping again in a sigh, Jules stiffened her spine. She just needed to be confident. She also needed to not let the cop's air of authority—as well as his muscled forearms and pretty dark-brown eyes—reduce her to the babbling idiot she'd become the last time he'd been at the diner. For goodness' sake, she'd messed up her name. Her *name*. If she wanted to survive in her new life, she needed to step up her game. Firming her jaw, she picked up a coffeepot and headed to Theo's table.

He watched her, his frown deepening with each step, and she fought the urge to slow or, better yet, turn tail and run.

"Morning." She turned the mug in front of him right side up with shaky fingers. His wary eyes—almost black and alarmingly perceptive—took in everything, including, she was sure, her obvious unease. "Did you need a menu?"

Jules caught herself before he could respond.

"Sorry." Her flush prickled her chest and moved up to her face to warm her cheeks. "Of course you don't need a menu. You probably know everything on there by now. Well, I'm guessing you do. I've only seen you here once, but Megan mentioned you're a regular."

Abruptly, Jules stopped talking. More of the nervous babble pressed on her lungs, wanting out. Afraid to open her mouth again in case she started talking and wasn't able to stop until she told this man—this police officer!—everything he shouldn't know, she forced a smile and stayed quiet. She was turning out to be a terrible felon.

"Number three," he said after another pause just long enough to make her uncomfortable. "Scrambled."

"Got it." Jules scribbled down the order, relieved to have something to focus on other than his too-intense gaze. He looked at her like he could see everything about her, and there were so many things she wanted to keep hidden. When she glanced up, she kept her eyes away from his, focusing on his left earlobe instead. "That'll be right out."

After picking up the coffeepot again, she began to turn around, relieved. A sound behind her, something halfway between a masculine grunt and a throat clearing, made her stop reluctantly. Jules focused on his other earlobe this time, trying not to show her renewed panic. "Was there something else you needed?"

"Where are you staying?" He bit off each word, making him sound like he was angry he had to speak to her.

The mild, unfocused fear blossomed into terror. Why

was he asking? Was he investigating her? His frown deepened when she took a beat too long to answer, and she rushed out her response. "Um…in Monroe."

"Where?"

Her paranoia was feeding her panic, and she gave a vague wave toward the north. "On the edge of town."

If he narrowed his eyes any more, he'd be squinting. "The blue house off of Orchard Street?"

"No." Her feet moved of their own volition, and she took a step toward the door. This job was too important for her to run out on her second day, but the cop's questioning was pushing her to the point where she just wanted to escape, paycheck or no paycheck.

"The old Garmitt place, then." It was a statement instead of a question, and the accuracy of the guess made her eyes widen despite herself. Jules knew fear and guilt must be plastered all over her face. "Heard someone had moved in there."

"Uh…" Her mind raced as she scrambled to think of the best way to respond, to save this conversation from the quickly approaching crash and burn heading her way. "I'm not sure." She barely caught herself before closing her eyes in exasperation. *That* was her clever save?

"Your address is Thirty-Two Blank Hill Lane." Again, he said what should've been a question with such certainty that it came out as a statement of fact. "Did you buy it?"

"No." Running was beginning to sound better and better. Jules was willing to do pretty much anything to get away from this man, this *cop*, who knew too much already.

"You rent then?" At her nod, he studied her. She stared back, determined not to say more. Every line in his body was held tightly, from the hard line of his mouth to his forearms to his erect spine. "What brings you to town?" he finally asked.

Her mouth opened, but nothing emerged as her thoughts bounced against each other in a chaotic mess. "This job?" Her voice was pitched too high, and the end of her sentence rose, turning it into a question. Jules resisted the urge to smack herself. Between her twitchy behavior and asinine answers, she knew that, even if he hadn't been suspicious before, he would know for sure now that something wasn't right. Her shoulders curled in as she wished for the power of invisibility. Either that or better acting skills—or *any* acting skills.

"What the hell, Theo?" Megan appeared out of nowhere, grasping Jules's elbow and tugging. Although she jumped initially, Jules relaxed and allowed herself to be pulled a few steps away from the extremely awkward conversation—or interrogation? "I finally find an employee who can do basic math and doesn't spit on people's eggs, and *she's* the one you inflict yourself on? Drink your coffee and be all broody, like you normally are. *Quietly* broody."

The tiny muscle in Theo's jaw pulsed with tension. Jules didn't breathe as she waited for him to react. There was strained silence for several seconds before Theo spoke.

"Which one spits?"

"You missed my point." Whatever else Megan was going to say was interrupted by the thump of the front entrance as it closed behind some new customers. "Be right with you!" Her gaze never left Theo's face. In turn, he never looked away or flinched. The non-panicked corner of Jules's brain was impressed with both of them.

"What's up?" Another cop came to a stop next to the booth, reaching to gently bump Theo's shoulder with his fist. Although the newcomer was wearing a congenial smile, there was a coiled tension to him. The way he placed his body almost, but not quite, between them and Theo said a lot. It was protective in a got-your-back kind of way, but it also showed that Theo had the lead, that the new guy wasn't taking over the situation.

"Theo's scaring my new waitress." Megan's glare shot toward the new arrival. "The one who can do math."

"And doesn't spit." Theo's deadpan delivery made Jules start, and an unbidden smile curled her mouth. Their gazes met, and the cop's eyes seemed to soften for the shortest of moments. Even before Jules was certain she saw it, it was gone.

"Are those your only hiring qualifications? Adding, subtracting, and saliva control? T, maybe we need to look for a new place for our breakfast meetings." There was humor in the cop's voice, although his gaze was ready and watchful, moving from Theo to Megan to Jules.

Turning toward the kitchen while keeping a firm grip on Jules's arm, Megan said over her shoulder, "*Your* food is safe, Hugh."

His snort followed them out of the dining area.

"Sorry it took me so long to rescue you," Megan apologized under her breath as she slammed through the kitchen door. Vicki glanced up from the grill, startled, but the cooking bacon quickly demanded her attention again. "I'd forgotten how weird everyone in this town gets with strangers. After you've been here a while, the newness will wear off, and things will go back to normal. And for Theo, normal is being all moody in his corner, muttering and glaring."

Jules's laugh sounded stilted, even to her own ears, and Megan gave her a concerned look.

"He didn't say anything offensive to you, did he?"

"Oh no." Waving a hand to dismiss the earlier conversation, Jules tried to force some sincerity into her reassuring smile. "He was just curious, I think. I'm just...awkward with strangers." *Especially strange police officers asking probing questions.*

Megan eyed her doubtfully. "So you're okay? You're not going to quit and leave me?"

Now that Jules's heart had a chance to slow down, her fear seemed a little extreme for the basic questions the cop had been asking. She reran their conversation in her mind and felt a little sheepish. There'd been nothing strange about his questions, considering she was new to town. Theo's manner had been abrupt, but from what Megan had said, that was his standard behavior. *He doesn't know*, she tried to reassure herself. *He doesn't know, or you'd already be in handcuffs in the back of his car.*

"Jules?" Megan's voice rose. "Are you staying?"

Yanking herself out of her warring paranoia and common sense, she sent her boss a smile. "No. I mean, yes, I'm staying, and no, I'm not quitting. Shouldn't we get back to the front now?"

"Yes," Vicki's testy voice answered from the grill. "Get out of my kitchen before I chop up your bony asses and add you to today's chowder."

Megan widened her eyes at Jules in a mock-terrified way, and Jules had to smother a laugh.

"We're going," Megan said, shooing Jules toward the front and following close behind. "Sorry, Vicki!" There was an only slightly mollified grunt behind them.

As soon as they emerged into the dining area, Jules shot a nervous glance toward Theo's table and swallowed a groan. Now there were *three* cops waiting for her. Her shoulders drooped for a second before she stiffened her spine. There were five more occupied tables in her section, and Jules needed to get to work. Giving Megan a final tiny wave, Jules headed toward the new customers, grabbing a fresh coffeepot on the way.

Deciding to get the scariest table over with first, Jules forced herself not to slow as she approached the cops. "Morning." She busied herself pouring coffee into the two new guys' mugs. "What can I get you?" Proud that her voice had wobbled only slightly, she topped off Theo's cup and then dared to look at the men.

That was a mistake.

They were all staring at her. Only the one Megan had called Hugh was smiling, but all three were watching her with assessing gazes. Jules gripped the handle of the coffeepot tighter. *Don't run, don't run, don't run,* she repeated in her head. *They don't know you. They don't know what you've done. Quit acting like an idiot.*

She couldn't help it. Panic was rising, threatening to blow off the top of her head. If her fingers squeezed the handle any harder, it was going to crumble to dust in her fist. "Sorry!" she blurted, knowing she was talking too fast but unable to stop. "Let me run and see if anyone else needs coffee, and then I'll put the pot back. I need two hands for my notebook and pen, since I'm still writing down orders. I'm sure I'll be memorizing them soon, and I'll know what you guys get without having to ask, but everything is new right now, since this is only my second day working here, so if you could just give me a minute…"

Sucking in a quick breath when she finally managed to pause, she took advantage of the cops' startled reactions and darted toward her next table.

"Wait!" Hugh called after her, but she pretended not to hear as she smiled at the man sitting three booths down.

She started to raise the coffeepot to fill his mug, but she hesitated when she saw how hard her hand was shaking. As she tried to calm her wild nerves, she focused on the man at the table. The best word to describe him was "nondescript." Jules got the feeling that she could stare at him for hours, but even then she'd only be able to give the vaguest description of his features. Average height, average weight, washed-out hair and eyes that weren't really any color at all, even features, and bland clothes. Forgettable. A study in beige. Looking at the man was almost soothing after the dramatic smack in the face that was Theo, with his flashing dark eyes, demanding questions, and muscular form. Shaking off the urge to peek over her shoulder, she forced a smile for the bland man. "Coffee?"

"Yes, please." He gave his mug a small nudge in her direction. The beige stranger had a voice as unremarkable as the rest of him. "I'm Norman Rounds."

"Jules," she replied automatically as she poured his coffee. Although she hadn't blurted out her last name, she still mentally reprimanded herself. *Julie Jackson. Julie Jackson. Julie Jackson.* Juliet Young was no more, and her family's safety depended on her remembering that.

Norman's voice brought her out of her head. "You're new."

"Yes." She felt so *noticed*. Maybe Dennis should've sent them to a bigger city, where they could've blended into the crowd.

"Where're you from?"

"Arkansas." The lie rolled off her tongue, and she resisted the urge to smile proudly. That was better. Now she just had to learn to do that when faced with a cute cop.

"Really?" Norman's tone barely changed, but the faintest note of skepticism made Jules's inner alarm begin to chirp. Why would he question that? He leaned toward her, and his expressionless face suddenly seemed unnerving rather than bland. "You running from something?"

Barely resisting the urge to lurch back a step, Jules frantically reran their conversation in her head. There was nothing she'd said that had given her away, so why had he jumped to that conclusion unless he knew something? Even the nosy, hot cop hadn't guessed, and she'd been a lot calmer—*normal*, even—with Norman Rounds. Did he know? She stared at him, as if her gaze could strip off his overly normal exterior and reveal his true intentions. Had her stepmother hired him? Was he a private investigator? He couldn't be—right?

Norman leaned even closer, and this time, Jules couldn't stop herself from taking a step back. She could barely keep herself from racing out of the diner, from grabbing the kids and running out of this whole *town*. As if sensing that Jules was about to flee, Norman froze, his unnerving gaze locked on her.

He doesn't know. If he did, he'd be dragging me out of the diner himself, or calling for the cops a few booths away to arrest me. With a huge effort of will, Jules stood still, clutching the coffeepot, trying to calm her racing mind and think of how to answer, what to say to keep him from being even more suspicious.

Norman shifted ever so slightly, his body tensing as the mild mask slipped even more. *He knows.* Although she tried to tell herself she was being paranoid again, that he was just a harmless, oblivious guy—albeit a strange one—it didn't work. Her instincts were shouting at her that she and the kids were in danger.

She opened her mouth, still unsure of the best way to reply, when a growly voice interrupted. "What's going on here?"

Her head whipped around. Theo was standing right next to her, so close that his arm was almost touching hers. This time, however, Theo's glare wasn't directed at her. Instead, all of his angry attention was focused on Norman.

"Are you bothering this woman?" Theo demanded, shifting so he was ever so slightly in front of Jules, as if shielding her from harm.

A rush of relief and gratitude hit her. Theo's take-charge manner was exponentially more attractive when he was defending her.

Norman's bland expression had returned, which upped Jules's suspicions even more. A normal person would at least flinch. As she knew from firsthand experience, Theo was hugely intimidating. "Of course not. Jules and I were just getting to know each other."

With Theo's back to her, Jules couldn't see his

expression, but there was disbelief in the tight lines of his shoulders. *His very broad shoulders.* Jules quickly shook the thought out of her head. Now was not the time. In fact, there was never a good time for her to be attracted to a cop.

"Why don't you just let her do her job, Rounds?" Theo's voice was even and calm, but there was a menace to him that would've left her shaking if it had been directed at her.

Instead of looking worried, Norman seemed almost amused. "Of course. Carry on, Jules. We can talk later."

"No," Theo snapped. "No talking later. Just eat your breakfast peacefully and then leave."

There was a tense silence before Norman said, "Sure."

After a long moment, Theo turned to face Jules, and she was startled by his proximity. It wasn't nearly as scary as it had been earlier, when Megan had saved her from him. Now *Theo* had turned into her hero…and the oddness of that made her smile. Theo's gaze lowered to her mouth, pausing there for a moment before he abruptly turned and headed back to his booth.

Jules watched him join the other two cops. Looking up, Hugh caught Jules's gaze. His expression changed before she could get a bead on what he was thinking, and he widened his eyes in an exaggerated pleading expression. "Can we order now? Please? We're so hungry it's possible we might *die* if we're not fed soon."

Residual relief made her want to laugh. The third cop whose name she didn't know looked amused, but Theo's scowl had returned, even more ferocious than before.

"Be right there," she called, her voice only slightly shaky. Turning back to Norman, she gave him a quick, insincere smile. "I'll be back in a minute to take your order." Before he could respond, she darted away toward the counter.

She returned the coffeepot to its warming station and pulled her notebook and pen from her pocket. As she hurried over to take the cops' orders, she marveled that she was actually *relieved* to be at Theo's table when, just five minutes earlier, she'd been anxious to leave it.

Now that she was away from Norman's odd and probing gaze, Jules began doubting her reaction. He was a strange guy, sure, but it was highly unlikely he was an investigator or that he knew anything about her except that she didn't sound like she came from Arkansas. She had to keep her guard up, though. In this new life of hers, pretty much anyone could be a threat. She tried not to glance at Norman three booths over as she smiled at the three cops—including her crabby, reluctant hero. "Sorry about the wait. What can I get you?"

It was all a matter of what—or who—was the *biggest* threat.

"Viggy, here!"

The Belgian Malinois huddled in a forlorn heap on the far side of his kennel. He didn't even turn his head at the command. As Theo stared at the dog, guilt and grief churning inside him, chewing away at his carefully constructed wall of numbness, he resisted the urge to punch the concrete wall dividing the enclosures. *Damn you, Don.*

"Can't really blame him."

Hands fisting, Theo whirled to face Hugh.

"Just saying," Hugh continued in his calm voice. "He's lost Don. It'll be hard for him to trust that you won't leave him, too."

Although Hugh pretended to be talking about Viggy, Theo knew the words were directed toward him, were *about* him. The well-meant but heavy-handed platitude made Theo want to punch Hugh in the throat. Theo should be used to that urge, since he'd been feeling it pretty much constantly—about everyone with whom he came into contact—for almost two months. Closing his eyes, Theo drew in an audible breath through his nose, grasping for calm. It wasn't in him anymore, though. There was no serenity, no peace. All he had to offer was guilt and rage and grief and barely leashed violence. He took a second breath, determined to control it.

"I know." That sounded almost calm, although the way Hugh's mouth tucked in at one corner showed that his friend knew Theo was faking it. Giving up on convincing Hugh that he wasn't a raging mess, Theo turned back to the dog.

"Viggy." There wasn't even a twitch of an ear. "Here."

"Calling him isn't working. You need to go get him, or he'll just keep ignoring your commands."

Although Hugh's tone was even and not judgmental at all, another surge of anger flashed through Theo. He knew too well how Viggy felt, the bone-deep sadness that made it impossible for anything else to matter. If he went and forced Viggy out of his corner, it wouldn't help. It wouldn't bring Don back. It wouldn't make Viggy accept that Theo was his partner now.

"No," he snapped. It sounded harsh, so Theo tried again, attempting to moderate his tone for the second time in as many minutes. "Thanks for the advice, but there's no point."

"The point is that you have to figure out a way to get through to him, or you'll never be partners."

Partners. His insides flinched. Partners died, leaving Theo and Viggy behind to try to scrape together what remained of their battered souls. Partnerships were overrated. It'd be better—safer—to continue to walk a solitary path. He glanced at the huddled dog, the very picture of misery. Viggy had already figured that out. Why was Theo even trying to bond with the dog? He could never replace Don, especially now that Theo was a hollowed-out, useless shell.

Unable to say anything or even look at Hugh, Theo turned and stalked out of the kennel. Alone.

CHAPTER 4

Five Days Earlier

AS THE SCHOOL RESOURCE OFFICER LED JULES TO THE office, she shivered. Although she tried to blame it on the cranked-up air-conditioning, she knew the cold air wasn't the reason. This was it. These were her last few seconds to change her mind, to not go down the road of crime. She knew there was no turning back, though. Sam, Tio, Ty, and Dee had to get out of that house.

With the SRO's attention fixed on the hall in front of him, Jules forcefully rubbed her eyes, trying to generate some redness. Her acting skills were minimal, and tears on command were way beyond her abilities. There was a reason why she'd been stage manager rather than the female lead in her high school's production of *Bye Bye Birdie*.

"Thank you," she told the SRO as she stepped through the office door he held open for her. He dipped his head to acknowledge her thanks and then left. Mrs. Juarez was behind the high counter, just as she'd been for the four years Jules had attended Lincoln High School, and probably twenty years before that.

"Hi, Mrs. Juarez."

Recognition lit the older woman's face. "Juliet Young! How good to see you again."

"You too." Despite the circumstances, Jules felt a flicker of nostalgia. "How are you?"

Mrs. Juarez rolled her eyes. "It's the usual zoo here. There are always those few troublemakers, but I suppose they make life interesting. Not that you would know anything about being a problem child, since you were always an angel. What brings you in here?"

It wasn't hard to put a quaver in her voice. "My dad... isn't doing well. Courtney is with him, so I told her I'd pick up the kids and take them to the hospital."

"Oh, I'm so sorry." Mrs. Juarez hurried around to the front of the counter and enveloped her in a hug, sending a wave of guilt crashing over Jules. "You poor things."

"Thank you." She forced a smile, feeling like the worst scum in the universe. The thought that Mrs. Juarez might be blamed for releasing the kids to her occurred to Jules, but she forced the fresh surge of guilt from her mind. "Could you get the boys out of class?"

After a final squeeze, Mrs. Juarez released her and bustled behind the counter to sit in front of her computer screen. "Of course. Let's see...Sebastian is in Mr. Hendrick's class first period, Horatio is with Ms. Garnett and...sorry, dear, what's your other brother's name?"

Jules was impressed she knew two out of three off the top of her head. "Titus."

"How could I forget that little scoundrel?" Mrs. Juarez chuckled, tapping at the keyboard. Ty must not have done anything *too* bad, though, judging by her amused tone. "Those twins are smart ones. Only thirteen and already freshmen. Very impressive."

As Mrs. Juarez made the calls to the three class-rooms, Jules caught herself before she could start to fidget, to shift from foot to foot and tap her fingers against her leg. She forced herself to be still, not wanting her twitchiness to give away her nervousness. If her father really had been hospitalized, it would be understandable for Jules to be upset, but there'd be no reason for her to be nervous.

It was just a few minutes before Tio arrived, quickly followed by Sam and Ty. Only Tio opened his arms for a hug, but Jules wasn't surprised. Sam didn't like to be touched, and Ty was at the stage where he found public hugs embarrassing. She squeezed Tio, pulling his lanky body close and getting a momentary release from the tension that gripped her insides.

"Thank you, Mrs. Juarez," she called over her shoulder as they left, trying to resist shoving the boys out the door. Their presence made the plan seem suddenly plausible, and she wanted to grab all three and tear out of the school.

"Of course, dear. Please tell your father I'm thinking of him."

"I will." Giving the receptionist a final, forced smile, Jules closed the office door behind them and hurried after her brothers. They obviously felt the same need to flee, since she had to jog to keep up with their long strides. That could've also been because even the twins, at thirteen, were already significantly taller than she was.

All four of them were quiet as they pushed through the exterior doors and stepped into the muggy heat. When Ty opened his mouth, Jules shook her head. Even outside the school, she felt the creeping sense of being watched. She wondered if she'd feel secure when they were in her car, or when they had left Florida, or maybe when they were ensconced in their new lodgings. Something told her she'd never feel completely safe again, but she quickly slammed the door on that thought. This was getaway time. She had to concentrate on that.

She opened the trunk with a press of the key fob button, and the guys tossed in their backpacks. Tio grunted as he swung his off his shoulder, and Jules's eyebrows rose as she looked at his overstuffed pack. The zippers looked like they were straining to stay closed. As she shut the trunk, she just hoped he'd included a change of clothes along with whatever other must-brings he'd packed.

The silence continued until they were loaded into the car, the twins in the back, and Jules had turned out of the parking lot onto a quiet residential street.

Sam's voice was the first to break the silence. "T-thanks, Ju."

Unable to resist, Jules reached over to squeeze his arm. She released him quickly, before he could get uncomfortable and pull away. "Sorry I couldn't get y'all sooner."

"That's because you had to go all outlaw to get it done," Ty said, bouncing in his seat. "That was awesome, like a prison break or something."

When Tio didn't say anything, Jules glanced at his tense face in the rearview mirror. "You okay, T?"

He didn't answer for several seconds. Jules bounced her gaze between the road and her youngest half-brother's face.

"It was difficult to decide what to pack," he finally said.

Jules chewed on the inside of her lip. It figured that this would be hardest on Tio, since Courtney mostly left him alone. Change wasn't his favorite thing. "I know. Are you in the middle of a project?"

"Seed dormancy. I'm working on reducing pre-harvest sprouting."

"Sorry you had to leave it." Attempting to lighten his mood, she sent him a smile in the rearview mirror. "Unless that's what you have stuffed in your backpack?"

Although she'd been joking, his response was solemn. "No. I brought the data files, though."

Her stomach lurched. "You didn't bring your laptop, did you?"

"Course not," Ty answered for him. "We didn't bring any electronics that could be traced. T's stuff is on a flash drive. Oh, and I turned on all our cell phones and hid them on the Gator the groundskeeper guy uses. That way, it'll look like we're at school if someone tries to use our phones to track us."

"Smart, Ty."

He shrugged, obviously trying to look less pleased at the praise than he actually was. "It was Sam's idea."

Turning into the St. Francis School parking lot, she glanced at Sam. "Good thinking, Sam."

His head was turned toward the window, so she couldn't see his expression. "I saw it in a m-m-m..." His frustrated exhale was audible. "On TV."

Frowning, she pulled into a visitor's parking spot. The stuttering worried her, but so did grabbing Dee, and kidnapping trumped all other problems at the moment. "I have new phones for you. First, though, let's get Dee."

Ty whooped and reached for the door handle.

"Hang on." All three boys looked at her. "Sad faces. Dad's in the hospital, remember?" Sam and Tio already had their mournful expressions in place, and Ty tried to mute his excitement, with mixed results. "Hmm. Ty, maybe just keep your head down. Y'all ready?" They nodded. "Let's go."

Just like at the high school, silence fell over their group as they entered St. Francis. The office was right past the door, and they filed inside, Jules at the front.

"May I help you?" The woman behind the desk wore a dark suit and a crucifix. Her nameplate announced that she was Sister Mary Augustine. Jules wondered whether lying to a nun was an automatic go-directly-to-hell card, and then pinched the back of her hand sharply to refocus her wandering brain.

"Yes. I'm Juliet Young, Desdemona Courtland's sister." She realized she'd forgotten to redden her eyes before leaving the car. "Our father went to the hospital this morning, and my stepmother asked if I could pick up Dee and bring her there."

This time, Jules didn't get a hug. Instead, Sister Mary Augustine frowned at her before turning to her computer. After a few tense seconds with the only sound being the click of the mouse, she shook her head.

"You're not on the list."

Jules's insides jumped. She'd been afraid of that. If Mrs. Juarez had checked her brothers' approved pick-up list, Jules wouldn't have been on that one, either. If not for stealthy visits and burner phones, she wouldn't have any relationship with her siblings at all. Ever since Jules had started her crusade to get custody, Courtney had gone from simply hating her stepdaughter to loathing her with the power of a thousand suns.

"Oh." She feigned surprise. "Well, her brothers are all here. Are Sebastian, Horatio, or Titus on the list?"

Sister Mary Augustine didn't even look at her screen. "No."

Desperation started to seep in, but Jules fought it back as she attempted to pull a solution from her whirling brain. "Even if we could get her to leave Dad's side, poor Courtney isn't in any condition to drive. Is there some way I could pick up Dee?"

Pressing her lips together in a tight line, Sister Mary Augustine shook her head.

"Maybe I could call Dee's mom and get permission?" Jules frantically tried to think of someone who could pretend to be Courtney. Too bad their father was "hospitalized," or Dennis could impersonate him for the length of a phone conversation.

It didn't matter anyway, since the nun was still shaking her head. "Only people on the list can remove students from the building."

Think, Jules! Think! No avenues of persuasion occurred to her, and she gave Sister Mary Augustine a weak smile. "Okay. Thank you."

Instead of responding to the courtesy, the nun just glared at them until they were once again in the hall. Even when the door was closed, she still scowled through the large window. It would be impossible to pass by the office without Sister Mary Augustine seeing them.

"New plan," Jules hissed quietly, ushering them away from the window. "Ty, you're the nun-distractor. Sam, I know you haven't had Driver's Ed yet, but do you think you could start my car and move it to the east side? When we came around the school, it looked like there's a door there."

"I th-hink s-so."

The uncertainty in his voice worried her, but she still dug her keys out of her pocket and handed them to him. He shoved through the front door as she turned to Tio. "T, you're with me."

His eyes grew wide.

"Ty, go." Jules tipped her head toward the office door.

He took a step and then stopped. "What should I say?"

"Anything! Just distract her for a few seconds so we can get by the windows. Pretend like you're sick or something. Once we're past, head to the car."

With a resolute nod, Ty reentered the office. Jules watched, waiting for her brother to pull the eagle-eyed nun's gaze away. Even through the closed door, she heard some realistic-sounding gagging noises. Sister Mary Augustine apparently found them to be convincing, as well, since her horrified attention focused on Ty.

Grabbing Tio's hand, Jules ran down the hall. She knew Dee was in Ms. McCree's fourth-grade classroom for everything except math and reading. Dee had also told her that this was Ms. McCree's first year teaching, and Jules hoped she could use that to her advantage.

She quickly figured out that the classrooms were arranged around a square with the lunchroom and library in the center. Each door was marked with the grade and teacher, making it easy to find Dee's room. Jules was panting from nerves and exertion, so she took a few seconds to get her breath before she knocked. Tio hovered nervously behind her.

A woman opened the door. If not for her lack of uniform, Dee would've thought she was one of the students.

"Hi." Her voice was still breathless from her dash. "I'm Juliet Young, Desdemona's sister."

"Hello." Ms. McCree looked confused.

"Our dad is in the hospital. Dee's mom sent me to get her."

"Oh." The teacher's face puckered, and Jules wondered if she was about to get her second sympathy hug of the day. "I'm so sorry."

Over Ms. McCree's shoulder, Jules could see her stepsister pulling on her backpack, and she had to smother a smile. Smart Dee knew the plan, and she was getting ready to go.

"Thank you." Jules forced herself back into a grief-stricken expression.

"You'll need to go to the office first, though."

"Oh, I did! There's a boy there who was throwing up, so Sister Mary Augustine told us to just come here and get Dee out of class."

Ms. McCree knotted her fingers together, looking anxious. "I'm not sure…"

"It's okay, Ms. McCree," Dee said, slipping around her teacher to stand next to Jules. "My sister's on the list. I should go to the hospital now to see my dad."

Jules resisted pulling Dee into a hug and took her hand instead. On her list of things to be concerned about later, Jules added the ease with which Dee lied, next to Sam's worsening stutter.

"Well, I guess that's okay." The teacher still looked

like she was about to change her mind, so Jules started moving away from the classroom.

"Thanks, Ms. McCree." With Tio close behind them, she and Dee speed-walked toward the side door she'd spotted earlier. Morning sunlight illuminated the glass pane set in the door, making it look like a beacon, and Jules increased her pace until they were nearly running. She reached out to push the door handle and then yanked back her hand. "Dee, the fire alarm isn't going to go off when we open this, is it?"

Dee shook her head, blond curls bouncing with the movement. "No. We go out this way to get to the soccer field."

Blowing out a relieved breath, Jules pushed down the handle and opened the door, holding it as Dee and Tio hurried through. She grinned when she saw the Camry sitting at the curb, the driver's door open for her. Sam was circling behind the car, heading for the front passenger seat, and Ty climbed out of the backseat rushing toward them, grinning with obvious pride of his nundistraction skills.

Jules's happy smile dropped when the car began to roll forward.

With a yelp, Sam grabbed at the open door to catch the runaway Camry. It slipped out of his grasp. Jules ran toward the car, but it picked up speed, the slight downward incline of the lot allowing it to roll straight toward a blue, new-looking hybrid.

"No, no, no, no, no!" Even in her panic, she kept her voice low, not wanting to draw attention from anyone inside the school. If her car crashed, however, people—like Sister Mary Augustine—were going to come running. Dee would be yanked back into school, the police and Jules's stepmother would be called, and that would be the end.

Jules ran faster, sprinting toward the Camry, her heart pounding more from fear than exertion. She drew closer, but it continued on its course, headed straight for the hybrid like a missile locked on its target. She could almost hear the crunching sound her car would make as it connected, the shrill squeals of the alarm, and she shot forward in a burst of panic-fueled speed.

Catching the driver's-side door, Jules dove into the car, her foot fumbling for the brake pedal. She hit it hard, and her head jerked forward at the abrupt halt. When she raised her gaze, the hybrid's bumper was hidden by the front of the Camry. The two cars couldn't have been more than an inch or two apart.

"S-s-sorry!" Sam ran up to the still-open passenger door, his eyes huge from the scare. Jules imagined hers were pretty wide, too.

"No problem," she said, sucking in air and forcing her hundredth fake smile of the day. With a shaking hand, she reached to pop the trunk. "You got it here, and that's the important thing. We can work on your parking skills later."

Sam dropped into the passenger seat, as if his legs refused to support him, and Ty climbed into the back.

"Whoa," was all Ty said. Jules knew he had to have been terrified for him to be robbed of words. Glancing in the rearview mirror, she saw Tio adding Dee's backpack to the three already in the trunk. He slammed it closed, and the two of them hustled into the backseat. Jules did a quick head count before backing away from the hybrid.

Her whole body was still shaking, and she tightened her hands on the steering wheel in an attempt to hide it.

She turned out of the school parking lot, glanced at Sam, and checked the rearview mirror again. Giddiness rose in her, sweeping away the vestiges of her earlier fear.

"Y'all?" All four of her siblings looked at her. "We did it." Her laugh was half-hysterical, and she quickly sucked it back in before she scared the kids. "You have officially been kidnapped."

Ty's cheer was joined by Dee and even Tio. Grinning—and possibly hyperventilating a bit—Jules looked at Sam. His head was tipped down, but his mouth curled the tiniest bit at the corners. That hint of a smile was the happiest she'd seen Sam in years. It made everything worth it.

Jules was a full-fledged criminal now, and it felt good.

CHAPTER 5

Present Day

THE CALL CAME THROUGH JUST AS THEO WAS ABOUT TO wrap up his shift. He pivoted away from the locker room door, turning up his portable radio as a surge of relief spread through him. This meant he could delay going home for a few hours. Since his K9 partner, Goose, had died of cancer a year ago, Theo's small house seemed echoing and empty. And now, after Don…

His head jerked back as the reminder took him unaware, and he immediately shoved the thought from his mind, forcing himself to concentrate on the dispatcher's words.

"…*repeat, officer requesting assistance at 4278 Green Willow Lane*."

Booted feet behind him made Theo turn just as Hugh passed him, thumping Theo on the shoulder as he went.

"What's up?" Theo asked, increasing his pace to keep up with the other officer.

"Wilson spotted a vehicle parked outside the Schwartz compound. Said it looks a lot like the van used by the Golden Sun Restaurant robbery suspect. He wants some backup before ringing the doorbell."

Theo snorted as they descended the stairs to the

underground garage where the squad cars were parked. "Don't blame him."

"Grab Vig before you head to the call. You know how Gordon Schwartz likes to stockpile things that go *boom*."

Resisting a wince, Theo turned toward the kennel on the opposite side of the garage. He took in Viggy's flattened ears and sighed. This wasn't going to go well.

As Theo put on the dog's protective vest and harness, Viggy stood listlessly, his tail tucked. A memory hit Theo like a punch to the belly, a flash of Don prepping Viggy the same way six months ago, laughing at something Theo had said. For that call, Viggy had been vibrating with excitement, ready to work, so confident and eager and just so fucking *happy*. The passive, dull-eyed dog standing in front of Theo now was just a shadow of that K9 officer. That was Theo, too—a shadow of the person he'd been a few months ago.

Theo gave a rough, humorless laugh. "We're a pair, aren't we, Vig?"

The dog didn't react, didn't even glance at him, and Theo swallowed a bitter surge of grief, gathering the numbness around him like a security blanket.

"C'mon, Viggy." The weary resignation in his voice would've worried him if he'd managed to care. "Let's get this over with."

With a reluctant Viggy in the back of his squad car, Theo pressed the accelerator, flying past vehicles that had pulled over in response to his overhead lights and siren. That low burn of anticipation he usually got when heading to a call wasn't happening, though. There was no surge of adrenaline, no bouncing nerves. He didn't feel anything.

Viggy shifted, drawing his attention for a split second before Theo returned his gaze to the road. It was strange having a dog in the back of his squad car again. After Goose died, Theo had successfully managed to put off getting a new dog for more than ten months. He didn't think he'd have the same connection with another K9 that he'd had with Goose, not ever again. Ever since Theo had picked up Goose from the training facility, the two of them had clicked. Goose had been an amazing partner—a once-in-a-lifetime K9 officer.

His eyes flicked to the rearview mirror again as guilt burned in his chest. Viggy had been a good dog, too— *was* a good dog. They just weren't right for each other. Vig was *Don's* partner. At least, he had been.

A dull pain throbbed in his stomach, and Theo tightened his grip on the steering wheel until his knuckles whitened.

As they left quaint downtown Monroe and headed toward the west edge of town, Theo slowed. The twists and turns of the narrow mountain road were treacherous even at normal speeds, and Theo didn't want to plow into one of the vertical rock faces that bracketed the pavement. Monroe was just west enough of the Front Range to be officially in the mountains, rather than in the foothills. Nestled in a valley, the town could be accessed by only two roads—one to the east and one to the west.

As he approached the turnoff to Blank Hill Road, the squirrelly waitress popped into his head...again. For some reason, he was thinking of Jules with unsettling frequency. Theo pictured her smile after he'd told Norman Rounds to back off. It had transformed her face, turning her from pretty to flat-out beautiful.

He realized he'd been slowing down, as if he were going to turn toward Jules's house, and he made an annoyed sound as he pressed harder on the accelerator. This preoccupation with Jules had to stop. Despite his resolution, he couldn't help but glance in the sideview mirror to catch a last glimpse of the Blank Hill Road sign.

Maybe he should swing by after the call was over. After all, he'd be driving right past again. The house she was renting was isolated, and it was obvious she was running from something—or someone. He'd do a quick check on her place and then leave. Jules wouldn't even know he'd been there.

His breath came out in a huff as he got close to the scene. He needed to stop obsessing. Her suspicious behavior just screamed she'd be trouble, and his life was enough of a mess right now. If only she hadn't smiled at him like that...

Theo cut his siren as he turned onto the road leading to Green Willow Lane but left his overhead lights flashing until he pulled up behind Hugh's squad car. The September sun was starkly bright and warm. Theo automatically checked to make sure the window fan ventilating the backseat was on and then froze. How many times had he done the same for Goose? Shaking off the nostalgia and grief, Theo strode toward Lieutenant Blessard, the incident commander. As he passed Hugh's car, Lexi, Hugh's K9 partner, barked twice.

"Bosco!" The lieutenant strode over to meet Theo. "You got Don Baker's dog with you? The search warrant just came through."

With a tight nod, Theo turned and returned to his car.

Lexi stayed silent that time when he passed Hugh's car. As Theo opened the back door and reached to attach the lead to the dog's harness, Viggy flattened his belly against the floor. Taking a step back, Theo eyed him. Vig was the picture of misery.

"I know, buddy," Theo said softly. Every time he looked at Viggy, Theo was hit with a stab of grief. The dog acted exactly how Theo felt. There wasn't time to wallow in their mutual sadness, though. They had a job to do. Their fellow cops' lives depended on him and Viggy doing what they were trained for, even if their hearts weren't in it.

"Let's go to work." Although he tried to infuse his voice with excitement, his tone remained flat, as did the dog. "C'mon, Vig. Out."

Theo pulled on the lead, but Viggy resisted for so long that Theo began to worry he'd have to lift the seventy-pound dog and carry him to the scene.

"Viggy..." He hauled on the leash again, and the dog reluctantly climbed out of the car.

"What's wrong with him?" Blessard asked from just a few feet away. Theo stiffened. He'd been so occupied with getting Viggy out of the car that he hadn't even noticed the lieutenant approaching.

Rubbing the back of his neck with his free hand, Theo kept a tight grip on the leash to prevent Viggy from slinking underneath the car to hide. "He's been this way ever since Don..." Theo had to stop when Don's name caught in his throat.

"Yeah." Blessard eyed the dog with sympathy. "Think we were all knocked sideways by that."

Clearing his throat didn't seem to help move the

impediment. "Ready?" he asked gruffly, wanting—no, *needing*—to change the subject.

"Let's do this."

Theo squared his shoulders and walked up the weed-choked two-track that led to the compound gates. The sun lit the ever-present mountain peaks towering over the trees, turning the whole scene into a postcard. Holding back a cynical snort, Theo glanced behind at a plodding Viggy. The two of them were as far from a picture-perfect pair as they could get.

With a sharp shake of his head, Theo tried to refocus. They just needed to pull themselves together long enough to go in, find the explosives—if there were any—and get out. But he couldn't stop himself from glancing back at the lackluster dog again, feeling an echoing pang of emptiness.

Yeah, this is going to be bad.

"Gordon Schwartz is talking with one of our negotiators. Said he's trying to convince Romanowski—our robbery suspect—to voluntarily come out and talk to us." Blessard spoke quietly, his usual carry-through-the-crowd voice muted. "Glad Schwartz didn't manage to talk him into that yet. We've been waiting for a while for a way to get a look inside of that place, see what kind of toys our buddy Gordon and his minions have been collecting."

Theo grunted acknowledgment before asking, "Any idea what kind of weapons he's got in there?"

"No." Lines of displeasure creased the skin between

Blessard's bushy gray brows. "We've gotten some unreliable witness accounts that claim his collection is anywhere from a couple of shotguns all the way to a fully stocked armory. Best guess is that it's somewhere in the middle-to-arsenal range. Schwartz is teetering on the edge of crazy, and I'd rather know what he's got stockpiled *before* we're involved in a standoff."

Theo made a wordless sound of agreement as they approached the closed compound gates.

"You're not coming in!" yelled a short, stocky man on the inside of the gate. Theo had seen him around enough to recognize him as Gordon Schwartz. "This is my home! You can't come inside my house without my consent. If you try to break in here, you fascist bastards will be trampling my constitutional rights!"

Hugh, the closest officer to the fence, raised a hand in a placating gesture even as his posture stayed alert. "You're not in trouble, Gordon. We just need to come inside to talk to Romanowski."

"He's coming out." Schwartz glanced over his shoulder, the tension on his face belying the certainty in his voice. "Give me a little more time. I'll keep talking to him, and he'll come out."

Blessard strode forward until he was standing next to Hugh. As Theo stopped well back from the gates, Viggy slunk to the end of his leash and sat as far from the compound as he could get, his ears flat and unhappy.

"Fuck your warrant!" The yell from Schwartz drew Theo's full attention, and a tense readiness rippled through the crowd of cops. With a whine, Viggy leaned against Theo's hold on the leash, his tail curled between his hind legs. Theo knew that, if Viggy weren't restrained, he'd be running back to the safety of the car. It hurt to see how timid the formerly confident dog had become. "It's nothing! It's a piece of paper. You know what piece of paper trumps your search warrant? The Constitution of the United States! And the Constitution says that I have the right to protect my home."

A year ago—hell, even two months ago—Theo would've been buzzing with adrenaline, alert and ready for whatever was going to happen. Now, he just felt a heavy wave of weariness press down on him. It was just another day, another call, another rotation of the hamster wheel, another chance for one of his fellow cops to get hurt or killed or messed up in the head. His muscles ached with the pressure of his resignation.

"Gordon," Hugh soothed, shifting so he blocked an impatient-looking Blessard from Schwartz's view. Theo marveled at Hugh's seemingly endless supply of patience. "We don't want to step on your rights. All we need to do is to go in, get Romanowski, and then we'll be off your property. Mrs. Lee was injured in that robbery. With the suspect walking free, she's terrified all the time. We need to bring in the guy who hurt her, so she can sleep at night. Don't you think Mrs. Lee deserves that?"

Schwartz's rigid posture softened slightly, and Theo felt everyone's tension ease. "Yeah," Schwartz mumbled. "I barely know the guy. I'd never hurt an innocent like that, not for money."

"We know, Gordon." Hugh reached through the gate and squeezed Schwartz's rounded shoulder. "We're on the same side—the side of justice."

Theo clenched his jaw, holding back a sardonic

snort at the cheesy graphic-novel dialogue. *The side of justice?* He was going to give Hugh so much shit for that later.

"You're just going to go in, grab Romanowski, and leave?" Schwartz repeated, still sounding wary but much more compliant than he had just a few short minutes before. Cheesy or not, Hugh's superhero speech was working.

"That's it." Hugh held Schwartz's gaze steadily. "First, though, would you agree to letting our explosives dog take a sniff around, just for the safety of our officers?"

His shoulders jerking back into his earlier tense posture, Schwartz shot a furious glare toward Viggy and snarled, "No dog. No way. I know how you people work. You'll come in here, into my house, and plant evidence against me. No one's coming in." His hand jerked slightly, and Theo had his gun holster unsnapped before he even paused to think. He wasn't the only one who'd noticed the threat. Theo saw that Blessard had his TASER drawn, holding it behind his left hip, out of Schwartz's view.

Hugh hadn't made a move toward his weapon. "How about this, Gordon. Why don't we let the dog go first? At the entrance to each room, we'll have the dog check things out, but we won't go in until we get an all clear. That way, we couldn't plant anything, even if we wanted to, and our guys will be safe from any explosions. Romanowski doesn't want us to bring him in. Who knows what he's doing right now. I need to keep my friends safe, just like you want to keep your friends safe. Sound like a plan?"

Even before Schwartz reached reluctantly for the

lock on the gate, Theo knew that Hugh had succeeded in talking him into letting them on his property. Giving a cowering Viggy a sideways glance, Theo felt his stomach begin to burn. Everyone's safety depended on their ragtag team of two.

They were so screwed.

CHAPTER 6

Five Days Earlier

THE BOYS LOOKED STARTLING ENOUGH WITH THEIR NEW buzz cuts, like junior military recruits, but Dee was the real shocker. Jules kept glancing in the rearview mirror of their new-to-them SUV, unable to keep her eyes off the small stranger in the backseat. Dee had the same problem. At the garage/car exchange/new-identity pickup, disappearance expert Dennis had given Dee a makeover and a pocket mirror, and her eyes had been fixed on her reflection ever since.

"You okay, Dee?" Jules asked, starting to get uneasy about the mesmerized silence behind her.

"Yes." Her eyes didn't move from the mirror.

"Do you like your new look?"

"I *love* it," Dee breathed. "I look so…different."

She did. Her long, blond curls were now a dark brown, cut in a pixie that made her blue eyes look huge. The fake pageant glamour was gone, replaced by a normal, cute little girl. She'd also changed out of her school uniform into a pair of jeans and a T-shirt.

"We look like real sisters now, too."

Jules shifted so she could see part of her own face in the rearview mirror. Her hair was the same color as Dee's, but Dennis had cut it so it went just past her shoulders. He'd also given her cute bangs. Except for the way Jules's blue eyes were narrow and tilted up at the corners rather than round, she and Dee did look a lot alike.

"We've always been real sisters, D," Jules said teasingly as she passed a semi.

"I know," Dee said to her mirror. "But now we really *look* like sisters."

"J-Ju." Sam's abrupt tone made her tense. "C-c-c…"

Glancing behind her, she knew what he was going to say even before he could force it out.

"C-cops."

The Highway Patrol car was right behind her. Even though she knew the cruise control was set at two miles per hour below the speed limit, she still had to resist the urge to slam on the brakes.

"Don't be an idiot, Jules," she muttered. "Just stay calm." Without touching the brake pedal, she signaled and moved into the right lane in front of the semi. The patrol car moved over as well, staying behind them.

As if he'd sensed the tension in the car, Ty woke from his doze with a snort. "What's going on?"

"Cops behind us," Tio said tightly.

"Shit."

"Language," Jules snapped.

"Seriously?" Ty gave a short laugh. "I think cops on our tail deserves a 'shit' or two. Maybe even a 'fuck.'"

"Swearing is a bad habit." Realizing she had a death grip on the wheel, Jules forced her fingers to relax. Her siblings couldn't know how close to blind panic Jules was. What if Mr. Espina hadn't had that talk with her stepmother? Worse, what if he *had* threatened her with exposure, and Courtney had called the cops anyway? Were the kids' pictures plastered over every TV and computer and phone screen from Tampa to Seattle? Her breath caught in her chest, suffocating her, and she made herself breathe normally. Hyperventilating while driving was a bad idea. She shoved her frantic worries into the back of her brain and tried to sound as calm as possible...which wasn't very calm at all. "Especially when your little sister is sitting right next to you."

"Sorry, Dee," Ty muttered.

"It's okay. Courtney swears a lot more than you do."

Choking back a mostly hysterical laugh, Jules asked, "Why do you call her Courtney?"

"You're seriously asking that now?" Tio interjected before Dee could answer. "When there's a law enforcement officer following our getaway car? Especially since Courtney most likely knows by now that you took us out of school, so it's highly probable there is a warrant out for your arrest on multiple kidnapping charges." Each word was precisely enunciated, which was typical for Tio when he was scared.

"If I don't relax," Jules said through her teeth, "then I'm going to do something stupid, like hit the brakes or jerk the wheel or, I don't know, roll down the window and flip off the nice cop behind us. I need you to cut me some slack right now."

"Sorry." He sounded young and subdued, and guilt rose in Jules for snapping at him. "Go ahead, Dee."

"I've forgotten the question," Dee said in a tiny voice.

Jules's eyes flicked to the rearview again. Instead of looking at the occupants of the backseat this time, she checked out the squad car. It was a reasonable distance behind them, and the lights weren't flashing—both positive things. All she had to do was not screw up and draw attention to them. "Um...I asked why you call your mom Courtney."

"I don't know." Dee was quiet for a few moments. "She just seems more like a Courtney than a Mom."

Despite the situation, Jules had to block a laugh that wanted to escape. "True."

"She seems more like a b-b-bitch than a C-Courtney," Sam muttered.

Now it was even harder not to laugh. "Sam! Language!"

"You need to give Sam points for truthfulness, though," Ty said.

Jules couldn't stop a snort from escaping. "Don't make me laugh, y'all, or I'm going to go full-on hysterical and won't be able to drive." A glance in the mirror showed the Highway Patrol vehicle still trailing them. "Should I take the next rest-stop exit?"

"What if he follows?" Ty asked. "We'll have to stop at the rest area, or it'll look like we're just trying to dodge him."

"You're right." Her hands had tightened again, and she peeled her fingers off the wheel before settling them loosely back in place. "Let's keep going then."

As the SUV and its escort continued down the interstate, they all went silent. Jules's gaze flicked to the rearview mirror again, and she froze. The trooper was right behind them. *Close* now. Trying to keep her breathing steady—or at least not start praying out loud—Jules had to force herself not to stare. As close as he was, he'd be able to see her jerky glances, each nervous movement just screaming "I'm guilty!" Every time her eyes disobeyed and strayed to the mirror, she caught a glimpse of her siblings' pale, frightened faces. Her breathing grew jerky despite her efforts at staying calm as she waited for the cop's overhead lights to flash, for the siren that would force her to choose—pull over or run.

As terrifying as the thought of trying to outrun the police was, the alternative was scarier. She'd go to prison, and her sister and brothers would return to that house.

That wasn't an option. If the trooper's lights went on, they were running. Every muscle in her body contracted, tighter and tighter with each dragging second until she was quivering with tension.

When she saw the sign, the ramifications didn't penetrate for a few seconds. As soon as she grasped what it meant, she laughed, and the sudden sound made Sam jump.

"Wh-what?" he growled.

"Welcome to Tennessee, Jackson family!" Behind them, the patrol car had switched lanes and slowed, preparing to turn onto an access road across the median. Comprehension eased the tension on Sam's face.

"I get it!" Ty almost yelled. "*State* Patrol!"

Everyone laughed, relief making them giddy. When Jules finally got her breath back, she had to brush at her watering eyes.

"Am I going to feel like that every time I see a cop?" she asked. "If so, I vote we go somewhere without a police force."

"Where's that?" Ty asked. "Canada?"

Reaching over Dee's head, Tio punched his brother in the arm. "They have cops there, dumbass. Haven't you heard of Mounties?"

"Language!"

"We can't say 'dumbass'?" It was Ty who protested. "I won't have a name for most of the people I know."

"You w-won't know them anym-m-more."

Everyone went silent at the reminder. Jules fought the urge to apologize for stealing them away from their friends, reminding herself they'd agreed it was for the best.

"Worth it," Ty said, echoing her thoughts.

"Totally," Dee agreed. "Now I don't have to pretend to be friends with Taylor Biggins."

"That obnoxious girl from the pageants?" Jules asked, vaguely remembering Dee mentioning Taylor's explosive tantrums.

"Yes."

"Why would you have to pretend to be friends with her?" Jules noticed her arms were shaking, probably from keeping her muscles tense for so long. "From what you've told me, I would've run whenever I saw her."

"Mrs. Biggins does the best hair." Dee's voice was matter-of-fact. "Courtney said I had to be friends with Taylor or her mom would drop me, and then I'd get stuck with Mrs. Papadopoulos, and she burns me with the curling iron when I don't sit still."

Everyone besides Dee sucked in a horrified breath.

"Does Courtney know that this woman burns you?" Ty asked. Each word was carefully precise, making him sound like Tio. When Jules glanced at him, Ty's face was tight, and he was staring at Dee with intense focus.

"Sure." Dee's casual tone made the answer so much worse.

"What did she say about it?" Jules asked, even though she was pretty sure she didn't want to know the answer.

"Sit still."

When her fingers started cramping, Jules realized she was strangling the steering wheel again. "I'm sorry y'all had to leave your friends—except for Demon Taylor—but I'm not sorry I kidnapped you."

"Me neither." Dee was the first to agree.

Ty was next. "Nope. Kidnap away."

"It's not the ideal situation"—Tio never used one word when he could use a dozen—"but it was necessary under the circumstances."

"Thanks, J-J-JuJu."

To her shock, Sam reached over and patted her forearm. It was a quick movement, his hand landing for just a second, but he'd actually touched her voluntarily. Her eyes burned, and she blinked hard to wrestle the threat of tears into submission.

"Okay," she said a little too loudly. "Enough talking about our real past. Let's make up a fake one. Where should we tell people we're from?"

"California," Ty suggested, making Jules snort.

"Only if you can control that drawl of yours."

"Drawl?" Ty protested. "I don't have a drawl!"

Even Sam laughed at that.

"We could be from Texas," Dee suggested. "From a ranch with horses."

Tio vetoed Texas. "The accent is wrong. Georgia would be a better match."

That made Jules shift uncomfortably in her seat. "Georgia feels too close. What's the most Northern state with a Southern accent?"

"Arkansas?" Ty suggested doubtfully, just as Tio said, "West Virginia."

Either one was fine with Jules. "Let's vote. Who wants to be from West Virginia?" Tio was the only "yes." "Arkansas?" Ty, Sam, and Dee all gave their enthusiastic approval.

"Arkansas?" Tio repeated disdainfully. "Really? Y'all want *Arkansas* to be our homeland?"

"I think it's good," Jules said. "I could be wrong, but I think fewer people would be familiar with Arkansas than West Virginia, which means less chance of someone catching a mistake if we make one."

Tio gave a deep, long-suffering sigh. "Fine. Can you hand me the atlas?" The Pathfinder they'd traded for the Camry had come equipped with an actual paper atlas. Until this trip, Jules hadn't used a paper map in years.

Pulling it from under his seat, Sam handed it over.

"What are you doing, T?" Dee asked, leaning toward him so she could see the atlas, too.

"Research. There's not much I can do without access to the Internet or books, but at least I can learn some Arkansas geography."

"Good idea. Why don't you check out our new hometown while you're at it?"

There were a few moments of silence before Tio asked, "Where *are* we going?"

Jules snorted. "It took y'all long enough to ask."

"It was enough that we were leaving," Ty said, and the others made sounds of agreement. "So? Where does this bus make its last stop?"

Excitement fought with nerves as she thought about the place they were going to make their new start. "Monroe, Colorado."

CHAPTER 7

Present Day

"WHAT IN THE HOLY FUCK DID YOU DO TO DON'S DOG?"

Uneasy silence followed Blessard's words, broken only by Gordon Schwartz's low snicker. Theo focused on the ugly green tweed couch, clenching and releasing his right fist as he tried to contain his anger. It would be bad to hit Schwartz, and probably even worse to take a swing at the lieutenant.

His gaze slid to the gap between the couch and the wall where Viggy had wedged himself as soon as Theo had released him with a command to search. No part of the dog was visible from Theo's position. Guilt and frustration coiled in his belly. Viggy had been the best explosives-detection K9 when he'd been partnered with Don. With Theo, Viggy wouldn't even search a room.

"I didn't do anything," he gritted, his churning emotions morphing into rage that coated his words despite his best efforts to control it. "Don did that."

Blessard made a scoffing sound. "What are you talking about? That dog was an explosives-seeking missile when Don was his partner. There wasn't anything wrong with him before."

"Exactly." Staring at the couch was not helping the

fury that wanted to erupt like lava, burning everything in its path. Theo met the lieutenant's critical gaze. "There wasn't anything wrong with the dog until his asshole partner ate his own gun and left Viggy alone."

Blessard flinched, his head jerking back like Theo had punched him. After his initial shocked look faded, a brick-red flush darkened the lieutenant's face. He opened his mouth but then closed it again after shooting a glance at a fascinated Schwartz.

"Later," Blessard muttered, and Theo answered with a nod that was more of a shrug. After all, what could the lieutenant do to him? Write a letter of reprimand? Take away Viggy? Theo never really had him anyway. Suspend him? At this point, he didn't know if he'd care if he lost his job. There was really no way Blessard could punish him. Theo had already lost everything that mattered.

Turning his back on his glowering lieutenant, Theo walked to the couch. Since he knew calling Viggy wouldn't work, he crouched down next to the sofa. Viggy, who'd mashed his too-thin body into the space between the back of the couch and the wall, panted nervously.

"C'mon, Vig." By reaching his arm as far as he could into the narrow gap, Theo was able to hook his index finger around the leash and draw it toward him. The sight of the crouched animal—the dog that, just two months ago, was brimming with confidence and eagerness to work—sent a spike of sorrow into Theo's heart. "Let's go home, Officer."

Viggy raised his head at the word "home," his expression alert for the first time in two months. Instantly, Theo felt like an enormous dick. To Viggy, "home" was

Don. There was no way for Theo to deliver on what he'd just promised.

Grief coursed through him, even as he wanted to punch a hole in Schwartz's drywall. With an audible exhale, Theo stood and pulled Viggy out of his hiding spot.

A thump and the sound of running boots made him jerk around and reach for his gun. Blessard was already in the hall, shouting, "Police! Romanowski, stop and drop your weapon!"

Feet pounded up the stairs as the lieutenant ran after Romanowski, and a half-dozen other cops followed. Theo was halfway to the door, determined to give chase, when a jerk on his arm brought him to an abrupt halt.

Viggy. He stared at the crouched dog, all his instincts and training shouting at him to back up his fellow officers. But looking at Viggy, Theo knew he couldn't do it, couldn't force the dog into the line of fire. Viggy was already traumatized. It wouldn't take much more to break him beyond repair…if he wasn't already.

A movement in his peripheral made Theo snap his head around to see Gordon slinking toward the hall, a pistol in his hand.

"No." Theo dropped the leash and moved to block Gordon's path. Grabbing the barrel of the other man's gun, Theo disarmed him with a quick upward twist before Schwartz realized what was happening.

"You can't take my gun." Gordon's eyes bulged with fury. "It's my constitutional right to carry that gun!"

Dropping the magazine into his hand and opening the slide by feel, Theo kept his eyes on Schwartz. "I'm not taking it." He tucked the pistol in one cargo pocket of his BDUs and the magazine in another. "I'm just holding onto it for you. You'll get it back when we leave." *If all the paperwork checks out*, Theo thought. "Take a seat."

Although his mutinous expression didn't lighten, Gordon sank down on an overstuffed recliner. Theo stayed by the door, in a spot where he could keep an eye on Gordon and another on the hall. More cops, including Hugh, thundered past the doorway. While the rest dashed up the stairs, Hugh paused when he spotted Theo.

"You good?" Hugh's eyes swept the room. "Where's Vig?"

"Behind the couch. I've got this. Go."

With a short nod, Hugh ran up the stairs.

"Is there anything up there we should be worried about?" Theo asked, trying to channel Hugh's negotiator skills. He was pretty sure he failed, judging by the way Gordon jerked back in his seat. "Guns? Bombs? Knives?"

"Everything's locked up," Gordon said. "And nothing's live."

When Theo looked at him steadily, Gordon scowled. "Why would I blow up my own home?"

"Romanowski can't access anything, then?" Theo relaxed slightly. Maybe his and Viggy's complete failure wouldn't be an issue.

"I told you," Gordon snapped. "Everything's locked up. All but the..." His face turned a pasty green color.

"What?" Theo barked, all thoughts of diplomacy gone. "All but *what*?"

A loud *boom* shook the house. Dust and small chunks of drywall rained down on top of Theo, and he staggered to keep his balance. There was sudden silence, a complete stillness, before all hell broke loose. Shouts and running feet came from above, and more debris fell from the ceiling. From his spot behind the couch, Viggy's whine slid into a howl.

Theo ran to the doorway, taking the stairs four at a time, terror and guilt accelerating his steps. *He*'d caused this. It was his fault. If he hadn't failed so dismally—failed the search, failed Vig, failed Don—then this wouldn't be happening. How many cops were hurt? How many were killed?

Officers started streaming past him, running down as he ran up. Theo scanned them quickly, looking for blood, but everyone looked uninjured.

"Hey!" one of them called to him. "LT wants everyone out. That blast could've damaged the structure."

Ignoring him, Theo tore down the second-floor hall, running toward the sound of loud voices. The air was thick with smoke and dust, tightening his lungs.

"Bosco!" Except for a layer of soot and dirt covering him, the lieutenant didn't look injured. "Get out of here!"

"How bad is it?" Theo asked, his gaze raking the officers passing them. "Where's Hugh?"

Before Blessard could answer, Hugh emerged from the doorway at the end of the hall, supporting a cuffed and dazed-looking Romanowski on one side, while another officer held his other arm.

"Out!" the lieutenant bellowed. "Everyone out!"

Now that he'd seen that no one was obviously injured, Theo remembered Viggy. He'd left him alone with Gordon Schwartz. Flying down the stairs as quickly as he'd run up them, Theo rushed into the living room to find Gordon, still white-faced, sitting where Theo had left him.

"That wasn't my fault," Gordon said. "If someone's hurt, it's not on me."

"Get outside. The house isn't safe." Theo scanned the room, vaguely registering that Gordon had followed his command. All his attention was fixed on finding Viggy. He spotted the end of the leash protruding from behind the couch. "It's over, Vig," Theo said quietly, crouching next to the sofa. Viggy was shaking so hard that the couch vibrated. "Let's go."

The dog didn't move. Dust sifted from the ceiling; they needed to get out. He pulled on the leash, sliding a resisting Viggy across the floor until Theo could reach him.

Theo knew there was no way Viggy would walk out of the house on his own. Wrapping his arms around the K9, Theo lifted him. Viggy stiffened as his paws left the ground.

"Shh," Theo soothed. "I've got you."

After a moment, Viggy went limp. Theo carried him out of the house and through the gates.

"Is Vig okay?" Hugh called from where he stood by the lieutenant.

No. He's not okay. We're not okay. "He's not hurt," Theo answered, his voice rough.

Everyone else was quiet, subdued, as Theo carried Viggy through the crowd of officers toward his squad car. Theo kept his gaze locked in front of him and let the numbness take over.

CHAPTER 8

Four Days Earlier

CLIFFS TOWERED ABOVE THEM TO THE LEFT AND dropped away on the right. Jules tapped a nervous rhythm on the steering wheel, hating that she was going twenty-five miles under the speed limit because the curvy mountain road into town completely freaked her out. At least the sun was high in the sky, so everything was well lit. Vaguely, Jules recognized that the view was beautiful, the craggy mountains surrounding them furred with evergreens and aspens until the bare, blue-gray peaks poked out above the tree line. She couldn't really appreciate the scenery, though. All she could do was concentrate on not driving her family off a cliff. Four or five cars were stacked up behind them, so Jules steered into a pullout and stopped to let them pass before entering the westbound lane again. To add to her humiliation, one of the vehicles that passed her was an extra-long RV. Another was a semi.

Ty snorted. "You're driving even slower than—"

"I know, Ty. Thanks," she interrupted, trying not to snap. Her sleepless night and driving marathon, capped by this treacherous mountain road, had drained her reservoir of good-natured comebacks and robbed her of her patience. Once she passed through a gap in the rocks barely wide enough for the two-lane road, houses and shops appeared, and the speed limit dropped to a much more tolerable twenty.

The kids were quiet as they looked around. "It's small," Ty said in a neutral voice.

Silence filled the SUV until Jules asked, "Is small good or bad?"

There was a silence as they considered the question. "I haven't decided yet," Tio finally said, and the others made sounds of agreement.

"Fair enough." Jules was too tired and, at the same time, too wired to have any kind of first impression of their new town. "Sam, could you be my navigator?"

Sam picked up the handwritten directions. "T-turn right on B-B-Bridesw-well."

"We passed Brideswell several blocks ago," Tio said.

With a sigh, Jules flipped her turn signal so she could go around the block and head back toward Brideswell. She was pretty sure this road trip would never end.

After that first false start, the directions were clear, and they found the right street number attached to a crooked mailbox. The deeply rutted driveway seemed to go on forever, twisting this way and that, the pine branches reaching out to brush against the Pathfinder. The closeness of the evergreens dimmed the sunny morning, and Jules's simmering anxiety rose to a boil.

As she turned left, avoiding exposed tree roots and rocks that threatened to grab the tires, the trees thinned, and the house came into view. The place had been white a long, long time ago, but all the exterior paint had faded to a wind-stripped gray. The front porch looked a little cockeyed, and the area in front of the house resembled a sparse hayfield rather than a lawn. A small, lopsided barn stood a short distance from the house.

Dee sucked in a breath. "There's a *barn*, Jules. Can I get a horse?"

"Uh…" The question barely penetrated as she tried to take in the huge amount of work the house would require. Going from a shoebox of an apartment to *this*…there was no way. She wasn't handy enough for this house.

"Can I?" Judging from the increased excitement in her little sister's voice, she'd taken Jules's hesitation for actual consideration.

"Let's try to keep ourselves alive for a while, Dee, before we start adding dependents, okay?" Parking in front of the sagging porch, Jules braced herself and got out. It was warm but dry—nothing like Florida had been. She slapped at a stray fly, managing to smack her own ear but missing the bug. As her siblings piled out of the SUV, she circled to the rear hatch. Movement helped. If she'd stood staring at the wreck of a house, she would've sat on the ground and burst into tears.

Tossing the computer bag strap over her shoulder, she passed the backpacks to their rightful owners, the weight of Tio's bag almost taking her down. Sam reached past her to grab her suitcase, and she gave him a smile of thanks.

"I thought you said no computers." Ty frowned at the case resting against her hip.

"This is just the bag," Jules explained. "And instead of a laptop, it holds all our brand-new paperwork, plus"—she dug out a key ring and dangled it in front of him—"the house keys."

Ty snatched the keys from her hand and ran to the porch steps, Tio close behind.

"Careful!" she called out, cringing as their shoes clomped noisily on the aged wood. "That doesn't look too stable." To her surprise, neither boy fell through the porch floor as they grappled to see who would be first inside the house. After watching to make sure the porch could hold her brothers, Dee made her careful way up the steps after them.

Sam kept pace with Jules, and she turned to him with a smile that was only partially forced. Dilapidated as it was, the house was theirs—hers and her family's. This had always been her dream, and she wasn't going to let a few loose shingles ruin the moment. "Ready to see the inside?"

His doubtful look was enough to make her laugh. Always-conscientious Dee had closed the door behind her when she entered the house, so Jules grabbed the doorknob. Straightening her shoulders, she patted the laptop bag holding their new identities and pushed open the door. The interior was dim after the bright, late-morning sunshine, and the kids' excited voices echoed off the walls deep inside the house.

Taking a long, slow breath, Jules stepped into their new life.

The house was a wreck—and yet gorgeous at the same time. Jules took a step farther into the entry and tripped when her toe caught on an uneven floorboard. Unbalanced, she grabbed the ornate railing that edged the staircase, steadying herself. Voices and alarmingly loud squeaks from overhead told Jules that the three younger kids had made their way upstairs.

The dated wallpaper was peeling and gouged in spots, revealing sections of an even-more-dated pattern. Cobwebs and dust covered every surface, and dead leaves and corpses of miller moths were piled in corners. Through a wide, arched doorway, she could see what was most likely a living room, although the age of the house made her want to refer to it as a parlor. Living rooms were in modern homes, places for televisions and wall-to-wall carpet. This looked more like a room where they'd gather around the fireplace and knit.

Jules snorted. She'd never held knitting needles in her life. Glancing at her brother's impassive face, she quickly sobered. "What do you think, Sam-I-Am?"

Instead of answering, he made his way down the hall, silently glancing through doorways as they passed a wood-paneled, shelf-lined room that Jules mentally dubbed "the library," a bathroom with an honest-to-God claw-foot tub, and a room she assumed was the dining room, judging by its proximity to the kitchen.

She followed Sam into the expansive room that bore no resemblance to her apartment's tiny galley kitchen. There were numerous cupboards, although several of the doors were hanging cockeyed or missing altogether. To her relief, the appliances, as ancient as they appeared, did not require firewood or hand cranking or whatever else century-old appliances had needed to operate. The room was large enough to hold a good-sized table and chairs.

Her attention left the worn counters as she focused on Sam. "We can fix it up." Pushing away the doubting voices in her head that were screaming at her, telling her that she had no clue how to even start, Jules tried to fake optimism. "A little paint, some...um, nails? It'll be like...well, maybe not *new* exactly, but better. Definitely better."

"JuJu." To her surprise, the corners of Sam's mouth were twitching up again. "It's p-perfect."

No amount of fake cheer could keep her forehead from wrinkling in confusion as she glanced around the battered kitchen. "Perfect?"

"Yeah." His smile grew, loosening the permanent knot in her stomach just a little. "Come on. We'd b-b-better get upst-st-st...up there b-before the kids claim the g-g-good b-bedrooms."

She couldn't stop herself. Rushing forward, she caught her brother in a hug. As soon as she felt him stiffen in her hold, she released him. "You're the best, Sam-I-Am."

His face flushed, he motioned her toward the hall-way. "Yeah, yeah."

There really were no "good" bedrooms. The upstairs was chopped into oddly shaped spaces with no apparent rhyme or reason. Several had slanted ceilings follow-ing the angle of the roof, creating areas where Jules, as petite as she was, couldn't even stand upright. What they lacked in quality and size, however, they made up for in quantity. She counted six rooms—but no second-floor bathrooms, to her dismay. Sam followed the twins' voices down the hall, disappearing into one room as Dee popped out of another and ran toward Jules.

"Jules," Dee breathed, her face glowing. "There's *another* upstairs. And you know how you get there?"

"How?"

"A *secret staircase*!" Her dramatic whisper increased

to a shriek by the end. Grabbing Jules's hand, Dee hauled her to what appeared to be a linen closet. When Dee yanked open the door, an impossibly narrow stairway was revealed. "See?"

"I see." Jules peered through the gloom that covered all but the bottom few steps. A shiver ran through her as she thought of all the things that could be lurking in the ancient attic—mice and bats and skeletons. Possibly serial killers. She fumbled just inside the doorframe. "Is there a light switch?" If not, there was no way she was squeezing herself into that narrow, dark space.

"Is there electricity?" Tio's voice asked from behind them.

Jules turned to look at him. "Do you mean 'is the electricity turned on' or 'is there any electrical wiring in this house'?"

"There's electricity," Dee answered for him as she reached to where Jules had been fumbling before. "See? It's buttons, though, not switches." The skinny staircase was illuminated by the harsh yet dim glare of a bare bulb. Jules exhaled with relief. At least there was power in this old wreck of a house. Dennis must be paying the bill. Would he expect her to change the bill over to her name? If so, it'd be the first test of her fake identity. Her throat felt like it was closing. Reaching up, she tugged at the V-neck of her shirt and coughed, trying to clear the imaginary impediment.

"W-what's wr-wr-wr…" Sam's huff of an exhale was short and impatient. "W-what's the matter?"

Too late, she dropped her hand to her side. "Nothing."

He just gave her a look and waited silently. Ty joined them, and all her siblings grew solemn as they watched her.

"Nothing," she said with more force. "I'm just thinking of everything we need to do to make this place livable."

"Beds," Ty said. Jules held back a cringe. She hadn't even thought about that.

"A TV." That was Dee's contribution.

"D-dishes."

"A computer. Oh, and Internet."

That'd be another test of her identity—*and* more monthly bills.

"Food." Ty's voice held the same longing that Tio's had when he'd mentioned the computer. "Soon, please. I'm starving."

"A horse."

She rolled her eyes at the last offering, trying to fight down her panic. After paying for their new identities, Jules had very limited funds to set up a household of five—four of whom were still growing out of their clothes. Her initial impression of the house was that it would take an enormous influx of cash just to keep it from falling down on top of them.

As if to underscore her growing anxiety, a heavy rumble of thunder echoed through the house. Jules shot a nervous look at the ceiling. If the roof was weather-worthy, she'd be shocked.

"C'mon, Jules," Dee urged, tugging on her hand. "Let's look upstairs."

Deciding that whatever lurked in the attic couldn't be worse than the worries that were multiplying in her mind, she allowed her sister to pull her up the narrow stairs. Each one creaked worse than the one before, and Jules's stomach lurched with every step. She expected to fall through the ancient treads at any second, and she clutched Dee's hand a little harder. The heavy clomping of the boys' feet behind them made her cringe.

As they passed through a door at the top of the stairs, she exhaled for the first time since they'd started ascending. Her relief at not falling to her death made her slow to take in her surroundings at first. When she finally looked around, Jules blinked in surprise.

She'd been expecting an unfinished, dirty attic, but the room—although definitely needing a good cleaning—reminded her more of an artist's studio than a storage space. A stained-glass window set in the triangular east wall lit the space with muted colors.

"Wow."

"I *know*!" Dee was practically dancing in excitement. "Isn't it the *best*? If I hadn't already picked the elf room, I'd *totally* want this room."

"Hey, there's stuff over here," Ty called from across the space. He'd opened a short door set in the wall and was pulling things out of the storage space. Dee ran over, and Tio joined them more leisurely.

"Elf room?" Jules repeated absently, watching Ty drag out an antique-looking trunk and a globe. She wondered how out-of-date it was, with no-longer-existing country borders and names. It might be a good history lesson, at least.

"Ju-Ju?"

Sam's serious tone made her focus on him. "What is it?"

"I w-want it. P-p-please."

It took her a second to realize he meant the attic, rather than the old globe. She'd already mentally assigned the room to Ty and Tio, since they'd always refused to be put in separate rooms, and she wasn't sure if there was a room on the second floor that would fit both of them. A single glance at Sam's tight expression and clenched fists was enough to immediately change her mind. "Okay."

For a long moment, he watched her warily, studying her face as if to make sure she was serious. Eventually, his shoulders relaxed slightly. "Thanks."

"It's going to be freezing in the winter and broiling in the summer, you know," she warned.

His almost-there smile was back. "I kn-know."

"I have no idea how we'll get a mattress up those steps." The thought reminded her of all the things they would need to get that day. Thunder, louder than before, crashed, sounding as if it was right above them. In the crackling silence following the boom, there was the tinny sound of a doorbell.

They all froze—none of them even breathing—until lightning lit up her siblings' faces, the stark light emphasizing the terror in their expressions. The sight reminded Jules that she was the responsible one now, the one who had to pretend not to be scared out of her mind that the cops were at the door, ready to break in and grab the kids, to drop them back into Courtney's clutches.

The horror of that thought snapped Jules out of her temporary paralysis. "Everyone stay up here. No, wait." There were no exits on the third floor. Jules made a frantic mental note to install some way to escape from the attic in the near future.

If she was hauled off to jail right now, though, that wouldn't be necessary.

Wrestling her panicked thoughts back under control,

she took a deep breath and let it out in a shuddering exhale. "Okay. Head for the kitchen and out the back door to the barn. Y'all can hide in there—or behind there, if it looks like it's going to fall down on your heads." She met Sam's frantic gaze and tried to force a smile. "Maybe it's just the welcome wagon."

The doorbell rang again, longer and more insistently that time, and Jules started down the narrow stairs, her heartbeat hammering in her ears. The kids followed her, their tentative footsteps a heartbreaking contrast to the pounding joy they'd shown running up them just minutes earlier.

Did I do the wrong thing? Jules wondered as her teeth found a raw spot on the inside of her lip. The physical sting wasn't as painful as the rush of guilt. She'd taken her siblings from a life of affluence, and in exchange, forced them to live in fear, always hiding, always having to look over their shoulders.

"I don't want to go back," Dee said in a tiny voice as they descended the stairs to the main level.

"You won't." The resolute way Sam said the words, without a stutter, erased Jules's doubts. Courtney might've been able to give them material things, but they'd have a better life with Jules, even if it was a life on the run.

At the base of the stairs, Jules turned toward the front door and then paused, looking sternly over her shoulder at the scared-looking group. "Whatever happens, you stay hidden. Got it?"

The younger three nodded, looking worried, but Sam sent her a tight-lipped frown that promised nothing. The doorbell rang for the third time, and she waved them toward the kitchen. Only when they disappeared through the doorway did she start to walk toward the front door, each step slower than the one before it.

The dirty, stained-glass panel running the height of the door revealed just the vaguest of outlines. Jules could tell that whoever was out there was big—very, very big. She hoped the dim interior of the house hid her from whatever giant lurked on the porch, waiting for her to answer.

Taking a deep breath, she let it out as she stretched up onto her tiptoes so she could see out of the peephole. Jules blinked, her lashes brushing the door, and the figure on the porch came into wide-angle focus.

She stopped breathing, stopped thinking. All she could do was stare. The cops were here. She'd barely gotten the kids to their new home, and she'd already failed her siblings. Her knees went watery, and her vision was strange, putting a gray film over everything, including the officer's nightmarish face, distorted by the peephole glass.

The world rocked a little, and she had to take a step back to catch her balance, cutting off her view of the cop.

This is it, she thought. Nausea flooded her, and she swallowed hard. Her brain spun with images of jail and the kids going back to Courtney...

No. The complete unacceptability of the idea cleared Jules's mind. There was no way she was going to allow that.

A heavy fist landed on the wood of the door, pounding several times, startling Jules and sending her skittering backward. Her heels hit the bottom stair, knocking her off balance so she sat heavily on one of the steps. As her heart pounded in her ears, Jules gripped the banister spindle and tried to think.

Should she reveal herself, walk outside and accept her fate, allowing Sam and the kids time to escape? Or should she not answer, delaying the inevitable? If she was arrested, Jules doubted the kids would run. Well, they probably *would* run—right toward her, trying to defend their sister.

She'd keep quiet then, ignoring the knocking and the doorbell. It might not give them much time, but maybe Dennis could find them somewhere else, somewhere that was actually safe, somewhere the cops weren't at her door within minutes of her and the kids' arrival.

The thumps on the door stopped, and Jules held her breath. Was the cop leaving, or was he just going to get reinforcements? The shadow behind the glass shrank and then disappeared altogether. Jules stayed frozen, waiting for the next step—more footsteps on the porch, a voice from a megaphone telling her to surrender, the door splintering after a hit from a battering ram.

Instead, there was silence. For several long, long moments, all Jules could hear was the rasp of her anxious breaths. Then, there was the rough roar of a diesel engine turning over.

Confusion knotted her eyebrows. That didn't sound like a squad car, or even a squad SUV. That was a truck—a big one. Pushing off the stairs, she took quiet, cautious steps to the door. The figure was gone, but a large object remained on the porch. Squinting, she tried to make it out, but the peephole didn't give her a good-enough view.

Biting the inside of her lip, she slowly, soundlessly

turned the lock and opened the door a crack. Jules peered out just in time to see the rear of a florist's box truck trundling down the driveway. Her gaze dropped to the object on the porch. It was a potted plant, wrapped in a bow with a card attached.

Her laugh rang out, and she clapped her hand over her mouth to mute the sound. Flowers. What she'd thought was a cop had actually been a delivery driver, complete with dark-blue uniform. Her heart drummed against her ribs with residual adrenaline, and she couldn't stop laughing into her muffling hand.

The delivery truck rounded a bend and disappeared from view. Still feeling spooked, Jules opened the door just wide enough to grab the pot. Once she'd secured the front door behind her, she brought the plant into the kitchen and opened the attached card with shaking fingers. Irrationally, she half-expected the flowers to be from Courtney, a sort of *I've-got-you* kind of mind game. When she saw what was written in the card, Jules's lungs finally relaxed enough for her to take a breath.

Welcome to your new life. —Dennis

CHAPTER 9

Present Day

THEO STARED AT THE PACKAGE OF STEAKS IN HIS HAND.
He didn't know why he was even considering them.
It wasn't like he'd suddenly have the initiative to dust
off the grill, fill his propane tank, and actually cook
anything. He'd grab something from the diner like he
always did, or he'd just wait until tomorrow at breakfast. It wasn't like he felt hungry, anyway.

Impatiently, he returned the package to the cooler.
The only reason he was at the grocery store was because
he wanted to delay going home. The quietness made it
harder to keep from dwelling on everything. His cart had
exactly one item in it—a chew toy for Viggy that Theo
had picked up from the sale display by the door. He
quickly looked away. It'd be a waste of money. Viggy
wouldn't touch it.

The aisle suddenly seemed too small, making it hard
for Theo to breathe. Needing to get out of the store, he
turned his cart abruptly before jerking to a sudden stop.
He'd almost crashed into another cart—a cart steered by
a certain startled-looking, squirrelly waitress.

They studied each other, his claustrophobia fading
as curiosity took its place. He couldn't put his finger on

why, but she intrigued him in a way nothing had for a long time. All the questions she'd evaded or answered with lies filled his head, and he was suddenly glad he'd stopped at the grocery store. A conversation with Jules, as frustrating and unilluminating as it promised to be, was so much better than the gut-wrenching emptiness of his house.

"Hello." She broke the silence first as her gaze darted around, searching for the closest escape route.

"Jules."

Her nervous gaze bounced off him and landed on the lone dog chew in his cart. "Not very hungry, I'm guessing?"

He liked her Southern drawl. It was almost relaxing. "No." Her cart, by contrast, was heaped with food, more than one woman could eat in a month. *Interesting*.

Although she must have noticed the direction of his gaze, she just shifted her weight and changed the subject. "Are you done for the day or just starting?"

"Done." He looked pointedly at her cart and then back at Jules. "Feeding an army?"

He didn't expect her to laugh. It startled him how it transformed her. Theo had thought she was beautiful before, but when she laughed... It took his breath away and made him forget his next question.

"You could say that."

He blinked, looking down for a moment so he could get his thoughts in some sort of order again. What was he doing? He was interested in her as a cop would be interested in a suspicious stranger. There was nothing personal about it. Even as the thought passed through his head, he knew it was a lie. Self-directed irritation made his next question come out more harshly than he'd intended. "Who lives with you?"

She flinched, her fingers turning white as they tightened around the cart handle.

"Sorry," he grumbled, rubbing a hand over his closely shorn head. He could be an asshole. Theo fully accepted that. He'd never been a bully, though.

Jules blinked, her grip on the cart easing. "Did you just...apologize?" Her accent gave "apologize" a few extra syllables, making the corner of Theo's mouth twitch. She really was cute. Then her shocked tone penetrated, and he scowled again.

"Yeah." He was capable of basic courtesies. At least, he *used* to be. "Why's that so surprising?"

She studied him again, but it seemed different this time, more...thoughtful. "You just didn't seem like a huge apologizer."

"I'm not a *huge* one."

Her smile returned as Jules tilted her head down a little, although she still held his gaze in a way that was almost flirty. "You look pretty big to me."

He found himself leaning a little over the cart handle, as if his body was trying to get closer to her. He was fighting a smile again. His end of this back-and-forth felt a little stiff and rusty, but enormously good, too. It was like when he took an old, corroded engine and brought it back to life. He opened his mouth to respond, but another cart crashed into the side of his.

"Imagine bumping into the two of you here." It was Hugh. Of course it was.

"Are you stalking me?" Theo demanded, glaring at Hugh, who just looked amused.

"Me?" he gasped, a meaty hand pressed against his chest. "Me stalking you? How do you know I wasn't here first? Maybe *you're* the one stalking *me*."

Theo narrowed his eyes. His glare could convince armed criminals to back down, but Hugh just kept grinning.

"What were the two of you talking about?" Hugh leaned on the handle of his cart. "Were you harassing our nice, non-spitting waitress again, T?"

The smoldering anger that sat in Theo's chest flared at the thought of Hugh trying to save Jules from him. It stung sharply that Hugh thought Theo couldn't be trusted even to grocery shop, for Christ's sake, without going on a rampage. It wasn't just Hugh, either. Everyone at the station, from his lieutenant to the rabbity guy in charge of parking control, treated Theo with the same caution they'd treat a bomb about to explode. Theo was sick of it. Before he could verbally rip Hugh apart, Jules spoke.

"He's not harassing me." Theo looked at her in surprise, his mouth snapping shut. "He's just telling me things I need to know. About the grocery store. Since it's new to me and all."

Theo cleared his throat to disguise his snort. Jules really was a terrible liar. And she'd lied to protect him, even though he'd been interrogating her earlier.

After a startled pause, Hugh leaned forward, focused on Jules. "Really? Tell me. I've lived in Monroe my entire life, and I didn't think there was anything to know about the grocery store. C'mon, share. I'm dying to know the Monroe Market secrets."

Shifting uncomfortably, Jules sent Theo a frantic "help me!" glance, and Theo suddenly understood the lure of a damsel in distress—especially a hot damsel who'd just lied to protect him.

"Don't you have shopping to do?" Theo asked, giving Hugh's empty cart a pointed glare. "Unless you're here just because you *are* stalking me."

Hugh grinned at him. "You wish you had a stalker as fine as me." He looked between Theo and Jules, his pointer finger following his gaze, back and forth like a metronome. "And don't think I didn't notice this sudden disturbing alliance between you two."

"You're delusional," Theo said, giving a side-glance at Jules while suppressing yet another almost-smile. It was a nice feeling, to have someone on his side, even in such a minor way. Hugh and Otto had been teamed up for months in a save-Theo-from-himself effort. Even though Theo knew it was well intentioned, it still made him feel like the outsider.

"Delusional, and a stalker. A delusional stalker," Jules added, her mouth quivering, as if she was hiding a smile. Hugh shot her a displeased glare, but Theo held out his fist to her. She stared at it, looking startled for a moment, but then grinned and bumped her knuckles with his. As soon as they connected, he knew he wouldn't be interrogating her anymore. He was still curious about Jules—intensely curious—but his interest had changed when she'd come to his rescue. He didn't just want to figure out what the squirrelly waitress was running from. Theo wanted to *know* her, to learn the little silly things about her, like why she needed all that food and what she did when she wasn't at the diner and how she looked first thing in the morning. The last thought made him swallow hard.

"My frozen stuff's melting, guys. I'd better run." With that, she backed up her loaded cart, did a U-turn, and headed for the registers. Theo watched her go.

"Thought you didn't like the new waitress."

Theo turned toward his partner, narrowing his eyes. "Quit stalking me." He shoved his cart down the aisle away from Hugh.

"I was *shopping*, you egotistical bastard!" Hugh yelled after him, the amusement in his voice making Theo clench his jaw and flip him off. Hugh's laughter followed him through the store. Even that irritation couldn't keep Jules from his mind, though. Despite his almost-empty cart and Hugh's presence and *still* not having anything to eat for dinner, Theo was glad he'd gone to the grocery store after his shift.

He'd made an ally.

A hot one.

Theo was staring at his bedroom ceiling when the howling started.

It was a low whine at first, barely catching his notice. As usual, Theo was spending the hour between two and three a.m. rerunning the last few days before Don's death. Sometimes he'd play the what-if game—what if Theo had said this? Or what if he'd done that? Tonight he was replaying the hours and minutes, catching every single clue he'd missed now that it was too late to do any good.

The high-pitched sound increased in volume, and Theo raised his head before letting it thump back onto the pillow.

"Stupid dog. Useless dog," he muttered, but guilt and his innate sense of fairness wouldn't let that stand. "Stupid *me*. Fucking useless *me*." As galling as it had been to hear, his LT had been right. Viggy had been a great dog and a great officer when he'd worked with Don. Theo was ruining him. He wasn't just useless; he was destructive. It was sheer luck that no one had been seriously injured in the explosion at Gordon Schwartz's house. Everyone would be better off if Officer Theodore Bosco wasn't around.

The whine amped up to a full howl, as if Viggy was providing a soundtrack to Theo's self-loathing. The neighbors would be calling dispatch soon, and then Otto would be making a house call. Before, Theo would've just gotten a cranky phone call, but the guys had been worried about him since Don had died. Although the rational part of Theo's brain understood why Hugh and Otto had been acting like anxious mother hens for the past couple of months, he still felt smothered. Every "Are you okay?" made him want to punch someone…hard and repeatedly.

He didn't know what to do with this kind of anger.

The howl switched pitches and increased in volume. With a huff of mingled annoyance and concern, Theo got out of bed, yanking on track pants before heading to the back door, turning on the porch light on his way. The second he stepped outside, the howling stopped, as suddenly as if someone had flicked a switch.

Theo peered through the gloom to see Viggy slip into his shelter, tail tucked. Feeling like he was suffocating on his pity and hopelessness, Theo headed back to his bedroom. He wasn't even through the kitchen before the mournful howl began again.

Shoving the heels of his hands against his eyes, he sucked in an audible breath before dropping his hands. He reversed his path and returned to the back door, not bothering to turn on the porch light this time. Again, Viggy went silent, darting back into his shelter as soon as Theo came into view. As he stood on the porch, the cool air of the now-silent night brushing over his bare skin, Theo's annoyance trickled away, leaving only guilt and sadness in its wake.

He picked his way toward the fenced enclosure, careful not to step on anything prickly with his bare feet. For a long time, he stared at the dark entrance to Viggy's shelter. Theo was suddenly exhausted, more tired than he'd ever felt, and he sank down to sit on the rough grass next to the chain link.

"I'm sorry, Vig," he said, his words sounding loud in the quiet darkness. "I should've done something. Not sure what, exactly, but there had to've been something I could've said or done or…something. I'm sorry for being an oblivious asshole and not seeing when Don was hurting so bad he thought death was the better option."

Viggy's muzzle poked out of the shelter, followed by the rest of his shape, silhouetted dark against darker. When he was several feet away from Theo, the dog sat and watched him.

"And now you're fucked up, and I'm fucked up, and I don't know how to fix it." Leaning forward, Theo felt the cool chain link press into his forehead. "Don't really see the point in fixing it."

With a low, almost soundless whine, Viggy lowered his front end to the ground and rested his head on his paws. The silence stretched, filled only by the low whistle of the constant wind, and it felt like he and Viggy were the only living things in the world. Loneliness hollowed him out, and he tried to think of something, anything, else.

Jules popped into his mind, and he relaxed fractionally. As messed up as he was, there couldn't be anything between them, but it was nice to have an ally, or maybe, possibly, eventually, a friend. From the little information he'd gotten from her, it seemed like she could use one, as well. Their grocery-store encounter gave him an excuse to talk to her, too. He found himself actually looking forward to going to the diner, and it had been a while since he'd looked forward to anything.

And he was back to thinking about Don. Viggy shifted and whined, as if sensing that Theo's mood had dimmed.

"I know you miss him." His voice came out rough, almost hoarse. "I do, too."

They sat together quietly until the sun turned the sky orange and the neighborhood began to wake. Only then did Theo stand and stiffly walk toward the house to get ready for another shift.

"This is a bad idea."

Viggy didn't respond, not even to shift positions in the back. Not that Theo needed confirmation that this was indeed a very, very bad idea. It had been a long, frustrating shift, and he needed to go home. Despite knowing this, he couldn't stop himself from turning onto the rutted driveway leading to the old Garmitt place—the one currently occupied by a squirrelly, yet extremely hot, waitress.

He told himself it was his duty to check on her, to make sure she was okay in that remote, ramshackle house. As scared as she was, Jules was obviously running from something, and the thought of what possible danger she could be in made him grind his teeth and push a little harder on the accelerator. Even as he tried to convince himself that his impromptu visit was for Jules's safety, Theo knew the real reason he was dodging potholes and tree branches along this godforsaken excuse of a driveway was because he wanted to see her. He *needed* to see her, to feel the stirrings of excitement and even happiness he always experienced when she was around. Before he returned to his tiny, too-quiet, suffocating house, and everything inside him returned to its usual deadened state, he was going to grab a few minutes with Jules, so he could feel *alive* for once.

As he rounded the final bend, he saw smoke billowing from the open front door. A curl of tension tightened his stomach, and he reached for his radio as his gaze scanned the house, searching for Jules. Her SUV was parked in the front, so she was probably home. The door was open, but she wasn't outside.

He brought the radio to his mouth, ready to call in the fire, but then he hesitated as he stopped his Blazer abruptly, right next to the front porch. This close, the smoke was much less alarming than it had appeared at first glance. In fact, the haze coming from the house was rapidly dissipating, thinning to almost nothing. Theo decided to check things out before he brought Fire and Med and everyone else running to what might be a false alarm. Stepping out of his SUV, he hooked the radio to his belt, sending a quick glance toward Viggy. Before they'd left the station, Theo had rolled the passenger window most of the way down to give the dog some air. Although it was a warm day, the house and surrounding trees shaded the vehicle. With the window lowered, Viggy wouldn't overheat in the few minutes it would take for Theo to figure out what was going on at Jules's house and quickly leave. Assured of Viggy's safety, Theo turned away from his Blazer and climbed the front steps.

The porch was old, and each riser gave an alarming, high-pitched creak as it took his weight. It was eerily quiet, especially considering the wide-open door and the smoke. Theo had second thoughts about not calling in the fire. Both times at the diner, Jules had acted scared. What if whatever—or *whomever*—she was trying to escape had caught up with her? Jules could've been attacked or injured or taken—

Theo firmly cut off his escalating thoughts, shoving out any what-ifs and firmly blanking not only his mind, but his emotions. He'd gotten pretty good at that over the past few months. His cool shell was firmly reassembled as he stepped over the threshold, quickly checking right then left before entering the house.

What a pit. Theo couldn't believe someone lived there. It'd been empty for at least five years—and looked it. The previous owners hadn't done much in the way of maintenance, either, and the final result was a house that needed to have a date with a bulldozer.

"Police!" he called into the open, still-smoky hallway. "Anyone here?"

There was no response, so he took a couple of steps

inside. The remaining smoke tickled his throat and gave the old place an eerie cast. Theo held back a cough. He walked down the hallway, checking in each room he passed, but except for a few items — a bright-green bean-bag in the living room, an old chest in the library, a cheap drinking glass with awkwardly cut flowers mashed into it on the windowsill in the dining room — the house was empty. Empty and smoky and wrong. With Jules's SUV out front and the door open, she should be here. He automatically unsnapped the top of his holster, resting his hand on the butt of his gun. He felt his muscles tighten with each new empty room he saw.

The smoke was lightening, but a haze still lingered, dimming the light struggling to find its way through the windows. There was an almost-closed door on his left, and he pushed it open. The hinges protested with a squeal, but the door reluctantly swung to reveal an empty, old-fashioned bathroom. He continued down the hall, his imagination going wild again with thoughts of what could've happened. Had Jules's past caught up to her?

The thought of something happening to Jules made his stomach clench, and he moved more quickly. As Theo got closer to the final door on the right, the one he was fairly sure was the kitchen, he finally heard people. Multiple loud voices piled on top of each other, making it difficult for Theo to hear what anyone was saying. Pausing next to the entryway, keeping his body hidden from whoever was in the kitchen, he listened, trying to pick out individual words.

"...if he comes back!" a child's voice wailed, rising above the babble of the others. Theo's muscles tightened. Who was "he," and why was the kid so upset at the thought of this man's return?

"…long gone…" Theo barely made out a few words from Jules, but he was certain it was her speaking. The rest of what she had to say disappeared into the cacophony of sound, and the short phrases Theo was able to pick out only confused him more. Someone mentioned an ignition point, and the child shrieked something about making someone homeless, and another person stuttered in a deep, male voice about clean up. Theo frowned, the term "clean up" leading him to think about corpses. All his earlier fears for Jules rushed back, and he couldn't hesitate any longer.

Theo surged into the kitchen.

A small crowd of people—*young* people—huddled around the ancient stove, ignoring the light stream of smoke that still drifted from it. No one was looking at Theo, and he immediately dropped his hand from where it had been resting on the butt of his gun. The sight of all the kids made him feel a little sheepish for overreacting.

"What's going on?"

The entire group jumped as if he'd given them an electric shock, all of them turning to stare at him with expressions that ranged from fear to wariness. Upon closer observation, he confirmed that they were kids, ranging in age from ten or so to late teens—the oldest being none other than his squirrelly waitress. Her hair was caught in two braids, and a smear of black ran across her right cheek. Even smudgy, she was hot.

Not liking the prickle of emotion she woke in him, he looked at the stove.

"Is the fire out?" he asked when it appeared that no

one was going to answer his initial question. When they still didn't say anything—instead staring at him, stock-still and wordless—Theo shifted his weight impatiently and reached toward his radio with the hand not holding his gun. "Do I need to call in the fire department?"

"No!" several of the kids, including Jules, chorused in unison. He kept hold of his radio, since the threat of Fire seemed to have brought everyone back to life. Theo could sympathize with their reluctance. Sometimes—a lot of times—firefighters could be a pain in the ass.

"It's out," Jules said, taking a step toward him and positioning her body between Theo and the kids. Her slight figure wasn't much of a barrier, but there was something in the way she held herself that reminded him of a fierce mama bear. "There wasn't really a fire. It was more…" She waved a hand toward the stove, as if what had happened was written on its ancient surface.

"It was more of an explosion," one of the younger boys offered, but his brother—a twin, Theo assumed by their almost identical size and appearance—cleared his throat.

"It wasn't actually an explosion," the second one explained earnestly. "The debris just ignited extremely quickly, mimicking an explosion. A small one."

Theo wasn't any more enlightened than when he'd first seen the smoke. "Debris?"

Jules cringed. "An old pack rat nest." A visible shudder rippled through her.

"The rat wasn't hurt," the youngest of the group, a girl who looked like a younger Jules, said solemnly. "He left a long time ago. We're hoping he doesn't come back, because it would be very upsetting if he did and found out his home had burned."

"Didn't you check inside the oven before you turned it on?" Theo asked, stepping closer to the stove so he could look inside. Unfortunately, that move brought him very close to Jules. Under a layer of smoke, she smelled really nice, like vanilla and sugar and baking things.

Her mouth-watering scent was overlaid by the stench of charred rodent, which refocused him. What was wrong with him, that he was sniffing squirrelly waitresses? He reached for the numbness, but for the first time, it eluded him, and he was stuck with feeling the irritated fascination Jules inspired in him.

"No." She glared up at him, her gaze hotter than he thought blue eyes could be. "I normally do *not* look inside an oven before I turn it on, because who would ever think a huge *rat* would build a house inside an appliance? An appliance in which we cook food. Food that we eat!" Her voice had risen to a decibel that made Theo's ears hurt, but he found himself fighting the beginnings of a smile. Jules was just so outraged that a rat dared take up residence in her stove. Judging by the condition of the house—especially the rough state of the kitchen—Theo was not even a little surprised that a rodent had made its home there. In fact, he wouldn't be surprised if one ran across the floor in front of them. Theo almost hoped one would, so he could play hero, and Jules could thank him in that sweet, Southern accent of hers.

Startled by the daydream, he shook it off and tried to distract himself by belatedly trying to place her dialect. She'd mentioned Arkansas, but her drawl didn't match.

"Where are you from again?" he asked. It was only then he realized his question would've seemed random and abrupt. Her surprise morphed into that same hunted look she'd had at the diner, and he swallowed his disappointment at the reminder that she *was* hiding from something—hiding, and apparently, dragging her family along with her.

"Arkansas," all of them chorused—all except the hulking, oldest boy, who protectively stepped closer to Jules, watching Theo warily. Theo narrowed his eyes. Their quick, in-unison answer just screamed that it was a lie. Something was not right about the Jackson family, and Theo felt an itch to investigate—an itch that had been dormant until he met her. He pushed back the urge, biting off questions he wanted to ask. Jules had stood up for him, and he'd decided to back off and trust that Jules had a good reason—a good, *ethical* reason—for running. It was hard to let it go, not only because of his raging curiosity, but also because he wanted to know more about Jules.

He wasn't sure if this was a good thing or not. If he opened himself up again, he was stepping down the road to heartache. Feeling nothing was easier, less painful. In fact, it was probably smart to leave this jumpy, lying little family. Now.

Before he could escape, the little girl's eyes lit up. "A dog!"

As Theo started to turn, Viggy shot past him, heading straight for the huddled family. The small girl stepped forward, hands outstretched.

"Stop!" Theo barked, not sure if he was talking to the dog or to the kid. In the scant seconds it took for Viggy to reach the child, Theo's stomach twisted. With Viggy acting as unpredictably as he'd been, Theo had no idea how the dog would react. He just knew it wasn't going to be good. "Viggy, here!"

The dog didn't even glance at Theo. His focus was locked on the girl, and he shot toward her, as straight as an arrow to a bull's-eye. Visions of vulnerable flesh bitten and bleeding flashed in Theo's mind, and he lunged after Viggy. His fingers brushed the harness strap across Viggy's back, but the dog scooted out of reach, twisting around the little girl's legs, stretching up to…lick her face? Giggling, the child crouched down to the dog's level, using both hands to scratch his ruff.

It took a stunned moment for the dog's action to sink in to Theo's brain, for the lack of screams to register, and the roar of blood in his ears to ease. The other kids, unaware of Theo's earlier terror, circled around the girl and dog, reaching to pet Viggy, who rolled onto his back to get his belly scratched.

Theo took a few breaths, still feeling the rush of adrenaline coursing through him. It had been a while since he'd felt anything, and his current state of alertness felt uncomfortable but also kind of, well, *good*. He closed his eyes for just a second, enjoying the flow of blood and the hard beat of his heart. It felt like his body was finally thawing after being frozen for a long time.

"What's his name?" Reluctant warmth filled Jules's voice. Theo's heart rate increased a little more, and he frowned, his eyes snapping open.

Quit lusting after the squirrelly waitress, he told himself firmly. His body didn't listen. "Viggy."

"He's your dog?" the little girl asked, smiling up at him from her place on the floor next to Viggy. "I'd like a horse, but a dog would be good, too. We can't get one yet, though. Jules says we need to focus on keeping all of us alive before we add any dependents."

An audible inhale from Jules caught Theo's attention, and he looked at her sharply. What about the girl's statement had upset Jules? Was it the implication that they didn't have much money, or had Jules meant "survival" in its most immediate form? Were their lives in danger? He examined her face closely, but Jules flushed and dropped her gaze to the dog.

"Is he?" The little girl urged, and Theo's focus shifted to her again.

"He's my..." He paused just a second. "He was my friend's partner."

The oldest boy looked up from his position crouched by Viggy's head. He'd been scratching the dog's upside-down ears, and his hand paused as he spoke for the first time. "H-he's a p-p-police dog?"

"Yes." Viggy waved a paw, urging the teen to continue, and Theo gave an amused grunt. The blissed-out dog, sprawled on his back with his tongue hanging out, was a completely different animal than the stressed, unhappy creature he'd been since Don's death. Theo felt a twinge of gratitude for the family who'd returned the dog to his previous self, even if it was only for a minute or two.

One of the twins regarded Viggy with interest. "Is he trained to find drugs, then? Or does he chase after the bad guys and take them down?"

For the second time in as many minutes, Theo felt the foreign urge to smile. He managed to contain it. "Explosives. And the second one. He's a dual-purpose dog."

"He sniffs out bombs? *Awesome*."

Theo's gaze slid to Jules, and he saw she was regarding him thoughtfully. "Did you need something?" she asked.

The question confused him at first, random answers bouncing around in his head. There were so many things he needed. He needed peace, he needed Viggy to get over Don's death, *he* needed to get over Don's death. Theo might even need Jules. He knew he wanted her. "What?"

"Why are you here?"

Feeling caught, he rubbed a hand over his mouth before answering. Even that extra couple of seconds didn't give him time to think of a good excuse for his presence, so he just blurted out the truth. "I wanted to check on you."

She flinched, and Theo grimaced. That hadn't come out right.

"Your house is isolated," he tried explaining, searching for the right words that would erase her hunted look. "You're out here alone." Great, now he was sounding like a psycho stalker. "I just wanted to make sure you were safe. I was…" He shifted uncomfortably. "I was worried."

After regarding him in silence for a few awkward seconds, Jules smiled. The fearful, timid waitress he'd met at the diner was nowhere to be seen, and he found he couldn't look away. The sight of Jules and the kids and a happy Viggy made his lungs tighten, and he forced his head to turn toward the stove again. The smoke had stopped, and it was time—past time—for Theo to go.

He opened his mouth to tell Viggy to heel, but he closed it again. The dog's normal reaction was to ignore him and curl into a miserable ball, and a part of Theo—a rather huge part—didn't want this family to see that.

"We'd better go." He focused on the younger girl. "Do you want to help bring Viggy outside?"

"Yes!" Her face lit, and she jumped to her feet. "C'mon, Viggy!" She ran out of the kitchen, the twins following. Theo watched as the dog bounded after the kids, his tail up and wagging hard. It was the first time in a long time he'd seen Viggy without his tail tucked between his legs.

"Thank you." At the sound of Jules's voice, Theo turned from the now-empty doorway. "For being so nice to them."

Theo blinked. He'd been nice?

"I'd really like to get them a dog," she continued, speaking faster. Her drawl and quick speech blurred her words until they were almost unintelligible. "It's just that, as you can see"—she waved at the oven with an unconvincing laugh—"we have so much to do with the house and getting the kids started at school, and with my new job and everything, it's just better that we wait to get a pet. That's what I meant about not wanting to get a dog right now. You know, what Dee said that I said, and I'm *so* babbling right now, so I'll just be quiet."

Her words ended abruptly, and she stared at Theo, her panic returning in an almost visible flood. Theo was a little disappointed. He hadn't missed the squirreliness. Plus, her rambling monologue had just convinced him that the reference to "survival" hadn't meant merely food and shelter. This family was in trouble. "Dee?"

"Yes. Deirdre." She took a quick breath, as if she was about to launch into another speech. When the oldest boy—the only one who hadn't run outside with Viggy—shifted slightly closer to Jules, she closed her mouth with an audible click and gave Theo a strained, closed-mouth smile.

Theo's gaze shifted to the teen. "What's your name?"

"Sam." There was no stutter that time. Theo met his eyes, and the boy looked back. There was something in his stance—a hidden flinch, a sense that he was torn between running and throwing a punch—that was troubling and familiar. Theo had seen something very similar when he'd interviewed abuse victims.

Theo's gaze moved to Jules. Although he could've been mistaken, could've been influenced by this stupid attraction he was fighting, he was pretty sure she wasn't the abuser. The protective attitude Sam had toward her didn't fit.

"You're all siblings?"

"Yes." Jules's chin tilted in a slightly belligerent way that Theo noted with interest. The gesture made him pretty sure her answer wasn't entirely truthful.

"And the twins' names?"

"Tyson and Thomas."

Her entire body was braced, as if she was waiting for a blow. After regarding her silently for a moment, Theo took a step back and gestured toward the doorway into the hall. "I should get Viggy."

Exchanging a quick glance, Jules and Sam walked out of the kitchen ahead of Theo. Sam gave Theo a few worried looks over his shoulder, but Jules kept her gaze fixed ahead, her spine a little too straight.

Happy, excited shrieks greeted them as they walked through the still-open front door. The three younger siblings had found a fallen tree branch and were playing fetch with Viggy. The stick was so long it threatened to bowl over anyone in the dog's path, and the kids had to dodge away, laughing.

Jules sighed audibly. "Sam-I-Am, we're going to have to get them a dog, aren't we?"

Despite her long-suffering tone, she was smiling, and Theo found it hard to pull his gaze from her face. Tense and serious, Jules was beautiful. Happy, she was... more than beautiful. Theo forced himself to turn toward Sam, who'd made an amused sound that wasn't quite a laugh. Both were watching their younger siblings with the same expression, a look that Theo had a hard time interpreting. There was love and worry and a ferocious protectiveness and so much more written on their faces, their emotions so naked and raw that Theo felt like a voyeur. He cleared his throat and glanced at the kids playing with the Malinois.

Viggy really was acting like a different dog. No, that wasn't right. He was acting like the dog he used to be. The usual grief and guilt started to twist in his gut again, and Theo turned abruptly toward his SUV.

Only after he raised the back hatch did he turn back to the family. "Viggy." His voice was too harsh. Theo knew that, even before Viggy's tail dropped from its happy carriage and tucked between his legs. "Load."

As the dog cowered, the kids went silent. Regret flooded Theo, filling him with a caustic burn that was all too familiar. Theo clenched his fists and took a breath, and then another. It was one thing for Hugh or Otto to see the mess Theo and Viggy had become. For whatever reason, Theo didn't want these kids to have to witness the wreck Don had left. He especially didn't want Jules to know. Why he cared what she thought was beyond him, but he couldn't help sending her a sideways glance to see how she was reacting.

Although her smile had disappeared, Jules didn't look scared or upset. Instead, she was looking back and forth between Theo and the dog with a thoughtful expression.

"He doesn't want the fun to end," she said lightly to her siblings. "Why don't y'all help get him into the car?"

Once again, she was saving *him*.

The kids immediately dove into the game, running toward Theo's Blazer while calling Viggy to follow. After a few seconds, he perked up slightly and trotted after the children. When he got closer to the SUV, he slowed, his whole body seeming to shrink in on itself.

Theo moved away from the open hatch and watched as the kids crowded around the back of the SUV, urging Viggy to jump inside.

"Load." The word came out too loudly, making the kids and the dog jump and look at him anxiously. Theo gritted his teeth, sucking in a breath through his nose before trying to moderate his tone. "The command is 'load.'"

The three kids relaxed and returned to their efforts. "Viggy, load!"

Reluctantly, as if Viggy was just as loath to return to the reality of grief and loss as Theo was, the dog jumped into the rear compartment. One of the twins—Tyson, Theo was fairly certain—lowered the hatch door. The ease with which these children had gotten Viggy to relax and play made Theo envious. At the same time it raised a flicker of hope that the dog would someday be the happy, confident Viggy he used to be.

"Thank you." His words were stiff, but they were lucky he'd managed to say anything at all. Theo felt his lungs tighten. This family—the hot waitress and dog-whispering children and their not-quite-hidden flinches—was starting to wake something inside of him. His emotions were bleeding through the armor he'd built to contain them, and it was making it hard to breathe. He needed to leave.

After a single step toward the driver's door, he paused. "The stove fire is under control?"

Jules grimaced. "Yes. All that's left is the cleaning."

"Have it checked before you try to use it again." The suggestion came out more as an order, but Jules didn't look offended. She did appear tired and a little sad as she gave him a forced smile that could have meant anything. Theo was pretty sure it wasn't the response he wanted. "Something could've been damaged by the fire, and that thing is ancient. You don't want to mess around with gas. Have your landlord get it checked."

"Okay!" Jules held up her hands, palms out in a gesture of surrender. "I'll have someone look at it."

Her promise was too vague to satisfy Theo, but there was nothing he could do except call the stove repairman himself. As much as he wanted to do exactly that, he barely knew this family. They'd never accept his help. With a stiff incline of his head to Jules and her siblings, Theo got into the driver's seat and started the SUV.

As he eased down the driveway, Theo glanced in the rearview mirror at the family watching him leave. He'd expected to feel relief at being away from their agitating presence, but he didn't.

All he felt was hollow.

"I like that dog," Dee said, watching the SUV disappear around the first curve in the driveway.

So had Jules. The dog's partner was a different story. It wasn't that she *didn't* like him, but "like" was such an inadequate word for what she'd felt. His continued visits to the diner and their unexpected alliance at the grocery store had made most of her initial cop-sighting panic fade.

Despite that, she'd been shocked to see him in her house, all her fears returning in a crashing wave, and she'd had to shove back the instinctual urge to tackle him and yell at her siblings to run. He'd just been concerned about their oven fire, though. And he'd been worried about her. Contented warmth flowed through her at the thought.

"Jules." The impatient note in Tio's voice told her it wasn't the first time he'd said her name.

She tore her gaze from the spot where she'd last seen the cop who was a little too fascinating—and around a little too often—for her peace of mind. "Sorry, T. What's up?"

"Can we go to the library?" he asked. "I'd like to see if someone scanned in an owner's manual for our stove."

She nibbled on the inside of her lip as she studied him, her mind working.

"Don't you want me to go to the library?" Tio finally prompted when her silence went on too long.

"No." She shook off her distracted thoughts. "I mean,

I'll take you. I'm just wondering if it's irresponsible of me to let you work on the stove. Shouldn't we have a professional…um, oven person look at it? Like Theo said, gas is nothing to fool around with."

He gave her a look of mixed condescension and long-suffering patience that sat oddly on his thirteen-year-old face. "I'll be fine, Jules. I know what I'm doing. At least, I will when I get that manual." He tilted his head toward the SUV meaningfully.

"Okay." She headed for the house to grab her keys and lock up, calling over her shoulder, "But if you get blown up, I'm going to be annoyed!"

Sam followed her inside, and she gave him an inquiring look.

"Th-Theo?" he repeated, frowning.

Examining her brother's extra-tense face, unsure of what, exactly, he was asking her, she said, "The cop who was just here."

"How d-d-do you know him?"

She grabbed the keys and her purse from the kitchen table they'd found at the thrift store. It was a little small for all of them, and the five chairs didn't exactly match—either the table or each other—but the set had cost a total of seventeen dollars. With their supply of cash dwindling painfully fast, affordability beat out aesthetics. "I wouldn't say I *know* him. He's at the diner every morning, that's all."

"B-but you c-c-call h-him *Theo*?"

She was still confused. "Yes?"

"Why?"

"Uh…because that's his name? What else should I call him?"

His fists clenched at his sides. "How ab-b-bout Of-f-ficer? Or G-Guy Who C-C-Can Ar-rest You for K-Kidnapping?"

"Sam." Her voice was soft, and she resisted the urge to squeeze his arm. As tense as he was, the last thing he'd want was to be touched. "It's okay. He doesn't know."

"M-mayb-b-be." He closed his eyes for a second as his jaw muscles worked, and she knew he was trying to get his stutter under control. "N-not yet. B-b-but he c-c-could f-find out."

She stared at him helplessly, unable to deny what he'd said. Theo could find out what she'd done, who they were, *everything*. "If he does, we'll run." It was weak, she knew, but it was all she could say to reassure him.

Sam didn't look at all reassured. "D-d-d-do you l-like him?"

"What?" The word came out a bit screechy, and she winced inwardly as Sam's frown deepened. "Of course not. That'd be crazy."

"It w-w-would be cr-cr-crazy." His grim tone made her drop her eyes. Maybe she'd thought about him a few times—and not in a he-could-arrest-me sort of way—but anyone with a pulse would indulge in a few daydreams when confronted by a man that good-looking. "Th-hat'd b-be b-b-bad, J-Ju."

"I know."

"*Really* b-bad."

"I *know*." Her response was barely more than a sigh as a tiny hope she hadn't even realized she'd been harboring slipped away. It hit her that this was her life now. Until Dee was eighteen and the threat of Courtney was gone, Jules couldn't date, couldn't have any close friends, couldn't get attached to anyone. If people got close, they'd ask questions. Jules had to be ready to take off at a moment's notice.

Loneliness crept up her throat, making it tight, but she swallowed the self-pity. It was worth it. Getting the kids away from Courtney was worth the sacrifice. She met Sam's worried gaze and held it steadily.

"I know, Sam." No matter how hot and protective and gruffly kind he was, Theo was also a cop, and she was a criminal. Jules had to stay away from him…no matter how hard that may be.

CHAPTER 10

WHAT WAS *WRONG* WITH HIM? THEO HUFFED OUT A humorless laugh as he slid out of his solitary booth and tossed down enough cash to cover the lunch he'd barely touched. A better question would be what *wasn't* wrong with him.

Megan lifted her eyebrows as he passed her on the way to the door. To his relief, she wasn't curious enough about his unusual lunchtime appearance to ask him why he was there. If she had asked, he wouldn't have had an answer—at least not one he wanted to share.

It was the squirrelly waitress's fault. He'd gotten used to seeing her every day, but their usual breakfast had been canceled when a traffic stop for a broken tail-light turned out to be a wanted meth dealer in a car he'd stolen from his ex-girlfriend.

Jules hadn't even been working, unless she'd been hiding in the kitchen the entire time he was there. That was a definite possibility, since he acted like a complete ass every time he saw her. But not seeing her made him cranky—well, crank*ier* than usual—and that made him even more pissed that he was allowing an almost-stranger to determine his mood.

He shoved the door a little too hard as he left the diner. The perfect September weather mocked his bad mood. The sun was a little too bright and cheery, the air just cool enough to feel good against his face. His frown deepening, he shoved on his sunglasses.

A familiar Volkswagen Jetta was parked next to his squad car. It took him a few seconds to remember who the VW's owner was. When it finally struck him, his step faltered, and he had the cowardly urge to duck back into the diner. It was too late, though. She was already headed his way.

"Hey, Theo." Sherry Baker, Don's daughter, attempted a smile, but it collapsed before it was fully formed.

Theo couldn't even manage that much. Instead he gave her a stiff nod. "Sherry." That was all he could say. If he tried anything else—an "I'm sorry for your loss," or even "How are you?"—his guilt and grief would choke him before he could get out more than a word.

To his surprise, Sherry didn't look offended. The last time he'd seen her had been at the funeral, where she'd been so angry, so devastated, trying desperately to find someone to blame...someone besides her father. Theo had accepted every accusing glare, knowing he deserved that and more...so much more. Don had been his friend, his mentor, his *brother*. Theo should've known, should've at least suspected. What kind of self-involved bubble had he lived in that Don's misery had escaped him so completely?

Except for the downward cast of her mouth, Sherry looked like she always had before. Her blond hair was washed and brushed, pulled back in a neat braid, and her sundress looked new. The woman in front of him bore little resemblance to that pain-racked mourner at her dad's funeral.

Now, she just seemed quietly sad. Oddly enough, Theo felt a jolt of envy for that sign of straight-up grief. He wished that was what he felt, rather than this seething mass of angry emotions that was corroding his insides.

"How's it going, Theo?"

How was he supposed to answer that? *Quite shittily, thank you for asking. I've even managed to fuck up your dad's dog. How are you?* Swallowing the words, Theo twitched one shoulder in a shrug. When Sherry's mouth flattened and her eyes glossed with tears, he knew it had come off as callous and uncaring rather than the truth: that he was so locked up by regret he couldn't even talk to her.

It was Sherry's turn to offer a jerky nod. "See you around, Theo."

He watched her go into the diner, his guilt multiplying into a giant churning mass so huge it felt as if his skin couldn't contain it. Clenching and unclenching his fists as the urge to punch something—or someone— surged through him, he stalked the rest of the way to his squad car and jerked open the door.

His bad day had somehow, magically, become so much worse.

Her body was an idiot. A self-destructive idiot. An *all-around*-destructive idiot. There was no other explanation for the way her heart leapt when she saw Theo sitting at his usual booth. He was watching her, so she knew he saw her stupidly huge grin and the way she barely paused to snatch up a coffeepot before heading in his direction.

It had to be hormones or pheromones or some

primitive instinct that made her body react to Theo that way. After all, it wasn't like he was even nice to her. Except for that one bonding moment in the grocery store, that one fist bump, that one mention that he'd been worried about her, and her body had gone haywire. Her brain knew better, but somehow she was at his table, grinning at him like the fool she really, truly was.

"Hey," she said, flipping his mug with unsteady fingers.

He gave her an upward tip of his head, and even that ultramasculine gesture made her melt in her comfy, completely unattractive shoes. She had to look away. There was no way she could stare at him and pour coffee. That would only result in second-degree burns and a huge mess.

"Your usual?"

"You know it already?" he asked.

Jules swallowed back the words before she could tell him that memorizing people's breakfast choices wasn't that hard compared to getting her accounting degree in three years. Instead, she just smiled and nodded. There was no excuse for her to stand there and stare at him anymore, no matter how much her stupid eyeballs wanted to, so Jules started to turn away.

"Wait."

She stopped midturn and looked over her shoulder at Theo. He didn't respond right away, and her brows lifted in question.

"Thanks," he finally said, gripping his mug but not taking a sip. "For yesterday. At the store. Hugh can be..." Theo grimaced and stared into his coffee, as if searching for the right word.

"A good friend," Jules finished, and his gaze jumped back to hers.

Although he scowled, there was a hint of amusement there, too. "I was thinking more along the lines of an obsessive stalker."

She laughed. "Sometimes, the line between a good friend and obsessive stalker is a fine one." With the hand not holding the coffeepot, Jules reached out and patted Theo's forearm. He instantly focused on her hand, the muscles in his arm tightening under her fingers. After a charged, silent moment, she pulled her hand away, oddly flustered.

"I'll just…um, get your order in." This time, he didn't stop her as she hurried away.

After returning the coffeepot to its station, she rushed into the kitchen. Pressing her hands to her face, she felt the heat of her burning cheeks and bit back a groan. Blushing, smiling, touching his arm…could she have made her budding interest in him any more obvious? Theo must've thought she was an infatuated idiot, and she was beginning to worry that he wasn't wrong.

"Need something?" Vicki called from her spot by the grill.

Yes. Some dignity. Maybe some pride. Definitely some self-control. "Nope. Just…taking a second. Oh, and Theo wants his usual."

"Got it."

When no insults or threats followed, Jules looked at Vicki curiously. She seemed to be in an unusually nonabusive mood.

"Before you go, would you mind grabbing another flat of eggs out of the walk-in?"

Jules tried not to make a face. She hated going into the walk-in cooler. She'd hated small spaces — especially small, *dark* spaces — ever since her father had remarried for the fourth time when Jules had been a shy fifteen-year-old. One of Courtney's favorite punishments had been to lock Jules in one of the linen closets. Most of the time, it had been only for a few hours. A few memorable times, though, Jules had been trapped in the tiny, dark space overnight. Although she'd mostly gotten over her claustrophobia in the years since she'd escaped from that house, something about the cooler made all Jules's old fears flare to life.

She had to suck it up, though. There was no way out of going into the cooler, unless she wanted to sound like a big baby. "Sure."

Flipping on the light switch, Jules closed her fingers around the metal handle. After taking a breath, she hauled back on the door. There was a brief hesitation before the heavy door released its seal and swung open, releasing a gust of chilled air. Jules shivered, although it was more from nerves than the cold.

She glanced over her shoulder and caught Vicki watching her. As soon as she saw Jules returning her gaze, Vicki focused on the grill, whistling tunelessly as she poked at some hash browns. Jules frowned but turned back toward the cooler. The longer she stood there, dreading it, the longer it was going to take. She needed to just go in, grab the eggs, and get out.

Jules stepped into the cooler, reluctantly letting the door close behind her. In three quick strides, she'd reached the egg boxes lining the bottom shelf. Crouching, she eyed the top of the container and sighed.

The box was taped shut, but she didn't want to go get a utility knife and have to *return* to the cooler. Instead, she just picked at a corner of the packing tape until she could pull it up and off the top of the box.

As she reached to open the flaps, everything went dark.

Jules froze. Her whole body flushed cold and then hot, and her fingers went numb. She couldn't feel the cardboard under her hands anymore, and she lost all sense of direction, all sense of balance. It was as if she were underwater, unsure of which way was up. Her legs gave out, and she sat down hard on the cold, tiled floor.

There. I felt that. She pressed her palms against the floor next to her hips, increasing the pressure until pain darted up her wrists into her arms. Strangely enough, she was relieved by the discomfort. It grounded her, made her feel like she was rooted to the floor, rather than floating in the dark space.

She heard someone gasping, short pants of air, and Jules realized the sound was coming from her. Even though no one else could hear it, she was embarrassed by how pathetic she sounded. She was much, much too old to be scared of the dark.

"It's just a power outage," she whispered, her voice coming out unsteady, her words interrupted by her shallow gulps for breath. "The door is right there." Her eyes blinked, trying to adjust to the absolute blackness, and a light-green glow caught her attention. At first, she thought it was nothing, just a blob of false light caused by her squeezing her eyes shut too tightly, but the green shape was there each time she opened her eyes to stare into the darkness. Finally, she realized it was the glow-in-the-dark emergency release handle.

Her relieved breath came out too close to a sob for comfort. Vicki would never let Jules live it down if she came out of the dark cooler crying. Her head still spun from fear and the dizzying darkness, so Jules crawled toward the green glow, her apron catching between the hard floor and her knees.

She'd made it. The emergency release knob was right at eye level, and Jules forced herself to stand. Crawling out of the cooler would be almost as bad as being in hysterics. Jules's hands followed the metal-lined surface of the door, helping her keep her balance as she rose to her feet. Once she was upright, she pushed against the door.

Nothing happened. It didn't budge.

Her breathing immediately sped up again. Was she *trapped* in the dark space? Jules could hear her heartbeat pounding in her ears, the thumps so close together that it created a steady thunder. Cold pressed against her like a living thing, filling her lungs with each rapid, futile inhale. There wasn't enough air. Each breath felt tight and empty, and she panted faster, trying to suck in oxygen.

Stop it! she snapped at herself. *There* is *air*. Fighting back the panic wanting to take control, Jules forced her breathing to slow. Gradually, her heartbeat followed enough for her logical brain to begin working. Maybe the door automatically latched in a power outage. She twisted the emergency release knob one direction and then pushed against the door again. Nothing. She tried the other way. The door remained stubbornly closed. Jules pushed and pulled and finally yanked so hard that the handle came off in her hand. She stared at the green, glowing, *useless* object in her hand and then burst into tears.

"Help!" she screamed, the panic rushing in and taking over. There were no rational thoughts left in her brain—just the desperate need to get out of the cooler. "Get me out!"

She pounded on the door, but its thick construction muffled her hits so even she could barely hear them. She wasn't going to get out. She'd be trapped in that shrinking space for *hours*, even days, until she died of hypothermia. *No!* She couldn't do it, couldn't be stuck in this tight, airless blackness for even one more second. Forget hypothermia; her heart was about to explode in terror. Bracing her hands on the door, she shoved with all her might. It didn't budge, immobile and horribly still...until suddenly the door was gone and everything was blindingly light and she was *falling*.

Theo caught her. Jules wasn't sure how she knew, but she did, the instant his arms wrapped around her and her face pressed into his uniform shirt. It was stiff with starch, and a button pressed hard against her cheekbone, but she'd never felt anything better. His hand cupped her head, pulling her tighter against his chest, and his other arm wrapped around her back. It took a few seconds for Jules to realize that Theo was shouting.

"You're a fucking psycho!"

Her head jerked back at that. She might be a kidnapper and a criminal and a liar, but she thought it was extremely unfair of him to call her a psycho. When she managed to focus her tear-blurred eyes on Theo's face, though, he wasn't looking at her. Jules followed his glare to Vicki, who was just a few feet away, doubled over with laughter. Jules blinked a few times, trying to tear herself free of the panic that still wanted to cling so she could figure out what was going on.

"C'mon, Theo," Vicki finally wheezed, wiping her eyes. "I was just joking around. God, that was hilarious. When I pulled the same trick on Megan, she just sat on a crate of potatoes and played on her phone until I got bored and walked away."

Theo snarled, "You—"

"What's going on?" Hugh burst into the kitchen with Megan at his heels.

"Theo's being a fun-wrecker. Again." With a final hiccup of laughter, Vicki turned to the sink and started washing her hands.

Megan looked at Jules, then the walk-in cooler door, then Vicki, and understanding washed over her face. She groaned loudly. "Vicki, Theo's right. You *are* a psycho. Did you do the whole turn-the-lights-off-and-hold-the-door-shut thing on poor Jules? You know she's scared of the walk-in!"

"That's what made it so funny!" When everyone just glared at Vicki, she threw her hands in the air. "You guys are no fun."

Megan turned to Jules. "Are you okay?"

"Yeah." With everyone's eyes on her, embarrassment was starting to set in. It didn't help that Jules realized she was still leaning against Theo's very muscular chest. His hand was smoothing circles on her lower back, and she would've been very happy to stay there for the remainder of the morning. At that moment, resting against him, Jules gave in. It wasn't just attraction; she was way too far gone for that. This was a huge, unmistakable, unignorable crush. She *liked* Theo…a lot.

When Megan and Hugh began to look more curious than concerned, Jules forced herself to take a step back, out of Theo's tempting hold. He resisted for a fraction of a second, but then let her go. "I'm fine." Her quivering voice turned her words into a lie. "I just don't like small spaces."

"Are you going to quit?" Megan asked, shooting an angry look at Vicki, who didn't seem to notice. She'd returned to her grill and had started whistling again.

"I'll stay if you promise I'll never have to go in there again." Jules jerked her thumb toward the cooler.

"Deal. Sorry about Vicki," Megan said. "I should've warned you that she has a messed up sense of humor."

Hugh nodded. "We all carry scars from Vicki's jokes."

There was a snort from the direction of the grill. "You're not scarred, dumbass. How did giving you swirlies in fifth grade scar you?"

He placed a hand on his chest. "My heart, Vicki. You scarred my heart." Letting his hand drop to his side, Hugh tilted his head. "And my pride. My pride definitely took a beating. I was so grateful that sixth-grade growth spurt finally made me taller than you."

"I could still take you," Vicki grumbled.

"You sure you're okay?" Megan asked Jules.

"I'm fine."

"Good, because there are hungry people waiting for us." Pointing at Hugh and Theo, Megan jerked her head toward the door. "You two, out."

Jules wanted to get back to work. All she'd do if they kept standing around was mentally relive her humiliating experience over and over. As Theo gave her one last, penetrating look and stepped toward the door, she caught his hand. "Thanks."

His gaze ran down her body, as if checking to see if she was intact, and then he gave her one of those short nods she loved so much. He squeezed her hand before releasing it as he moved away. She watched him, remembering the feel of his shirt against her cheek. The terror of being trapped in the dark walk-in cooler had been almost worth being held against his chest.

Shaking her head, she forced herself to look away from his retreating form. Why did he have to be so... heroic? Her crush on Theo had just grown a thousand times bigger.

At the heavy knock, all conversation around the dinner table ceased. Everyone went still, not even chewing. Since her freak-out in the walk-in cooler that morning, Jules had been jumpy, and an unexpected visitor didn't help matters. Their new life in Monroe was so fragile. The unknown person at the door could be the one who would destroy it. Jules exchanged a look with Sam, and then he ushered the other three kids out the back door toward the barn. Taking a shaky breath, she walked toward the front door.

I won't let them get the kids, she told herself as she approached the entryway. *I just need to buy them time to get away*. Her hand shook as she flattened it against the door, rising on her tiptoes to look through the peephole. Her lungs and heart stilled for a second, only to rush into motion again when she recognized the person on her porch.

Light-headed with relief and a giddiness she felt only around Theo, she yanked open the door. "Hi."

"Hey."

"What are you doing here?"

For some reason, his scowl deepened. "This porch is a death trap."

Confused, Jules looked down at the boards under his feet and then back up to his face. "Okay. Should you be standing on it then?"

His snort could've been a laugh if he hadn't looked so cranky. "Probably not. I...uh..." He shifted, looking away, and Jules could've sworn he seemed uncomfortable. But he was Theo, and from what she'd seen, Theo wasn't ever uncomfortable. Angry? Yes. Hostile? Sure. But uncomfortable? This was a first. "I brought some boards and my tools." When she just stared, even more confused, he gestured toward the porch floor. "To fix it."

"You're going to fix our porch."

"Yes."

"Why?"

"I told you. It's a death trap." He shifted impatiently, and the wood squeaked under his boots. "You could fall through. Or one of the kids could get hurt."

As she looked at him, a wave of strong emotion washed over her. He was there to *help*, to do something she couldn't to protect the kids, to protect her. She felt like she'd been treading water since she'd met with Mr. Espina, trying desperately to keep them all from drowning, and now Theo was there, offering her a hand. It was just a porch, but it was *help*, and it made her feel so much less alone.

Stepping forward, she wrapped her arms around his chest and hugged him hard. He stiffened, letting out a surprised grunt, but she held on, pressing her forehead against his worn T-shirt. Tears of gratitude rushed to her eyes, and she blinked hard, trying to keep them contained. Releasing him, she stepped back, giving him a shaky smile.

"Are you crying?"

"No."

"It's just a porch."

"I know." Her smile stretched bigger even as her eyes filled again. "Thank you."

"I'm not fixing it if you cry," he threatened, making her laugh.

"I'm going to go get the kids," she said with a final sniffle.

Theo glanced toward her SUV, probably thinking she had to pick them up. "Where are they?"

"Oh, um…just playing in back." She forced her brain to get back on track. Just because he was fixing her porch didn't mean she could slip up and reveal that they were hiding in the barn. "Did you want me to keep them out of your hair?"

He shrugged. "They can help."

Jules beamed at him.

"What?"

"You are such a sweetheart."

His wary look shifted back into his usual scowl. "Am not."

With another laugh, she turned away, moving

toward the back door so she could give the kids the all clear. He really was. A porch-fixing, heroic, heart-stealing sweetheart.

"Maybe we could be homeschooled?" Ty asked hopefully.

As the five of them stared at the two-story building, a mustard-yellow box with just a few narrow windows on each corner, Jules was tempted to agree. Then she thought about the reality of trying to teach her siblings—especially Tio—and she sighed.

"C'mon, y'all." She shoved the driver's door open with more confidence than she felt. "Dee, you too." Even though just a few people were around, and the few extra-early students were headed into the school, Jules didn't want Dee to be left alone. It was going to be hard enough having them out of her sight for the whole day while they were in school.

Ty groaned, but Tio got out of the backseat more enthusiastically. Sam didn't say anything, but Jules could feel his tension. If he'd been drawn any tighter, Sam would've snapped like an overstressed steel cable. Catching his sleeve—but being careful not to grab his arm—she held him back a few steps, allowing the twins and Dee to walk slightly ahead of them.

"Dennis is good at what he does," she said very quietly, so only Sam could hear. "We have new names, new social security numbers, new ages, new lives."

Sam stared straight ahead, the muscle in his jaw working.

"She won't find us." She looked for any sign that her words had reassured him, but his expression hadn't changed. "If there's any chance she even has a clue where we are, we'll run again. I'm sure Dennis has a new-life warranty of some sort."

It was a sad attempt at a joke, but it made Sam finally meet her eyes. "I'm okay, J-JuJu. It's j-j-just..." He gestured toward the ugly building. "N-n-new school."

"Oh." It shouldn't have been such a surprise that Sam was worried about such a normal thing as his first day at a new school, but it was. They'd been freaking out over getting away and staying away from Courtney so much that Jules had forgotten any other worries existed. "You'll do great, Sam. All the work will be old hat to you. If anything, you'll be bored."

Sam came as close as she'd ever seen to rolling his eyes. "Sure, J-Ju."

The twins and Dee waited at the main doors for Jules and Sam to catch up. Feeling like a parenting failure, she asked, "Are you nervous about starting school, Ty?"

"Nah." His shrug was a hair too nonchalant as they passed through the door into the dimness of a hallway. "I'm not scared. Not that excited about getting homework and stuff, but school is school. Kids are kids. Some are nice and some are assholes."

"Language!"

Tio looked at her seriously. "It *is* the most appropriate term for some people in our demographic."

Since she couldn't really argue with the truth of that, Jules changed the subject. "What about you, T? Any first-day jitters?"

The look her brother gave her was completely

uncomprehending. "Why would school make me nervous?" For him, school had always been his safe place.

"Good," she said. A sign that said "office" pointed to the right. "That's…" Her attempt at a pep talk died as they turned the corner.

"*Th-there's* one r-r-reason to b-b-be n-nervous about school," Sam muttered under his breath as they all came to a startled halt—all except for Dee.

"*Viggy!*" she called, lurching forward. Grabbing a handful of her shirt, Jules caught her little sister just in time.

"Dee! Viggy's working!" she whispered, excitement making her stomach buzz despite her efforts at staying calm. After Theo had fixed their porch the previous evening, she'd spent a sleepless night alternating between grinning like a besotted idiot and scolding herself for being a besotted idiot. At around three in the morning, she'd resolved to try her best to avoid Theo, so her crush on him would fade. Apparently, the universe was not cooperating with her plan. Theo—looking like hot, broody forbidden fruit—was already turning away from Hugh and moving toward them. Viggy was trying to plunge forward to get to Dee, and Theo's arm strained, his biceps bulging under his uniform shirt as he held back the dog. Jules's attention was caught by the way his sleeve looked on the verge of ripping, as if it was struggling to contain the impressive muscles underneath.

Theo stopped a few feet from them, greeting them with a short jerk of his head as he half-wrestled, half-ordered Viggy into a sit. When Dee lurched forward again, yanking against Jules's hold, Jules realized she still had a grip on the back of her sister's shirt.

"Dee," she said, focusing on the girl in front of her so Theo's...*Theo-ness* didn't take away her ability to speak. "Stop."

"But I want to pet him." Viggy's tail thumped against the floor, as if in approval of that plan.

"He's on duty." That deep, clipped voice made the hairs on Jules's arms stand up straight, and it wasn't from fear. "He can't play with you when he's on duty. He needs to focus."

"Oh." Dee drooped a little, but she didn't make any additional efforts to get to Viggy.

"What's he focusing on today?" Jules asked, trying to keep the question light and casual and not get distracted by how good Theo looked in his uniform.

Theo eyed her with a look filled with so much interest that she had to bite the inside of her lip hard to keep from babbling and filling the silence. "Looks like a false alarm," Theo finally answered.

False alarm, Jules repeated in her head, confused until she remembered what Viggy's job was. "A bomb threat?" Her voice went a little shrill on the last word. Her paranoia about the kidnapping made her forget that there were other dangers in the world, and she needed to protect her siblings. After all, they were *her* kids now.

"Happens a lot." Theo seemed awfully casual about the *threat* of a *bomb*. "It's usually some kid who's pissed at a teacher or wants a free day."

Jules's brain seized on what she saw as the most important word in that sentence. "*Usually?* Shouldn't you have evacuated the school, just in case?"

"We try to keep it low-key unless we believe it's a legitimate threat. Otherwise, we're just giving the kid who called it in what he—or she—wants," Theo explained. "If I thought there was a chance there really was a bomb, Viggy and I wouldn't be in here. We'd get everyone out of the building and call the bomb squad in Denver."

Although his words were reassuring, Jules still felt jumpy. She glanced around, trying not to think of all the possible hiding spots—that locker, that recycling bin with the lid, that janitor's closet. She nibbled on the inside of her lip as she forced herself to quit looking and focus on Theo's face. If she was honest, that last part wasn't a hardship.

"Jules." Tio tipped his head toward the office. The flow of students had increased, although most of them were making a wide berth around the cop and his dog, and Jules wasn't sure how long it would take to complete the admissions paperwork. She'd hate it if the kids had to walk in late to their first class. Being the new kids was bad enough without drawing extra attention. There was already a lot of staring going on, although Jules wasn't sure if that was due to them being strangers or the K9 cop in their midst.

Taking a step toward the office, she said, "I need to get the kids registered."

His nod was just a short dip of his chin. "I'll wait."

Jules stopped and blinked at him, trying to keep from smiling. One glance at Theo, and her newly formed resolution was tossed out the window. If only he wasn't quite as nice to look at, maybe she could resist him. Or if he wasn't so nice, period.

"C'mon, Jules!" Tio began nudging her in the direction of the office.

"I'm coming!" As she walked, keeping a firm hold on Dee just in case her sister decided to bolt for the dog, she refused to glance behind her, refused to check if he was keeping his word and waiting. She definitely didn't want him to wait.

She *shouldn't* want him to wait.

As she completed the necessary paperwork, she mentally thanked Dennis. Everything was perfect. There were immunization records and transcripts and custody papers. The administrative assistant—who had severe glasses and not a hair out of place—even gave her an approving look, murmuring, "Very organized."

They managed to get all three boys registered and sent off with a student "buddy" to find their lockers. Jules watched them go, feeling a little scared and helpless that they'd be out of her reach.

A squeeze on her hand brought Jules out of her distracted worry. "They'll be okay," Dee said quietly.

"I know." Giving her sister a small grin—the best she could manage—Jules added, "I just like to keep them close."

Looking much older than eleven, Dee tightened her grip again. "They're used to taking care of themselves."

That made Jules frown as they left the office. "They shouldn't be."

"Right. That's why you stole us."

Even though Dee had used her quietest voice, Jules still bugged her eyes out at her. "Ix-nay on the ole-stay alk-tay."

"Orry-say!" Dee whispered, making a zipping motion over her lips.

"Done?" The deep voice made her jump, and Jules

barely held back a startled shriek. When she turned to Theo, Jules couldn't help but marvel at how he got better-looking every time she saw him. Despite his scowl—*or maybe*, a contrary part of her brain whispered, *because of it*—he really was the poster child of masculine beauty.

When his eyebrows unsnarled enough to lift in question, Jules realized he was waiting for an answer. "Um… yes. Sure. Right. We're all done getting them registered. The boys, at least. I mean, for this place, so everyone except for D. The elementary school starts later, so we decided to come here first. It helps that the junior and senior highs are both in one building, this…um, building, I mean. Because, if they were separate, we'd need to go to a third school." She was painfully aware that she was rambling, and that Theo and Dee and even the dog were staring at her like she'd lost her mind, but Jules couldn't manage to stop the flow of words. "Yeah. So, anyway…did you need to talk to me?"

"I'll walk you out."

"Don't you need to do"—Jules waved a hand in the general direction of the lockers, recycling bin, and janitor's closet she'd eyed so suspiciously before—"bomb stuff?"

There was the tiniest movement at the corner of his mouth, just the barest twitch of his lips, but it was enough to startle her. Was he actually almost smiling?

"Bomb…*stuff* is done. Hugh and I are the last ones here, finishing up the paperwork." Any sign of amusement was gone now, and Jules decided she'd imagined that hint of a smile. "No sign of any explosives. It was just a prank call."

"Did Viggy figure that out?" Dee asked, looking at the dog with equal parts fascination and awe.

The frown was back, heavier than before. "No."

Jules flinched slightly at the snap in his voice, startled by the abrupt change in his manner. In their last few encounters, Theo had been different with her...gentler.

"No," he repeated in a softer tone, as if he'd noticed her reaction. Jules suspected there wasn't much he *didn't* notice, which could be a problem. After all, she had a lot she wanted to hide. "Cliff County leant us one of their explosive-detection dogs. Viggy's..." He looked down at the dog. Viggy was sitting slightly crouched, as if he was trying to appear smaller than he was. His jaw tight, Theo brought his gaze back to Jules. "Never mind. Don't you need to get over to Cottonwood Elementary?"

"Right!" Jules glanced at Dee, who was still focused on the dog. The hot cop had a knack for getting her to forget where she was and what she was supposed to be doing. That also could be a problem. "C'mon, Dee. Let's get you educated."

When Theo fell into step next to her, Jules gave him a surprised glance. From his fierce scowl, she'd assumed he'd no longer be accompanying them outside.

Although he kept his body low to the ground, Viggy walked on the other side of Theo willingly enough. Jules wondered what the story was. Had the dog had a bad experience? Had Theo, as well? Was that the reason for his perma-scowl? Jules felt her stomach twist as she thought of what possible tragedies could've left such a mark on the two.

"Someone look at your stove?"

Once again, the question startled her. Jules didn't

know if it was his gruff manner of barking out conversation, or if she was still jumpy about the whole bomb-threat thing, and the being-away-from-her-brothers thing. "Yes."

"A professional?"

"He knew what he was doing." It wasn't an outright lie. After finding a manual for the stove online at the library, Tio had managed to get it working without any additional explosions. By the time he'd finished fiddling with it, he was confident in his stove-fixing abilities. It was Jules who was a nervous wreck the whole time he was working.

Theo gave her a hard look, as if waiting to see if she was going to confess to her half-truth, but Jules put on her most innocent expression. After a long moment, Theo gave an accepting—or possibly skeptical—grunt. Taking a few long strides, he reached the door first and held it open for her and Dee.

Jules blinked against the morning sun until her eyes adjusted. Florida had been sunny, but Colorado was even brighter than the sunshine state. She figured it was something to do with the altitude or the clean mountain air or something.

The first thing she saw when she was no longer blinded was that Theo had slid on his sunglasses, which made him improbably *hotter*. Jules bit the inside of her lip hard. She needed to nip this crush in the bud immediately. Even if she hadn't accepted that any relationship was not in the cards for years, just being friends with this man was a bad, bad idea.

Her eyes lingered on the way his upper arms stretched his uniform shirt. It took all her willpower to rip her gaze away and refocus on Dee, who was humming to herself, skipping a few feet ahead of them, happily oblivious to the fact that her older sister was being an idiot.

"What do—"

There was a strange sound, something between a crack and a thump, and then she was on the ground, a very large, very heavy cop on top of her. The sidewalk was hard beneath her, and Theo was just as hard above her, and Jules couldn't figure out why he'd tackled her. She turned her head, meaning to ask him, but the intense, grim look on his face stopped her. Something was happening. Something *bad*.

"Stay down!" he ordered before rolling to his feet and running the few steps to Dee. She turned to look at him, her eyes and mouth rounding with surprise as he snatched her off her feet. Spinning around, Theo hunched over the little girl, as if protecting her. Jules's brain still refused to work, refused to make sense of what was happening.

The sound came again, louder this time. A sharp pain bit into her calf, and she twisted to stare at the spot. A drop of dark-red blood welled before trickling across her leg. Her gaze darted from her injured calf to a hole in the asphalt walkway just inches away. There was a hole in the sidewalk. A *bullet* hole.

The sight finally knocked her brain back in gear, and she knew what was happening.

Someone was shooting at them.

CHAPTER 11

"DEE!" SHE CRIED, THE WORD SCRAPING AGAINST HER THROAT. Before she could do anything other than lie there, stunned, Theo was running back toward her, carrying Dee with an arm around her middle. His other hand clutched Viggy's leash, holding the dog tight to his side. He used his body as a shield between Dee and the shooter. "Inside! Go!"

His commanding tone had Jules scrambling to her feet even before her brain processed the words. Theo fell in behind her, urging her forward with the fist clutching Viggy's lead pressing against her back. Although she knew she was running, moving as fast as she could go toward the door, Jules's legs felt so, so slow—nightmare slow. Her breath caught in her chest as she sprinted toward the school entrance, trusting that Theo would be right behind her, keeping Dee safe.

Hugh slammed through the doors, gun drawn but held low. "Get inside!" he bellowed, his usual good-natured expression sharp and focused. He ran, slightly crouched, toward the stone school sign. Taking cover behind the monument, he scanned the area behind them, squinting against the bright sun.

The entrance grew closer, although it still seemed agonizingly far away. Her breaths clawed their way out of her throat in rough heaves, and Jules couldn't stop her brain from picturing a bullet tearing through Theo's broad yet vulnerable back and into Dee—sweet, lovable Dee. Even though she knew, she *knew* that Theo was wearing a bulletproof vest, the image kept running itself through her frantic brain.

They were only five strides away from the entrance, then four, then three. Hope began to trickle into Jules, even as each gasp for air caught in her lungs like a sob. They were so close. Dee would be all right. She had to be all right. Jules repeated in her mind like a mantra, *Dee will be safe. Dee will be safe. Dee will be safe.*

Just two steps away now. Jules reached for the door handle, ready to jerk it open, when the glass panel next to the entrance exploded into an opaque cobweb of shattered glass, the safety film the only thing keeping it from spraying them with fragments. Jules automatically jerked away, her back bumping into Dee and Theo.

"*Shots fired at the high school*," Hugh's voice barked from Theo's radio.

"Inside!" Theo snapped, drowning out a rush of tense radio transmissions. He used his body to propel her forward again. Her hand shook as she fumbled for the handle, jamming her knuckles against it before she managed to grip the metal. Her fingers felt thick, clumsy, as she closed them around the handle and jerked open the door. There was barely enough room for her to fit through the opening before he was shoving her into the entry.

"Take them," Theo ordered, shoving the end of Viggy's lead and Dee toward her. Jules automatically grabbed both the dog and the girl. "Go! Get away from the door." Turning, he reached toward his holster as he sprinted back outside.

Clutching Dee and Viggy's leash, Jules watched Theo run back into the line of fire. He'd saved them. And it might be the last time she'd see him alive.

Slightly crouched, Theo ran, his gun up and ready as he scanned for the shooter. He'd never thought Monroe would have a school shooting. They'd trained for an active-shooter situation, but it had seemed like such a remote possibility. An attack like this was something that happened elsewhere, somewhere they didn't know every kid and parent at least by name.

He rushed toward Hugh. The six-foot-high stone slab bearing the words *Monroe High School* was the best cover in the area, providing both concealment and fairly good protection from the bullets. Theo just had to cover an open stretch of ground in clear view of the shooter to get there.

Gunshots rang out, so distinctive yet so foreign here, at what should have been a peaceful place. A dart of pain sliced his forearm, and he went faster even before his brain processed that a bullet had grazed him. The sound of gunfire was louder, and the section of his brain that had gone on autopilot—hours and hours and *hours* of training kicking in and directing his actions—told him Hugh was returning fire, attempting to give Theo the few seconds he needed to reach cover.

It felt as if he were miles away, but suddenly he was there, next to Hugh, and he had to slam on the brakes so he didn't run full tilt into the stone. Panting, more from adrenaline than from exertion, Theo crouched behind the sign.

"Shooter's position?" Theo asked as his breathing steadied.

"No fucking clue." Dropping his magazine, Hugh reloaded his Glock. "Second floor of Tornado Block, maybe?"

"Not the second." Theo brought up a mental image of the dilapidated apartment building that looked like it was a strong wind away from collapsing completely—hence the nickname. "No openable windows on this side. Unless he's on the roof. Or behind the dumpsters at the southeast corner."

"Angle's wrong for him to be ground level." Hugh shifted slightly, which was the equivalent of a jiggling knee for most people. The man knew how to be still.

"Roof then." Theo's gaze scanned the area, as much as he could see with the stone barrier blocking his view to the north. A flicker of movement behind the school doors caught his attention. Jules and Dee had run through those doors. Panic darted through his gut at the thought that they might be coming back through them.

Hugh's grunt was affirmative.

"What's the... Shit." One of the doors swung open, and someone charged outside. It was Jules's oldest brother—Sam. The teenager's gaze darted around, his face drawn with fear. Theo's muscles tightened as he crouched, ready to run out to get Sam to safety. A bullet struck the corner of the sign they hid behind, and Theo ducked automatically. Hugh was going to have to give him some cover so Theo didn't get picked off the second he took a step toward Sam.

"What's the shit?"

Shit, shit, shit! "Check it out. At your four." The

person had quit firing, and Theo risked a glance toward Tornado Block, ready to sprint into the open.

"Shit!" Hugh echoed Theo's thoughts. "Cover me." Then he was running toward Sam.

The voice in his head had changed to *fuck, fuck, fuck!* "Hugh, you asshole," Theo hissed even as he crouched, getting into position. Leaning out just far enough to see Tornado Block, Theo scanned for any movement, any sign of the gunman, while mentally swearing at Hugh. Theo was the one who should've gone to get the boy to safety. It would've been easier to run across that open space than to watch his partner do it. If anything happened to Hugh... Theo had to cut off that line of thinking before it completely destroyed his focus.

The seconds ticked past, horribly slowly. Theo kept his gaze and his weapon aimed at the top of Tornado Block. The mechanical equipment scattered over the flat roof offered too many hiding places. He paused, catching the slightest flash of light reflecting off metal. Was that the shooter? He stared at the spot until his vision blurred.

At the sound of swearing, Theo risked a quick glance toward his partner. Although Hugh had reached Sam, the teen shied out of his reach.

"They're inside!" Hugh yelled, giving Sam a push toward the front entrance. His words must have convinced Sam, because he started running in that direction. Hugh followed, trying to provide some cover for the kid.

The *snap* of a gun caught Theo's attention, and he immediately began returning fire. He aimed where he'd seen the reflected light and pulled the trigger. There was a slight movement on the other side of the rooftop condensing unit, and Theo lined up his sights on the new spot before shooting again.

A quick glance showed that Sam had reached the entrance and was ducking through the door. The glass above him shattered as a bullet connected with the pane. Theo expected Hugh to follow the boy inside, but he didn't. Instead, Hugh turned and ran back toward Theo.

"Hugh, you dumbass!" Theo hissed as he pulled the trigger again and again, trying to provide whatever cover he could for his partner—his partner who should've stayed in the safety of the school rather than risk returning to Theo.

In his peripheral vision, Theo could see Hugh getting closer, could hear his rough breathing and running steps hitting the ground. Theo's attention was focused on the shooter, however, and he pulled out another magazine from the holder on his belt and did a tactical reload. It took barely three seconds before Theo was shooting again.

Just a few steps away, Hugh gave a startled grunt. Theo turned and saw his partner fall, a surprised expression on his face. It felt like all the air had been punched out of Theo's lungs—as if the bullet had slammed into him, right along with Hugh.

Without thinking, before he could even regain his breath, Theo was there. Jamming his pistol back in its holster, Theo grabbed fistfuls of Hugh's uniform shirt and pulled. The heavy form didn't want to budge, but it finally, grudgingly, started sliding across the grass.

Theo took one backward step and then a second, dragging his partner toward the safety of the sign. A bullet hit the ground just inches from Theo's foot, debris showering his pant leg. Another clipped the sign, digging a chunk from the stone.

There was a tearing sound as a seam in Hugh's shirt gave way, and Theo shifted his grip, hooking his hands under Hugh's arms instead. Hugh was using his right leg to help, pushing it against the ground. Another bullet hit the ground close—too close—to Hugh's leg, and Theo took several rushing steps back, not stopping until all of Hugh was behind the sign.

Dropping Hugh's shoulders, Theo scanned his partner's sprawled shape, looking for where the bullet had hit. It didn't take long to find. The navy material over his thigh was soaked with blood, and a small hole punctured the center. Theo pulled out his pocketknife and lifted the wet fabric away from Hugh's skin before slicing through his uniform pants, cutting and ripping until the wound was exposed through the enlarged hole.

Blood flowed from the wound, and Theo felt a familiar pressure in his chest that stopped him from breathing. He pressed a hand firmly against Hugh's thigh as he grabbed his portable radio from his belt.

"Officer down!" There was too much blood. It leaked out around Theo's palm as his other hand fumbled to manage his radio with fingers that felt clumsy and thick. Had the bullet struck the femoral artery? Jesus. He prayed it hadn't.

"Copy, officer down." There was the slightest of quavers underneath the dispatcher's calm tone, and his words came a little too quickly. "Unit number?"

"Fifty-six seventy-four." Theo's thumb, slippery from blood and sweat, slid off the "talk" button, cutting him off in the middle of his transmission. "Goddammit!"

He adjusted his fingers around the radio, unintentionally pressing down harder on the wound with his other hand. Hugh groaned, and Theo immediately lightened the pressure. "Sorry, buddy." He'd pulled back too much, though, and a gush of blood poured from the wound. His teeth clenched so tightly that his molars squeaked together, Theo pushed his palm hard against Hugh's leg again, forcing himself to ignore his partner's yelp of pain.

Turning back to the radio, he repeated his unit number before saying, "Fifty-six thirty-three has been shot in the thigh. He's bleeding heavily and needs Medical."

"Copy."

"Negative." Lieutenant Blessard's sharp voice broke in before the dispatcher could say anything further. "Med's staging until we get word from the Emergency Response Unit that the scene is secure."

Glancing down at the blood coating everything—way too much blood—Theo swallowed a growl. The shooter had been silent since Hugh'd gone down with a startled grunt. The stone sign offered some cover, but it also blocked Theo's view of anything except a chalk-white-and-blood-red Hugh. "Negative on that negative. He needs Med here *now*."

"We're not sending medics in to get shot at, Bosco." Blessard dropped all attempts at radio etiquette. "Keep pressure on the wound, and I'll kick some ERU ass into high gear. They'll send out the Beast for you. We need to secure the scene before anyone else can get out there."

Clenching his teeth to hold back a profanity-heavy retort, Theo gripped the portable so tightly his fingers turned white.

"It's okay, Theo." Hugh's voice was rough and breathy and didn't even sound like him. "They're moving as fast as they can." He paused to suck a breath in through his teeth. "LT's right."

"Fuck that."

"Bosco!" Blessard growled, but Theo had already reclipped the portable to his belt. He'd need both hands for this. "Bosco!"

"Dude." Hugh gave a gasping laugh as his eyes started to close. "You're in so much trouble."

"Wake up!" Theo barked. "C'mon, you lazy ass. I need you to do some of the work."

Although Hugh forced his eyes to open with obvious effort, he was so pale there was a green undertone to his tan skin. "What...are you...talking about? You're the... lazy one."

"Give me your hand." Theo was almost snarling by this point. He'd lost so much this past year. He knew, just *knew*, that he couldn't survive losing Hugh. If Theo let another partner die, that would be the end of him. "Hugh, you fucking asshole! Give me your god-damned hand!"

There was a pause, just a single second of stillness, but long enough to make Theo's heart stop.

"Such language." Hugh tsked, his voice weak but present, the hint of a teasing smile on his face. He slowly raised a visibly shaking arm.

Relief flooded Theo, making his heart thud with such force it felt like it was pounding against his rib cage. He grabbed Hugh's hand and positioned it over his own where he was futilely trying to stanch the bleeding. "Press here. Hard as you can. Got it?"

"Got it."

Theo slid his hand free and pushed Hugh's palm against the gushing hole. He didn't think it was possible for Hugh to blanch any paler, but somehow he managed it. Theo hardened his heart against the grimace on his partner's face. "Harder. Don't be a baby."

That got a pained chuckle, but Hugh's shaking hand obediently pushed more firmly against his leg. After a final glance at Hugh's face to determine exactly how close he was to passing out, Theo yanked his uniform shirt over his head. Without bothering to remove his badge or nametag or even the pen in his chest pocket, Theo hurriedly folded the shirt into a rough bandage and wrapped it around Hugh's thigh.

"Move your hand," he ordered, and Hugh did, his arm dropping like a dead weight to his side. Theo pulled the shirt tight and then tied it on the side of Hugh's leg. The improvised bandage immediately became stained with blood. "Think you can run with help?"

There was no answer, except for the continuous chatter on the radio. Glancing at Hugh's face, Theo saw his partner's eyes were closed and his head lolled to the side, looking so lifeless that Theo's stomach twisted hard.

"No," he said, although no sound emerged. It felt like he'd had the wind knocked out of him. Shaking off his terror that Hugh wasn't just unconscious, Theo gritted his teeth and rolled his partner onto his stomach. Kneeling by his head, Theo hooked his arms under Hugh's and stood, grunting with the effort.

"You're a big bastard," Theo muttered, his voice gritty with effort. All that bulk was dead weight, too, making him feel even heavier.

Theo winced at the term "dead."

"Knock it off," he muttered as he bent, taking Hugh over his shoulders in a fireman's carry. As he straightened, Theo took a second to steady his burden before blowing out a hard breath.

"Ready, buddy?" Hugh didn't answer. "Me, neither." Despite that, Theo stepped out from behind the safety of the sign.

He couldn't run, not while wearing his two-hundred-plus-pound partner like a cape, but he moved as fast as he could. Each step felt exposed, every foot he covered in the seemingly endless space between him and the cluster of emergency vehicles made him want to duck back behind their stone cover. Why had he thought this would be a good idea?

Theo wasn't worried about his own unprotected parts. It was Hugh. His partner's vest seemed too small and useless. Sure, it covered some vital organs, but what about his head or his neck or that femoral artery Theo worried was already nicked?

He expected the lieutenant to be screeching at him, but his portable had gone silent. Blessard had probably ordered the radio silence, so as not to draw the shooter's attention. There were no shouts coming from the first-responders' camp, either—just an expectant, waiting silence.

His boots hitting the ground sounded too loud, as did each breath as it tore in and out of his lungs. The space between them and the police staging area was still too far—hopelessly far.

Clenching his jaw and tightening his grip on Hugh's limp form, Theo kept moving, one step after the other, braced for the bullet that would bring him down, or worse, hit Hugh, ending Theo just as surely.

The thought pushed him to move faster, despite the unconscious man weighing him down. His feet shuffled forward in an attempt at a run. The vehicles were getting closer, near enough to see Otto's distinctive form running toward them. Other cops grabbed at him, but he shook them off like they were pesky mosquitoes and kept running.

Stay back, Otto! Theo shouted in his head, but he didn't have the breath for anything except taking one step at a time. He tried to hurry, tried to get Hugh to safety before Otto could get hurt as well, but his body would not obey, would not go any faster, and they were still much too exposed when Otto reached them.

Otto was a monster of a man—four inches taller than Theo's six feet and with an extra fifty pounds of muscle. Between the two of them, they quickly shifted Hugh so his arms were over their shoulders, his weight divided between them. With enormous relief, Theo realized he could run that way, and he picked up speed. The staging area grew closer and closer, and a faint tendril of hope worked its way through Theo's dread.

Theo felt the punch to his ribs before he heard the shot. He lurched sideways, only Otto and Theo's grip on Hugh keeping him from falling. Otto visibly braced, supporting all three of them for a moment until Theo regained his balance.

"I'm fine," Theo barked in answer to Otto's concerned look. "Let's go!"

They resumed their dash to safety, but every breath sent fire through Theo's side. The distance between them and the staging area suddenly looked impossibly huge. His toe caught, making him stumble, and agony shot from his side through his whole body.

"You good?" Otto asked.

"Fine." The word was a grunt. Theo needed all his air, all his energy, everything he had inside of him to keep going without dropping Hugh's dead weight. *No,* he thought fiercely. *Not dead.* He had to believe Hugh would live, or Theo wouldn't be able to make it.

"Stay with me, Theo," Otto said.

Digging for his last reserves of strength, Theo plowed forward. The gap between them and safety narrowed with each painful, dragging step, and then they were surrounded, helping hands reaching for them, taking Hugh away, tugging on Theo's arm in an attempt to get him to sit down.

Theo shook off the EMTs. "Help Hugh. I'm fine."

"I'm concerned with how you're breathing," Claire, a serious-faced EMT in her forties told him.

"Bosco!" Lieutenant Blessard snapped, elbowing through the surrounding crowd. Theo braced himself for a lecture about ignoring orders and dragging Hugh into danger. "Sit your ass down and let them check you out."

Surprised into compliance, Theo sat on the back bumper of a fire rescue truck. When an EMT—this one a redhead named Scott—reached toward the front of his vest, scissors in one hand, Theo waved him off and pulled at the Velcro fastenings, holding back a frustrated sound when his fingers wouldn't stop shaking. "How's Hugh?"

"Alive." Although the LT's tone was as gruff as always, the pat he gave Theo's shoulder was almost gentle. An ambulance siren started to wail, making Theo jump and then wince as pain shot through his chest. Claire and the lieutenant exchanged a concerned look, and Theo held back an annoyed snarl, mentally cursing himself for showing his discomfort.

"That him?" Theo asked when the ambulance had gotten far enough away that the siren wasn't deafening anymore. Frustrated by his fumbling fingers, he yanked at the vest, but all he achieved was an agonizing jolt through his ribs.

The lieutenant made an affirmative sound as he reached to help remove Theo's protective vest. Theo started to protest, but swallowed his words as another shock of pain made all his muscles tighten. He wanted to skip the exam and go right to the get-to-the-hospital part, so he could find out the latest on Hugh's condition.

"Where the hell is ERU?" Even as Theo growled the question, he spotted a convoy that included the Emergency Response Unit's armored vehicle snaking its way toward their staging area.

Lieutenant Blessard pulled the last Velcro strap free so the vest opened like a clamshell, freeing Theo. Although the cool air felt great with just a sweat-soaked T-shirt covering his chest and back, his ribs gave a vengeful throb, as if the vest had been containing some of the pain. Theo bit the inside of his cheek as he struggled to keep his face expressionless. When Scott reached toward his T-shirt with scissors, this time Theo allowed him to cut the fabric. Putting his arms above his head to finish undressing seemed next to impossible.

"Better go debrief," the LT muttered, but he didn't move as the T-shirt was stripped away. Instead, Blessard kept his gaze dispassionately fixed on Theo's side. A downward glance showed Theo that it was already bruising, the immediate red mottled with black. Claire pressed around the injured area, and Theo sunk his teeth into his inner cheek so hard that he tasted blood. He'd always gotten along with Claire, but he hadn't realized she had such a sadistic streak. "Broken?"

"He'll need an X-ray," Claire answered the LT. "But I'm guessing they're just bruised."

"Good." Blessard strode toward the arriving ERU members. "I'll check in with you later."

"Enough." Theo twisted away from an especially vicious poke. Unfortunately, the evasive movement hurt even more than Claire's examination. "Can we just get to the hospital already?"

"You're going willingly?" Claire's eyebrows shot up to hide behind her bangs. "I figured we'd have to strap you down and sedate you like an ill-tempered wild boar."

Standing up, Theo decided he didn't really care for jokey Claire. He headed for the only remaining ambulance, the one he assumed would be his ride. "Let's go."

Before he climbed in, he sent a glance toward the front of the school. It sat silent and looked as empty as if it were the middle of July. He knew the kids and teachers were huddled inside locked classrooms. Theo wondered about Jules, her little sister, and Viggy. Where had they ended up hiding? Were they scared?

Shaking off his useless preoccupation, he stepped into the back of the ambulance, a breath catching in his lungs as his ribs screamed from the movement. Why was he so concerned about people he barely knew? Theo couldn't answer that question, any more than he could stop worrying about them the entire ride to the hospital.

When Theo turned and ran back toward the sign, Jules had to keep herself from lunging after him. He'd been her shield, and now, standing behind fragile glass doors, Jules felt horribly exposed. She shook off the desire to chase him. With Dee and Viggy to think about, Jules needed to be their protector now.

Clutching Dee's hand and Viggy's leash, Jules tore through the empty hallway, automatically heading for the office. Theo's absence made her feel raw and vulnerable, as if she'd had body armor that had been stripped away. Jules had to resist the urge to glance behind her, but focused on her goal instead, Dee and Viggy running on either side of her.

The office door was locked. Jules gave a short sob of fright and frustration, but then forced herself to think. The school must be in lockdown. Jules huddled against the wall for a moment, but the hallway didn't feel safe. Someone could come at them—the *shooter* could come at them—from too many directions. Her hunted gaze scanned the area, the sure-to-be-locked doors lining the hall mocking her with their close inaccessibility.

"There!" she cried, hauling Viggy and Dee past the office and down the hall.

"Where?" Dee gasped.

"Here." Darting into the girls' bathroom, Jules didn't stop until they were in the farthest stall, huddled against the wall. It took forever for her breathing to slow enough to hear any sounds other than her oxygen-starved gasps. Finally, she was able to listen. There was only silence. They sat for what seemed like an eternity. Viggy was the first of the three of them to shift, lying down and putting his head in Dee's lap.

"JuJu?" Her sister's voice was tiny, despite the echo in the tiled bathroom.

Resisting the urge to hush Dee, Jules looked at her solemn face.

"Viggy shouldn't be in here," Dee whispered, massaging the dog's ears. "He's a boy."

For some reason, Dee's lame joke struck Jules as hysterically funny. Pent-up adrenaline pushed for relief, and she struggled to silence her laughter. It didn't help when Dee began to giggle, as well. They eventually trailed into silence, and they waited, still and quiet, not even shifting positions on the hard, uncomfortable floor.

After what felt like hours later, a loud tone sounded over the PA system, making all three of them jump. Dee let out a tiny scream, and Viggy lifted his head. A few minutes later, small sounds came from the hallway outside. The noise gradually grew in volume until it sounded like a normal high school between classes, with an added note of anxiety that Jules attributed to the lockdown. Blowing out a shaky breath, she climbed to her feet and offered a hand to Dee.

It was over. They'd survived. As Jules's brain processed this news, her legs went a little rubbery with relief. Niggling worries remained, though, growing until she couldn't ignore them.

Were Theo and Hugh okay? And who had just tried to kill them?

CHAPTER 12

EVEN LYING IN A HOSPITAL BED, HUGH LOOKED ENORMOUS. The only sign of his brush with death was the greenish-pale cast to his skin, and that was mostly hidden under his tan. Theo scowled down at the sleeping man. For some reason, Hugh's oddly healthy look bothered him, made Theo feel like the whole nightmare hadn't happened less than a day earlier.

"Whatcha doing, creeper?" Hugh rasped without opening his eyes. The amused quiver at the corner of Hugh's mouth pissed off Theo even more. "You going to smother me with a pillow or kiss me like I'm Sleeping Beauty?"

Silently, Theo turned to leave, but Hugh caught his arm before he could step away from the bed. When Theo reluctantly turned back around, he saw Hugh's suggestion of a smile had turned into a full-fledged grin.

"C'mon, man." Hugh's voice still sounded rough, but it was definitely amused. "I'm in the hospital after almost dying. There was lots of blood and everything. This is the one time you have to be really nice to me."

At the mention of blood, Theo went cold. He was immediately back there, trying to hold back the flood that trickled through his fingers, draining Hugh's life away. Theo stared at the IV stand next to the bed, focused on the half-filled bag of clear liquid. All his

fear and helplessness tangled together in his stomach,
but Theo squeezed his hands into fists and stomped the
emotions into bits, until all he felt was the usual rage.

"Theo?" Hugh's tone wasn't joking anymore.

"Fuck off," Theo muttered, attempting to turn away
again, but Hugh's fingers tightened. It would've been
easy to free himself of Hugh's grip, but there seemed
something so wrong about taking advantage of the other
man's weakness when he was in the hospital. When he
had nearly died.

Theo's throat tightened, restricting his breathing.

Hugh gave his arm a little shake. "Why are you
pissed? I figured you'd be happy—okay, so maybe
not *happy*, since the whole dancing-on-a-mountain-top
thing really isn't your style, but at least mildly content—
that I'd survived. It was thanks to you I made it. If I'd
lost much more blood…" Hugh finished with a wordless
squeeze right below Theo's elbow.

That grip felt like it was at his throat. Despite its good
intentions, despite its gentleness, that hand was strangling him. Theo barely managed to force out a lie. "I'm
not pissed."

Hugh actually laughed. It was the shadow of his
former laugh, but it was still a laugh. Theo stared harder
at the IV stand, rubbing his hand against his skull, back
and forth across the short strands of hair that were just
long enough not to be bristly. "Liar. You're in a constant
state of pissed off. What's wrong?"

"What's wrong?" Theo repeated. The sheer ridicu-
lousness of the question forced him to finally fix his
glare on Hugh. "What's *wrong*?"

"Yeah." That touch of humor was back, and Theo

wanted to punch it out of him. "Besides this mess, of course." He gestured to his blanket-covered form.

Theo opened his mouth, the angry words rushing into his throat, but then he clamped his lips together without letting them fly. His rage wasn't logical. If he tried to explain it, to yell at Hugh for laughing when he'd almost *died*—the way Don had *died*—the words wouldn't make any sense. Swallowing the tirade that wanted to spill from him, Theo just muttered, "That mess is enough."

His smile fading, Hugh studied him for a moment. "Yeah, it is. Sorry."

Hugh's serious response stole his anger, just blew it out from underneath Theo, creating a void. Other emotions started to creep in—fear and grief and sheer gratitude that Hugh hadn't died. They were overwhelming, stripping Theo raw and leaving him vulnerable.

Unable to hold Hugh's gaze for a new reason that had nothing to do with anger, Theo returned to studying the IV. Once again, he had no words. All he could do was give a choppy jerk of his head to acknowledge Hugh's apology—an apology that made no sense. After all, he hadn't done this to himself. Not like Don.

"So what's going on? They find the asshole yet?"

Pathetically grateful for the change of subject, Theo said, "No. By the time ERU made entry, he was gone."

"Shit." Hugh shifted his weight with a stifled wince that Theo pretended not to see. "They get anything? Prints? A witness? A signed confession? A piece of chewed gum? A gun?"

A corner of Theo's mouth twitched. Leave it to Hugh

to be lying in a hospital bed after being shot and *still* dreaming of unicorns and rainbows. "One casing the shooter missed when cleaning up. Forty-caliber."

His face brightening, Hugh opened his mouth, but Theo knocked him off his hopeful horse before he could ask the question. "No prints."

His disappointed expression quickly slipped away, replaced by thoughtfulness. "Forty-cal? I would've sworn he was using a rifle."

That had been bugging Theo, too. "Could've been a Kel-Tec."

"True."

Theo stood, holding back a groan as his ribs and muscles protested the motion after a sleepless night sitting in the very uncomfortable hospital waiting-room chairs. "Have to go pick up Vig."

"Did someone drop him at the station yesterday?"

For some reason, Theo was reluctant to talk about Jules. The other guys knew her as the new waitress, but that was it. As odd as it was, Theo felt like Jules and her family were his—just his. He didn't want to share her. Hugh was waiting for an answer, though, his expression growing more curious by the second. With a silent sigh, Theo admitted, "Jules took him."

It took a second before comprehension dawned, quickly followed by a smirk. "New waitress Jules? *Hot* new waitress Jules?"

Theo just stared at him flatly. For some weird reason, that made Hugh laugh.

"Go for it, man." Hugh chuckled again. "Oh, and could you—"

Before he could finish the sentence, Theo was already

pulling a wad of paper from one of the cargo pockets on his BDUs and thrusting it at Hugh.

"Incident report?" At Theo's affirmative shrug, Hugh grabbed it from him, his face lit up like it was Christmas. "You're the best. How'd you know I'd want it?"

Theo didn't bother answering. After working together for so long, Theo had just known. "I asked Otto to bring it early this morning. I'll grab copies for you of any follow-up reports as they come in."

"This is great."

Shrugging off Hugh's appreciation, Theo headed for the door, but paused before opening it. "Thanks," he muttered at the door handle.

"For what?"

"Holding on." Yanking the door open, Theo escaped into the hall so fast he barely caught Hugh's response.

"You're welcome, partner."

"They couldn't have been aiming at you. No one wants to *kill* us." Ty tipped his chair back to balance on two legs. "I vote we stay."

Sam frowned. "Th-th-they st-st-still haven't c-c-c-c...f-found the sh-shooter."

"They will." At least, Jules really hoped they would.

Looking up from where she sat on the kitchen floor with Viggy's head in her lap, Dee said, "I don't want to leave. We just got here."

"I don't want to go, either." Tio was sitting in the seat next to Ty, although all four of his chair's legs were solidly on the floor.

Looking around at her siblings' faces, seeing everything from worry to hopefulness to Sam's closed-off, unreadable expression, Jules felt inadequate. How was she supposed to be a parent and make these kinds of decisions? How could she manage to let them head off to school every morning, a school where she'd been hiding in the bathroom a day ago because someone was *shooting* a *gun* at them? Would a new place be any better, or was this just life? Was death and danger around every corner going to be an ongoing part of their new, post-kidnapping existence? It had seemed like such a peaceful, pretty town.

"Jules?" Dee said tentatively. "Can we stay? Please?"

Jules squeezed her eyes closed for a moment so she wouldn't have to look at their hopeful faces. They depended on her, and she had not a single clue what she was doing. Opening her eyes again, she took a deep breath.

The doorbell rang.

All the air in her lungs escaped in a relieved rush at the interruption, allowing her to delay her decision—this huge decision that would affect all of their lives—for a little bit longer. Immediately after, however, familiar panic sparked to life, fueled by her siblings' anxious expressions.

Giving them a look she hoped was reassuring, she headed to the door. The kids knew the drill already. They waited in the kitchen and listened. If they heard Jules say they were at the park, then they were supposed to slip out the back door and run to the barn to hide. After fifteen minutes, if Jules hadn't joined them, they were to grab the money hidden in the loft and run.

Each step tightened her stomach more as she

approached the front door. Holding her breath, Jules peeked through the peephole. When she saw who it was, her muscles relaxed and a smile crept onto her face. Who would've thought that, just days after she'd become a felon, the sight of a cop would be a relief?

Brushing off the nagging thought that it was stupid to feel excitement fizzing in her belly, Jules opened the door. Her crush—or whatever it was—on Theo was one of her stupider moves, dumber even than working for Luis Espina. She *knew* this, but she still couldn't help grinning at him.

He scowled back at her, but for some crazy reason, that only made her smile widen. His crabbiness was just part of Theo, and she liked it. It made no sense, but she couldn't help herself. It was the worst time and the worst place and the worst everything, but she still *liked* Officer Theodore Bosco. A lot. It was hard not to after he'd thrown himself in the line of fire to save them.

"Hi."

His answering grunt made her beam, even as she mentally rolled her eyes at herself.

"You okay?" Her gaze scanned him, wanting to see with her own eyes that he was in one piece. As soon as they'd emerged from the school bathroom, Jules had heard that a police officer had been shot. It had taken a frantic twenty minutes to find out that the injured cop was Hugh, not Theo. To her shame, relief had coursed through her at the news. Although she'd hated that funny, cheery Hugh had been hurt, Jules had just been so glad it wasn't Theo who'd been shot.

"Yeah." And he did appear to be uninjured. At some point since the shooting, he'd changed out of his uniform into well-worn jeans and an equally broken-in T-shirt. Jules tried to focus on their conversation, rather than how very good he looked in civilian clothes. "You? Your family?"

"We're all fine, thanks to you and Hugh. How's he doing?"

The corners of his mouth twitched into an almost-smile. "Well enough to be a pain in my ass."

Relief made her laugh a little too loudly. "That's good. We've been worried. Thank you for what you did for us yesterday."

Appearing a little uncomfortable, he gave a tight nod as his gaze dropped to the side.

"You saved our lives." Tears that had been hovering too near the surface for the past twenty-four hours threatened to spill over once again. "I was still trying to figure out what was going on when you dragged us back to the school. We could've easily been killed in the time it took for me to realize that someone was shooting at us. If something had happened to Dee…"

As her breath choked off in her throat, Jules stopped that train of thought, since talking about how much danger her little sister had been in, how close she'd come to *dying*, was a sure way to lose control of her teetering emotions. "So, thank you. It's such a stupid, tiny thing to say, when what you did was so amazing, so brave, so *huge*—"

He'd been looking more and more awkward as her speech continued, until he finally cut her off. "Please stop talking."

Startled, she did.

"Sorry." Theo scrubbed a rough hand over his head.

"I didn't mean… You can talk, just stop thanking me." Glancing at her face, he twisted his mouth in a grimace. "Sorry."

"It's okay." She could see how her gushing could have made him uncomfortable. He was just lucky she wasn't hugging him again, because she could barely restrain herself. There was a pause, and Jules realized she'd been keeping him standing on the porch. "Oh, sorry! Did you want to come in?"

Stepping back, she waved him inside. After a minute pause, Theo stepped forward into the entryway. He always seemed so *wary*, Jules thought, watching him. That and his cranky demeanor hid the sweetness she knew was in there. He was so good and strong and heroic and looked really, really nice in his T-shirt… Only when he eyed her did she realize she was staring.

"You're here for Viggy!" she blurted, feeling her cheeks warm and knowing she was probably as red as the lights on top of his squad car. Of course he wasn't there just to see her, to check in after the traumatic events of the previous day. Her smitten mind had turned the situation to fit her daydreams, when he was just running a necessary errand. "He's in the kitchen. Actually, everyone's in the kitchen."

As usual, he waved for her to go first and then followed her down the hall. It was hard not to let self-consciousness change her gait when she knew he was right behind her, watching her.

"Any news on the shooter?" she asked over her shoulder.

"None I can tell you." When she looked at him again,

slightly taken aback by his abrupt words, he amended his statement. "Yet."

Her mouth twisted down as she eyed him. "So you haven't caught him?" Jules figured that if the cops had brought him in, they'd be very willing to share that news right away. If the shooter was still on the loose, it made her decision about whether to go or stay even harder. Theo gave her a steady look, and she couldn't stop her frown from lightening into a wry smile. "Fine. You can't say anything yet. Will you let me know when you get the okay to talk?"

After regarding her for another few seconds, he lowered his chin in the smallest of nods. Not quite satisfied, but knowing that was all she was going to get, she turned back around and continued down the hall.

Everyone stared at them when they entered the kitchen. Dee was standing, leaning against Sam, who had an arm around her and his other hand resting on Viggy's head. The dog was pressed against his side. The twins were still sitting, but there was a similar tension in both, as if they were ready to bolt out of their chairs at any second.

"Theo's here to pick up Viggy," she announced, her voice sounding too loud in the otherwise silent kitchen. Still wrapped up in the relief that it was Theo and not someone else—a PI or a different cop or even her stepmother—that she hadn't considered the kids' reaction to losing their houseguest. After an extended argument about where Viggy would sleep the previous night, he'd ended up taking over two-thirds of Dee's bed. Now, she braced herself for a tearful good-bye—on Dee's part, at least.

Jules had underestimated her sister, though. Her

words brought the tiniest of quivers to Dee's bottom lip before she brought herself back under control, forcing a pageant-like smile that looked eerily real, even to Jules. Seeing that mask of a smile, Jules decided at that moment that they were getting a dog. Sure, they were on the run, but how much harder could it be to hide five people and a dog, rather than just five people?

Theo looked around the kitchen with the same cautious attention he'd given the entry and the hall, as if he was expecting enemy forces to jump out of the fridge. To Jules's surprise, he didn't make any move to hook up Viggy's leash.

"Are you hungry?" she asked, unable to help it. Ignoring the burning lasers of Sam's gaze cutting into her, she smiled at Theo. "I'm not working this morning, so we're eating breakfast together for once. You're welcome to join us."

Seeing the scowl on Theo's face, Jules braced herself for his rejection, but he gave one of his habitual, small, downward tilts of his chin—a nod. Her smile was huge. She could feel it, and she sort of regretted how happy his being there made her, but a part of her didn't care about anything except that she'd get to have Theo for the next hour or so.

Theo's company, *that is*, her mind quickly corrected, and she could feel the heat returning to her cheeks as the other ways she could have Theo rushed through her brain in an uncontrollable wave. Caught up in her mental mortification, she forgot about avoiding Sam's eyes and met his gaze full-on. His huge frown told her exactly what he thought of her excitement.

"Can we have bacon, please?" Dee's careful request brought Jules out of her thoughts.

She frowned at her sister. "Bacon? Since when do you like bacon?"

Dee shot a quick side-glance at Viggy. "I love bacon. I've always loved bacon."

Jules let the complete and utter falsehood go, turning to the ancient refrigerator that they'd learned made alarming whining noises on a semiconstant basis. Today, the usual sounds were joined by a few loud thumps.

"It's going to explode," Ty warned.

Tio sighed. "It won't explode."

"It sounds like it's going to explode."

"It might break," Tio said, "but it most likely won't explode."

Pausing with her hand outstretched, reaching for the handle, Jules gave her brother a look. "Most likely?" she echoed.

His head tilted to the side, and his eyes got that slightly unfocused look that meant he was doing math in his head. "About an 88 percent certainty."

Her hand still frozen in midair, Jules did some math of her own. "That means there's a 12 percent chance that a refrigerator will take us all out."

Tio waved a hand as if brushing off her concern. "But it's more probable it'll just break. And if it were to explode, it would be minor."

"A minor explosion. That's...good."

"You need new appliances." Theo's gruff voice startled her a little, since the explosion discussion had distracted her. "Call your landlord."

"I will." Dennis was definitely going to hear about this. He'd promised her a safe place to live, and to her, "safe" included having appliances that wouldn't explode. Glaring at the avocado-colored surface, she yanked open the door and retrieved the bacon.

Sam silently accepted the package from her, taking the opportunity to give her a *look* when his back was to Theo. Since Jules was facing him—and Theo behind him—she kept what she hoped was a bland expression. Sam didn't have to tell her she was being an idiot. Jules was perfectly aware of that fact.

"T, you're on egg duty. Ty, please cut up some fruit." She'd learned not to give Ty any task that involved actual cooking, unless she wanted to test the smoke detectors. Again. "Dee, set the table, please." Dee gave Viggy one last belly scratch before standing. "Wash your hands first."

Although she headed for the sink, Dee gave Jules a chiding look. "Viggy is a very clean dog."

"I'm sure he is." Pulling out a couple of slices of bread, Jules popped them into the toaster. The loaf was already two-thirds gone, she noticed. Her stomach gave a nervous twinge. The five of them went through food so fast. Maybe she could add another few shifts at the diner to her schedule. "But I'd rather skip the dash of dog hair on my eggs, thank you very much."

Dee laughed and collected the plates. As she set the table, she sang quietly to herself. Ty and Tio were having a conversation about eggs. Only Sam held his silence, keeping his gaze focused on the cooking bacon.

Jules sent a quick glance in Theo's direction and had to quash a smile when she saw how bewildered he appeared as he looked around the crowded room. He was probably telling himself exactly the same thing she'd been repeating in her mind: this was a bad idea.

That was just too bad, though. He was hers for breakfast, and she was going to take all the Theo-time she
could get.

Staying was a bad idea.

Theo had no idea why he'd agreed, why he'd even
come inside this strange, handyman's nightmare of a
house, rather than just grabbing Viggy and leaving. It'd
been over twenty-four hours since he'd last slept, and
everything was starting to get a disorienting halo. He
blinked several times, trying to normalize his vision, but
then he gave up. Nothing but several hours in bed was
going to fix him.

Then why was he here, watching the chaos of this
family in their clown-car of a kitchen? Jules looked over
her shoulder at him and smiled, and he knew exactly
why his dumb ass hadn't left immediately.

Clearing his throat, he offered, "I can help."

She gave him an appraising look from those narrow,
too-sexy-for-his-own-good eyes, and he felt as if
she could see his soul-deep exhaustion. Although he
expected her to refuse his help, she offered him a plate
piled with several slices of toast. "You can butter."

Accepting the plate, the butter, and a table knife, he
glanced around, looking for enough counter space to
create a station. Apparently seeing his dilemma, Jules
waved him over to the spot next to her—the spot *right*
next to her. He hesitated long enough for her to notice,
and she raised a questioning eyebrow. With a soundless
sigh, he wedged in beside her. They were close, so close

he could feel heat radiating from her side, could smell her scent—vanilla and spice. He recognized it from when she'd lean in to put his plate in front of him at the diner, and he caught himself moving closer to get a better whiff.

"Jules," Dee said, bringing Theo back to the present situation. He jerked back, as far away as he could get from Jules in the narrow space they were sharing, and buttered toast with much more focus than the task required. "If you were an animal, what kind would you be?"

Tilting her head, as if she was thinking, Jules finally answered, "A bird."

"Good answer!" Dee sounded pleased. Glancing at the girl, Theo wondered at her resiliency. Just yesterday, they'd been forced to run for their lives. Now Dee was cheerily setting the table and daydreaming aloud. Theo was impressed by her ability to bounce back. Personally, he felt more like a deflated basketball. He wasn't sure he'd ever bounce again.

Spatula in hand, Tio made a humming sound. "What kind of bird? A hawk?"

"Not a hawk," Jules said definitely, adding another two slices to the toaster. "I couldn't eat mice."

Dee nodded. "Because they're so cute?"

"Uh, right." Jules shot Theo a sideways look that made him have to hold back a snort of amusement. It startled him that she'd almost made him laugh, especially after the past grueling hours. "And because eating mice is gross."

"You're right." Dee paused between placing forks next to each plate to make a face. "So what kind of bird?"

"A robin?" Jules suggested.

Ty fake-retched. "You'd eat worms but not mice?"

"Good point." Sending Theo another amused glance, Jules tried again. "What about bluebirds? Do they eat bugs? Even if so, I pick a bluebird. They're so bright and flashy." Theo liked how she would look at him, as if they were sharing an inside joke.

"Just the males," Tio piped up, scraping scrambled eggs into a big serving bowl. "The females are a dull grayish-blue."

"Typical." Jules eyed Theo from under lowered lids with an expression he wasn't sure how to interpret. "The guys are always prettier."

Clearing his throat, Sam said, "I-I'd b-be a shark."

Theo glanced at him in surprise. That was the first he'd spoken since Theo had gotten there.

"Sharks don't sleep." Tio's tone indicated approval of his brother's choice. "They just swim and eat."

"And nothing attacks a shark," Ty added enthusiastically. "They're the badasses of the ocean."

"Language," Jules sighed, but no one seemed to pay attention.

"Except for humans," Tio corrected Ty. "People hunt sharks."

Sam scowled and jabbed fiercely at the sizzling bacon strips. "Typ-p-pical."

A heavy silence settled over the kitchen, until Dee broke it. "What animal would you be?"

When no one answered, Theo glanced at Dee to see her gaze fixed on him. In fact, everyone was looking at him, waiting. His mind blanked, as if he were back in high school and had just been called on to solve a calculus problem. The waiting pause lengthened, became uncomfortable, and he opened his mouth and blurted an answer without thinking. "A dog."

Dee looked satisfied by his response, but Sam frowned. "B-b-but d-dogs have no contr-tr-trol over where they l-l-live or anyth-thing. What if you h-had m-m-mean owners?"

"I'd bite them and leave." Again, the words were out before he'd considered them. At Jules's choked sound, Theo slanted a glance at her, trying to determine if she was offended or amused. Her head was down, focused on the toaster, but he was pretty sure she was fighting a grin.

There was no question that Dee approved, judging by the deeply commending look she gave him. "Good. Good dog."

That made Jules dissolve into laughter. Watching her, Theo felt warmth spread through his midsection. There was something about watching Jules giggle that made him want to keep her happy. Her gaze met his, and her laughter faded, but her smile remained. Theo realized he was actually smiling. It had been a long time, and it felt strange. Really good, but strange.

A clearing throat made him turn his head. Sam was watching him with a thoughtful expression. When Theo raised his eyebrows in question, Sam turned back to the bacon. His silence seemed different from a few minutes earlier, though. It was a little less…hostile.

A gentle elbow in his side brought his attention back to Jules. "Slacker," she murmured, tipping her head toward the pile of still-to-be-buttered toast that had collected during the previous discussion.

Although he tried to regain his scowl, it wasn't

available. Theo settled for giving her a mock frown and resuming his task. The conversation continued, and Theo let it flow around him. The sound of their chatter, the repetitive motion of the butter knife, the sight of Viggy sprawled out near Dee's feet, the knowledge that Hugh was going to be okay—all of those things lulled him, filled him with a sense of something he'd been missing for so long.

It was peace.

Jules couldn't help it. Even though there were a thousand things to do, she found herself outside the archway into the living room…again.

"Just a quick peek," she muttered under her breath, and then mentally scolded herself for being…what, she wasn't sure. A voyeur? A creeper? A dumbass who was already in over her head and should immediately return to installing the window fan in Sam's attic room?

Despite her internal talking-to, she leaned sideways, just far enough to see the figure sprawled on the couch. It was a big couch, but he managed to make it look small in comparison to his sleeping bulk. After breakfast, Theo had begun swaying with exhaustion. Although he'd made noises about going home, she'd been able to steer him to the couch without too much opposition. Only seconds later, he was sleeping, his breathing heavy, just short of snoring. Jules had covered him with a blanket and tiptoed away, only to keep returning to eye the sleeping man.

He was normally so guarded, so angry, that seeing

him vulnerable as he slept was a revelation—a dangerous one. If she went all mushy for the scowling, hostile Theo, Jules knew she had no chance of protecting her heart from this sweet and sleeping version.

This time, Theo wasn't alone. Dee was sitting on the floor, reading a library book, her back against the couch next to the sleeping man's feet. Viggy was lying next to her. His tail thumped the floor in greeting, making Dee look up and give a tiny wave. Jules returned the wave and slipped out, heading back upstairs to try to make the stifling third-floor space a little less unbearable.

Something about the scene of the sleeping man and reading girl and relaxed dog niggled at her, though. It wasn't just Jules who was getting too attached. Somehow, the idea of leaving Monroe had become infinitely harder. They were all settling in—to the house, to the town, to a local cop who'd saved her more than once and fixed their porch and protected them from flying bullets and answered Dee's childish questions with utmost seriousness and respect.

There wouldn't be anything simple about leaving anymore.

Jules managed to make it almost forty-five minutes before she found herself next to Theo again. Dee and Viggy were gone, and Jules could see them through the window, playing in the front yard. Theo had turned onto his side, and the thin blanket Jules had draped over him earlier had slipped off and lay puddled on the floor. Secretly glad of an excuse to get near him, Jules crept into the room, snagging the blanket off the floor. As close as she was, Jules could see the dark stubble shading his olive skin, and her gaze locked on his mouth.

When he was awake, his lips were thin, just a slash on his hard face, but sleep softened them. They were surprisingly full, and Jules had a hard time tearing her gaze away.

She managed, though, and covered him. Although she was tempted to smooth the fuzzy fabric, to feel his hard contours beneath the layers of blanket and clothing, Jules resisted. It would be too creepy, worse even than just peeking at him while he was sleeping. As she tucked the blanket over his shoulder, she allowed her hand to smooth it over his upper arm—just once.

Her gaze slid over his strong neck and along his jaw, pausing at that tempting mouth and to his eyes...his wide-open, completely awake eyes.

Heat flared in her face, sweeping over her skin, as she realized he'd been awake, that he'd seen her actually groping him. Sure, it'd just been his arm, and just the tiniest of pats, but still. She'd stroked him while she'd thought he was asleep. Theo was going to think she was all sorts of stalker-y.

At least he didn't look angry, or creeped out, or any other expression that would make Jules think he minded. He just seemed a little bemused and hungry— really hungry.

Jules's breath caught, and she leaned in. It was as if Theo had a gravitational pull that was tugging her closer and closer against her better judgment. Her stomach warmed, and her skin buzzed, arousal and attraction and affection all layered together, drawing her toward Theo and erasing all the reasons she shouldn't be doing this. She felt the hot breeze of his exhale against her lips, and it made her realize she was almost kissing him. Jerking back, she stood on unsteady legs so suddenly that she had to take a step back to catch her balance.

As she was pulling away, Theo sat up and turned so his feet found the floor. With a huge yawn, he stretched and stood, making Jules take another step back to put some more space between them. After what had just happened, she didn't trust herself not to hurl her kiss-starved self at him.

The silence felt thick as they stared at each other. It was too much. Jules had to do something, and since kissing was out, she went with babbling. "Did you have a good nap? It's been a few hours, so you must've been tired. I mean, I know you were up for a long time to make sure your friend was going to be okay, but..." In the middle of the sentence, Jules realized she had no way to finish it, so she let her words trail off and waited for his reaction. She fully expected him to run away, since she was acting like a freak.

To her surprise, Theo gave her a tiny grin, more of a twitch of his lips than a smile, but it still warmed her from the inside out. "Thanks."

"You're welcome?" Her voice rose in surprise at the end. "I mean, you're welcome to sleep here any-time." Her blush, which had been fading, flooded back with a vengeance. Although she was tempted to run off at the mouth again, to try to verbally take back the unintended innuendo, Jules knew it would just make it a million times more embarrassing. Instead, she changed the subject. "So...Dee is out front playing with Viggy."

"I see that." He tipped his head toward the window, which framed the little girl and the dog. Theo stretched, and as his muscles popped and shifted, Jules's throat went suddenly very, very dry. "I should go."

She so wanted to protest, but he didn't need some criminal perving on him, especially when she knew she should stay far away. Instead of chaining him to the couch like she wanted to do, Jules trailed Theo to the front door.

He opened it and then paused, turning to look at her. Jules waited, her muscles tight in anticipation of what he was going to say.

"Thank you again."

"You're welcome again. And thank *you* again for saving our lives."

That tiny smile came again, and then he was walking away. Jules had to bite down hard on the inside of her cheek to keep from calling him back.

CHAPTER 13

"WHAT ARE YOU DOING HERE?"

Theo scowled at Hugh, who was trying to maneuver into the bench seat across the booth from him. He was making a mess of it, knocking his crutches against the table and finally falling onto the seat in an awkward motion that made him wince. "Me? I'm not the one with a hole in my leg. Are you supposed to be driving?"

"I walked." Hugh settled into place, and the pain lines on his face eased slightly.

"Hobbled."

Hugh flipped him off and Theo raised his eyebrows. Normally, Hugh would've laughed at that. "Didn't they give you pain meds?"

"Yeah." Hugh grimaced. "They did."

"Why aren't you taking them?"

It was Hugh's turn to look surprised. "Because they make me puke. How'd you know?"

"It's obvious from your pissy mood. Can't they give you something else that doesn't make you sick?"

Hugh scowled. It wasn't a look Theo was used to seeing. On his own face in the mirror, sure, but not on cheery Hugh. "Quit nagging. You sound like my grandma."

"Fuck you." Theo couldn't put much heat behind it.

Even though a week had passed since the shooting, he was still in a constant state of relief and gratitude that Hugh hadn't died. After that first rush of rage at the hospital, it was hard to get truly angry with him.

"You wish." It was Hugh's standard answer, but it lacked the cheeky warmth that usually imbued the comeback. "Where's the new waitress?"

"Jules." The correction was out of Theo's mouth before he could stop it.

"Right." A hint of familiar humor lit Hugh's gaze. "*Jules*. So have you seen *Jules* around, or is she in the kitchen, reading your stealthily passed note and checking off whether she likes you or not?"

To his horror, Theo realized his cheeks were getting hot.

"Are you *blushing*?" Hugh hooted in delight.

To Theo's relief and embarrassment, Jules chose that moment to hurry up to the table. His stomach dove and leapt in a disconcerting way, as if Jules was his own personal amusement-park ride. That thought heated his face even more.

"I'm so sorry!" Jules sounded breathless, which made Theo's brain continue down the path it had already stepped on to. "This has been the craziest morning. The kids go back to school today, and Megan called me earlier to tell me that Laura, the waitress who was supposed to work this morning, was sick, so I couldn't drop them off, so my brain is half here and half riding the bus to school with them, and I've already dropped Mrs. McCurdy's eggs and rye toast with just a little butter on the floor, and—"

Reaching out, Theo grabbed her hand—the one that

had been waving in emphasis, fluttering around like an anxious bird. He gave it a squeeze and received a grateful smile in return.

"Hey, *Jules*?" Hugh's voice had an underlying note of amusement. Although Theo tried to feel irritated about that, he was just happy Hugh wasn't looking bitter and pained anymore. "I'm really, really hungry. In fact, I believe my belly button might actually be touching my backbone."

Unable to hold back an amused snort, Theo muttered, "Belly button touching your backbone? If I'm your grandma, then you're my grandpa."

Although Jules sent him a baffled glance, she went with it, giving Hugh a mock-concerned look. "That sounds like a serious medical problem. I'm not sure food is going to fix it."

"It will. I'm sure of it. The power of belief is strong."

She rolled her eyes, but reached over to squeeze Hugh's upper arm. A jolt went through Theo—a jolt he ignored, because it felt too much like jealousy for his peace of mind. "Seriously, though, how are you doing?"

"Except for those instruments of torture"—Hugh gestured toward his crutches—"I'm just fine." When she gave him a disbelieving look, he grimaced. "Better, then. I'm getting better."

"I can't thank both of you enough for what you did." All teasing dropped from Jules's voice as she looked back and forth between Hugh and Theo. "For saving Dee and Sam and me." Her laugh held the threat of tears, and Theo shifted uncomfortably. He hoped she wouldn't cry. If she cried, he'd have to hug her, and then he'd never hear the end of it from Hugh.

"Jules?" Norman Rounds called from his booth, distracting her from impending tears *and* awkward hugs.

"Be right there," she responded, giving Theo an apologetic grimace. "Your usuals?" At their nods, she hurried to the beckoning man. Theo watched her go, not even trying to pretend that he wasn't enjoying the view. When she reached Norman, however, Theo frowned.

"Rounds has been in here a lot lately," he told Hugh in a low voice.

Without even looking toward Norman's table, Hugh answered, "Yep. Showed up in Monroe six months ago and has been squirreled away in Gordon Schwartz's compound ever since—well, until lately. I'd caught glimpses of him around town once in a while, but this daily breakfast thing is different."

"Why the change?"

"No idea. Maybe the bromance honeymoon period's over and Gordon refuses to cook for him anymore."

Before Theo could say anything else, Otto dropped into the booth next to him. "Why are you here?"

"I just asked him the same thing," Hugh said, giving Theo a mock-chiding look. "You have another week to go before your mandatory leave is up. It'd be longer if you told the truth about how much your ribs are hurting."

"I'm not at work," Theo growled. "I'm getting breakfast. And he was talking to *you*. You know, the one with the extra hole."

Otto raised a hand, cutting off Hugh's retort. "*You*"—he jerked his chin at Hugh—"should be at home. And *you*"—this time his sharp gaze fixed on Theo—"should also be home."

"I'm getting breakfast!" Theo repeated, a little louder that time.

"And flirting with the new waitress," Hugh added. "*Jules*."

Theo turned his fiercest scowl on Hugh, but it just made his partner smile wider.

"He held her hand."

Otto's eyebrows lifted so high they almost touched his hairline.

"I know," Hugh said, as if Otto had made a comment. "We didn't think it would happen, but our little boy is all grown up. Remember when he said all girls have cooties and he'd rather die than kiss one?"

If he hadn't been positive Megan would take unholy glee in banning him from the diner, Theo would've climbed over the table and started pounding on Hugh, bullet wound or no bullet wound.

"Quit trying to distract me," Otto grumbled, although his mouth had twitched at the corners. "How'd you get here?"

"Great." Hugh flopped back in his seat dramatically, but then winced, presumably when his leg protested the jerky movement. "I have two new grandmas now."

"He walked," Theo answered for Hugh absently, his attention distracted by movement at the stranger's table. Norman Rounds reached out and grabbed Jules's wrist, pulling her closer to him as he spoke rapidly. Theo stiffened. "Let me out."

"Why?" Hugh asked, while Otto just looked at him.

"Out." When both men still looked at him expectantly, Theo exhaled, short and sharp, and jerked his head toward the stranger's table. "He's militia, and he's touching Jules."

After a single glance, Hugh and Otto got to their feet, and Theo rushed out of the booth behind them. Theo tried to move around them and take the lead, but the two men formed a wall, even with Hugh swinging uncomfortably on his crutches.

"Hello," Hugh greeted Norman, who immediately dropped his hold on Jules. Nudging her gently out of the way, Hugh lowered his body into the seat next to the gaping man. "Hope you don't mind if I sit here. My leg is throbbing something fierce, and I really need to get my weight off of it."

Jules took several steps back, as if she was happy to put some space between her and Norman. "Oh no! Do you need anything? Like an ice pack or something? I have some ibuprofen in my purse. Oh, what am I saying? I'm sure it's hurting more than over-the-counter pain meds could even touch. Is there any way I could help?"

As Hugh shifted, taking up more of the room on the seat and trapping the still-startled Norman in the corner, he gave Jules an entreating smile. "Just my breakfast? Please?"

"Of course." She gave Hugh another one of those shoulder pats that made Theo unreasonably jealous. "Right away."

Theo watched her hurry off before sliding into the booth across from Norman. For once, when Otto followed him in, Theo didn't complain about being trapped. This time, it was someone else—Norman, to be exact—who was the animal caught in the cage, and Theo was one of the hunters.

"Hello," Hugh said amiably, shifting another inch toward Norman. Now that he'd recovered from his surprise, Norman wasn't acting like most people would have. Instead of cringing or getting hostile, Norman just pasted on a bland smile that eerily matched Hugh's. "I don't believe we've formally met."

"Hold up." Megan grabbed her arm as Jules rushed past, swinging her around with the force of her momentum.

"I promised the guys their breakfast," Jules protested. "They just got creepy Norman to quit being handsy with me, plus—and much more importantly—Hugh was shot in the leg while saving my brother. The least I can do is make sure they get fed. Vicki's in a mood and can't promise to put a rush on their order, and kind of... Well, she demanded that I get out of her kitchen, so I grabbed some biscuits and gravy to tide the guys over. I put it on my tab."

"Those three will be fine waiting a few minutes for their food. Did Hugh do his starving-puppy imitation?"

"Well..." He *had* looked a bit like a starving puppy.

"Besides," Megan continued before Jules could answer, "they're doing their thing."

"Thing?" Jules looked over at where the three cops had joined Norman in his booth. Since she'd been distracted by Hugh's mention of his leg hurting, and Theo just being Theo, and relief at getting away from Norman's tight grip as he babbled about needing to tell her something important, she hadn't wondered why the guys had sat down with Norman. "What thing is that?"

"Their cop thing," Megan said, as if it were obvious. "And it's about time. Norman Rounds has been here every morning for the past two weeks, staring at you with his weird creeper stare, and now he's started grabbing you. That's not okay for anyone to do, but especially Norman. He's one of Gordon's bomb nuts, so he's not one you want to have as your very own super-special stalker."

"Bomb nuts?" Seriously? As if she didn't have enough to worry about, now Megan was telling her that a guy who was into bombs had a crush on her? This was bad.

"Yeah. Gordon has a group of guys living at his place, and they build things that go *boom* while discussing how much the government sucks. Theo will have a talk with him about how there's only one creeper allowed to stalk you at a time, and Theo's called dibs." Ignoring Jules's stare, Megan continued. "Those two are your only tables right now. Why don't you go sit down, eat your biscuits and gravy, and ignore those guys for a few minutes. If anyone else comes in, I can babysit your section while you take a breath."

Shaking off the disturbing information overload Megan had just dumped on her head, Jules glanced around. It was true. There was a lull, rare for this early in the morning. Even in the short time she'd been working as a server, she'd learned to grab breaks when the opportunity presented itself. Jules wasn't about to turn down Megan's offer, especially as frantic as the day had already been.

"Thank you, Megan." With a final, curious glance at Norman's table, where the three cops seemed to loom over the strange man—as much as three people sitting down could loom—Jules obediently headed for an unoccupied booth in the corner. She chose the side that had an excellent view of whatever was going down at table twelve. Jules was curious to see what "doing their thing" entailed.

Norman had become an early morning regular at the diner, always sitting at table twelve, and she'd started to dread seeing him walk in. She would've asked Megan to switch sections with her, since the other woman didn't seem to be as bothered by Norman's weirdness—or much of anything, actually—but then Jules would lose the cops' table, too. She was willing to put up with Norman in exchange for an excuse to talk to Theo every day.

Speaking of Theo, he was saying something to Norman, who looked…how Norman always looked. Bland. Possibly mildly amused. Although Jules had a more oblique view of Theo's face, she didn't have to see his expression to know he was frowning. In fact, his entire body was scowling.

It would've been better if she could have heard what they were saying, but the men kept their voices low. She gave up trying to figure out the gist of the conversation and just enjoyed her biscuits and gravy, as well as her chance to stare at Theo as much as she wanted without anyone noticing.

As soon as she had that thought, she caught Hugh's amused glance and held back a sigh. *Busted*. Well, even if her gawking had been noticed, at least she still had her food. Jules tried to stay focused on her plate, but her disobedient eyes kept glancing at the cop—*her* cop.

Finally they slid out of Norman's booth and started back to their usual table. When Theo glanced around and spotted her, he reversed direction and headed her way. Her stomach did its usual spin and dive at the sight of him, so big and intense and focused on her, and she put down her fork. With all the butterflies in her belly, there was no room for any more biscuits and gravy.

Theo stopped at her booth. Instead of sliding into the seat across from her, as Jules half-expected him to do, he sat right next to her, using his muscled bulk to nudge her over. She slid to the right, making room for him, trying not to be too conscious of the heat radiating from his side or his amazing smell or the way her heart flapped around like a crazed bird at his proximity.

He tipped his head at her abandoned breakfast, and she made a "help yourself" gesture. Tugging the plate — which still held the majority of her biscuits and gravy — toward him, he took a bite, keeping his gaze steady on her. There was something so intimate about him eating from her plate, using her fork — the same fork that had been in her mouth — that she felt heat rise in her cheeks and hoped her blush wasn't obvious. Her throat was so tight she knew her voice would sound weird if she spoke, but she also knew she needed to say something; otherwise, she'd explode. Words were a sort of release valve for her overinflated balloon of a brain.

"What was—" Her voice came out husky—like, *phone-sex-operator* husky—and her face burned hotter. Clearing her throat, she tried again. "What was that whole thing with Norman about?"

Chewing, he studied her thoughtfully for a long moment before swallowing and then replying. "Just getting some answers."

"Did you ask him why he's so weird?" She was blushing hard now, but she couldn't help it. The side of Theo's knee brushed against hers, melting her brain until all she could do was shriek single-word thoughts like *Knees! Touching!* "Or why he only wears beige? Black, I think, would be more practical if he wanted to go monochromatic. Stains wouldn't show on black."

"No."

"You don't think black would be better?" Why was she still talking?

He stopped eating for a moment so he could look at her. His frown seemed to be more confused than angry, for once. "No, I meant I didn't ask him... This is a strange conversation."

"Sorry."

His expression softened as he studied her. "I don't mind."

Jules wasn't quite sure how to respond, and his careful regard was making her jittery—although in the best way possible—so she glanced around as an excuse to break eye contact. Hugh was giving her hungry-puppy face from their usual table, while Otto looked on in long-suffering, yet tolerant, amusement. "I should get back to work."

Theo followed her gaze to his partner. "He can wait. Kids okay with going back to school?"

"The kids, yes," Jules said with a grimace. "I'm the one who's freaking out. They're ready—more than ready. I keep watching for signs of trauma, but they're not there. The kids are sick of me asking if they want to talk about it. Dee finally said she didn't need to, but she would if *I* needed to."

Theo made a sound that might have been a laugh if it hadn't come from Theo.

"It was so hard not to lock them in the basement this morning so they couldn't get on their bus." This time, he choked a little on his latest bite of biscuit. "Not that I would do that...especially since the basement door doesn't have a lock on the outside. It's just tough not to keep them home, where it's safe."

"You want to protect them." He said it like it was a good thing, an admirable thing, like she was trying to be a good sister rather than the unstable, clinging-to-the-edge mess she felt like she was right now.

Officer Theodore Bosco was a shockingly good listener. Jules gave him a sideways look. Such a short time ago, he'd seemed like the enemy. After he saved her life, and her sister's life and her brother's life, though...after he fixed their porch and said he'd like to be a dog and then snored on their couch, everything about him had turned in her mind. Now, it felt as if he was on their side.

That wasn't good. No matter how big a hero he was, he would still arrest her if he knew what she'd done—what she was still in the process of doing. Theo was a good cop. He wouldn't have any choice.

"I really should be getting back to work." Although she tried to make the words sound casual, Jules must've failed, because he gave her a sharp look. She slid toward the opening in the booth that was blocked by his solid form, thinking he'd shift out of her way. He didn't. All Jules accomplished was getting her body close to Theo's—very, very close.

"You know," he said quietly, tipping his head toward hers so they were the only ones who could hear his words, "this doesn't give me much incentive to move." His gaze dropped to where her thigh touched his. Heat radiated from him, warming her entire side, making her want to get closer. Theo's gravitational pull had activated again, drawing her in until their planets collided.

Thinking about colliding with Theo made her flush, and she guiltily raised her gaze to his, hoping desperately that he'd missed how she'd just ogled him. By the humor and heat in his eyes, she knew he could read every lustful thought in her head.

Jules could feel her face burning in embarrassment... and for other reasons.

Megan hollered across the diner, "Quit holding my waitress captive, Theo! Indulge in your bondage fantasies later, when there aren't hungry people to feed."

There was a bark of laughter from Hugh. Although Theo looked annoyed, he didn't seem to be at all embarrassed. Jules, on the other hand, felt her skin burn from her chest to her hairline. Worst of all were the images instantly flooding her mind. The heat wasn't all from humiliation. There was some excitement brewing there, as well.

Luckily, Theo was too busy scowling at Megan and sliding out of the booth to notice Jules's embarrassment. Ducking her head, she stood and grabbed what little remained of her biscuits and gravy. Before she hurried to the kitchen, though, she couldn't stop herself from sneaking a quick peek at his face.

He wasn't looking at her. Instead, he stared, expressionless, over her shoulder. Jules turned to find out what had put that look on his face, but she moved a little too quickly and bobbled. Theo caught her upper arm, steadying her. She automatically put out a hand, and it landed on his belly. Her breath stopped as soon as her fingers landed on his solid belly, only a T-shirt blocking skin-to-skin contact.

"Theo." The woman's voice was sweet and feminine, and it yanked Jules back to the present in a disconcerting rush. Turning toward the speaker, she dropped her hand too quickly, blushing as hotly as if she'd been caught fondling his naked stomach. Her embarrassment increased when she saw the woman was insanely perfect, enough so that her beauty melted Jules into an insecure heap. "How are you? I heard about the shooting. How terrible! I'm so glad you're okay."

Theo's response was more a grunt than a word, and his tension was so obvious that it made Jules intensely curious. Was she an ex-girlfriend? Or—and her heart dissolved at the thought—maybe a *current* girlfriend? Jules could easily see it. The woman was gorgeous. Tall and willowy and even-featured, like a model who specialized in the girl-next-door look.

"Who is this?" The too-attractive stranger turned to Jules with a friendly smile and held out a hand. "I'm Sherry Baker."

Off-balance from imagining Theo and this woman together, Jules automatically accepted the handshake but waited a second too long to answer. "Oh, I'm Jules! I mean, um…Julie Jackson." She tried to hide her wince. The last time she'd bungled her new name so badly was when she'd been interrogated by Theo. It made it worse when Sherry gave her a sympathetic smile, as if she knew too well what it was like to act like a babbling idiot. It'd have been much easier to hate Sherry if she hadn't seemed so stinking nice.

"Sherry," Otto said, startling Jules, who hadn't

noticed his approach. For a big guy, he sure moved quietly. He must have taken Sherry by surprise, as well, because she quickly twisted around.

"Hey, Sherry." Hugh swung up on his crutches. "How're things?"

Glancing between the two newcomers, Sherry laughed. "What a reception! Hi, Otto, Hugh. I didn't see you two when I came in. Oh, Hugh—I can't believe you were shot! I think I must've left the lieutenant fifty messages after I heard. I was going crazy with worry until he finally called me back yesterday to tell me you were going to be okay. How's the investigation going? Any idea who it was?"

"Thanks," Hugh said lightly. "I'll be fine. We're following up some leads, but there's nothing definite yet." Jules studied his face, pretty sure the tension in his expression wasn't from pain—not all of it, at least. She wondered if she'd guessed wrong about which cop was interested in Sherry.

"Jules!" Megan bellowed from across the diner. "If you don't get back to work right now, I'm never going to offer you a break ever again, and by 'never' I mean 'not until the end of time'!"

Jules took a step toward the kitchen. "I'd better get back," she said. "It was nice to meet you?" To her embarrassment, her voice rose at the end, turning the pleasantry into more of an insult. Sherry's smile faltered, and Jules felt like a rude toad. It wasn't Sherry's fault that residual, unwarranted envy still churned in Jules's stomach, making her regret eating the biscuits and gravy. She gave Sherry an apologetic grimace, and the other woman's expression brightened again.

"You, too, Jules."

Jules started to take another step away from the group, but Theo caught her hand, squeezing it briefly before releasing. That was the second time in less than an hour that Theo had held her hand, Jules realized, and her smile grew huge as she met his gaze.

Thanks to that realization, Jules was almost skipping as she returned to work. There had been hand-holding and thigh-touching and same-plate eating. Jules had no idea what—if anything—all of that meant, but she was happier than she'd been in a long time, and she was determined to enjoy that feeling as long as she could.

CHAPTER 14

"How about a Great Pyrenees?" Dee asked on the tailside of a yawn, wiggling down on the bed. It was too warm for covers, even with the window open, so they were bunched at the bottom of the mattress. "My book said they're excellent family dogs. They guard sheep when they're...well, in the mountains, I suppose. We'd be like their sheep. They'd protect us."

Jules wished something as simple as getting a dog could keep their family safe. "Did your book happen to mention how big they get?"

Dropping her eyes to the side, Dee gave an unconvincing shrug. "The girls don't get more than, like, eighty pounds or..." Her voice dropped to a mumble.

"What was that?" Jules cupped her ear, leaning closer. "Eh? I didn't quite catch that last part about how they get to be super-dooper enormously huge and would take up all the room in our big new SUV, even where the driver is supposed to go." She poked a teasing finger into her sister's ribs, exactly where she knew Dee was the most ticklish.

Starting to giggle, she twisted away from Jules. "We'd just have to teach her to drive."

"Or you could find a smaller breed to obsess over," Jules suggested. "Keep reading that dog book."

"Okay." Dee yawned again.

"Love you to bits, Dee."

"Love you, too."

"Good night."

"'Night, Jules."

Although she'd been sitting on the side of her sister's bed for the past twenty minutes, Jules was reluctant to leave. It had been almost impossible to let the kids finish their first full day at school and not run in and drag them all out of class—kind of like when she'd kidnapped them, she realized. Even if the mention of homeschooling had been a joke, it was enormously tempting after the shooting.

Dee, who had closed her eyes, peeked at Jules before quickly snapping her eyes closed again. With a snort, Jules stood. "Don't stay up too late reading."

Keeping her eyes shut, Dee gave a tiny, guilty smile. "I won't."

Jules knocked on the odd, small elf door before ducking into Tio's room. As she'd expected, it was empty. Crossing the room, she stepped into the open closet, pushed a few shirts aside, their hangers scraping against the rod, and knocked again, this time on the side of the opening they'd created.

Ty, lounging on the bed, and Tio, sitting in the hardback chair—which, along with the adjacent desk, had been another thrift-store find—glanced over at her as she entered. Their weighted silence hung in the air, and she soundlessly sighed as she took a seat on the foot of Ty's bed. "What's up?"

"Nothing." Their synchronized answer just made her more suspicious.

"Is it something that will endanger your health, lives, and/or safety?" she asked and received two negative head shakes in return. "Okay. Just try not to damage anything—or anyone. How was school?"

"Fine." The chorus had returned.

Crossing her arms, she settled herself a little more firmly on the bed. "I can stay here all night."

Ty was the first to crack. "School was school. My English teacher is a thousand years old, but Mrs. Lee— she's my math teacher—is kind of hot. I like getting to repeat stuff from last year. Sometimes, I actually get what's going on. I'm thinking about trying wrestling instead of football."

Blinking, Jules absorbed that flood of information. "Wrestling? Okay. You know, you can do both, if you want. Wrestling won't start until January, right? We'll figure out a way to pay the fees."

"Yeah." The boys shared a private look, and Jules wondered what kind of plotting they were up to. "With everything being all new here and stuff, I'm going to skip football."

"That's probably smart." She turned to Tio. "Your turn, T. Hot math teacher? Old English teacher? Changes in extracurriculars? Share."

"There's a science club." His hushed tone was almost reverent.

"That's great, T." A spark of pleasure lit in her chest. She'd dragged them away from privileged lives and dropped them into a small Colorado town. Except for the shooting—which was, granted, a fairly big "except for"— things had been going pretty well for them so far. There was potential for contentment. "How's the teacher?"

"He'll be good, I think. Although"—his mouth twisted a bit—"he's also the wrestling coach." He ducked as a balled-up sock flew at his head.

"Hey!" Ty complained, lobbing a second missile at his brother. "Just because someone's athletic doesn't mean he's a dumbass."

"Ty's right," Jules said, and then sent him a quelling look. "Although he could've picked a better way to express it. Keep an open mind, T, and I bet you'll be happily surprised by your teacher."

"And if he does suck," Ty added, "we'll have the entire wrestling season to get revenge."

With a groan, Jules stood. It was too late to start a revenge-is-wrong discussion, especially since she felt like she'd been beaten by a very large, very heavy stick. She'd resume her attempt to drill morals into her brothers tomorrow. "No revenge," she simply said, and that would have to do for the moment. "Don't stay up too late."

"We won't." The chorus was back again.

Leaning down, she kissed Ty's forehead before he could wiggle away, and then walked over to give Tio a side hug. "So, you think you can be happy here?"

T's return hug was quick but unbearably sweet, although it was Ty who answered. "We *are* happy here, JuJu."

That warmed her heart as she headed for Sam's room. Even though he would've heard the squeaks and thumps and occasional muttered curses as she climbed the narrow stairs, Jules knocked and waited for Sam's invitation before she entered his room. Like Tio, he was sitting at his desk, although he didn't look nearly as happy as T to be doing his homework.

"Hey, Sam-I-Am," she said, crossing to flop down

in the armchair next to him. "Oh, it's so much cooler in here than it was. That fan is miraculous."

"Yeah." He glanced toward the window fan that had cost her skinned knuckles and two hours of frustration. "Th-thanks for th-that. It's easier to sleep n-now."

"Probably kills some of the noise from the twins below, too."

Although he gave a half smile, he said, "I c-c-can't hear m-much up here."

"I'm jealous." Jules studied him carefully. He was so guarded, it was hard to guess what he was thinking or feeling. "How was school?"

"Ok-kay."

"Okay good or okay bad but you don't want to worry me?"

That brought another crooked smile. "J-just ok-kay ok-k-kay."

"Well, okay then." She grinned back at him. "The other three seem to be adjusting well, although the Ts are up to something."

"Wh-when are they n-n-not?"

"Good point." Jules brought her feet up so she could sit cross-legged. "Are you going to be bored repeating sophomore year again?"

"N-no. The cl-cl-cl-cl…" He let out a frustrated breath. "Ev-veryth-thing's d-different. And I g-get t-t-to learn t-to d-drive."

"Makes up for a lot, doesn't it?" Although she said it lightly, Sam gave her a direct look, his expression serious—even more so than usual.

"You d-don't n-need to m-make up for anyth-thing, J-Ju."

"I feel like I do," she admitted. "I mean, I took y'all away from so much."

He snorted. "Yeah. So m-m-much sh-shit."

"Sam!" she protested, although she laughed. He just shrugged unapologetically.

They settled into a quiet moment, until Jules broke the silence.

"You'll tell me if things are not okay, right? So we can figure out how to fix whatever's wrong?"

Sam studied her for a moment before answering.

"Yeah, J-JuJu. I pr-promise."

A few hours later, Jules started awake, her body jerking into instant awareness. She lay unmoving, trying to quiet her breathing so she could hear what had woken her. Everything was silent. Even the usual groans and squeaks of an elderly house were absent. Somehow, the absolute stillness was more unnerving than any sort of suspicious noise would be.

After a long minute of fruitless listening as her muscles grew tighter with each passing second, she slid out of bed and turned on her lamp. The bedside clock, an old-fashioned thrift-store find Jules had loved from the moment she'd spotted it, showed it was almost twelve thirty. Closing her eyes with a sigh, she accepted that waking up in three and a half hours was going to be rough.

She couldn't sleep now, though, not while this unnatural silence was eating at her nerves. Opening her eyes again, she grabbed her cell phone and slipped into the hall, trying to keep her bare footsteps quiet. With each press of her weight, the ancient floorboards whined and complained with small cracks and squeaks. Tiptoeing up to each room, she peeked inside, comforted by the Ty-, Tio-, and Dee-shaped lumps on each bed.

Glancing at the door to Sam's third-floor room, Jules decided against checking on him. The stairs were noisy enough to wake him if she attempted it, and she didn't want to disturb his sleep just because she was having a paranoid moment.

Instead, she checked the other second-floor rooms. The nearly full moon streamed into the uncovered windows, making the light spaces brighter but the shadows deeper. Even her almost-silent footsteps seemed to echo in the empty rooms, and Jules kept having to stop to listen, unsure if she'd made a sound or if it came from somewhere else.

By the time she crept down the stairs to the first level, her heart was racing and her breathing came fast.

"Stop it," she hissed at herself, and then jumped at the loudness of her whisper. The absurdity of that made her laugh quietly, and her heart slowed slightly. Now that the risk of waking her siblings was lessened, she forced herself to walk briskly through the hall to the living room, rather than tiptoe in like a jumpy mouse.

Moonlight slanted through the windows, breaking the room into geometric shapes of light and darkness. Familiar objects—the couch, Dee's open backpack, a book on the coffee table—looked foreign in the strange illumination. Drawing herself up, Jules made her feet step into the room, and she checked each shadow, each dark corner, until she was satisfied no boogeymen were hiding in there.

In each first-level room, she did the same, until she ended up in the kitchen. When she glanced at the door to the basement, her stomach dropped to her feet. There was no way she was going down to the cellar-like, dirt-floored, lit-by-a-single-bare-bulb, creepy-as-heck basement in the middle of the night. Jules didn't care if there were multiple serial killers taking refuge in the subterranean space; that was how people got their dumb selves killed in horror movies.

With a shudder, Jules turned away from the basement door. Through the window above the sink, a dart of movement caught her eye. Startled, she stepped back, but then caught herself. A few weeks ago, she might have been able to avoid checking it out, to run back to bed and hide under the covers. Now, though, she was responsible for four other people, younger people, vulnerable people. If something—or someone—was outside, she needed to know so she could decide what to do.

Her phone slid in her damp grip, and she switched it to her other hand. Dialing 9-1-1, she kept her thumb next to the *send* button and took a hesitant step toward the window, and then another. When she finally was close enough to see outside, she leaned in, watching for another movement.

The evergreens and aspens danced in the wind, their branches lifting and swaying and making Jules wonder if that was the motion she'd noticed. It didn't seem right, so she kept watching, her gaze scanning over the forest and the listing structure of their barn.

She'd thought the moonlit living room was creepy, but their backyard was ten times as scary. There were so many dark spaces where someone could be hiding,

so many flashes of movement that Jules was almost—
almost—positive were the wind in the trees. It was hard to
see much from the window, though, much less distinguish
what was always there from what might be suspicious.

Her teeth caught the inside of her lip as she headed
for the back door. "There's nothing there," she muttered.
"Just open the door, take a quick look, and then you can
go back to bed, knowing for *sure* there's nothing there."

The knob was slick in her hand, rattling loosely as
it turned. As she pulled open the door, a gust of wind
pressed against her, as if urging her back into the house.
Setting her jaw, she stepped onto the back porch, and
one of the boards creaked under her weight. Closing the
door behind her, Jules let her gaze scan the area. With
the trees and weeds and even the barn swaying in the
wind, finding something—some*one*—moving in all that
chaos seemed impossible.

Standing outside of this remote house in this mountain town, Jules felt alone and very, very small. How
was she supposed to protect her family when she was
jumping at every imagined noise? The task seemed
impossible. Maybe kidnapping them had been a stupid
move, a destructive move, something that would damage
them all.

At that thought, she dragged herself out of her gloomy
imaginings. She'd done the right thing, the *only* thing
that could've been done. Her siblings had thanked her,
and they all seemed surprisingly content in their new,
more bedraggled life. It was just the dark and the wind
and the strangeness of a new place that was getting to
her, making things seem hopeless.

She needed to go back to bed, not only because she

had to be up in a few hours, but also because the middle of the night was not a good time to weigh major life decisions. Everything seemed heavier in the wee hours of the morning.

As she started to turn to go back inside, the movement caught her eye again. Jules whipped around as she strained to focus on the shifting shadow—one that was definitely not a tree branch. She clutched her phone tighter.

If she called the police, there would be reports and questions and her name would almost surely be run through some database. Dennis seemed to be good at what he did, but Jules would rather not test that, not for an unconfirmed shadow on a windy night. Instead of hitting the *send* button, she held her breath and watched the spot where she'd seen the movement.

There it is! Something had moved, a shape that was too big to be a cat or a bunny or any sort of nonthreatening creature going about its innocent business in the woods. She'd been so worried about human dangers that she hadn't even considered that Colorado was home to all sorts of predators, including bears and mountain lions and—

The shadow moved again, the black-on-black shape moving out of the trees, and Jules jolted, the thought of tearing claws and ripping teeth filling her brain, making her lurch back until her shoulder blades hit the door with a painful *thump*. As her hand reached for the door handle, the thing—whatever it was—charged toward her.

She grabbed for the doorknob, a shriek building in her lungs, but it evaded her fingers, and she was unable to look away from the dark shape plunging toward her. Her fingers smacked against the doorframe, but she didn't feel it, couldn't feel anything except her terror and the scream filling her lungs like overextended balloons. It was so fast, yet she felt like she was bogged down in a slow-motion nightmare. The thing came closer and closer until it lunged onto the porch with her, wriggling with excitement and twisting around her legs.

"Viggy?" she croaked, heart still racing. In response, the dog sat on her foot, a bony part of his haunch digging painfully into her instep. The ache brought back her reasoning skills, and she bent to simultaneously pet him and shove him off her foot. "Holy moly, Vig, you scared the stuffing out of me!"

As her initial panic settled, a new fear rose in its place. Why was Viggy here? Had something happened to Theo? Jules wished she'd gotten his phone number, although there was no way in Hades she would've been brave enough to ask, even if she could have come up with a good excuse. After all, how was she to know his dog would end up on her back porch in the middle of the night?

Peering at her phone, she cancelled the call with fingers that shook with residual adrenaline. Pulling up her Web browser, she found the police department's nonemergency number.

When the dispatcher answered, Jules asked hesitantly, "Can you get a message to Officer Theo Bosco?"

"What message is that?"

"His dog is at my house."

As the dispatcher asked for her name and address, all Jules could think about was that the call was being recorded, leaving yet another breadcrumb for their stepmother's investigators to find. She squeezed her eyes closed tightly. It was just one more reason that letting Theo and Viggy into their lives was a horrible, horrible idea.

Viggy whined, and Jules opened her eyes. The sight of the dog, looking at her with sweet eyes and his head cocked to the side, made Jules realize it was too late. A certain cop and his K9 partner had already implanted themselves firmly into her heart.

Swallowing a sigh, Jules gave the dispatcher her address.

⸻

The phone rang, startling Theo out of yet another daydream about Jules. His first instinct, as nonsensical as it was, was that Jules was calling him, and a surge of anticipation shot through him as he grabbed for his phone.

"Hey, Theo, it's Jackie from Dispatch."

Theo grimaced at his own idiocy. Of course Jules wouldn't be calling him. She didn't even have his number. "What is it?" His tone was short from disappointment, and Theo held back a wince. It was a good thing he didn't work nights, or Jackie would've made him pay for his attitude. She would've sent only the worst calls his way, and his shifts would've been miserable until she forgave him—or until someone else pissed her off.

Jackie was talking, and Theo forced his attention back to the call. When her words started to penetrate, Theo was startled out of his self-recriminations. "Viggy's *where*?"

Even as she repeated herself, Theo was rushing downstairs and shoving through the back door.

Sure enough, Viggy's kennel was empty.

"The caller's address is—"

"I know it," Theo interrupted, knowing he was being rude again but too distracted to care. On one hand, it was embarrassing and worrying to have his canine partner escape his custody, but a part of him was glad to have the opportunity to leave his sleepless bed and visit Jules. "Thanks."

He headed for his SUV, ending the call after that halfhearted attempt at civility. As usual for that time of the night, the streets of Monroe were quiet. If any wildness was happening, it was behind closed doors. Glancing at the darkened houses, he wondered what crimes were being committed, what arguments were being held, what desperation was being felt. *That's the problem*, Theo thought as he turned onto Jules's street. How was he supposed to help people when they hid their problems, acting like everything was fine until it all went to shit? Things were fixable up to a point. After that point, all he could do was grieve.

Shaking off his introspection, Theo slowed to a crawl when he saw the start of Jules's driveway. He scowled. The mailbox listed to the right, just waiting for the gentle breeze that would send it to the ground. The landlord needed to step up and start fixing some of these issues. A crooked mailbox was one thing, but Jules shouldn't be having to deal with faulty appliances and a leaking roof and the hundred other dangerous situations in the making. At least the porch was no longer a death trap, but Jules and the kids shouldn't have to wait until Theo had time to fix everything around the place. He resolved to get the landlord's phone number from Jules so Theo could give the slumlord a...gentle nudge to start some home improvements immediately.

He lurched across a final pothole and came to a stop outside her house. The porch light turned on, and the front door opened, the entrance framing a pajama-clad Jules. At her feet sat Viggy, who was looking as innocent as a runaway dog could look.

Jules stepped onto the porch, followed closely by Viggy. The dog—*his* dog, the one that ran off and forced him to visit Jules in the middle of the night—stretched out on one side of the entrance. Closing the front door behind them, Jules took a couple of steps to the front of the porch, closer to Theo. The wind whipped her hair around her face and plastered her sleep shorts to her body in a very enticing way. Theo tried not to look obviously eager as he joined her, but he was pretty sure he failed at that. He did take the six porch steps in two strides, after all.

Once he was standing next to her, Theo was at a loss. Even before he'd disappeared into a cloud of rage, talking to women had never been his strong point. Now, faced with Jules in all her sleep-mussed glory, Theo had nothing. His mind was a blank.

"I thought he was a serial killer," Jules blurted.

He was so grateful to her for breaking the silence that it took a second for her words to make sense. Except, even then, they didn't make sense. "Who?"

"Viggy."

"You thought my dog was a serial killer?"

"It was dark!" she protested, starting to laugh. "A

strange noise woke me up, and then something moved in the trees, so I went outside, and then Viggy ran toward me and scared the holy spit out of me."

"The holy spit?" he teased, before the rest of what she'd told him registered, and all humor left him. "Wait. You thought you saw someone, so you went outside to check?"

Jules winced, ducking her head and peeking at him through a silky fall of hair. Theo tried not to focus on how she even made cringing cute. "I know. It was stupid."

"Yes."

That made her frown. "It wasn't *that* stupid. I mean, it wasn't really a serial killer. What if I'd called 9-1-1? Cops would've arrived, gun blazing, and all for Viggy."

No one made him smile as much as she did. No one else made him smile at all. He pretended to scratch his nose in order to hide it. "Guns blazing?"

Just like that, her temper was gone, and she was laughing again. "Don't you mock my colorful vernacular, Officer Bosco!"

"I just don't think I've ever done anything with my gun blazing. What does that even mean?"

"I'm not sure. But it does sound very dramatic."

"And unsafe."

"Yes. That too."

Her laughter faded, leaving them in a weighted silence. "So Viggy is your dog, then? I thought you said he was your partner's?"

"He was." A wash of grief ran through him, erasing any traces of laughter. "He was Don Baker's dog."

"Was?" she asked tentatively, looking at him in a way that made him feel like he could tell her anything,

anything at all, and she'd get it. She'd get him. Jules settled onto the top step, patting the spot next to her.

As he struggled to find the words, Theo sat down next to her. "Don was my partner, my friend…more than that. He was like a dad to me." His throat got tight, making it hard to continue, but he forced out the words. It seemed important, somehow, for Jules to know this, for Jules to know *him*—the real him, not the angry mess he'd become. "He killed himself two months ago."

Her breath caught, her hand flying up to cover her mouth. "Oh no. I'm so sorry!" Her free hand reached out and caught his. As she squeezed, he braced for the flare of anger to hit him, for the need to escape to overwhelm him, but it never did. Instead, he felt relief, as if telling her about Don had opened up something inside him, allowing all the anger and pain to escape.

"Since I lost my K9 partner to cancer last year, Hugh assigned Viggy to me. It's been…tough." Theo almost laughed at the understatement.

"He seems to be doing better, though," she said, still holding tight to his hand. "You both do."

Sometimes it felt that way, but other times all the frustration and rage and grief threatened to drown him. It felt right to tell Jules, though. Even though he'd known her for such a short time, but there was something about her—and her whole family—that settled him, brought him peace.

Jules's fingers tightened around his again, and he looked down at her. His blood instantly started to warm. Peace wasn't the only thing she made him feel. He squeezed her hand as he studied her, feeling as if he could look at her all night and not get bored. Everything about her was beautiful—her eyes, her cheeks, her laugh, the smooth fall of her hair, her mouth…especially her mouth.

Theo couldn't stop staring at her. At first, her full lips were curled up at the corners in a sympathetic smile, and then they grew serious, parting slightly. His breath stopped, his lungs stalling out and refusing to work anymore. He shifted toward her, unable to resist. It felt as if there was an invisible but powerful thread connecting them, reeling him closer. The wind gusted, tossing her hair across her face again.

Jules reached up a hand, but Theo beat her to it. He caught the stray strands, tucking them behind her ear. In the process, his fingertips just barely grazed over her cheekbone and around the shell of her ear. Her skin was cool, and goose bumps rose on her arms.

Frowning, Theo let his hand drop. Her gaze followed it down and then found his face again. Her breaths were coming quick and light, and the rise and drop of her chest was extremely distracting. Shoving away his confusing jumble of emotion for the moment, he released her hand so he could pull his hoodie over his head. Jules was staring at his stomach, making Theo realize the movement had made his T-shirt ride up, exposing his abs. He tugged it back down, loving how Jules's face dropped in obvious disappointment when his skin was no longer showing. She shivered again, and he remembered what he'd been about to do.

"Here," he said quietly, lifting the sweatshirt so he could put it on over her head. "You're cold."

She raised her arms once she realized what he intended, allowing the "Monroe Police Department" sweatshirt to envelope her, the bottom hem falling to the porch floor, the fabric puddling around her hips. For some reason, Theo liked seeing her in his sweatshirt. He decided he'd give it to her. That way, during the long, lonely, sleepless nights, he could imagine her wearing it.

A surge of heat ran through him, and he cleared his throat, trying to refocus. "Warmer?"

"Much." Her voice was throaty, lending the word a secondary meaning, one that Theo wasn't sure was intentional or not. Either way, it brought his attention back to her mouth. This time, when he leaned closer, there was no chilled skin to distract him. His gaze was locked on her and hers on him, and he could see she felt the same pull of the invisible thread, that same irresistible tug that linked them together.

It didn't matter then whether he had the right thing to say. Silence was fine.

Fraction of an inch by fraction of an inch, he came closer and closer, until he was enveloped in her scent—spicy vanilla—and her heat and the puffs of excited air that warmed his throat.

Finally, he was there.

The first spark of their lips meeting startled him, making him jolt and pull away just a little, until he couldn't feel her breathe anymore. Almost as soon as he separated from her, he was back, needing to kiss her more than he'd needed anything.

Then she moaned. It was a tiny sound, cute—like so many things she did—and hot and perfect. It vibrated against his mouth, and he was done thinking or debating or being angry or anything else. All he wanted to do was kiss Jules Jackson, who was very likely *not* Jules

Jackson. At this moment, he didn't care if she was Al Capone's zombie in drag. Whoever she was, whatever she was running from, it wasn't going to stop him.

He gently nipped her full bottom lip, and she gasped. Theo took full advantage, deepening the kiss. Stroking both hands down her sides, he shifted forward, erasing the last half inch between their upper bodies.

The feel of her pressed against him was overwhelming. Theo had to break the kiss for a moment, just so he could suck air into his oxygen-starved lungs. At some point—he was not sure when—Jules's hands had slid to the back of his neck, and she was massaging the muscles there. It ramped up his arousal, but at the same time, it soothed him.

After a few ragged breaths, he kissed her again. Immediately, he was consumed. Need and pleasure raged through him, burning as they flared to life after months of numbness. It was like his emotions had fallen asleep, and now they were waking with a wonderfully painful tingling. Theo kissed her harder, his hands flattening at the small of her back so he could press her against him.

She groaned into his mouth, and he loved hearing that, loved knowing their kiss was affecting her this way. Theo felt so wrapped up in her, always thinking about her, wanting to be with her, and it was a heady sensation to know she wanted him just as much. He stroked up and down her spine, running his hands over the small but strong muscles in her back. Jules scraped her nails lightly over his head, and it was his time to shudder.

Even as lost as he was in her, Theo heard the click of the latch. Ripping himself away from the most intense kiss of his life, he stood and whirled toward the sound, keeping his body between Jules and whoever was interrupting.

"Theo?" Jules's husky voice questioned at the same time Dee barreled onto the porch, making a beeline for Viggy as she squealed with excitement.

"Hi, Theo." Dee greeted him absently, all her attention on the dog.

"Dee." He'd regained most of his composure, although hearing Jules's audible breaths was not helping in that regard. "Did we wake you?" He wondered how loud they'd gotten. Although it had only been a kiss, he'd been completely immersed in the moment. It had felt so huge, so explosive, he didn't know how anyone could've slept through it.

"Yes, but that's okay." Dee hugged the dog. "If you hadn't, I wouldn't have gotten to see Viggy. What are you doing here?"

Since *making out with your sister* seemed age-inappropriate, Theo just said, "Viggy decided to visit you."

"On his own? He ran off?" Her arms squeezed tightly around Viggy. The dog didn't seem to mind. On the contrary, he leaned into the girl with a low groan. Dee's expression was guarded as she asked, "Did something happen?"

"To make Viggy want to leave?" When she nodded, Theo continued. "No. I think he just wanted to see you."

Dee's face lit up, and she turned her attention back to Viggy, talking inaudibly to him.

"That was kind," Jules murmured, standing and leaning into his back. Her breath warmed his skin through his T-shirt. Theo got goose bumps. He wasn't sure how to respond, so he didn't—out loud, at least. Turning, he looped an arm around her waist and tugged her in front of him, pulling her close. She leaned back against him, and he couldn't resist wrapping his arms around her.

The wind had quieted to a light breeze, and Theo just reveled in the moment, in the warm body pressed to his front, the cool night, the stars that were so bright they almost didn't look real. The constant grief and rage churning in him had quieted for now, and Viggy looked happy.

It wouldn't last. For this minute, though, it was enough.

CHAPTER 15

As she bussed the table, picking up the few coins wedged between two plates and trying not to think about all the things her family needed and how quickly that seventy-one cents would be spent, her stomach buzzed with excitement.

He'd actually kissed her. No, *they* had kissed. There'd definitely been some mutual lip action. Her cheeks grew warm as she rewound—for the hundredth time that morning—every second of their time together on the porch.

Her eyes darted to the clock on the wall, and she held back a grimace when she realized the three cops wouldn't be there for another forty-five minutes. Jules wanted to see him, wanted to know if they were going to sneak each other secret looks and touches, or if the kiss was something Theo wanted to forget. If his gaze would slide right past her, as if it were a normal day, and they were normal people, and something miraculous hadn't happened earlier that morning.

Wiping down the table, she snorted. *Miraculous?* It had been a kiss. A good kiss—an amazing kiss—but that was all. It hadn't cured cancer or turned water into wine or stopped a plague of locusts. It was a kiss. A toe-curling, brain-erasing, life-altering kiss, sure, but still just a kiss.

A flash of blue uniform had her turning even as the sensor on the door beeped, announcing a customer. Disappointment made her shoulders sag when she realized it was Hugh, not Theo. Guilt quickly followed, and she gave Hugh an extra-bright smile to make up for her mental lack of enthusiasm. She liked Hugh—quite a bit, actually. He just wasn't the cop who made her heart quicken.

By the way Hugh was charging toward her, though, it looked like she was exactly the person he wanted to see. The crutches didn't seem to slow him down, even when he was forced to maneuver through the tables. His obvious intent made her nervous, and she tried to take a step back, but her calves bumped one of the wooden chairs. She bobbled, hurrying to put her bussing tub down before she dropped it and all its contents. By the time she'd recovered her balance, he was right in front of her.

Although he was smiling, there was a determined look on his face that ramped up her nerves. Jules tried to appear like his speedy approach hadn't bothered her, as if she wasn't seconds from tossing the contents of the bus tub at him and vaulting over the table to freedom.

"Jules," he said, his sharp gaze taking in everything. Somehow, she just knew that *he* knew that she was ready to run. "Just the person I wanted to see. Do you have a minute?"

"Actually," she rushed out, her voice too high-pitched, "we're really busy this morning. Could this wait until later?"

"'Fraid not." His smile turned apologetic, but his tone was firm. Whatever this was, Jules was not getting out of it. All the horrible possibilities—he knew who they were, what she'd done—rushed into her mind, weakening her knees, and she sank into the chair behind her.

"Sorry. Mind if I sit?" she asked belatedly.

"Of course not." Leaning on his right crutch, he used his left to push another chair away from the table so he could drop into it. "Good idea."

There was a short silence, although it felt very long to Jules. Her gaze darted around again, wishing for a tour bus of seniors to stop by before heading farther into the mountains, or maybe a preschool crowd of teenagers, or even for Megan to come out of the kitchen and yell at Jules to get back to work. Any of those would be acceptable options, all better than waiting to hear what was making Hugh's smile look like he'd duct-taped it on.

"So...what's your story, Jules?"

The question made her throat seize. Even if she'd known how to answer that question, even if she'd *wanted* to answer that question, it would've been impossible to speak. Instead, she settled for giving him a quizzical look—at least she hoped it was a quizzical look. Jules was pretty sure it leaned closer toward deer-in-the-headlights.

"Come on, now." Hugh leaned back, making the chair squeak in protest, and laced his fingers behind his head. The pose brought all the muscles in his arms and chest into stark relief, but Jules didn't really find it sexy. She *did* find it intimidating. Even with a bullet hole in his leg, Hugh would have no problem restraining her. "You randomly show up in town, jump at every sudden movement, and get a job I'm guessing you're a college degree or two overqualified for. What'd you do?" He was watching her closely, and she struggled to keep the panic off her face. "Or what was done *to* you?"

She fumbled for words, trying to think of the best way to prove him wrong, to turn him off the track he was on before it led him inevitably to a kidnapping in Florida. "I haven't done anything wrong."

A judge might disagree, but she felt it, deep in her gut. The kids had needed saving. She'd saved them. In the weeks since they'd arrived in Monroe—even when facing a school shooting and a falling-down house and a new town—none of her siblings had ever even hinted at wanting to go back to Courtney, to their old life. Jules knew she'd done the right thing.

Not that her certainty helped now, faced with Hugh's coolly assessing gaze.

"Good," he said. "That makes it easier. Just tell me why you ran, why you're hiding, and I'll be able to help you."

"I…" For a single, insane moment, Jules was tempted. Hugh was a good guy. He could understand why she had to take the kids, right?

The door sensor beeped, and she whipped her head around to see Norman coming in. He started to head to his usual booth, but then he noticed Jules and Hugh, and his footsteps slowed. Just for a second, his bland countenance focused and sharpened, making him look like a completely different person.

Jules inhaled quickly, and Norman dropped his gaze, returning to the beige, slightly *off* customer she saw every day. Even though she was pretty sure he wasn't a private investigator hired by her stepmother, he still set off her internal alarms. When she'd grabbed the kids and run, she'd been so focused on the possibility of her step-mother finding them that Jules hadn't even considered that their new life would hold other dangers. Although she wasn't sure what kind of threat Norman presented, all of Jules's instincts were insisting he was dangerous. Turning her attention back to Hugh, she saw he was glancing back and forth between her and Norman, as if he'd noticed her reaction and was trying to figure out the reason for it.

The pause had allowed her to regain her common sense, and the moment of craziness passed. Hugh was, first and foremost, a police officer. If he even had the smallest suspicion she'd kidnapped her siblings, he'd be arresting her. Immediately. That temptation to confess was just a moment of weakness, a wish that someone would help them, would share the burden of responsibility that weighed so heavily on Jules.

"What were you about to say, Jules?" Hugh asked. His tone, a mix of command and persuasion, was the same, but any chance of her confessing was gone.

"Just that I need to get back to work." Standing abruptly, she rushed toward Norman, making as large a circle around Hugh as possible. Unfortunately, it wasn't wide enough, and he caught her wrist, gently but firmly pulling her to a stop. The fingers locked around her wrist reminded her viscerally of handcuffs, and she fought the urge to twist free.

"Jules." There was no softness to his voice or his hold. "Know this. If you break Theo, I will break you. Understood?"

There was no way she could answer immediately. Too many emotions spun through her, from bewilderment to fear to shock to anger. When she finally managed to arrange her scattered thoughts into a sentence that made sense, Hugh had already gathered his crutches and was swinging his way toward his usual booth.

"I would never hurt Theo."

Hugh paused to give her a measuring look over his shoulder, but he didn't respond except for a grunt that could've meant anything, from "I believe you," to "You're a Theo-breaking liar." Then he crutched the rest of the way to his booth, leaving her feeling shaken and scared and guilty.

It was a good reminder, though. Theo was every bit the cop Hugh was. She was an idiot for ever thinking there could be something between them. No more kisses, she resolved. Kissing Theo was like a gateway drug. It started small, but if she let it continue, it would be so easy to slide into other things. Then, all of a sudden, she'd be in love, and it wouldn't be Theo who'd get broken.

It'd be Jules.

The encounter with Hugh threw her off her game for the rest of her shift. She mixed up more orders and fumbled more plates than she had on her first, nerve-racked day. It didn't help that Norman Rounds stayed all morning, his creepy gaze locked on her.

In the lull before the lunch rush, she slipped into the kitchen. She needed a short break before putting on her happy-waitress face again. The customers' main topic of conversation was the school shooting—who could've done it, why the police hadn't caught the shooter yet, which family had started homeschooling afterward. The memory of that awful day still brought bone-deep shivers when she thought of what could've happened, and every mention of it made her relive the horror of that day.

Vicki wasn't at her usual spot by the grill. Jules could hear her talking to the delivery guy right outside the propped-open back door. It was a relief to be alone for a few seconds, and Jules leaned against the wall, closed her eyes, shoved away persistent thoughts of Theo, and just breathed.

"Hey."

Her eyes popped open to see Norman Rounds standing right in front of her, and she had to bite back a startled shriek. "What are you doing back here? You're not supposed to be in the kitchen."

"I need to talk to you." He took another step toward her so he was much too close, and she shifted sideways. Norman followed, blocking her against the wall.

"Please go back to your booth." Her gaze darted to the open back door, and she debated calling for Vicki. The cook would probably just think it was funny, though, to watch Jules try to escape from Norman.

"Wait," he said, his gaze locked on hers. He was just so *creepy*. There was a prep sink to her right, blocking her in, so she dodged to the left. Norman blocked her escape again. "Wait! Just listen! I need to—"

Jules tried to duck around him, but he grabbed her by her upper arms, holding her in place. As soon as his hands latched on, she opened her mouth, ready to scream.

"Knock it off, Norman." Sherry Baker's calm voice cut off Jules's shout for help before it could emerge.

Dropping his hold on her arms, Norman spun around to face the other woman. "She's obviously not interested. In fact, I think she and Theo are together, and you probably don't want to be pissing him off."

"I wasn't..." Norman shot Jules a frustrated look and then stomped out of the kitchen, giving Sherry a wide berth.

"Thanks." Jules knew her smile was a little shaky.

Shrugging off her thanks, Sherry smiled back. "Norman's harmless, but he shouldn't have grabbed you like that. If Theo had seen..." She rolled her eyes in an exaggerated way.

"Oh, Theo doesn't..." She could feel a burning flush creeping up her neck toward her cheeks. "I mean, we're not dating."

"Not yet." Sherry's smile turned teasing. "I've known Theo a long time, and the way he looks at you..." She fanned her face, making Jules laugh despite her flustered state. "So hot."

Despite Hugh's warning, despite Jules's own misgivings, a warm spark lit in her belly. "Really?"

"Oh yeah." They shared another grin. "Now feed me. I'm dying for one of Vicki's turkey clubs."

"I'm on it." As she led the way out of the kitchen, Jules realized that the wreck of a day might've been salvaged after all. She was pretty sure she'd just made her first Monroe friend.

It was one thing to resolve to stay away from Theo when she wasn't faced with his broad shoulders and a rare, precious smile. Viggy sat next to him, his tail thumping on the porch boards. It took less than two seconds for her to cave, to smile back and open the door wide enough for them to step inside.

"We're about to have dinner," she said, unable to keep her gaze from roaming over Theo hungrily. He was in jeans and another hoodie that was identical to the one she'd stolen from him. Although Jules had planned to wash it and give it back, she couldn't bring herself to do either. It was warm, comfortable, and smelled like him, and she couldn't bear to change that—or give it up. "Want to join us?"

"Yes."

"It's tuna noodle casserole." As she started to lead the way to the kitchen, she glanced over her shoulder and caught him staring at her butt. Her voice went a little husky. "Just thought I should warn you."

"Consider me warned." His gaze slid up her back and their eyes caught.

Of course, Jules tripped on the warped floorboard at the kitchen entry. Flushed and flustered, she regained her balance and hurried to the stove, pretending she had to check the contents of a pan. After a moment of staring at broccoli—because who could get breathless about a vegetable?—Jules was ready to face Theo again. When she turned, he was right there, his eyes locked on her mouth. She was immediately breathless all over again. He leaned in closer—or maybe she did—until their lips were just a breath apart.

Ty and Tio came charging inside through the back door, and Theo straightened, taking a step back. Jules didn't know whether to curse the twins' timing or thank them.

"Hi, Jules! Hi, Theo! Hi, Viggy! We're going to get cleaned up," Ty yelled as they charged through the kitchen and into the hallway. The clatter of their feet on the stairs sounded like a thousand booted soldiers making their way to the second level.

"Ow," Jules complained, rubbing her ear with one hand. "Why was he shouting? I was two feet away from him. I think I just lost my hearing in this ear."

Theo took a step closer again. Taking her fingers in his, he gently pulled her hand away from her ear and leaned in. She held her breath.

"Should I test it?" he said quietly, near enough to her ear that his breath touched her skin.

Jules shivered. "Um...what?"

"A test." He leaned even closer. Now she could feel the warmth of his lips. "A hearing test."

"This doesn't feel like any hearing test I've taken before." Her voice had gone from slightly rough to full-on throaty. "I'm wondering about its medical legitimacy."

"That's because it's a field hearing test." She loved how he played along, understanding when she was teasing and when she was serious. She knew, too, that he wasn't like this with anyone else—only her. There was something heady about being the one who was able to make serious, angry Theo laugh and joke. "Only to be used by trained first responders." His voice had lowered to a rumbling hum, and his lips were actually brushing the ever-so-sensitive shell of her ear.

"Good thing you're here, then. Being a trained first responder and all." Jules knew she shouldn't be flirting, but this teasing version of Theo made it impossible not to respond.

"Hey." Sam's voice brought her off her flirty cloud and back to earth with a thump. On the pretext of getting a serving bowl from the cupboard, she reluctantly eased her body away from Theo's, only then realizing how closely they were standing, with her side almost plastered against his front.

"Hi, Sam." She still sounded breathless, and Theo hadn't even touched her—not really. "Homework done?"

A crease formed between his brows. "N-not yet."

"Need a hand? I can break out my rusty chemistry skills."

"N-n-no, th-thanks." He got a pitcher out of the cupboard and started filling it with water from the tap. "Hey, Theo. D-does Viggy n-need a w-w-water b-bowl?"

"Sure. Thanks, Sam." Theo leaned against the counter next to Jules, close enough that she was continually aware of him. She held back a snort. Who was she kidding? She'd be hyperaware of him even if he were in another room.

"D-did you f-f-find the sh-sh-shooter?"

Theo's expression turned grim. "Not yet."

"Jules!" the twins shouted in unison. Jules knew that tone. That was the something-else-is-broken tone. Her shoulders sagged before she stiffened them. No matter what had broken or collapsed or fallen off or stopped working, it was better than not having the kids with her. Even if the house toppled down around their ears, at least they were together.

"Sorry." She gave Theo an apologetic smile. "Dinner might be delayed a few minutes."

He took a step toward her. "Need help?"

"No." She frowned. "Maybe. I'll call you if it's

something beyond my abilities. My fix-it record is actually pretty good."

Sam snorted. "All you d-d-do is p-put duct t-tape on st-tuff. Or k-kick it."

When Theo coughed, Sam looked over at him, and the two exchanged a look that was so full of manly condescension that Jules propped her fists on her hips, now determined not to ask Theo—or Sam—for help. "Sam," she said, her voice sugar sweet, and Sam gave her a wary look. "Since it might take a while for little ol' me to *duct tape* whatever it is that's broken, why don't you finish your homework in the meantime."

He made a face but answered politely enough. "Yes, m-ma'am."

"Jules!" The shout from upstairs had a hint of hysteria to it, so Jules hurried out of the kitchen, hoping she'd be able to solve whatever was wrong. Now it was a matter of pride.

A half-hour later, she proudly sailed back into the kitchen. Passing through the doorway, she opened her mouth to brag about how the toilet had been successfully unclogged—no duct tape necessary—when she stopped abruptly, the words catching in her throat.

Theo was sitting next to Sam, their heads bent over an opened textbook.

"If I c-can't *see* it, I j-just d-d-don't g-get it." Sam's head was propped on one hand, the fingers working against his buzzed scalp.

Theo picked up a pencil and tugged Sam's notebook closer. "Here's a hydrogen atom. Here's another one. They each have one electron." Jules leaned against the wall, her heart filled to bursting at Theo's patient explanation. "When they share those electrons, they form a covalent bond and become a hydrogen molecule."

Sam's rumpled forehead smoothed slightly, although he still looked confused. "Wh-what m-makes it a c-c-covalent bond?"

"Sharing the electrons, rather than just taking them."

"I'll n-never r-r-rememb-ber th-that."

"Sure you will. Think of 'co' as in working together. Like 'cooperating' or 'coexisting.'"

Jules's brain instantly supplied a host of other options, such as "co-parenting" and "cohabitation." Feeling warm, she cleared her throat to derail those thoughts, and both of the guys looked up at her. "Y'all hungry?" Her voice was huskier than normal. "Although the casserole is probably burnt to a crisp by now."

"I turned off the oven," Theo said, getting up and crossing the kitchen to turn it on again. "It'll need heating up, but it should be okay."

Of course he did. Because Theo is wonderful.

How was she supposed to resist him when he looked like he did and saved people's lives and rescued dinner and helped Sam with his homework? It was impossible.

"Theo, could I see you in the hall for a second?"

Although he gave her a wary look, he followed her out of the kitchen. As soon as they were out of Sam's line of sight, Jules shoved Theo against the wall. With both hands knotted in his shirtfront, she yanked him down until she could reach his mouth. Then she kissed him. Hard.

For a fraction of a second, he froze, his muscles tight and his lips unresponsive. Jules didn't even have time to feel awkward, though, before Theo wrapped his strong arms around her, yanked her so close her front was plastered against his, and completely took over the kiss.

It was even better than she'd remembered from the night before, and she'd remembered it as feeling pretty darn good.

One of his hands cupped the back of her head, while the other arm was a steel band locked across her lower back. He turned, rotating them with dizzying speed, so Jules's back was now the one pressed against the wall. As his tongue played with hers, it felt as if she was surrounded by him, like he was body armor protecting her from the world.

Being safe was the best feeling. No, the best feeling was his lips on hers, his teeth dragging gently over her lower lip, their bodies pressed against each other. Feeling safe was just a really, really nice bonus. His tongue slid against hers, sending a mix of heat and happy chills through her.

Jules released his shirt so she could move her hands to the back of his head, run her fingers through his short, short hair, and massage his scalp. She felt an almost-silent groan rumble through his chest, felt the vibrations in her body and against her lips, and Jules clutched him to her more tightly.

There was a clatter of footsteps on the stairs, and Jules wanted to whimper. How was she supposed to let go of Theo now, when she'd discovered how very, very nice it was to hold him? The thought of the kids seeing them kiss, of having to explain exactly what she and Theo were doing, gave Jules the strength to step back.

He resisted for a brief moment, but then released her, although his gaze remained fixed on her lips, and his eyes were so hungry she almost hurled herself back into his arms. The twins and Dee raced around the corner, putting an end to any thought of continuing the kiss. The kids didn't ask why Jules and Theo were out in the hall, but just tore into the kitchen.

"Hi, Theo!" Dee called as she passed, although her attention was already fixed on the dog. After a final, heated look that warmed Jules from her toes to her eyebrows, Theo ushered her back into the kitchen. All three younger kids were clustered around Viggy. Once the initial round of petting was done, they moved toward the table, but Jules, still feeling flushed and spacey and extraordinarily happy, blocked them with her body. "Hands."

Reversing direction, they stampeded to the bathroom to clean up. Theo and Sam, who'd cleared his homework while they'd been in the hall, helped her get everything on the table, and she felt a warm rush of contentment as she watched them. As unexpected as it was, Theo seemed to fit effortlessly into the family, as if they'd been holding a spot open with his name on it. Even Viggy, who'd stretched out across the ancient linoleum, had become one of them. Shoving away her fanciful thoughts, Jules headed for her chair, only to find Theo there, holding it out for her.

"Thank you," she said as she sat, the gesture making her wonder what it would be like to go on a real date with Theo. The return of the youngest three distracted her from the pang of longing that hit her, a wish to be a normal, law-abiding woman, someone who could be with Theo without wondering when he was going to find out about her past. A memory of Hugh's accusing words flashed through her mind, and stomach clenched, she looked down at her plate.

"Jules." When she glanced up, Theo was watching her. "You okay?"

"Sure." Painting on a smile, she brushed off his concern. "I'm great. How about y'all? What happened in school?"

"I got a job!" Dee bounced in her seat.

"A job?" Jules repeated, feeling her eyebrows climb toward her hairline. Was there a child-labor-based sweat-shop in Monroe she didn't know about? "Doing what?"

"Mrs. Vang said she'd pay me five dollars a day to feed her cat while she's on vacation. She said she'd have to talk to you first, though, to make sure it's okay." Dee clasped her hands together and pressed her fist under her chin. When Dee put her mind to it, she could outdo even Hugh in the hungry-puppy-eyes department. "So is it? Okay?"

"Who is Mrs. Vang?"

"One of the lunch ladies. I know we don't have much money, so I want to help. I put up some dog-walking fliers at school, and Mrs. Vang saw one, and she's going to Hawaii next week, but she doesn't want to bring Mr. Sylvester to the usual boarding place, because they charge so much and he hides for a long time after he gets home because he's so mad at Mrs. Vang for leaving, so she's going to see if it's better if he can stay home. So, is it okay?" Jules was pretty sure Dee didn't breathe once during the entire monologue.

"Dee," Jules said firmly. "We talked about this. It's my job to make money. It's all y'all's job to go to school and be kids and have fun."

Dee's face fell, and her bottom lip quivered for a second before she put on her pageant mask.

If Dee had thrown a tantrum or cried or whined or acted like a normal kid, Jules could've held strong, but her sister's stoic acceptance of disappointment was unbearable. "But I'll talk to Mrs. Vang."

"Really?" Dee's eyes got even larger than normal.

"Yes." With a look Jules tried very hard to make strict, she added, "But nothing's set in stone until I talk with her, okay? So try to keep the excitement to a minimum." Even as she said it, Jules knew she was too late. If Dee had been any more excited, the top of her head would've blown off.

"Okay." She took a big bite of casserole, smiling the whole time. "Thank you."

"You're welcome. And don't talk with your mouth full, please." Jules had lost any last hints of sternness, though. Dee's huge grin was too contagious.

"We have a job, too," Ty blurted. There was a thump from under the table, and he winced.

"Tio, did you just kick your brother?" Jules demanded.

"Yes."

"Why?" She darted a glance at Theo, wondering what he made of their antics. To her surprised pleasure, he wasn't wearing his usual scowl. In fact, he looked almost relaxed…and amused. He was definitely amused.

"To remind him to keep his mouth shut."

"Why should he keep his mouth shut?" Jules was simultaneously grateful for and exasperated by Tio's blunt honesty. "What exactly is this job of yours?"

They exchanged one of their looks. Finally, Tio answered, "I'd rather not say."

"Why not? It's not something illegal, is it?" As soon
as the words were out, Jules felt like the world's biggest
hypocrite. After all, by taking the kids and keeping them,
she'd committed—and was continuing to commit—
crimes much more serious than whatever scheme they'd
come up with to make money…at least she *hoped* they
were more serious. She sent another glance at Theo, who
looked to be taking a great interest in the conversation.
Great. Now, if the twins were breaking the law, a cop
would know about it. Jules had a feeling she was in the
running for worst parental figure ever.

The twins did their look-communication thing again,
but it was more thoughtful this time. "We do not believe
so," Tio finally said.

"You don't believe so," Jules echoed.

"Why don't you tell us exactly what you're doing,
and I'll let you know if you're breaking the law." Theo's
even words caught the twins' attention, as if they'd forgotten a cop was in their possibly law-breaking midst.

"It's not illegal," Ty said reluctantly after yet another
silent conversation with his brother. "I'm, like, 99 percent sure."

Tio frowned. "I'd put that closer to 84 percent."

With a sigh, Theo made a get-on-with-it gesture.

"We're offering protection services," Ty blurted, the
words tumbling quickly from his mouth, as if he wanted
to get them out and have it be done.

Blinking, Jules tried to absorb his answer. It wasn't
what she'd been expecting, although, with the twins,
she never knew what to expect. "Protection services?
Like…the mob?" Guilt rose up in her again. Was
this because of her influence? She'd tried to keep

the whole mess of her involvement with Luis's business away from her siblings, but it had been a fairly high-profile case. Once she'd refused to turn on Luis, the FBI had no incentive to keep her name from the media, so the kids almost certainly knew at least the basics of the situation.

To her relief, both twins were shaking their heads. "Not extortion," Tio explained. "We're not charging for protection from us. We're charging for protection from others."

"It's like an anti-bullying campaign," Ty added. "Only...with punching."

"Punching." Jules repeated faintly.

"Just as a last resort," Tio corrected, giving his twin a look. "Mostly we rely on the threat of violence for intimidation purposes."

Theo rubbed his hand across his mouth, as if he were hiding a smile.

"Okay, stop." Propping her elbows on the table—having dropped her fork onto her plate long ago—Jules grabbed a handful of hair on either side of her head. "Tell us, using easily understood words and phrases, *exactly* what you are doing."

"If a kid pays us fifty bucks, we make sure he doesn't get picked on anymore."

"So, basically," Jules said slowly, trying to figure out what the best—most parental—response should be, "you're hiring yourselves out as bodyguards."

"Correct." Tio turned to Theo. "Hiring personal protection is not illegal, I believe?"

Theo studied the twins for a long moment before asking, "Where does the punching fit in?"

"Like T said, just as a last resort," Ty answered a little defensively. "Usually they back right off when they hear a kid hired us. And they've always hit first. Well, they *tried* to hit first, at least. It was self-defense."

"Isn't there a no-tolerance stance on fighting at your school?" Theo asked mildly, and Jules turned to the twins as horror filled her.

"You are not going to be kicked out of your school, do you hear me?" Her accent thickened as her voice rose. "We joke about homeschooling, but that's not an option. How am I supposed to teach you two? How am I supposed to teach *T* anything? He's so much smarter than I am already!"

Reaching over, Theo gave her arm a gentle squeeze. Her panicked gaze met his, and she instantly calmed. There was something about his steady presence that made her feel like everything would be okay.

"We won't get kicked out, Jules," Ty said. "We're careful not to get caught."

"Besides, the punishment for a first offence is a week of in-school suspension," Tio added, although not nearly as soothingly as Ty. "We'd have to get caught four times before we were kicked out of school."

Jules's laugh was more than half-hysterical. "Great. That's very reassuring."

"I l-like it," Sam said. "They're helping b-bullied k-k-kids."

After a final squeeze, Theo dropped his hand from Jules's arm and returned to eating. He looked not at all bothered by the twins' self-employment strategy.

"So?" Tio asked him, more with clinical interest than with any anxiety. "It's not illegal, is it?"

"Avoid the punching part," Theo said, "and no. It's not illegal."

With a satisfied nod, Tio resumed eating.

Ty eyed Jules. "Are you going to make us stop?"

Sitting back in her chair, Jules regarded him and Tio as she thought. "No," she finally said. "Just please, *please* don't get kicked out of school."

"We won't."

Somehow, Ty's assurance wasn't that convincing.

"How about you, Sam?" She turned to the only sibling who hadn't revealed an entrepreneurial scheme. "Are you starting up a secret poker club you'll run out of the basement?"

"I w-wish." He frowned and poked at his casserole. "The gr-grocery store, that lawn service pl-place, even the g-g-gas station…everywh-where I've ap-p-plied has said n-no. M-m-my hours are wr-wrong."

"Because of school?" Jules asked. Her stomach finally had settled enough for her to handle eating, although cold broccoli wasn't very appetizing. Still, she ate it. They spent too much money on food to waste it.

"Yeah." An idea made his eyes light. "M-mayb-be I c-c-could—"

"If you're about to suggest that you drop out of school," Jules interrupted in the iciest voice she could manage, "you better swallow those words right back down again, shove them in a closet, lock them inside, and throw away the key. We'll manage on what I make at the diner."

"B-but…" He trailed off when she gave him her fiercest look. She'd been on the fence about the twins' bodyguard gig, but on this, she was adamant.

"You like dogs?" Theo asked Sam, who gave him a confused look.

"Um...sh-sure."

"I know that Nan is looking for help at Bastian Kennels. Her place is just a couple of miles south of here. It'd be before and after school, so it should work with your schedule."

"Yeah?" His face brightened briefly before dimming again. "I d-don't have m-m-much exp-perience with d-dogs."

"Probably won't need it," Theo told him. "It'll be grunt work to start with—feeding and cleaning, mostly. You won't be helping with training or grooming until you've been there a while. Want her number?"

"Yes, p-p-please." Sam looked tentatively hopeful, although his gaze followed Theo warily, as if he were expecting the job offer to be ripped away at any moment. His caution broke Jules's heart, and she had to look away from her brother so she didn't burst into tears.

"Okay." Her voice was slightly rough, and Theo gave her a probing look, which she avoided with great effort. "Now that everyone is employed or has the potential of being employed, who wants ice cream?"

Everyone enthusiastically chorused their requests, except for Theo, who just smiled at her before turning back to discuss details with Sam. Her heart warmed at the rare sight. Despite his profession and his usual antisocial attitude and his friend's overprotectiveness, Jules was glad he was there. Paying two dollars for an extra chair at the thrift store had been worth it to have a place for Theo. He belonged there, belonged to their family.

Overcome with sudden joy, she got up to get the ice cream. As she passed behind Theo, she couldn't resist running a hand from one shoulder to another. It was yet another memory she could cling to after they had to run again—run and leave Theo behind.

CHAPTER 16

BULLET WOUND OR NO BULLET WOUND, THEO WAS READY to punch Hugh in the head. No, in the throat. That way, his partner would have to stop talking.

"Nothing? Not even running her license?"

Theo's jaw ached with the effort it took to unclamp his molars enough to speak. "Drop it."

"I'm not dropping it." Of course he wasn't. Theo stood and started to pace Hugh's deck. The rock fell away beneath them, exposing a startling view of the evergreen-studded cliffs that rose from where Lion Creek had worn a fold in the mountain. The rest of Hugh's house wasn't much, but that view from the back deck made developers and real estate agents from all over Colorado knock on his door with offers. Hugh had grown up in that house, and he'd inherited it when his grandparents died. Theo couldn't see him ever selling it. "Are you listening to me?"

At Hugh's demand, Theo turned to face him. "No."

"No, you're not listening to me, or no, you won't run a background check?"

"Both."

Hugh looked ready to hurl a crutch at him like a javelin. "Why not? Why not protect yourself? The woman is running from something; that's obvious. Who knows what she's done? She could be one of those black widows, who marry men for their money and then kill them."

Theo actually laughed out loud at that. "So she picked blue-collar Monroe, rather than Breckenridge or Aspen or Vail, to find her next victim, and a cop, rather than someone who actually has money? If she's a black widow, she's not very good at it."

Although Hugh made a frustrated sound, a grudging smile broke through his scowl. "Fine. So she's probably not planning on killing you for your money. The point is that she's running. Don't you want to know who's chasing her before you get trampled?"

A part of Theo, the cop part, was still almost unbearably curious about Jules's past. It was overwhelmed by the much-stronger urge to bury his head in the sand and pretend there wasn't a huge, blinking neon sign telling him something was very wrong. If he dug into it and found it was something bad, something he couldn't ignore, he'd be forced to act. And he didn't want to act. He wanted to keep visiting that dilapidated shithole of a house because he was actually starting to like the place. He liked her brothers and sister, liked the way Viggy became his normal dog-self around them, and Jules… he more than liked Jules.

"You're ignoring me again."

"I'm trying," Theo grunted, crossing his arms over his chest.

"Why?" True frustration filled the word. "I don't get it. You *hate* not knowing shit. And now you're living happily in la-la land, playing house with this woman who's obviously lying to you. Why aren't you protecting yourself?"

Silence hung over them, the only sound the lingering echo of Hugh's words bouncing off the cliff faces as Theo looked at his partner, trying to sort out a rational response in his mind. It was hard to explain—even to himself—this bone-deep assurance that Jules was a basically honest person, that her reasons for whatever she had to do in her past were solid. He didn't need to hear the entire story. Jules was good. There was no doubt in Theo's mind.

"It's true that I don't know the specifics of her past, but I'm starting to know Jules. She's kind, and she loves her brothers and sister. I'm not ignoring my gut. It's telling me she doesn't have it in her to hurt me or anyone else—intentionally, at least."

It was Hugh's turn to study Theo. Finally, Hugh sighed. "I hope you're right, buddy. I really do."

Theo hoped so, too.

Something was out there.

It was something that had woken her, a forgotten sound or feeling or instinct that had made her eyes snap open at two in the morning. It was something that had forced her to check all the scary, dark corners of the house until she ended up in the kitchen, peering out into the darkness, watching shadows where shadows shouldn't be.

"It's probably only Viggy," Jules told her galloping heart as she eased open the back door. Her heart ignored her, beating even faster. She didn't blame it. It was the "probably" part that scared her.

Sticking her head outside, with most of her body still in the kitchen in case she had to duck inside to safety before slamming and locking the door as quickly as possible, she quietly called, "Viggy? Viggy, you out there?"

Everything went silent. There was no crashing of a large dog through the underbrush, no answering bark, nothing. It was almost like the forest was holding its breath. Even the aspen leaves, which almost never stopped shifting and moving, were still. It was eerie and threatening and Jules didn't like it.

Retreating into the kitchen, she stared at her cell phone screen immediately after turning the ancient dead bolt and hearing it *thunk* into place. It felt strange calling him, even though it was for a legitimate reason. Still, her fingers shook slightly when she pulled up his number and hit *send*, and she was pretty sure it wasn't from residual jumpiness about moving shadows.

"Jules." As soon as she heard his gruff voice, she calmed, to the point that she started feeling silly for overreacting. If it wasn't Viggy, whatever she'd seen moving in the trees must've been, if not her imagination, something natural and normal and no reason to get hysterical. "You okay?"

"I'm fine." Even though she felt a little silly about calling him for no reason, it was still nice to hear his voice. Closing her eyes, she pictured his face, pictured him here with her, his reassuring hand squeezing her arm. The last of her anxiety trickled away. "I just thought I saw Viggy in the trees behind my house, and I was wondering if he'd made a break for it again."

"No," he answered immediately. "Vig's here with me. We're on duty."

"Oh!" She'd gotten so used to him being off during his two-week leave after the shooting that she hadn't even considered he might be working. "I thought you were on days, normally."

"I am, but there was some shift shuffling happening. Hugh's out, of course, and three others are down with the flu. Guess it's going around. Try not to breathe other people's air for a while."

She laughed softly as she stepped outside, not wanting to wake any of the house's still-sleeping residents. With Theo on the line, all the scariness of the dark shadows and the waiting silence of the trees dissipated. "I'll try. Has it been a busy night, then?"

"Yeah." He gave a huff of impatience, and she smiled, imagining his cranky expression. "Just a lot of bullshit calls that kept us running. It's been quiet for the last hour, so Vig and I are parked behind the Suds 'n' Go, and I'm trying to get some reports finished up."

"You're hiding?" she teased.

"Trying to. Can't hide from dispatch, though. If they send me a call, I'm stuck."

"Poor baby." She smiled again. It was surprisingly easy to talk to Theo on the phone. For some reason, she figured he'd bark a few words at her and then hang up without saying good-bye. "When does your shift end?"

"Six."

"Are you coming to breakfast?" Her heartbeat sped up as she waited for his answer, and Jules knew she was too eager to hear him say "yes." Her resolve not to get involved with this cop tended to dissolve as soon as she saw him or spoke to him or touched him or, to be completely honest, thought about him.

His voice roughened, not with irritation, but with a certain husky tenderness she'd just started noticing when he talked with her. "Wouldn't miss it."

"Good," she whispered, flushing, her face hot even in the cool mountain night air. "I should let you finish your reports."

His groan made her laugh again. "I'd rather talk to you."

Her face flamed even hotter, and she used her free hand to fan herself—not that it helped. "Um…okay."

This time, it was Theo who laughed, a low chuckle that raised goose bumps along her spine, up her neck, and under her hair. "Good night, Jules."

"Good night, Theo. Be safe."

Long after the call ended, she sat smiling at her phone screen.

A shiver brought her back to reality, and she slipped back into the kitchen. It was hours before she had to leave for work, but there was no way she was going to get back to sleep. Jules figured she might as well do something productive, rather than lying in bed, staring at the ceiling, replaying the phone conversation in her head, and smiling like a maniac. There was no reason she couldn't clean the kitchen while replaying the call and grinning. She was an excellent multitasker.

She reached for the light switch when she heard a creak above her head. Possibilities raced through her thoughts as she froze, staring at the ceiling, her arm still outstretched. *It's just the house settling, or one of the kids headed to the bathroom, or…*

Or there's someone else in the house.

Once the idea popped into her head, it wouldn't

leave, no matter how many times Jules told herself she was being paranoid.

Just check it out, she told herself as her hand dropped to her side and she moved toward the dark doorway. *You'll see it's nothing, and then you'll be able to sleep. Or at least you'll be able to clean and think of Theo.*

Theo. The reminder made her realize she'd missed something. Viggy was with Theo. If the dog wasn't in the woods, then what—or who—was?

Her heartbeat ramped up until it thumped in her ears, masking all other sounds. Swallowing hard, her throat suddenly very dry, she forced her feet to move to the window. *Check outside first, and then go look upstairs.*

She peered into the darkness. The moon was half-full, but that almost made things worse. The wind had picked up again, and every swaying evergreen tree cast a shifting shadow that overlapped other shadows, creating a moving, layered grid of semidarkness. After seeing countless crouching boogeymen that morphed into normal, nonscary things like rocks and trees and scrub, Jules gave up. She wasn't going to see anything out back, and she certainly wasn't going to leave the kids and go monster-hunting by herself in the dark woods.

Turning away, she moved quietly into the hall. The house had its own dark corners and frightening, shadowy pockets, and she realized she was tiptoeing as she reached the stairs. It was silly. She was in her own house—her own creaky, noisy, possibly haunted house—and there was no one there who shouldn't be. Although she drew her shoulders back, determined to believe there was nothing to fear, her feet still touched each stair tread softly, and she cringed at each creaky step.

On the second floor, she slipped down the hall, telling herself she was being quiet so as not to wake the kids, but knowing in her heart she was a chicken and a liar. The room right above the kitchen was at the end of the hall, one of two unoccupied bedrooms. Jules reached for the doorknob. Even in the dim light, she could see her hand was shaking.

Biting her lip, she turned the knob and pushed open the door.

The room was empty. Empty and cold. A night breeze blew chilly air through the open window, making the normally limp, old curtains billow and cast dancing shadows across the wall. Why was the window open? Her heartbeat hiccupped, and she told herself firmly that there were four other people in the house, any of whom could've opened the window earlier that day.

Sending a nervous glance at the half-open closet door, Jules took a step toward the window, but decided to check out the closet first. As overcautious as it was, she didn't want to turn her back on a possible hiding spot.

The closet door resisted sliding open but finally yielded, squeaking as it moved along its track. Moonlight filled the space, revealing nothing but an empty closet. Jules's heartbeat settled slightly. She crossed to the window quickly. Now that she knew the room was empty, she wanted to shut it, to have that barrier between her and whatever was moving in the trees.

As she closed the window and wrestled the rusty latch back into the locked position, she looked out into the backyard. The roof of the small porch was right below her, and she bit her cheek, trying not to think about how easy it would be to climb from the porch railing to the roof to the open window—

"J-J-JuJu?"

She jumped and spun to see Sam in the doorway. Pressing a hand to her thundering heart, Jules glared at him. "What are you doing up?"

He frowned right back at her. "You w-were b-b-being k-kind of loud."

"Sorry." Jules took a deep breath and let it out again before forcing a smile. "I'm just being a nervous Nellie. You should go back to bed."

Instead of responding, he just crossed the room to look over her head out the window. "Is someone out there?"

"No." The answer came too quickly to be believable, and she grimaced at his skeptical expression. "Really, truly, there's no one out there. I'm just letting the night worries get to me. Let's go to bed."

After studying her for a long moment, he nodded, but he didn't head for the third-floor stairs.

"Where are you going?" she asked.

"Wh-where are *you* g-going?" he shot back.

"I figured I'd sleep with Dee."

"I'll s-sleep in T-Tio's b-b-bed. You know h-he's in T-T-Ty's r-room."

Something inside Jules finally relaxed. They'd all be together. "Let's leave the doors between the rooms open."

"Of c-course."

_____

It was hard to return to the drudgery of reports after talking to Jules, listening to her sexy sleep-roughened laugh and the warm note in her voice as she'd told him good night. He wondered if she'd made up the possible Viggy sighting to have an excuse to call him, and then Theo frowned. If she hadn't, if Jules really had seen something moving in the woods, what had it been? Just a mule deer or a coyote, or could it have been something more dangerous, like a mountain lion or a bear or a person skulking through the trees? Although Monroe was a fairly quiet town, it did have its share of troublemakers and criminals. He should stop by, check things out.

"Better look around, just in case," he said out loud, making Viggy raise his head. Although the dog wasn't plastered against the seat like the first few times Theo had taken him out, his body language was still screaming that he was unhappy.

"Want to go see Jules?" he asked, feeling like an idiot. Viggy wouldn't understand him. For some reason, though, Viggy thumped his tail weakly against the seat. Despite knowing Viggy couldn't understand English, and that the dog had responded to something in Theo's tone, rather than the words, he chose to take Viggy's reaction as affirmation that he was doing the right thing. "Okay, then."

Ignoring the little voice in his brain that was mocking him for his pathetic attempt at finding any excuse to visit Jules, he shifted into drive. He'd just pulled out of the car wash parking lot when his radio came to life.

"Unit 5449 requesting assistance on a traffic stop in the three-hundred block of Timson Street."

Theo was less than a mile away. As he picked up the mic to tell dispatch to put him on the call, he resigned himself to waiting to see Jules. At least he knew she'd be at the diner later. Dispatch copied his transmission, and Theo flicked on his overhead lights, accelerating down the abandoned street. With as little traffic as there was, he kept his siren silent. No need to wake the sleeping neighborhood, he figured.

"Ready for this?" he asked Viggy. There was no tail thump that time, just a mournful look that Theo caught in the rearview mirror. "Sorry, buddy. You'll have to wait to see your fan club. Otto needs our help." His foot pressed harder on the gas, and a tiny shock of excitement bubbled up in him. It was familiar, yet foreign, since he hadn't felt anything except for numbness on a call for months. Theo welcomed that surge of adrenaline. He'd missed it. Turning the corner onto Timson, Theo saw the front of a newer Ford pickup. Behind it, Otto and another man were silhouetted by Otto's squad car headlights.

"Vehicle belongs to Gordon Schwartz," the dispatcher continued, and Theo's shoulders tightened. Schwartz meant possible explosives, which meant Lieutenant Blessard was going to want Viggy to do a check. Theo glanced in the rearview briefly as he pulled in behind Otto's vehicle. Vig's tail was firmly tucked, and he'd started panting tensely, the very picture of canine anxiety.

Quickly letting dispatch know he was on scene, Theo got out of the car, turning on his portable radio as he did so. Otto had Gordon out of his pickup and in cuffs, and Theo cautiously approached, his gaze scanning the scene to make sure someone else wasn't going to pop out on them. As he passed the truck, he looked in the bed and then the cab. Gordon was screaming at Otto until he caught sight of Theo.

"You!" Gordon gave a bitter laugh. "Why don't you sic your vicious attack dog on me? Oh wait, because it'd run and hide! Perfect dog for a fucking useless, tax-stealing pig who wants to stomp on my constitutional rights!"

Theo cocked an eyebrow at Otto, who gave an almost invisible eye roll in return, making Theo have to swallow a smile. The big guy was usually the king of poker faces, so Gordon must've been aggravating him. Otto started searching him, and Gordon's yelling ramped up several decibels, especially when Otto carefully extracted a Beretta Nano from the cargo pocket of Gordon's BDUs.

"You're violating my second *and* my fourth amendment rights, you fascist asshole!" Gordon screamed.

Otto handed the compact pistol off to Theo. He cleared it, and then placed it and the magazine on the hood of Otto's squad car. There were four other cleared handguns there, and Theo shook his head. The guy was prepared for a battle. Theo had no doubt they'd find a lot more when they searched his pickup, too.

"Theo," Otto said, projecting his voice to cut through Gordon's rant. When Theo looked at his partner, he saw Otto was holding out yet another gun, this one a 9mm Glock. Theo accepted gun number six as Gordon's protests rose to an outraged howl.

By the time Otto had finished patting down Gordon, there were nine handguns and eleven fully loaded magazines decorating Otto's hood.

"Watch your head," Otto rumbled as he assisted Gordon into the backseat of his squad car. Gordon, who'd gone pretty much silent by the time Otto had removed the eighth gun from his possession, responded with an anatomically impossible suggestion.

Ignoring Gordon, Otto closed the door and moved around to the front of the car, where Theo was eyeing the results of the search.

"Once we search his truck," Theo said, eyeing the weapon collection, "we could open a gun store."

Otto gave an amused grunt. "The man likes his weapons."

"Why'd you stop him?" Even as Theo asked, his gaze was moving, peering past the immediate area lit by streetlights and the headlights on their squad cars into the blackness beyond. They were in the closest thing Monroe had to a warehouse district. A boxy building that housed a gymnastics school butted up next to the expansive lot of a landscaping company, and the piles of gravel and decorative rocks cast strange shadows stretching to the ten-foot chain-link fence.

Although this was better than being in a residential neighborhood, where the flashing lights would've woken the residents and brought gawkers by the truckload, there was something about the shadowed darkness of the hulking buildings that was making the back of his neck prickle with warning.

"It started as a suspicious vehicle call," Otto explained. A quick glance told Theo that Otto was scanning the area, as well. Apparently, Theo wasn't the only uneasy one. "Someone driving by saw Gordon's truck. It was running, but the headlights were off. When I got here, there was someone standing on the left side of his truck, talking to Gordon, but they ran off as soon as I pulled up. I approached Gordon, saw he had a pistol in a hip holster in clear view of God and everyone, so I arrested him for brandishing." Otto rubbed his forehead above his right eyebrow. "No licenses on any of those guns, and he doesn't have a CCW. Said he doesn't believe in asking the government if he can carry, and he doesn't see any reason to conceal his weapons. There might be a few extra charges to add to the brandishing."

Eyeing the extensive collection decorating Otto's hood, Theo asked dryly, "You think?"

"Not looking forward to searching that truck."

Theo glanced at the pickup. From what he'd seen during his very brief inspection after he'd first arrived, the topper-covered bed was filled with junk. The cab had looked only slightly better. "Yeah."

"Think Viggy would be up for a quick check?" Otto eyed Theo hopefully.

"Nope." Although Theo hated to turn Otto down, he was pretty sure Viggy wasn't ready. All a failed attempt at searching the pickup would do was destroy the dog's already shaky confidence. Theo never should've tried to get Viggy to search Gordon Schwartz's compound. It'd just set the dog up for failure, and Theo felt a surge of guilt at the memory. He hadn't protected his K9 partner. "He's not ready."

Otto accepted it easily, right before a thump from behind them brought both of their heads around. Gordon had gotten turned around on the seat and was kicking at the window. Both Otto and Theo groaned.

"Mind if I run him to jail?" Otto asked, already headed for the driver's seat as he looked over his shoulder at Theo. "I don't want to have to wrestle him into the leg restraints."

Theo waved him on. "Go ahead. I'll keep an eye on the truck until you get back, and then I'll help you search." He didn't say it out loud, but the creeping feeling of being watched hadn't eased. Theo wasn't about to turn his attention away from his surroundings to focus on a search, not without someone to watch his back.

"Thanks." Otto climbed in the squad car and drove quickly down the street, leaving Theo in the dimly lit night with a terrified dog, looming buildings, and a jumpy sense that he wasn't really alone.

Shaking himself out of his hyperalert state, he returned to his squad car. Grabbing Viggy's leash, he hooked it to the top hook in the harness. Viggy backed up, ready to brace against the forward pressure, his forehead wrinkled with tension.

"C'mon, Vig." Theo forced cheer into his voice. It felt easier, more natural this time than it had in a long time. Viggy even cocked his head to the side, and his nervous panting stopped. "Want to play?"

At the word "play," Viggy's posture eased a little, coming out of his crouch a little. Encouraged, Theo remembered the stuffed toy he'd tucked into the glove compartment one day when he hadn't been able to stand the sight of it. He pulled out the bedraggled plush penguin.

"You've seen better days," he muttered, examining the toy under the dome light, but then snorted a laugh and looked at Viggy, who was regarding him cautiously. "Guess we all have."

Viggy hopped out willingly. Thinking back to that day when he thought he'd have to carry the dog to the scene, Theo was grateful. They'd made *some* progress, at least. As they approached the truck, though, Viggy dropped farther and farther back, until he reached the end of his lead and stopped.

"C'mon, buddy," Theo urged, and Viggy reluctantly walked forward again. When they were just a few feet from the truck, Theo stopped and glanced down at the dog's crouched, miserable-looking form.

"Viggy," Theo said, and the dog stared up at him, panting in the tense, nervous way that made Theo feel guilty and sad. "Sit."

There was a half-second pause, as if the dog hadn't been expecting an obedience command, but then Viggy lowered his haunches to the ground.

"Good boy!" Theo enthused, offering him the penguin. Still eyeing Theo as if he suspected it was all a trick, Viggy shifted forward, so slowly if felt as if he were in slow motion, and closed his teeth gingerly around the leg of the penguin. As soon as the dog took hold, Theo tugged on the stuffed toy, gently until Viggy's hold got stronger, and he started pulling back. "Good boy!" he called again, swinging the penguin from side to side, swinging Viggy's attached jaws along with it.

"Viggy, release," Theo said, and Viggy let go of the penguin, his gaze fixed on Theo. "Viggy, sit."

Again, he sat, this time as soon as the command left Theo's mouth.

"Good dog, Vig!" Theo offered the toy again, and Viggy latched on immediately. As he tugged, Viggy's tail slowly rose, swinging cautiously from side to side until it was wagging enthusiastically. Theo laughed, a sound of pure joy and relief, at the sight of Viggy playing, of Viggy happy—and not just with Jules's family this time. He was listening to Theo, responding to him, as if they really were dog and handler. For the first time, Theo had a spark of hope that they could really be partners.

"Viggy, release," he said, and he did, looking up at Theo with an open mouth, his tongue lolling out in a doggie grin. "Good boy."

Although it was tempting to keep going, to try other commands, to lead Viggy to the pickup and point, indicating that he should check for one of the eight component odors that most explosives contain, Theo just led Viggy back to his squad car. They'd made a huge step forward, and it was time to stop before Theo ruined all their progress by pushing too hard. They'd worked together, and Viggy'd had fun. That was enough. That was more than Theo had expected.

After returning Viggy to the back of his squad car, Theo moved closer to the pickup to wait for Otto's return. As he stood in the near dark, the sensation of being watched creeping over him again, Theo realized that, strangely enough, he was smiling. Maybe there was a chance that he, like Viggy, could be happy again.

Maybe.

CHAPTER 17

THERE WAS A BOOT PRINT.

Although Jules knew in her head that there were a thousand perfectly logical, completely innocent reasons someone had left a print in the soft dirt right next to the first line of evergreens framing their backyard, her gut just knew this was bad. Really, really bad.

Had the boot-wearer been watching her last night? Had he climbed through the open window and been *inside* the *house*? No. Jules couldn't allow herself to even consider the idea. If she did, she'd grab the kids, stuff them in the SUV, and leave. It wouldn't matter where they'd go, though. She'd never feel safe again.

She moved around, searching for more prints, hoping to at least see what direction the person came from or went, but the rest of the ground was too rocky or hard-packed or covered with pine needles to hold a print. Jules returned to the footprint and studied it. Should she tell Theo? Even as she thought it, she dismissed the idea. Whoever had left it hadn't committed a crime. The trees weren't even part of her property, so she couldn't even call it trespassing.

"Wh-what are y-you l-l-looking at?"

Jules shifted so she was standing on the print. "Caterpillar."

Sam's expression was skeptical, and he walked closer, scanning the ground around her feet. "Wh-where is it?"

"I stepped on it."

Now she could tell he really didn't believe her. "L-liar."

She laughed and purposefully walked back toward the house, hoping her shoes had scuffed the print enough that Sam wouldn't spot it. He worried too much as it was. "Where are the kids?"

Although he eyed the spot where she'd been standing, he didn't seem to see anything out of the ordinary. Jules's tight shoulders eased slightly in relief.

"Out fr-front."

"Good. It's a beautiful day." It really was. The sun was warm, but the air had a crisp undertone that hinted of fall. Between the bugs and the humidity in Florida, Jules had avoided being outside most of the time, but Colorado was different. It made her want to hike and do all sorts of outdoorsy things. "We should get bikes. Let's keep an eye on Craigslist."

Sam just hummed, traces of his early suspicion still clinging to him.

"Jules!" Ty's urgent shout made her heartbeat pick up immediately. He, Tio, and Dee came running around the side of the house. "We heard a car coming up the driveway!"

"Did they see you?"

"I don't think so," Ty said, shooting a worried glance over his shoulder, even though the driveway was hidden by the house. Although Jules hated that the kids were so suspicious and wary that they'd been spooked by the sight of an approaching stranger, it was important that they stay cautious. After all, being too trusting could get them caught.

"Good." Jules glanced at Sam, who was already ushering the other three toward the barn. "I'll go check it out. Remember, if you hear yelling or if fifteen minutes go by, and I don't give you the all-clear, grab the emergency stash hidden in the loft and go."

"W-we kn-kn-know the d-d-d-drill."

Jules watched them for another second before hurrying to the back door. Rushing through the house and into the living room, she yanked the curtains closed until there was only a tiny space between them. The room was instantly full of shadows, reminding Jules of creepy nighttime searches, and she tried to throw off her unease and focus on the actual—well, possible—threat outside.

Peeking through the opening between the curtains, she saw the truck pull up in front of the house. It was an older pickup, its paint faded oddly to an uneven robin's-egg blue. The sun reflected off the windshield, hiding the driver from her. She caught herself leaning closer to the window, trying to get a better look, and Jules hurried to step back before she made the curtains move and caught the attention of the person outside.

No one got out of the truck, and Jules waited, breathing too quickly. She realized she was clutching the edge of the curtain and forced her fingers to slowly release their death grip. The drapery swayed once it was free, and Jules held her breath until it stilled. Had that been visible to the person in the truck?

The pickup door swung open, making her suck in a breath, so roughly that it hurt her throat. She watched, biting the inside of her cheek, as a man climbed out and turned toward the house. When Jules saw his face, her head jerked back like someone had slapped her. It was Norman Rounds.

Although he'd seemed weird and grabby and slightly stalkerish at the diner, showing up at her house made Norman a hundred times scarier. Why was he here? How did he know where she lived? The things Megan had told her about him, about his connection with the local, bomb-loving militia group, echoed in her mind, and she took an involuntary step back.

From her new position, she couldn't see him through the crack in the curtains. It was so much worse not knowing what Norman was doing, but she couldn't seem to make herself step closer to the window. Sudden, loud knocking made her jump.

Jules went still, torn. She wasn't about to answer the door, but should she wait for him to go away? Her SUV was parked behind the house, so he couldn't be sure she was home, unless he went around back looking for her. The idea of Norman Rounds prowling around by the barn where the kids were hiding was terrifying.

She could call Theo. The idea was so tempting that her hand went to her back jeans pocket where her phone was tucked. What could she tell him, though? That Norman Rounds was at her door? It seemed like an overreaction. Maybe paying friendly visits was just a small-town thing. Maybe he needed to borrow a cup of sugar—or some plastic explosives.

A hysterical giggle wanted to burst out of her, but she clapped her hand over her mouth and swallowed the laugh. When there wasn't a second knock, she stepped close to the window and peeked through the tiny crack between the curtains.

Norman was standing right outside the window. Lurching back, Jules sucked in a rasping breath. His head had been turned away as he'd scanned the yard, so he hopefully hadn't seen her. She strained to listen, dying to know whether he was still standing there. If she looked out the window again, and Norman wasn't looking away this time, he'd see her for sure.

After either seconds or minutes ticked by, Jules forced her feet to take her back to the window. She had to know where he was and what he was doing. It was worse to stand there, blind and clueless, than it was to risk him seeing her if he'd not moved from that spot.

Please don't be there, she mentally pleaded, and then twitched the curtain aside. Her thundering heartbeat eased, and she took a long, relieved breath. Norman was gone.

Then she realized his truck was still parked in front of the house. Pushing the curtains farther apart, Jules frantically raked her gaze across the entire front yard. There was no sign of Norman. Her breath started fluttering in her throat as she hurried into the library. She ran to the window, not caring at the moment that he could see her through the gauzy curtains if he was there, and looked out over the side yard. It was empty.

If he wasn't in front or the side, then he was in the back—where the kids were hiding. She ran for the kitchen as she pulled out her cell phone. Her hands shook as she tried to call, her fingers fumbling with too-small buttons on the cheap, prepaid phone. It slipped out of her grip and skittered across the wooden floor.

"Please don't be broken," she muttered, grabbing it from where it had come to rest against the hall baseboard. "Please, please, please..." Holding her breath, she pushed the *send* button and waited. When it rang on the other side of the call, she let out the air in her lungs in a *woosh*. Darting to the kitchen window, she caught a quick glimpse of someone rounding a corner of the barn before they disappeared behind the leaning structure. "Oh no..."

"Jules." Theo's gruff voice was the best sound in the world.

"Theo! Norman Rounds is here, and he knocked, but I didn't answer, and now he's roaming around, and the kids are out back, and—" She knew she was talking too fast, that Theo probably couldn't even understand her, but she couldn't seem to halt the flow of words.

"On my way," he clipped, interrupting her. "Stay inside."

"But—"

"Stay inside. I'll be there in four." He ended the call before Jules could argue again. It didn't matter, though. Norman was out by the barn, and the kids were in the barn, so Jules couldn't just stay inside and let the kids fend for themselves. Rushing to the back door, she started to push it open when she heard the rumble of an engine coming from the front of the house.

She hesitated for a second, but another glance didn't show any movement from the barn, so she hurried back into the living room and peaked through the curtains.

The back of Norman's pickup disappeared around the first bend in her driveway. Relief rushed through her body, leaving her feeling limp and noodley. Leaning against the wall for support, she watched for a couple of minutes, until she was sure he wasn't coming back.

When the driveway stayed empty, Jules moved toward the back door again. It had taken so long that the kids were probably scared out of their minds, especially if they'd seen or heard Norman snooping around the barn. As she crossed the kitchen, her vision narrowed, growing gray around the edges, and Jules realized she was breathing in quick, short pants. She stopped by the back door, leaned her head against the cool glass, and took several deep breaths. She couldn't let her siblings see her so obviously shaken up. Once she was breathing somewhat evenly and felt a little more under control, she shoved through the back door and took a step onto the porch.

There was a deep *boom* that Jules felt more than she heard, and the barn exploded.

She staggered back, her back bumping against the siding. Blinking, she focused on the barn—on what used to be the barn and was now a burning husk of a building. It didn't feel real. Jules stared at the burning structure, unable to comprehend that it wasn't a movie, that it was *her* barn that flames were eating, in *her* yard, with *her* brothers and sister inside…her brothers and sister…

Oh, God.

With a scream, Jules ran toward the fire.

She had to get them out. She had to save them. They were in the barn because *she'd* told them to go there, because Jules had thought it would be a safe place to hide, and now they were—*No!* She couldn't allow herself to believe that. She'd get them out. She would save them. They would be okay. If they weren't, if she'd torn them out of their previous lives, brought them here only to lose them all... Jules didn't know how she'd be able to go on.

The heat was incredible. It reached out and pressed against her skin, but she still ran toward it. Every breath she took felt like she was setting her lungs on fire. The smoke was thickening, making her eyes sting and water and blur. As she ran, she blinked rapidly, trying to see, trying to make out any figures in the burning remains of the barn.

She hesitated at the entrance, a huge, uneven hole gaping where the sliding door used to be. The flames roared as the fire eagerly consumed the old wood, so loud that Jules could hear it even over her thundering heart. With the too-bright flames and rolling smoke, it was impossible to see anything—anyone.

Taking a deep breath of roasting, smoky air, Jules held in a cough and stepped into the burning barn.

She barely made it a step before she was falling backward. Something had grabbed her arm, pulling her to the ground. Jules tumbled down, her numb body not feeling any pain as her back and then her head connected with the ground. All she knew was that she needed to get up, to get to the kids, to get them out, but something was still holding onto her arm.

Turning her head, she saw Viggy had her forearm caught in his jaws. She vaguely felt betrayed, but her urgency to get back up and to the barn overrode everything else. Before she could try to pull free, there were human hands on her, pulling her back, dragging her away from the barn. With a boom that felt and sounded almost as loud as the original explosion, the roof caved in, sending flaming beams and shake shingles crashing down, burying the spot where Jules had just stood. Hopelessness flooded her, and Jules started to cry.

"Viggy, release!" It was Theo. Theo was the one keeping her from saving her family. She barely noticed that her arm was suddenly free. "Good boy. Jules! Talk to me. Where are the kids?" His hands were turning her over and pulling her into a sitting position. "Jules!"

"In there!" she sobbed, renewing her struggles. Maybe it wasn't too late. If she told him, maybe he'd understand she needed to get into the barn to save them. "They're in there!"

"Jules, no." His voice had changed, the urgency shifting to shock.

"Let me up," she demanded, trying to pull away from the gentle, yet relentless hands holding her. "I need to get them out!"

His grip didn't ease. "There's nothing left." He pulled her against his chest, wrapping his arms around her, even as she still fought to get free. "The building's gone, Jules. There's nothing left of it."

He was wrong. He had to be wrong. If the building was gone, then her family was gone, and she couldn't allow herself to believe that. Shoving at his chest with both hands, she managed to wrench herself out of his hold, only to be caught again.

"J-J-J-Ju!"

The stuttering shout made her freeze, terrified to hope she hadn't imagined it, until it came again.

"J-Ju! W-w-we're h-here!"

Her head whipped around, following that wonderful, wonderful yell, and she saw Sam and Ty and Tio and then finally Dee running out of the trees. She pulled away from Theo's slackened hold and ran, not toward the burning skeleton of the barn, but toward her sister and brothers, her beautiful, living, not-burned, not-dead, not-even-hurt family.

They crashed together, falling as they collided, each one joining until they were in a five-way hug. Jules clutched them to her, her hands running over each precious head and back, pressing kisses on any place she could reach, letting her touch reassure her that they were truly alive and in her arms.

"That's it!" she cried, her voice thick with tears. "I'm never letting y'all out of my sight ever again. Forget school. Forget going to the bathroom by yourselves. Y'all will be within reach and in view at all times, got that?"

"I like the no school part," Ty said. "But hell no on the supervised showers."

Jules gave a soggy, shaky laugh and kissed the top of Dee's head. "Language."

"Your arm is bleeding," Tio said, and they all looked at it.

"Oh, right." She wiped at the small trickle of blood. "That's just where Viggy bit me."

"He *bit* you?" Dee repeated, her eyes wide. "Why? What did you do?"

Her laugh came a tiny bit easier that time, although she couldn't stop patting and squeezing the kids. "Why do you think I did something?"

"Because he wouldn't bite you for no reason."

Not really wanting to explain that she'd tried to run into the burning barn, Jules changed the subject. "Are y'all okay? No one's hurt, are you?"

"W-w-we're f-f-fine," Sam said.

"We were far enough away to be out of the blast radius." Tio sounded calm enough, but he leaned against her side like he used to when he was eight years younger and needed comfort. He lowered his voice so only she could hear. "We waited for you for fifteen minutes, and then we took the emergency money and started walking through the woods toward our meet-up spot, like we planned. We heard the explosion, though, and were worried that it was the house, so we ran back here." His even tone shook slightly on the last word.

"You should move farther away from the fire," Theo said from where he was standing a few feet away. Viggy sat next to him.

As they climbed to their feet, Jules smiled at Theo, trying to show him the heaping piles of gratitude filling her heart. His face was sober as he moved forward to help her stand on shaky legs. Now that she knew the kids were safe, her body felt limp and heavy, and she knew she was one what-if away from bursting into tears again.

The kids rushed toward the house, staying well away from the fire even as they watched it in fascination. Theo and Jules followed more slowly. When Jules tripped for the third time, Theo wrapped an arm around her back, and she leaned into him, grateful for the support...and for so many other things.

"Thank you," she said quietly enough that the chattering kids couldn't hear. "If you—and Viggy—hadn't stopped me, I'd have run right into that fire."

He pulled her even more tightly against him, and she felt the pressure of his lips on her hair.

"I'm just glad you got here in time." The nightmarish thought of what would've happened if he hadn't arrived in time made her shiver.

"Me too." His voice was raw, hoarse, and he kissed her head again. "Me too."

The sound of sirens caught her attention, and she looked up at him. "Did you call for help?"

"Yeah. I heard the explosion as I was pulling up in front of your house. I told dispatch to send Fire here and send everyone else to track down that bastard Rounds. Then I dropped the radio mic and ran."

A fire truck circled around the side of the house, driving across the lawn and stopping a safe distance from the still-burning barn. Another truck joined it.

"Firemen!" Dee squealed.

When Theo grumbled something under his breath, Jules looked at him curiously. He grimaced. "Fire can be a pain in the ass."

"But firemen are so hot."

That just made his frown turn ferocious. "Pain in the ass."

Squashing a smile, amazed that she could even *think* about smiling after the past agonizing minutes, Jules leaned against Theo and watched the firemen extinguish the remains of the barn.

Dee stood next to her as an EMT cleaned up Jules's arm and covered the two shallow puncture wounds with Band-Aids. The three boys were sitting on the back porch, watching as the firemen put away their equipment. Theo was across the yard, examining the soggy, blackened remains of the barn with some other cops and a tall woman who'd introduced herself as the county fire marshal. Other officers were searching for Norman Rounds, but he'd disappeared. Theo's lieutenant was working on getting a warrant to search Gordon Schwartz's place, since they figured Norman was most likely hiding out at the militia leader's compound.

One of the firemen approached, giving Jules a small, but friendly, smile. He was a big, burly guy, and despite Jules's fascination with Theo, she had to admit he looked really good in his bunker gear.

"Hi," she said. "Thank you for putting out the fire." Her words sounded inane to her own ears, but it had been a long, hard, stressful day already, so small talk was beyond her at the moment.

"You're welcome." He nodded at Dee. "Want to see the fire trucks up close?" Turning back to Jules, he added, "If it's okay with you, that is."

When Dee turned to her with wide, hopeful eyes, Jules smiled. "Of course. Thank you...?"

"Steve Springfield."

"I'm Jules, and this is Dee." The EMT had finished, so Jules was able to stand and wrap an arm around Dee.

"Nice to meet you. I have a daughter about your age, Dee. Do you go to Cottonwood Elementary?"

"Yes. What's her name?"

"Maya."

"She's in my class. We're both new this year," Dee said in her serious way. "I like Maya. She's nice."

He gave Dee a kind smile that made Jules love him a

little. "Thank you for being friends with her. The move's been hard for the kids."

"Where'd you move from?" Jules asked, and immediately wanted to retract the question. She didn't need to be exchanging life stories with anyone. Every time she talked about their made-up history was a chance to screw up and make someone suspicious.

"Simpson. It's a small mountain town a couple of hours away. We liked it there, but things just got too… well, dangerous."

As much as Jules wanted to ask about what he meant by dangerous, she swallowed her questions and just said, "It's nice to meet you."

Steve escorted a happily chattering Dee toward the fire trucks, and Jules watched them until her view was blocked by Theo.

"Hey." Just looking at him made her smile.

"What'd the new fireman want?"

She blinked at the hostility in his tone. "To show Dee the fire trucks."

"Uh-huh," he said, not sounding like he believed it. "A good excuse."

"For what?"

"For introducing himself to you."

She snorted. "Please. He's a married guy with kids."

"Widower."

"Oh," she said sympathetically, glancing over to where Steve was helping Dee climb into the cab of one of the trucks. When she looked back at Theo, he was glowering at her.

"Don't get all mushy just because he's a single dad."

For some reason, his crankiness made her smile. "I'm not. I'm mushy because he's a hot fireman single dad."

His expression was too much; Jules couldn't hold in her laughter any longer.

"I'm kidding! Of course I'm kidding." Theo didn't look convinced, so she hooked a finger in his belt and gave it a teasing tug. "Hot firemen single dads don't do it for me."

"Sure, they don't."

"It's true." Another tug brought him close enough for her to lower her voice. "I have a thing for hot cops...*one* hot cop in particular."

That lightened his cranky frown and made his eyes turn hungry. "Yeah?"

As crazy as it was for her to get involved with a cop, it was so, so true. "Oh yeah."

Except for when a certain cop came for his breakfast, Jules's shift had dragged. Her brain had bounced between elated anticipation and anxiety, depending on if she was thinking about Theo or exploding barns or the whereabouts of Norman Rounds or...well, Theo. As she wiped a recently vacated table, Jules reminded herself that she couldn't get involved. *How involved is involved?* she wondered, and then frowned at the convoluted question. What if she just kept it light, just a surface relationship? Then he'd never need to know about her past, because he wouldn't care enough to ask.

Jules snorted. Of course he'd ask. He'd been asking

since the very first time she'd met him, and he'd known nothing about her. If she wanted to be with someone who wouldn't be curious about her reasons for moving to Monroe, she shouldn't have picked Theo. Although she really hadn't *picked* Theo. He'd just sort of slipped into her life and saved her life a few times and taken over every thought in her head—well, except for the thoughts required to worry about the kids and getting caught and everything that needed to be done to the house and—

"Jules, I think it's clean."

Starting, she looked up to see Megan smirking at her. "You've been wiping down that table for the past five minutes. It's clean. I promise. It was clean four minutes and fifty-five seconds ago. I do appreciate your dedication, though."

It felt like Megan could see her thoughts, like all the obsessing she'd been doing was scribbled across her forehead. "Sorry."

Megan waved off her apology. "Did you want to take off? I can take your tables."

Frowning at her boss, Jules said, "Are you sure? It's pretty busy."

"Yes, I'm sure." Megan smiled, a big, crocodile-esque grin that made Jules shift back a step.

"Why are you smiling at me like that?" she asked.

The freaky grin sagged around the edges. "Like what? I'm just being friendly."

"No, you're being scary," Jules said. "Why?"

To Jules's relief, the last traces of Megan's fake grin fell away, and she returned to her usual grumpy expression. "Fine. Can you open for me tomorrow?"

"Was that your attempt to butter me up?" Jules

laughed. "Next time, just ask. You don't have to scare me into submission first. And yes, I can open tomorrow." She'd opened the diner only once, but Megan had a detailed check sheet to follow, so it wasn't hard.

"Great. Thank you." Megan scowled. "But also, screw you for saying my smile is scary. It's cute and endearing."

Jules coughed. "Scary."

"Whatever." Megan turned and headed toward one of the booths where someone was waving at her. "Now go, before I forget my gratitude and retract my offer."

Jules opened her mouth, about to tell Megan that she could stay and finish her tables. It had occurred to her that all she had at home was a quiet house that needed a trillion things done to it and her crazy, rampaging worries to stew over. After considering it, she'd rather continue her slow-as-molasses, endless shift at the diner.

Before she could say anything, the sound of the door sensor caught her attention. When she saw Theo standing there, staring at her with eyes so intense that she couldn't breathe, she decided she didn't need to finish her shift after all. She'd found her distraction from her multitude of duties and worries, and he was stretching the sleeves of his worn T-shirt in a truly beautiful way.

All she could do was stare as he got closer and closer, his long strides eating up the distance between them. In no time at all, he'd reached her frozen form.

"Hey."

She swallowed. "Hey." It somehow came out both raspy and squeaky, and she tried not to wince.

"How are you?"

Although she rolled her eyes just a tiny bit, his

concern still made her smile. "As I said yesterday afternoon, and last night when you called, and later last night, when I brought coffee out to the nice officer you had watching my house during your shift and he asked me how I was, and this morning when you asked… was it six times or seven?" When he didn't answer, just frowned at her instead, she continued. "I'm fine. Better than fine. Everyone's okay, so we're wonderful. The kids are complaining that I'm hugging them too much, but I told them they're just going to have to suck it up."

He was quiet for a moment, studying her as if doing a visual health check, before he gave her a tiny smile back. "You heading home soon?"

There was a weight to his words. Instead of being merely a simple question, it was heavy and sexy and nerve-racking, all at the same time. Her throat went dry, and she could only manage to nod.

"When?" Again, he managed to imbue that one word with so much more.

"Megan told me to leave." When he cocked his head to the side, his eyebrows drawing together as if puzzled, she clarified, "Um…now."

"Want to go?"

Did she? Did she want to go and do all those wonderful and terrifying things his husky tone suggested? "Oh yes."

His smile came then. Unlike Megan's, Theo's smile was honest and gorgeous and made her stop breathing. "Let's go then."

He reached out and twined his fingers in hers. Between his grin and the hand-holding, Jules was lucky to retain enough presence of mind to grunt out an affirmative sound. That's all she needed, though, before he was tugging her out the door and into the blinding sun.

The light shocked some sense back into her. It wasn't quite enough to make her tell Theo to have a nice day and find his own ride home, but it *was* enough to remind her that she needed to grab her stuff. She squeezed his fingers and tugged her hand free.

His expression blanked. It startled her, how all the hope and happiness and anticipation could slip away so quickly, leaving this mask in its place. Jules felt an intense urge to take back the motion, to put her hand in his again and leave it that way forever. The only problem with that idea was she couldn't reverse time, and also, she needed her stuff. They wouldn't get very far without her car keys.

"I'll be right back. I just have to grab my things." Turning away while she still had the willpower, she hurried to the back, where she'd put her wallet, silenced phone, and keys in one of the kitchen nooks before she'd started her shift. Her stuff was tucked back far enough in the highest one that no one could see that they were there. As her fingers fumbled for her possessions, she frowned.

Had she placed them so far back that morning? It'd been early—before five—when she'd arrived, so she probably hadn't been completely conscious. Shaking off her unease, she pulled her wallet and keys toward her, and then hopped to be able to reach her phone, which had been pushed back the farthest. Quickly, she flipped open her wallet to check that her Julie Jackson ID and the small amount of cash was still there, and her heart settled when she saw that everything was in place. Relieved, she pulled off her apron and tossed it into the dirty laundry bin. Calling out her good-byes to Vicki and Megan, she rushed toward the front, embarrassingly eager to return to the cop waiting for her.

As she hurried through the diner, her gaze fixed on Theo's silhouetted form outlined through the door glass, the moment of oddness slipped from her mind. Everything inside her was fixed on the man standing right outside the diner.

He held open the door for her, and she slipped past him into the sunshine. Although he let the door swing shut behind them, his feet didn't move. Instead, he stayed in place, his gaze locked on hers with an intensity that put goose bumps on her arms. Finally, she couldn't take it anymore. If he kept staring at her with those hungry eyes, she was going to jump on him in the diner parking lot and give Megan, the customers, and any passersby a show.

"Theo." When he looked at her, she tipped her head toward her SUV. "Ready to go?"

With a clipped nod, he finally moved. Jules couldn't drag her eyes away as he walked toward her—no, he *stalked* toward her. She shivered happily. When had this happened? How had this happened, that this gorgeous man had come to the diner to find her, so they could...? Her brain ground to a halt as she tried to mentally complete the question. So they could what?

Then he was there, in front of her, tracing his hand down her forearm so he could take her fingers in his, and Jules didn't care *what* they were going to do. She was just happy to be here, hand-in-hand, with Theo. Looking from their linked fingers to his face, she felt her smile slip away.

"When was the last time you slept?" From the looks of it, it had been a few days.

Theo raised one of his shoulders in that aggravating half shrug that didn't mean anything, but—she was learning—he often used it to try to dodge a question he didn't want to answer. That meant he'd been awake for a while—a long while.

"So..." She'd automatically headed toward where she'd parked her SUV, and since they were attached at the hand, he'd gone that way, as well. "We're taking my car, then?"

"Yeah." Theo used his free hand to rub his eyes before sending her a sideways glance that was cuter than it should've been. Apparently, Theo did the guilty-little-boy look well. "Viggy's at home, and like you said, it's been a while since I've gotten much sleep. It'll be better if you drive."

Frowning at him, she said, "You should be home in bed, then."

"Doesn't help." At her confused look, he added, "Insomnia."

"Oh. I'm sorry." There was a moment as they reached her Pathfinder, both pausing for a second, as if reluctant to let go so they could climb in opposite sides of the vehicle. Realizing how ridiculous they were being, Jules tried to tug her hand free with an amused snort. Theo's fingers tightened, holding her captive, and her smile faded as her pulse sped up. For a second, they stared at each other, anticipation gathering around them in a thick fog, but then Theo released her, and the spell dissipated.

Silently, they got into the SUV, and they remained quiet for most of the drive. Inside Jules's mind, though, the rush of thoughts was very loud, as if she had an entire fleet of sorority sisters in there who were all trying to give Jules advice at the same time at the top of their lungs. When Theo finally spoke, it was a relief to focus on something other than her spinning thoughts.

"I want someone to watch your place again tonight. We still haven't found Rounds."

"Okay." Jules didn't mind. Although it was strange having someone she didn't know sitting in her driveway all night, it was a huge relief. If she and the kids had to stay alone in that house with Norman on the loose and mysterious shadows moving in the trees... Jules shuddered. She wouldn't sleep at all. "I'll bring him—or her—coffee. And maybe a snack."

"Do that." Reaching over, Theo poked her side with a gentle finger. Although she was normally very ticklish, shock kept her from reacting, other than to stare at him. Had Theo actually tried to tickle her? "Right now, watch the road."

"Sorry." Jules snapped her attention back to the street, but her brain was still whirling. Surly Theo was tempting enough. She wasn't sure if she could handle friendly, teasing Theo without her head—and heart—exploding.

As she turned onto her driveway, her breath started coming quickly. After the first curve in the rutted gravel path, they were surrounded by rocks and trees, hidden from everyone. The isolation of the property made her so much more aware of being alone with Theo. It was a good kind of excitement, but that tiny voice in her head—a voice that sounded a lot like Sam—wouldn't shut up about the stupidity of getting involved with a cop.

Pulling up next to the house, she turned off the engine. When she peeked at Theo, he looked back with heated eyes, a tiny smile touching his mouth.

Who am I kidding? She gave a mental sigh. *I'm already involved with a cop.*

Getting out of the car, climbing the porch steps, unlocking the front door...all the things that were becoming routine in her new life had a new tension now that she was with Theo. Before she could step inside, he was there first. Even though he was a cop, someone who could bring her world crashing down, could break apart her family just as easily, Theo made her feel safe. Having him as a wall—a strong, solid wall—between her and any dangers that might be lurking in the house was such an intoxicating feeling that she was afraid she'd already become addicted.

She wanted to be strong and independent. For her siblings' sakes, she *needed* to be strong and independent. It was just such a relief to have a little help.

"You okay?" Theo asked, eyeing her carefully.

Jules realized she'd stopped in the doorway, half-in and half-out. Flushing, she moved all the way inside and closed the door before turning the dead bolt. "Yes."

He was still watching her, but his expression changed. Concern morphed into focus, and he took a step closer. Jules watched, like prey hypnotized by a predator, as he moved in, not stopping his advance until every part of his body, from his legs to his belly to his chest to his lips, were just a fraction of an inch from hers. Her breaths were quick and shallow; her breasts brushed his chest with every inhale.

"I don't want to want you," he murmured, the heat of his words warming her lips. It took a second for the meaning to penetrate her brain. When it did, her gaze locked onto his, and she raised her hands to his chest, intending to push him away.

"Then don't." She meant her voice to sound challenging, rather than husky. The feel of his pecs beneath her palms startled her into stillness. Her hands flattened against his chest, but her touch turned into more of a caress than a shove.

"Too late." He moved infinitesimally closer, and his lips barely grazed hers when he spoke. It made it very hard for her to concentrate on what he was saying. "You know what's worse?"

"What?" Jules asked, distracted as her desire rose. If he didn't move, didn't close that tiny gap between them so they were finally kissing for real, she was going to either scream or kiss him herself.

"I actually like you."

Despite her growing impatience, his words made her smile, especially the bemused exasperation in his tone that made what he was saying sound so sincere.

"You know what else?"

"What?"

"My dog likes you, too."

Her laugh was soft and surprised. In the middle of such intensity, she didn't think she could feel amused, especially by Theo. "And I like your dog. Not as much as Dee, though. She *really* likes your dog. In fact, I think she might be in love."

At the word "love," his dark eyes went soft and hot at the same time. Without another word, he finally, *finally* closed the gap and kissed her. Because of the long lead up, his extended, teasing almost-kiss, she'd expected it to be gentle, exploratory. It wasn't.

It was explosive.

The touch of their mouths was the ignition switch, and Jules's brain went white as all her thoughts were blown out of her head. Only Theo remained, his lips and tongue and the press of his body flattening her against the door. She burrowed her fingers through his short hair, pulling him impossibly closer, trying to fall even more deeply into him.

With a groan that set off vibrations she could feel down to her toes, Theo snaked one arm around her waist and slid the other over her hip to her thigh. With an effortless ease that Jules—even in her kiss-clouded state—couldn't help but appreciate, Theo lifted her off the floor.

Immediately, she wrapped her legs around his waist, wanting the pressure and friction of that position. His hands ran up the back of both thighs, kneading and squeezing her hamstrings. With a groan, she pressed closer, locking her ankles behind him and her arms around his shoulders.

He leaned his weight into her, sandwiching her between his powerful body and the unyielding door. Her shoulder blades rubbed against the wood panels, an aching pressure that only drove her arousal higher. And during everything, he kept kissing her—and she kept kissing back.

Jules couldn't stop. She could barely stand to pause long enough to suck in a quick breath before diving back in for more. In those seconds, it felt as if her physical connection with Theo was more important than her need for air.

Pressing his hips even more firmly against her, pinning her securely against the door, Theo released his grip on her legs and caught two handfuls of her blouse at her waist. He tugged upward, and Jules untangled her arms from around his shoulders to help. Impatiently, she wiggled and pulled, probably hindering his efforts more than helping, but she wanted the intrusive fabric gone. There was a *pop* as a button flew off and a tearing sound as a seam gave way, and then her shirt was over her head. Theo tossed it away.

Without pausing, he yanked off his T-shirt. He ducked his head to begin kissing her again, but she held him off, entranced by his chest, needing to touch the lightly furred expanse of muscle. As she looked her fill, running her palms across his chest and making him groan and jerk under her touch, Theo reached behind her and unhooked her embarrassingly serviceable bra.

As the last barrier between their upper halves fell away, Theo caught the back of her head and yanked her in for another kiss, his mouth taking over hers in that irresistibly bossy way of his she was beginning to know and love. Her breasts met his chest, skin to skin, and she gasped into his mouth at the incredible shock of pleasure that flashed through her at the contact.

He continued to kiss her in that all-consuming way, holding her with the weight of his body pressing her into the smooth wood of the door—living hardness in front of her and inanimate hardness behind—as he unfastened his jeans and shoved them down his hips. When

Jules heard the crinkle of plastic and guessed it to be a condom wrapper, reality hit her, and she pulled back.

Theo went still except for his chest heaving against hers, and he eyed her carefully. "Okay?"

This was it. He was giving her an out, an escape path, if she wanted it. If she were smart, she'd take it—pull away and excuse herself and never see him outside the diner again. The thought brought such a rush of sadness that she flinched.

Misinterpreting her reaction, Theo squeezed his eyes closed and gave a short jerk of his head. "Okay."

When he started to lower her to the floor, though, she clung, her arms and legs tightening around him. "What?" Her voice was almost nothing, a husky, scratching murmur that barely made it to her ears.

He paused, hope reigniting in his expression. "Did you want to stop?"

"No!" Her answer was out before she could consider it, before she could listen to the nagging sane voice in her head, the one telling her to put down the hot cop and back away slowly. "No. I really don't."

Theo waited another few seconds, watching her expression as if checking to see if she would change her mind. When Jules, her entire body buzzing with arousal, got tired of waiting, she palmed the back of his head and jerked him toward her. Jules tried out the role of aggressor, giving him the same bossy kisses he'd given her, but that didn't last long. With a low growl, Theo took over again, his mouth even more ferocious than before.

He must have managed to get the condom on while kissing her, because the next thing she knew, his hands were under her uniform skirt. He shoved her panties to the side, and she cried out as the touch of his fingers lit her up inside. Her hands worked on his neck, kneading the tight muscles, as her body strained to get closer to his touch.

Then his hands were at her hips, holding her steady as he buried himself inside of her. They both went still, frozen against the front door, as her body adjusted to him, to the incredible sensations that he caused. It was that same mix of exhilaration and safety and affection that Theo always made her feel, only more—a thousand times more. The way he watched her, the way he held so tightly and yet so carefully, as if she was something precious, made her breath catch. Jules hadn't expected to feel this way...not ever. Now there was Theo, and he was touching her like he cherished her, and making her dream come true—a dream she hadn't even known she'd had. Her heart squeezed with so much love for this heroic man that it was agonizing and amazing, all at the same time.

As if he couldn't wait any longer, Theo started to move, his hands almost painfully tight on her hips. She clung to him as they found a rhythm, unable to believe what was happening, or how right it felt, or how perfectly they fit together, moved together. The entire time, he still kissed her, as if he couldn't stop, couldn't tear his mouth away from hers. Jules didn't mind at all.

He shifted his hips slightly as he drove deep, hitting a spot that sent shock waves of pleasure through her, and Jules made a hungry sound. His muscles tightened in response, and he closed his teeth on her bottom lip. The slight sting made her gasp and then moan. From Theo's answering growl and the way he moved faster and harder, he loved her eager noises.

As she lost her grip, her hands slipping from his taut, sweat-slicked back, she tensed, instinctively worried about falling. He didn't drop her, though. His hold didn't waiver at all, and Jules relaxed, quickly falling into the abyss of pleasure once again. Now that her hands were free, she explored, drawing her fingers up the straining tendons of his neck and scratching lightly at his scalp.

A shiver vibrated through him, and he inhaled sharply. His kiss intensified as he thrust into her, making Jules forget about everything but the feel of his body against hers, *inside* her.

The pressure built in her, almost scary in its intensity, and she shifted against him. He tightened his grip, keeping her steady. That security, that strong hold, eased her worry and allowed her to let go, to let the pleasure flood her cells and drown everything else until all that was left was sheer joy.

She cried out against his mouth, gripping him as tightly as he was holding her, and he groaned, his rhythm changing, speeding up as he looked for his own climax. Still, he kissed her, not releasing her mouth until they slid down the door and landed on the floor in a sweaty, boneless, blissful heap.

It wasn't until her muscles began protesting their position that Jules reluctantly stirred, lifting her head to meet Theo's eyes. Her laugh was just a puff of air. It would take a while to recover from having her mind blown so completely. "You look so sleepy."

He gave her a smile, a real smile, and what little part of her that wasn't already in a puddle on the floor melted again. "Want to take a nap with me?"

"Yes." Her answer was out almost before he'd

finished his question, and it was Theo's turn to give a little laugh. He stood, scooping her off the floor in the same motion, making her yelp and then giggle.

"How are you carrying me?" she asked as he headed up the stairs. "Why aren't your muscles mush? Because mine are mush. Mushy mush." She laughed again, giddy because Theo was holding her and they'd just had incredible sex, and she felt safe for the first time in a long, long time.

He smirked at her. "So you're done, then? We'll have to work on your stamina."

When he hesitated at the top of the stairs, Jules pointed in the direction of her bedroom. "My stamina's fine. Excellent, even. I could go another five rounds. I just said that about the mushy muscles so you didn't feel bad if you were feeling weak."

He laughed as he maneuvered them through the doorway. Although it was a little rusty, his laugh was the best sound she'd heard probably ever. "Nice of you."

Jules tried to respond but couldn't, because Theo was in her bedroom. *Theo* was in her *bedroom*. And then he took a few strides and tumbled onto the bed with her. Theo was now in her bed. In. Her. Bed. Amazed, she stared at him lying next to her.

"Five rounds, huh?" His smile was sweet and crooked, and Jules's muscles suddenly didn't feel like mush anymore.

CHAPTER 18

"You're happy." Dee's glare was almost accusatory.

"I am." Even now, an hour after Theo had left to pick up Viggy and get ready for work, she felt almost giddy. She sang to herself—sang and smiled and stared blankly into the pantry. She was supposed to be thinking about dinner options but couldn't think about anything except Theo. As silly as it was, Jules was stupidly happy.

"Why?"

"Why not?"

Dee considered this. "Because the water heater is broken, so we have to take really cold showers?"

That did dim Jules's happiness. Until she'd actually experienced one herself, Jules hadn't realized how very, very cold a shower could be. She'd figured not having hot water would be annoying, but endurable. It was not endurable. She could stand the spray only for a few seconds before her lungs stopped working.

"I'm going to have to call someone to fix that." She dreaded the thought only slightly less than she dreaded taking another icy shower. Not only would it cut a significant hole in their dwindling supply of cash, but having a stranger in the house felt risky.

"Your landlord should fix that," a testy voice said from the doorway, and Jules spun to face Theo. It felt like her blood was carbonated, filled with tiny bubbles of excitement that rose to her brain whenever he appeared.

"Hey!" she said, trying to keep her giddiness under control. When he smiled at her, though, all her efforts were for naught. "How'd you get in?"

"Ty let me in."

"Did you forget something?"

"No."

"Then…" She paused, but Theo didn't fill in the blank. "Why'd you come back? I thought you had a shift tonight."

"I do. I wanted to see you first." He held her gaze as he spoke without coyness or shyness or anything except flat-out honesty.

She couldn't stop staring at him with what was probably a very silly grin on her face.

"Hi, Theo." Dee's voice snapped Jules out of her daze. "Is Viggy here?"

"He's in the car." At his answer, Jules realized Theo was dressed for work. She also realized he looked really, really nice in his uniform, even if it reminded her of why the two of them would never, ever work. "You can go see him if you want."

Dee's enthusiastic squeal made both of them wince as she ran from the kitchen, her feet pounding down the hallway in a rowdy, very un-Dee-like way. Jules loved it. "Thank you."

"Don't thank me." Theo moved toward her, his smile slipping away as an intense look took its place. "I have an ulterior motive."

"Yeah?" Suddenly, inhaling was difficult, which would explain why the word came out sounding so breathless. "What's that?"

He was in front of her now, a uniformed wall of muscle and lustful intentions that made the bubbles of excitement in her stomach go a little crazy. "I wanted to see you. Alone."

"What?" she teased. "You used Viggy for nefarious purposes? Officer Bosco, how could you?"

"Easily." Cupping her face in both hands, he lowered his lips to hers.

It was immediately apparent that her brain hadn't exaggerated how wonderful this was. He backed her into the curved surface of the ancient fridge, kissing her with an almost frantic edge, as if he needed it for his survival. Making a small sound, she pressed closer, her fingers grasping the stiff material of his starched shirt on either side of his waist. She felt like she needed to hold on to something, needed him to anchor her before arousal and happiness launched her into space.

"G-g-get off of h-h-her!"

At the sound of Sam's voice, she crashed down to earth as quickly as she'd rocketed away from it. Sam swung for Theo, but Theo caught Sam's wrist before the blow could land. He pulled it behind his back and turned Sam, gently but firmly pressing him against the wall in a motion so quick that it stunned Jules.

"Let him go," she said, and Theo did, although he stayed between them. Sam lurched back several steps, and Jules shifted so she could see her brother. He looked…stunned. Stunned and gutted.

"Theo…" Moving around so she could face him, she saw she didn't need to finish the sentence. She could tell by Theo's expression that he already understood.

After a sharp, assessing look at Sam, he said, "I need to head to work. See you tomorrow morning."

"Okay. Be careful."

Sending her a warm, tender glance that was almost as good as a good-bye kiss, Theo left the kitchen.

Sam's glare was not nearly as sweet. As he tried to follow Theo out, Jules grabbed his arm. "Nope, Sam-I-Am. We're talking."

Although he didn't look happy about it, he let her tow him to the kitchen table and plopped down in his usual chair. Jules lowered herself into the chair across from him, and they sat in silence for a few minutes. She shifted, not knowing how to begin this sure-to-be-awkward discussion. It turned out that she didn't have to.

"H-how c-c-c-could you?" The words burst from Sam in an explosive rush.

"How could I what?" Even as she asked, she knew what his answer would be. After all, she'd accused herself of the same thing over and over. How could she endanger her family's new life by getting involved with a cop? How could she put this crazy infatuation before her siblings' safety and happiness?

"K-k-k-k..." His inhale shook. "Touch h-him like th-th-that. H-how c-c-c-can you st-stand it?"

Shock made her go silent. They stared at each other, Sam breathing hard, as if he'd sprinted a mile. The goal had always been to get custody, to get the kids away from Courtney. She'd never thought beyond that point. Jules had always just assumed that, once her siblings were living with her, once they were in a safe place, they would be okay. And that, she saw now, sitting across from her wonderful, sweet, tortured brother, had been really dumb of her.

What could she do, though? For now, therapy was out. With the big secret they were keeping, it would probably do more harm than good. It was up to her, then, to muddle through. Suddenly, Jules felt useless. If she couldn't fix the stupid water heater, then what hope did she have of fixing her brother? As she searched for words—the perfect words, the words that would make him feel right and whole again—the silence stretched between them, and Sam started to look alarmed.

"D-d-did h-he f-f-f-force you?" he demanded.

"No!" Mentally, Jules swore at herself for already messing up. "No, sweetie, no. I wanted to kiss him."

That didn't lighten his horrified expression. "Wh-wh-why?"

"Um…" She never thought she'd have to explain attraction to her little brother. Jules would have paid a lot—all of her tips for a month—not to have this conversation. "Because I like him. He's kind and brave and handsome and he saved our lives. At first, he was really surly—well, he still can be surly—but when he smiles, or listens to Dee like what she's saying is really important, or checks the house for any danger before I come in, or looks at me like I'm the most interesting and beautiful woman in the world… Well, then I want to kiss him." She didn't mention that she also wanted to kiss him when he was at his crabbiest. Since Jules didn't even understand it herself, it would be impossible—and embarrassing—to explain that to Sam.

He didn't say anything, just continued to stare at her with that baffled, betrayed expression.

"Haven't you ever wanted to kiss someone?"

"No." His answer came quickly, with no hesitation. His certainty made her heart break for him.

"Sam..." Pausing, she took a deep breath, praying that what she was about to say helped, rather than hurt. Sam had been hurt enough. "What Courtney did—"

He scooted his chair back so quickly and violently that it slammed into the wall behind him with a loud bang. "I d-d-don't w-w-w-want t-to t-t-t-t...d-disc-c-cuss th-that."

Frantically trying to think of the best thing to do—to push it or let it go, to change the subject or make him face it—Jules ended up just nodding and dropping her hands into her lap. "That's fine, Sam-I-Am. If you ever do want to talk about it, though—"

"I w-won't."

"Quit interrupting your elder," she scolded, trying to put a light note in her voice as she reached over and flicked his nose. He looked startled. "I'm here if you want to talk about anything. Got it?"

After several long seconds, he grudgingly shrugged. "G-got it."

"Good." She paused and then told herself to quit being a chicken and act like a parent. "What you saw me and Theo doing—"

"Y-you d-d-don't have t-to t-t-tell m-me th-th-this. I *kn-now* it's n-not the s-s-same, okay? I j-j-just s-saw you with h-h-him, and..." He trailed off with a frustrated sound, as if he couldn't find the right words.

"Sure, *now* you say that." His grudging smile at her teasing sent a flood of relief through her. "And quit interrupting me. What you saw, that was completely consensual. We both wanted it, and we were both enjoying it. At least, *I* know that I was enjoying it, and by the sounds Theo was making, I'm pretty sure he was enjoying it—"

"J-JuJu!" Sam groaned, but he was actually laughing a little.

Smiling, Jules continued. "Hey, you asked!" Her smile faded, and she leaned across the table. If Sam hadn't been out of reach, she would've grabbed his hand. "And I'm going to say this last part, and you're going to listen, and then I won't bring it up again unless you want to talk about it, okay?"

He looked a little anxious, but he didn't try to stop her from continuing.

"What you saw just now, between me and Theo, is not the same thing as what was done to you. It's not even close." All trace of a smile was gone from his face, and he just stared at her, every muscle in his face and body tense. "Kissing and touching and sex—those things should come from a place of affection, of love. What Courtney did came from a place of sickness—hers, not yours—and a misuse of power." Sam started to shake his head and say something, but Jules continued, flattening his protests with her words. "I just want you to know that they're not the same, not even close, so you don't look at me and Theo and think we're hurting each other like Courtney hurt you. When you find someone you love, who loves you right back because of the wonderful, amazing, *lovable* person you are, I don't want you to think that you're hurting them. It's not the same as the awful things Courtney did, got it? It's not the same." Her words came faster and faster as tears pressed behind her eyes, seeking release.

"J-J-Jules."

"What?" She sniffed and blinked rapidly several times.

"Stop t-talking."

Her laugh was watery, but it was a laugh. "Fine. Just one more thing."

He sighed dramatically, making her laugh again.

"I love you, Sam-I-Am."

His crooked smile made her want to cry again, but she managed to push the tears away.

He shifted, his gaze bouncing around the kitchen. Jules could see some of the tension seep out of him, and she knew they'd moved out of crisis mode and closer to regular teenage awkwardness. "S-so…"

"So what?"

There was the tiniest hint of mischief in his expression, and she had to fight down the almost irresistible urge to jump over the kitchen table and hug out his guts. "A c-c-cop, Ju? Really?"

"I know!" It came out as a wail, and she allowed her forehead to fall to the table onto her crossed arms. "How did this happen?"

"How did what happen?" Ty asked as he wandered into the kitchen.

"JuJ-Ju's in love w-with a c-cop."

"Hey!" Her head shot up as she protested. "Who said I'm in love with him?"

"You d-d-did. J-just n-now."

Jules reran their conversation in her head, and her head dropped back to the table. "I did, didn't I?" she wailed.

"You're in love with Theo?" Although Ty sounded startled, there was no judgment in his voice. Jules's mental critic was a lot harsher than her siblings.

"No."

"Y-yes."

"Cool." Apparently, Ty was accepting Sam's take over her own. "This way, when we start driving, we'll never get a ticket. Just remind the cop that we're Jules's brothers."

Jules groaned as Sam and Ty continued their conversation without her input, and the dirty, lovely side of her brain compiled her own list of benefits of dating a cop. When she couldn't stand either the external or internal conversation anymore, she stood.

"Where's Tio?"

"Library," Ty said through a mouthful of apple. They were getting low on groceries again, Jules had noticed. "He asked if you'd pick him up at five."

Glancing at the clock, she saw it was five minutes before five and gave Ty a pointed look that went right over his head. Going to grab her keys, she asked, "Is this a recreational trip, or is he doing homework?"

"Water heater research."

Jules groaned. "I hate when he tinkers with the gas appliances. I should just call a repairman."

With a shrug, Ty banked the apple core off the side of the trash can. It fell neatly inside. "He likes doing it. It's a challenge."

"A ch-challenge that m-m-might blow up in h-his face," Sam grumbled, but he looked much more relaxed than before. "L-literally."

"Ahh!" Jules yelled, covering her ears as best she could with her keys in her hand. "Stop talking about explosions, y'all! The stove, the barn—can we please go a few days without something blowing up? Honestly, is that too much to ask?"

As she left the kitchen, both Sam and Ty were laughing, and Jules had to smile. Moving to Monroe might not have fixed everything—and everyone—but things were better.

Things were better, and she'd sacrifice a lot to make sure they stayed that way.

CHAPTER 19

"PULL A PAN OF CARAMEL ROLLS FROM REACH-IN COOLER at four," Jules muttered out loud as she read the diner opening checklist. "Leave on bread rack to proof."

She yanked open the small refrigerator and pulled out the pan of caramel rolls. True to her word, Megan hadn't made Jules go into the evil walk-in cooler since Vicki had trapped her in there. Relieved that she didn't have to venture into the claustrophobic space, especially when she was at the diner alone, Jules gave Megan mental thanks and checked the next item on the list.

"Pull chairs off of tables." Easy enough.

As she slid the chairs from their upside-down position on the tables, there was a flash of light, almost immediately followed by a crack of thunder. She jumped. Although she usually didn't mind lightning, Jules was still getting used to Colorado's violent, short-lived thunderstorms that brought buckets of rain and often hail. She was more used to the quieter sort of storm that lingered, sullen and muggy, all day.

A patter of raindrops on the roof turned into a steady drumming. With the front lights off, the diner was dim, and the flicker of lightning lit the interior in eerie, uneven flashes. Her hands shook a little as she reached for another chair, and she forced a laugh at her silly fears.

A *thump-thump-thump* on the window made her scream. Whirling around, she saw a figure in a raincoat standing close to the plate-glass window.

The bluish cast to the security light drew strange shadows, hiding the person's face. Jules's heart hammered in her chest, and she took an uncertain step back, still holding the chair in front of her. A small corner of her mind told her that she must look ridiculous, like she was trying to imitate a lion tamer, but the rest of her brain was frantically trying to figure out what to do.

The figure at the window lifted a hand and waved. The enthusiastic, harmless-looking gesture killed most of Jules's panic, and she set down the chair. Then the person tipped her head, allowing the security lights to illuminate her face, and the rest of Jules's concern washed away. She knew this person. It was Sherry Baker, Hugh's maybe-possibly future girlfriend.

Sherry knocked on the window again, and Jules realized that she was just standing there, staring at the woman as the rain hammered down outside. Jules hurried over to open the door.

"Oh, thank you!" Sherry gushed as she hurried inside. She placed a large bakery box on a table, wiping water from its glossy, white top. "It's pouring out there. I didn't think I'd find anywhere that was open. Would you mind if I stayed in here until the rain lightens up a bit?"

"Of course." Jules closed the door and relocked the dead bolt, feeling a little uncertain. Although she didn't think Megan would mind that she'd let Sherry inside before they opened, it still felt strange, as if Jules was doing something wrong. "What are you doing out this early?"

"Oh well…" Sherry made a rueful face. "The studio where I do crossfit, Energy?" When Sherry looked at her, Jules nodded. She was pretty sure she'd driven by the small gym on her way to Dee's school. "I usually go there very early to work out, but I forgot they're doing remodeling this week, so they're closed. My battery died, and my car wouldn't start, so I figured I'd just walk to my friend's house—he's just a couple of miles away. Bad idea." Sherry gave a little laugh. "I didn't even make it halfway before the rain started pouring down so hard I couldn't see. That's when I saw your car here, so I thought I'd see if I could get you to let me in."

"Make yourself comfortable—well, as comfortable as you can get."

"Thank you." Instead of sitting, Sherry wandered around the space. Jules couldn't help but notice that, even soaking wet and enveloped in a bulky rain jacket, Sherry was gorgeous. No wonder Hugh seemed interested. The woman was so stunning that Jules felt dowdy in her waitress uniform and comfortable, yet very ugly shoes.

Shoving her feelings of inferiority to the back of her mind, Jules resumed pulling chairs off the tables. "So… your friend lives close?"

"Yes. I'm not sure if you know him," Sherry answered absently as she peered through the blinds covering the glass door, probably at the sheets of rain pouring from the sky. "Gordon Schwartz."

The name sounded familiar, but Jules couldn't put a face to it. "I don't think I've met him yet." Maybe it came from being a cop, but Theo seemed to know every person in town. If this Gordon was more of a boyfriend than a friend, then Jules was going to have to shelve

the matchmaker-type plan she'd hatched featuring Hugh
and Sherry. She stifled a laugh. After such a short time
of being with Theo, she'd already become one of *those*
people, the ones who wanted to make every person as
couple-y and sickeningly happy as she was.

"Understandable. You're new here, and Gordon
likes to keep to himself." Then, as if Sherry had read
her mind, she added, "Speaking of friends, it looked
like you and Theo Bosco have progressed past the
buddy stage?"

Instantly, Jules's face flamed hot, and she fumbled
with the chair she was moving, dropping it the last few
inches to land upright, but with an embarrassingly loud
clatter. "I…um…why do you think that?"

Sherry laughed. "Please. If you could've seen the pair
of you the other day. I don't think Theo's ever *cuddled*
anyone like that before in his life."

"Um…" *What do I say to that?* Jules thought. It was
still so new that it felt odd and awkward to talk about her
and Theo. Just thinking about her and Theo was enough
to fluster Jules, so discussing it was not going to go well.
She decided to change the subject. "What about you and
Hugh? You two seem to light up some sparks."

She laughed again. "Me and Hugh?" Sherry asked.
"No. I don't think I could date a cop. Besides, my dad
never wanted that for me."

Pounding on the window made them both jump.

Jules peered out to see another waterlogged figure. *It
must be the day for rainy-day refugees*, she thought with
a small huff of laughter. The person turned his head, and
his face was lit by the streetlight. Jules's chuckle cut off
abruptly as she jerked back a step.

"Who is it?" Sherry asked.

"Norman Rounds." Her heartbeat had taken off at a gallop, and she started breathing quickly—too quickly. Jules reminded herself that she and Sherry were in a locked building. Help would arrive long before Norman could reach them. "I should call Theo."

"Why?" Sherry sounded surprised. "He's a little strange, but he's harmless. Norman's good friends with Gordon. I'm sure he just wants to get out of the rain. You don't need to let him in if he worries you, though."

"He blew up my barn!" The words came out too loud and high-pitched. She needed to stay calm. Jules exhaled a shaky breath, trying to think rationally.

"Norman blew up your barn?"

The pounding resumed, and Norman started yelling something, but the thunder and the clatter of the rain on the roof made it impossible to understand. Jules was a little grateful for that; she didn't think she wanted to know exactly what her crazed, bomb-happy stalker was shouting.

Eyes wide, Sherry moved back, away from the door.

Jules reached for her phone, but her hand brushed her pocket-less uniform skirt. "Shoot." The word sounded so insufficient for the situation that she almost laughed. Her phone was in the back, and she didn't have Theo's number memorized yet. "I'm going to call 9-1-1 on the diner phone."

She took a step toward the counter when a loud *crack* made her spin around. Norman had a brick in his hand, and he was swinging it toward the large window. As it connected, Jules let out a shriek, her gaze locking on the small crack that had formed under the blow. How long could the window hold up against his assault? He hit the glass with the brick again, and the sound snapped Jules out of her paralysis. Whirling around, she ran for the phone.

Grabbing the handset, she started to dial when a smashing sound made her jerk, her fingers mashing too many of the wrong buttons. Her gaze flew to the window, but except for a few cracks, it was in one piece. The shades on the door rattled, and Jules realized with dawning horror that Norman had broken the glass in the door, and he was shoving the shades aside so he could reach for the dead bolt.

She couldn't look away from that groping hand, rainwater diluting the blood oozing from multiple small cuts and running over his fingers. He gripped the dead bolt, and Jules knew a 9-1-1 call wouldn't help them. The police couldn't get there in time.

Dropping the phone, she ran for the kitchen door. "Sherry! This way!"

There was no response, no sound of running feet behind her, and Jules turned. Sherry was unmoving, frozen in place between two diner tables, watching as Norman unlocked the dead bolt. Reversing her steps, Jules ran toward Sherry, intending to grab her and haul the woman into the kitchen and to the back door. It was their only chance to get out of there, to get away from Norman.

She was only ten feet from Sherry when the door opened and Norman stepped inside. His jacket hood shadowed his features, turning him into a nightmarish figure, and Jules couldn't hold back a cry.

Finally, Sherry moved. Lifting her right arm, she aimed a black pistol at Norman and pulled the trigger.

The blast was loud, so loud that all the other sounds went quiet for a moment. Jules skidded to a stop, turning her head from Sherry to Norman's form sprawled on the floor. Shock kept her brain from understanding for several seconds. When comprehension finally started seeping in, she was torn between checking on whether Norman was dead and running just in case he wasn't.

Running won.

"Sherry," Jules said, her voice echoing strangely in her head. "Let's go. We need to get help."

Sherry finally turned, arm still outstretched. Staring at the gun that was now pointed directly at her, Jules stopped breathing. "No. We don't. Norman's been a pain in my ass since he came to town, always butting into other people's business. I thought planting explosives in your barn and pinning it on him would finally get him out of my hair, but here he is again." She shot his crumpled form a quick, disgusted glare. "Interfering bastard."

"What?" It was a stupid thing to say, but it was the only word Jules could force past her lips. Sherry's words weren't making any sense. *Nothing* was making any sense. Sherry blew up their barn to frame Norman? What was happening?

"Please close the blinds." Sherry smiled, a friendly, completely nonhomicidal smile that made everything even more disorientating.

Jules could only stare at her. It was hard to believe it was real. In fact, it was hard to believe the whole morning was real, that she was standing inside a cozy diner with the rain pattering on the roof and a possibly dead guy lying on the floor and a woman she was starting to think of as a potential friend pointing a gun — a gun! — at her. It seemed more like a dream. Jules waited to be woken by one of the kids or a sound or just her own fear, but nothing changed.

She was still standing in the diner, Norman still bleeding by the door, and Sherry still had her gun.

"Didn't you hear me?" It was strange. Even though Sherry was holding a deadly weapon, her voice stayed sweet and even. It was Jules whose thoughts were verging on the hysterical, while Sherry sounded perfectly reasonable. "Please close the blinds."

Perfectly sane.

Numbly, with hands that shook, Jules walked to the window and dropped the blinds, turning the slats so they completely covered the window. She considered trying to leave them partially open, so someone could see in if they happened to be walking by at four thirty in the morning, but there was no way to conceal it from Sherry, who was watching her intently from just a few feet away.

So she closed the blinds, hiding the two of them from the outside world.

"Thank you," Sherry said, and the small part of Jules's brain that wasn't screaming with fear marveled at how polite her captor was. "Now come this way, please." She gestured toward the back.

Jules's knees wanted to fold, to soften and place her on the floor, but she stiffened, forcing her legs to carry her as she walked in front of Sherry toward the counter. It was harder not being able to see Sherry, just knowing that she was right behind her, holding a gun pointed at Jules's back. Her skin felt itchy with nerves, her body knowing that something very bad could happen at any second, but she couldn't brace herself for it.

"What do you want?" she asked, more so Sherry would speak than wanting to know. Having the silent, menacing presence behind her was too nerve-racking. She needed Sherry to talk, to make some sort of sound.

At first, it seemed Jules's plan wasn't going to work, but then Sherry finally answered, "I'm never going to get what I want."

That was unhelpfully cryptic, Jules thought semihysterically. She frantically searched her brain for words, for the right statement or question or argument to make Sherry see Jules as a person, as someone with a right to her life.

If she died, what would happen to Sam and Ty and Tio and Dee? It wasn't just fear that was circling inside of Jules, twisting like a cyclone. There was also rage. How dare Sherry threaten to take Jules away from her family? How dare she hold a gun on her? Just a jerk of her finger, and Jules would be gone, leaving her sister and brothers to suffer...again. And Theo—

She sharply cut off that train of potential grief.

As she shuffled forward, trying to move as slowly as possible without getting shot, Jules welcomed the anger. It ate away the fear and sharpened her mind. She needed to be smart, to get through this so she could stay alive and give her siblings that chance at a new life she'd promised them. And as crazy as it was, she wanted to give this thing with Theo a chance to survive.

"Do you have a reason for doing this?" she asked out loud. Jules was proud that she sounded so strong, so undaunted. "Or are you just flat-out bat-shit crazy?"

From the hissing inhale behind her, it seemed Jules had struck a nerve. "I'm not crazy."

"So what's your justification?" Jules demanded, righteous anger flowing through her and giving her courage. "What's so important that you can blow up our barn and shoot Norman and risk my life for it? Risk my brothers' and sister's lives? What?"

"He took him from me!" Just like that, the politeness, the calm, was gone, and Sherry was full-out yelling. The fear returned as Jules imagined the gun swinging with Sherry's hand as she gestured wildly. It would be so easy for Sherry's finger to jerk back, sending a bullet tearing through Jules, through her back, her spine, her lungs, her heart...

"Who did?" Jules came to a stop as she tried to make her tone even, but it was hard with anger and fear warring inside of her. "Who took him?" *And what does that have to do with me?*

"Theo." She spat out the name, punctuating it with a jab of the gun barrel in Jules's back. "Theodore Bosco."

Jules cried out, as much from the surprise of the sudden, violent contact as from pain, stumbling forward a step to escape the pressure on her spine. "Theo?" she repeated, panting, once she was able to speak again. "Who took Theo from you?"

"No!" Sherry shouted, making Jules's whole body contract in anticipation of the shot. Sherry didn't fire, though...not yet. "Theo is not the *good guy*. Everyone thinks he's a hero, but he's not. He's not."

Even though Jules knew she should try to pander to the woman pointing a gun at her back, she just couldn't say it, couldn't agree with her. "Theo *is* a hero. He saved me, my sister, my brother, and Hugh from that gunman."

"You were never in any danger," Sherry scoffed. "No civilians were. And Hugh was supposed to die."

All the air left Jules's lungs in a whoosh. "What?" she finally managed to croak as realization began to seep into her brain. "You know who the shooter is?"

"Keep moving." Sherry's words, accompanied by another jab of the gun to her spine, made Jules realize she'd come to a halt again in front of the entrance to the kitchen. Jules pushed through the door as her thoughts bounced wildly with escape plans. Images of her shoving the swinging door back in Sherry's startled face or cracking her over the head with a sheet pan ran through her brain in the half second it took to pass through into the kitchen. The proximity of the gun— and the blatant scariness of the gun—kept her docile, though, at least externally.

"Who was the shooter?" Jules asked. She knew on some level that Sherry was sharing too much with her, that every new fact Jules learned lessened her chance of survival, but she still needed to ask, needed to know who had tried to kill her and Dee and Sam and Theo. "Why did he want to kill Hugh?"

"I didn't want to kill Hugh," Sherry snapped back, and Jules's eyes widened. *Sherry* was the shooter? Then she realized the silliness of her surprise. After all, Sherry was currently holding her at gunpoint, proving she had access to guns and was willing to use them. "I *had* to."

"Why? Why did you shoot him?" Jules winced inwardly at her confrontational tone, but it was sinking in that *this* was the person who had endangered all of their lives. The memory of Dee, looking bewildered as someone shot at her—shot bullets at a little girl!—rose in her mind, and rage started to take hold again.

"He needs to know." The words were so soft that Jules, straining to hear, started to turn toward the other woman. The pressure of the gun barrel against her back made her freeze. She hoped the conversation would distract Sherry, keep her from realizing that they were just standing there. Jules wasn't sure where Sherry was taking her, but she knew it wasn't good. If Jules could delay it, she would. "He needs to know what it's like to lose someone he loves."

"What?" Anger for Theo was building, adding to the existing blaze. "How can you say that? He's suffered so much already. I assure you, he knows perfectly well what it's like to lose someone he loves."

"Bullshit!" That hysterical edge was back in Sherry's voice, but Jules was almost too riled up to care. "I'm the one who lost my dad. *I'm* the one who's hurting, not him!"

The mention of her dad's death softened Jules slightly. Although Jules's father hadn't died, she understood what it was like to lose a father. After all, everything that had made him her dad had already slipped away. His Alzheimer's had slowly, painfully stolen him from her. "I'm sorry about your dad, but Theo—"

Sherry interrupted before she could finish. "He knew! He had to have known. They were together all of the time!"

"What?" Jules halted again. She wasn't sure if it was fear or adrenaline making it hard to understand Sherry, but she felt like she'd just been knocked into the deep end of the pool. "I don't understand. Who knew what?"

"Theo knew." Every time Sherry said his name, she spit it out, like it tasted bad. "All those months, when Dad's depression was getting so bad, Theo must've known something was wrong. He knew, and he didn't do anything!"

Although Jules opened her mouth, nothing came out. Her brain was too busy absorbing the new information to be able to form sentences.

Sherry didn't have that problem. The words came rushing out, like a newly cleared drainpipe. "You think he loves you, but just wait. You'll be hurting, and he'll just ignore it, pretend you're fine, until you're dead."

"I don't… Why are you blaming Theo?" Jules finally pulled it together enough to ask. "Why not you or your mom or the other cops? Couldn't someone else have recognized your dad's depression and tried to get him help? Why is Theo the only one you're blaming?"

Judging by the angry silence behind her, it had been the wrong thing to ask. Again, Jules braced herself for the shot, but it still didn't come. "Because"—Sherry's voice was too quiet, and a nervous shiver ran through Jules, leaving prickling goose bumps in its wake—"Dad was never around. I couldn't have seen it. Mom couldn't have seen it. He was always with his precious partner, Theo. He got all of Dad's time, all of his attention, so he was the one who knew Dad the best. He should've seen it. I shouldn't have had to walk in on that, to see Dad's body after he ate his gun. Why did he get all the good times with Dad, and I only got *that*?"

Despite the gun, despite the shooting, despite her bone-deep anger, Jules felt a tiny spark of sympathy for Sherry—but that was quickly extinguished by another jab of the gun barrel into her back. Jules started walking again.

"In there."

The heavy door of the walk-in cooler loomed in front of her. Jules bit down on the inside of her lip hard enough to draw blood. Her whole body felt numb, unfamiliar, as if it wasn't her own. Her feet were glued to the floor, refusing to move forward.

"Go. Now!"

The pressure of the gun between her shoulder blades reminded Jules that there were scarier things than going into the walk-in cooler, although her clammy palms and racing heart disagreed. Feeling like she was moving through sludge, Jules moved forward. Her hand shook as she closed it around the handle, and it took another prod with the gun barrel before she was able to yank open the heavy door. The dark space yawned in front of her, reminding her to turn on the light, and she fumbled for the exterior switch. Even with the tiny room lit, however, she couldn't keep herself from stopping just inside the door. Sherry's hard shove propelled her forward until she was as far in the cooler as she could get, wedged in the *L* of two shelves filled with cases of eggs and milk and bacon.

"Hands behind your back."

As she grudgingly complied, Jules made a last-ditch effort at talking Sherry out of whatever she was about to do. "I don't understand what locking me in the cooler has to do with your revenge on Theo."

"I told you." Sherry sounded impatient as cold metal circled Jules's wrist. *Handcuffs*, she thought, her mind flooding with panic at the idea of being cuffed. Every muscle in her body tensed. "It's too easy just to die. He needs to live and suffer. Killing Hugh would've done that, but that didn't go as planned. Your death will be even better, though, because it'll be his fault."

Metal touched, cold and smooth, against her other wrist, and a realization hit Jules—Sherry was using both hands to put the handcuffs on her. That meant she couldn't be holding the gun. A thrill of possible escape ran through her. Without thinking, she threw her head back, cracking Sherry in the face with her skull.

It hurt. In the movies, head-butts looked effortless, but the reality sent shock waves of pain through her head. Sherry yelled, a nasally sound of pain, and her grip on the handcuffs loosened. Whirling around, Jules ripped free of her grip and confronted a bloody-faced Sherry. Without hesitating, Jules charged forward, hands locked behind her back, toward the cooler door and freedom. Her shoulder bumped hard against Sherry's side, sending them both off balance. Jules collided painfully with the edge of a shelf before scrambling forward, desperately hoping to escape before Sherry recovered.

Don't fall, don't fall! She repeated the mantra in her head, knowing it would be next to impossible to get up quickly with her hands secured. Using her sore shoulder—the one she'd just used to take Sherry out like a linebacker—she pushed the cooler door open and half ran, half stumbled out of the tiny, cold room.

She heard Sherry swearing until the door closed behind her, cutting off the other woman's tirade. Jules took a precious few seconds and forced her brain to think, to come up with the best plan. There was no lock on the cooler door, and no way to keep it closed without holding it shut like Vicki had. Nothing except light-weight carts were close by, so she couldn't even block the door. With the cuffs restraining her hands, it would be time-consuming at best and impossible at worst to dial either the diner landline or her own cell. Norman Rounds's possibly dead body was sprawled by the front door, blocking it, so that was out.

After a moment of sheer, *I'm-not-going-to-make-it* panic, she remembered the back kitchen door and headed as fast as she could to the rear exit. It had a simple, emergency-exit bar that she could push open with her body. Once she was outside, she could run the half mile to the gas station down the street.

Dodging around counters and workstations, she worked her way through the kitchen, her gaze fixed on her goal—the door. Her elbow clipped a speed rack, sending it rolling sideways and forcing her off-balance. She scrambled several sideways steps, the hard, tiled floor looming in her peripheral, reminding her that, if she fell, she was done.

As soon as she managed to get her feet under control again, she darted for the door. It got closer and closer, blocked only by a large, wheeled garbage bin. With her side, she shoved the bin, but its grocery-cart-style wheels didn't want to move sideways, grudgingly rotating a quarter circle instead. Jules twisted to fit between the bin and the wall, and she was there, the wide emergency-release bar hard and cold against her arm as she pushed.

"This was not part of my plan."

Sherry's voice came from right behind her, and Jules automatically snapped her head around to stare. A dark blur swung at her face. She tried to duck, but it was too late.

Everything went dark.

"You never listen to me." Hugh scowled, shifting uncomfortably on his kitchen chair. Although Hugh would never admit it, Theo could tell his partner's leg was killing him. "No one ever listens to me. Then bad things happen, because you didn't listen, and do I say 'I told you so'? No. I let you cry on my shoulder, and then you feel better and go back to never listening to me."

Otto glanced up from the eggs he was scrambling. "Why are you sounding more like our grandma than usual?"

From his spot leaning against Hugh's kitchen counter—where he'd been since he'd given up trying to find something edible to go with the eggs Otto had brought—Theo laughed.

"And why is Theo laughing?" Otto asked.

Hugh's frown deepened exponentially. "Exactly."

"No," Otto said, pouring the eggs into a pan. "I'm really asking. Why is Theo laughing?"

"Theo," Hugh said in a pointed tone, "would you like to explain to the class why you're laughing?"

Theo shrugged, trying to stop smiling. It wasn't working. "Otto's funny."

Hugh imitated an obnoxious buzzer sound. "Wrong! You're laughing because you didn't listen to me."

"I'm confused," Otto muttered at the eggs. "And why couldn't we go to the diner this morning like usual? There's no food here."

"There are eggs."

Otto gave Hugh a flat stare. "*I* brought the eggs.

Last time we came here, there was no food, so I brought eggs this time. Good thing, since"—he paused meaningfully—"there is no food here."

"Well, your place is too far out, and Theo's is a closet disguised as a house, so it has to be here."

"Or the diner," Theo said. "I agree with Otto. Why couldn't we go to the diner like usual?"

With a glower directed at Theo, Hugh said, "Of course *you* want to go to the diner. That's why we had to meet here for breakfast, instead. This is an intervention."

As Theo groaned, Otto admitted, "I'm confused again."

"Is this about Jules?" Of course it was. Now that he thought about it, Theo was surprised Hugh, the stubborn bastard, hadn't pushed the issue sooner.

Looking back and forth between them, Otto asked, "Jules? The new diner waitress?"

"Yes," Hugh said. "This is about *Jules*."

"What's the problem with her?" Otto put some eggs onto the only two plates Hugh owned, and then started eating his portion directly from the pan. "She seems nice. Jumpy, but nice. I'm guessing there was an asshole husband or boyfriend back wherever she came from."

Hugh grabbed one of the plates and stabbed his fork into the eggs more violently than was really required. "That's the problem. We don't know where she came from or why she's running or even who she really is. And head-in-the-sand Theo here isn't even bothering to look."

"She'll tell me when she's ready," Theo said, pushing away from the counter so he could grab the last plate of eggs. "But I agree with you, Otto, about your asshole-ex theory. One of her brothers shows signs of abuse, too."

Now it was Otto stabbing his eggs with unnecessary force. That information had poked him right in his soft spot for kids and animals.

"Nan just hired him to help at the kennels, so you'll be seeing him around there." Theo took a bite of his eggs. "Are you still working with that rescue Malinois?"

"Yeah." The question didn't seem to cheer him up. "She's going to take some patience."

Theo grinned at him. "Good thing you have plenty of that."

"We're off track," Hugh said grumpily. "And, Otto, you know I hate my eggs scrambled. You couldn't have gone over easy?"

Otto put the pan down on the counter with a *thunk*. "You could've had your eggs any way you wanted if we'd *gone to the diner*."

"They're not even open yet. Besides, we need to talk about—" Otto's and Theo's radios chirped at the same time, and Theo hurried to turn his off before there was feedback. At the same time that the dispatcher's voice sounded, Theo's cell phone rang.

As he answered, he tried to listen to the call coming in on the radio with half an ear, but Lieutenant Blessard quickly took all of his attention.

"Bosco!" he barked. "You fix that dog of yours yet?"

Irritation warred with concern. "He's coming along, but I don't think he's ready for the field yet. Why?"

"Officer Lopez responded to a shots-fired call and found Norman Rounds with a bullet hole in him. Med picked him up, and he's holding on, but he's not in any shape yet to tell us anything. Not sure who shot him, but he's ass-deep in that militia group, so I want the place checked out before our crime scene people start crawling around. I requested help from the bomb squad in Denver. They're at another incident right now, so it'll be an hour—minimum—before they can respond. Mind taking a walk around with your dog, see if he alerts to anything?"

Putting aside the startling news that someone had shot Rounds, Theo considered his lieutenant's request. After their progress at Schwartz's truck, Theo was feeling optimistic that Viggy could come back to his former self. This might be the perfect, low-stress opportunity to try a search. If Viggy wasn't up for it, they'd just withdraw and wait outside in the safe zone for the Denver bomb squad. It wouldn't have the confidence-destroying consequence like the attempted search of Gordon's compound.

"Yeah," he said. "That sounds like a good plan. Thanks, LT."

There was a pause before Blessard cleared his throat. "Right. Well, you're...welcome, I guess."

Theo held back a laugh. If he'd known that thanking his lieutenant would bewilder the man so much, he'd have done it earlier. "What's the address?"

"It's the Monroe Diner."

CHAPTER 20

THEO FROZE FOR WHAT FELT LIKE A LONG MINUTE BEFORE he turned, his gaze hunting the clock display on the microwave. It was 4:49 a.m. His lungs released in a relieved huff. Jules didn't start until five, and she rarely got in more than five minutes early. She hadn't been in there. She was fine.

"Bosco? You there? Bosco!" The lieutenant's irascible tone echoed through his phone. "Damn shitty cell reception. Bosco!" The cell went quiet and then beeped, indicating that Blessard had ended the call.

Theo called Jules, listening to it ring as he turned to tell Hugh and Otto what was happening. The other men were already moving—Hugh toward the back door to grab Lexi from the yard, and Otto to the front, where his squad car was parked. The robotic voice of Jules's generic voice-mail message began reciting her number, and Theo impatiently waited for the message to end before he clipped out, "It's Theo. Call me as soon as you get this."

"Was that LT?" Otto asked as Theo hurried after him, catching the door after Otto pulled it open.

"Yeah. The first call, at least. Norman Rounds was shot at the diner."

"Got that from dispatch." As they separated, heading

toward their respective cars, Otto called over his shoulder, "LT give you any details?"

"Just that Rounds is alive, but barely. He wants us to check for explosives before the crime scene team goes in." Theo climbed into his squad car and fired the engine with one hand while he called Otto on his cell with his other. As soon as Otto answered, Theo started talking like there'd been no interruption of their conversation. "LT thought it'd be a good retraining opportunity for Viggy." The dog sat up in the backseat at the sound of his name.

"Good idea." Otto took the abrupt start to the call in stride. "Who's in there this time of day? Megan?"

"Yeah. Maybe Vicki, unless she's running late like usual." Although it felt slightly stalker-like, Theo had developed the habit of driving by the diner on his way to work—or from work, depending on his shift. If he timed it right, he'd see Jules hurrying into the diner. Megan's Volkswagen was usually there, but Vicki's motorcycle was generally absent until she roared into the lot a few minutes after five.

"Not Jules?"

"Not Jules," Theo repeated firmly, trying to reassure himself as much as Otto. There had to be a good reason why she wasn't answering her phone. They would have already evacuated the building, of course, and the lieutenant would've told him if anyone else had been injured, but he hated that she was nearby if there was any possibility of danger. Although he didn't want Megan or Vicki to be harmed in any way either, Theo couldn't stop obsessing about Jules. He'd feel better when he got on scene and was able to see that she was safe.

And she would be safe, he told himself as he called her again. Of course she would be safe. He couldn't consider any other option. He just wished she'd answer her damn phone.

By the time he'd pulled up to the diner a few short minutes later, he'd left three more messages on Jules's voice mail. Before getting out of his car, he shot her a quick, Call me now text, and then rushed over to the lieutenant.

"Everyone's out?" Theo asked.

Blessard gave him an *are-you-insane* look. "What are you going on about, Bosco? Of course we've cleared the building."

"Good." Theo scanned the parking lot as he spoke. The rising sun had painted the sky red behind the mountains, silhouetting the patrol officers working on setting up a perimeter. "I'll—"

His words and heart stopped at the same time when he saw the Pathfinder sitting on the far side of the lot.

"Where's Jules?" he demanded as he frantically searched for her among the small crowd of people milling around outside of the perimeter.

"Who's Jules?" Blessard asked, but Theo was already jogging toward the SUV. "Bosco! Get back here!"

Theo was so focused on the Pathfinder that he barely heard his lieutenant's yell. Before he even reached it, he knew it'd be empty. The second he'd spotted her SUV, he'd known in his gut that she was inside the diner. Why, though? Why hadn't she been evacuated? Turning, Theo saw Blessard had followed him.

"What's going on?" the lieutenant demanded. "Is there someone still inside?"

"Jules." Just saying her name made his stomach

cramp with fear. "Julie Jackson. She's a waitress here. That's her vehicle. Who cleared the building?"

Instead of answering him directly, Blessard turned and shouted at one of the uniformed officers erecting a traffic barrier across the entrance to the diner's parking lot. "McNamara!" The cop lifted his head. When Blessard waved him over, McNamara started walking toward them. Unable to stand still, Theo strode to meet him.

"You searched the diner?" At the other cop's nod, Theo continued hammering him with questions. "Was there a woman in there—early twenties, dark hair, about five-four, one-twenty-five?"

"Uh...no, sir," McNamara stammered, clearly intimidated. "No one was in there—except Rounds, of course."

"You checked everywhere? Bathrooms, kitchen, closets?"

Even before he answered, McNamara's shamefaced look told Theo what he needed to know. "Well, I...I looked around and called out."

Whirling around, Theo jogged for his squad car. His heart was pounding, and there was a buzzing under his skin.

"Now what are you doing, Bosco?" His lieutenant sounded cranky, as usual, but there was a note of worry underlying his voice. Theo had worked with Blessard for years, and his LT knew him, knew that Theo was not likely to overreact. In the past few months, the problem had been that Theo wasn't feeling anything, and he faced every situation, dangerous or not, with the same impassive facade. Theo's reaction now was akin to another officer's hysterical screaming, so Theo didn't blame Blessard for his concern.

"Grabbing Vig," he said. "If it goes well, he'll let me know if we have any explosive materials to worry about. If it doesn't go well, he'll at least help me search for Jules." Opening the back of his car and attaching the leash snap to the middle ring on the dog's harness, the spot that told Viggy it was time to work, Theo took a breath, trying to steady his breath—and heart and stomach and brain. "He likes her."

"Sounds like he's not the only one." The lieutenant gave Theo a sharp look. "You okay doing this? If you're not up for it, I'll grab someone else. No shame in being too involved to keep a clear mind in the field. That's what your partners are for."

Even though Blessard's words were well meaning and considerate—at least for him—Theo felt a flare of impatience. If there was any chance that there were explosives in the diner, he needed to get in there and get Jules out—now. "I'm fine," Theo snapped, and then softened his tone with an effort. "Thanks, LT."

Blessard studied him. After a second that felt like an eternity, the lieutenant gestured toward the diner. "Go get her, then."

The command released his legs, and Theo grabbed Viggy's plush penguin from the front passenger seat, jammed it in one of his BDU pockets, and jogged toward the diner. As if he knew something important was happening, Viggy trotted at his side rather than being hauled behind.

"Please find it," Theo muttered under his breath, sending the dog a sideways glance. Even though they'd had a breakthrough, they didn't have anywhere close to a solid partnership yet. And they need that to help

Jules. "If there's something to find, find it. And help me find *her* before something bad happens. Please." Viggy glanced up at the sound of his voice, wagged his tail a single time, and then faced front again.

Pushing the door open, Theo set his jaw. He'd let Don down when the other cop had needed him, and now Don was dead. He wasn't about to do the same to Jules. Whatever her secrets, there was something between them, something new and exciting and incredible. He was going to keep her as long as he was able, and even a bomb wasn't going to stand in his way.

Glass crunched under Theo's boot, and he bent to pick up Viggy so the dog wouldn't cut his unprotected paws.

"Here we go," Theo said.

Carrying his new K9 partner, Theo stepped into the diner.

Jules woke with a start, going from unconscious to conscious in one painful jerk of her head. She opened her eyes, but it was still dark. For a moment, she wondered if she'd lost her sight, and then reason set in again. She was just in a dark room. A dark, cold room. When she tried to move her hands, she felt resistance, and metal clanked against metal before pain radiated up her arms.

A greenish glow across the room was familiar, and she blinked blurry eyes a few times to bring it into focus. The glow-in-the-dark shape was the emergency release handle she'd yanked off when Vicki had trapped her in there. Megan must have fixed it. That and the cold that had already seeped into her skin and muscles and was working on chilling her bones made her realize exactly where she was. Sherry had knocked her out, dragged her into the cooler, and handcuffed her to a shelf.

Panic started crawling under her skin, and Jules forced it back, taking long, shaky breaths until she could think again. She couldn't allow herself to freak out. All that would do was waste time and ruin any possible chance of getting out of there. Despite her pep talk, she could feel the irrational fear building, pushing against her lungs and not letting her get enough air.

Breathe, she told herself, biting the inside of her cheek until the pain shocked her out of her panic. *There is plenty of oxygen in here. There is nothing to be scared of.* Sherry and her gun were gone, and Jules was still alive. The worst was over.

Why, though? If Sherry wanted to make Theo pay, why hadn't she shot Jules, killed her? Jules had been unconscious, at Sherry's mercy. Why wasn't she dead? As nauseated as this thought made her, Jules forced herself to think, to figure out what Sherry was planning.

Her gaze settled on the cake box, the same box Sherry had brought into the diner. Her mind jumped to the barn, to the reverberations of the explosion shaking the ground, to the leaping flames consuming what little was left of the building. Jules couldn't take her eyes off the innocuous-looking box.

"Crap."

———————

"Jules!" The lowered blinds cut off all the rays from the rising sun, so only the low lighting kept it from being pitch-black inside the diner. His gaze hunted for Jules even as he moved away from the broken glass and lowered Viggy to the floor. "Jules!"

There was no answer. He needed to find her. First, though, he needed to find the bomb—if there was one. There was no sense running around, blindly searching for Jules and getting all three of them—Jules, him, and Viggy—blown sky high in the process.

"Search."

Viggy stared at him, crouching a little, his tail starting a slow descent between his legs. As the dog's tail lowered, so did Theo's hope. He crouched in front of Viggy and slid his hands over the furred head and down to his scruff. Theo buried his fingers in the fur and loose skin on either side of Viggy's neck.

"C'mon, buddy." He laid his cheek flat against the top of his dog's head, felt the ridge of his skull and the movement of his heavy, nervous panting. "I know I don't deserve it, that I've sucked as a partner. Do it for Jules, though—for Jules and Sam and Ty and Tio and Dee, okay? They need you to come through for them right now."

He lifted his head to see Viggy in almost the same position, although he'd stopped panting. The dog stared as Theo stood, trying to pretend his legs weren't shaking as he walked over to one of the booths and pointed to the side of the bench seat. "Search."

Viggy didn't move. The two stayed locked in their frozen positions, staring at each other, and a bead of sweat trickled down the side of Theo's forehead to sting his eye. When the dog took a step toward him, Theo had to force himself not to jump. Instead, he stayed still, his pointing finger shaking with adrenaline and tension.

With each of the dog's hesitant steps forward, Theo held his breath. Finally, *finally*, Viggy was close enough to touch. Theo didn't put out his other hand, though. Instead, he remained locked in place, muscles quivering with tension, as Viggy, his partner, stretched to sniff the seat where Theo was indicating.

"Good." The word came out in a shaky rush of relief—more than relief. "Good dog." Theo moved to point at another spot, this time on the bench across from the first, and Viggy checked it but didn't signal that he'd detected any trace of explosives. Steadily, they moved around the room, searching, and Viggy's tail started to rise, then wag. By the time they reached the counter, Viggy was acting like he had when he'd played ball with Dee—a happy dog that loved what he was doing.

When Theo moved to point at one of the cupboards lining the wall behind the counter, Viggy didn't follow. Instead, he stayed by the door to the kitchen, looking at Theo and dancing impatiently.

Theo didn't hesitate. He shoved open the door and let Viggy into the kitchen. Without waiting for any direction, the dog moved quickly through the kitchen, heading directly for a heavy door in the wall, snuffling along the bottom.

It took Theo a few seconds longer to weave through the workstations, shelves, and bins to get to the door. He yanked on the handle. At first, he thought it was locked, but then the heavy door reluctantly released its seal and opened.

Cold air flowed out of the small, dark room, and

Theo reached for the flashlight on his belt as Viggy rushed inside.

"Viggy? Is that you? Theo!" It was Jules's voice coming from the shadowed corner of the cooler.

Utter relief flowed through him at the sound, and he directed his flashlight so he could see her huddled form. He took what felt like his first full breath since spotting her Pathfinder parked outside. "Jules, what are you doing in here?"

"Hugh's crazy-pants no-longer-possible-future girlfriend shot Norman and locked me in here!" Although she huffed a laugh, it sounded more than half-hysterical.

He frowned, confused, and felt for the light switch on the wall outside the cooler. "Who?"

"Sherry!"

His hand froze before his finger could push the switch to the "on" position. "What? Sherry? She's not Hugh's girlfriend." Of all the ricocheting thoughts in his head, that wasn't the one he'd expected to come out. "Did you say she *locked* you in here?" He turned to inspect the door he'd just opened. "It's not locked."

"No, but these handcuffs attached to this shelf sure are." There was a rattle of metal against metal, and Theo jerked out of his paralysis. Grabbing a nearby bin, he yanked it over, wedging it against the frame so the door wouldn't close.

"Let me see," he said, sweeping the beam from his flashlight across the floor in front of him as he crossed to the back of the cooler. As he got closer, he fanned the light across her feet and then her legs, bent in front of her as she sat on the floor. She twisted her face away from the glare of the flashlight.

Theo frowned. Viggy was sitting next to her, as he'd expected, but he wasn't focused on Jules. Instead, he was facing the opposite shelf, every muscle in his body alert, staring at a cardboard box on the second shelf.

Viggy wasn't just sitting. He was signaling. There were explosive materials in that box.

"Good boy, Vig!" Theo praised, trying to force his voice to sound pleased, rather than panicked. His fingers were numb as he dragged out the stuffed penguin from his pocket. "Good dog!" After the shortest game of "tug" in the history of domesticated dogs, he tossed the penguin through the cooler door into the main kitchen. Viggy bounded out of the cold space after it.

Theo looked at the top of the box Viggy had been focused on, but the flaps were folded over tightly. "What's in this box, do you know?"

"Sherry brought the box into the diner with her." Jules's voice was thin and high.

"Sherry brought it?" His brain was refusing to make connections, to draw lines between facts and reach conclusions. How could he accept that Sherry, Don's surviving daughter, had shot a man and then locked Jules—his Jules—in a walk-in cooler with a bomb?

Pulling a pen from his pocket, Theo stepped over to the box that had held Viggy's interest. He gingerly lifted one of the flaps just enough for him to point the flashlight into the box. As soon as he saw the wires, his last hopes that it was all a misunderstanding dissolved, and he lowered the flap carefully.

Jules shifted, drawing Theo's attention in time to catch her wince. "These cuffs hurt. Do you think you can get them off?"

"Let me see," he said, crouching next to Jules so he could shine the flashlight on her bound wrists. He needed to get her out of there, away from the bomb. Anger built in him as he ran his finger along the edge of the cuff where it dug into Jules's skin. Sherry hadn't bothered to double-lock the cuffs, so they'd tightened to the point that they were cutting off circulation to Jules's hands. Moving as fast as he could without scaring Jules, he pulled out his handcuff key and tried to fit it in the lock. "Fuck."

"What's wrong?"

"These cuffs are an off-brand." He resisted the urge to swear again, and maybe throw something. "My key won't work on them."

"Oh." Her voice came out small. "How can I get out of them, then?"

"We'll get Fire out here with one of their cutting tools and snip that chain. Once we get you outside, they can work on taking off your new bracelets." He turned on his portable radio. After the initial beep and two seconds of silence, Lieutenant Blessard's voice echoed through the walk-in cooler. From his tone, which was just short of a yell, Theo had a feeling Blessard had been trying to reach him for a while.

"…your status? Goddammit, Bosco, turn on your fucking radio and tell me if you're alive or not!"

Theo rattled off his unit number. "Can I get someone from Fire to meet me at the front entrance with some heavy-duty bolt cutters? Something that'll cut through a cuff chain."

"Fire Rescue One copies," a new female voice responded over the radio, a siren echoing in the background. "We're three minutes out."

The lieutenant spoke again. "I'll send them in as soon as they arrive. Where are you in the building?"

"Negative!" Theo snapped, and then repeated more calmly, "Negative. Do *not* enter the building. I will meet you at the front door to get the cutters."

After a momentary pause, Blessard asked in a controlled voice, "Did the dog find something?"

With a quick glance at Jules who, even in the dim light, Theo could see was looking more and more terrified, he muttered, "Affirmative."

"Get out now, Bosco."

"Working on it, LT." When Jules made a small, scared sound, he crouched down next to her again and cupped the back of her neck in a clumsy attempt at comforting her. He vowed to himself that he would get her out. Whatever it took, he'd get her out alive. "I'd recommend moving the perimeter back another two hundred feet."

"Out now, Bosco! The bomb squad is on its way."

"That'll take too long. It's an hour drive, and I bet they haven't even left Denver yet." The lack of response confirmed it. "All three of us will be out as soon as possible."

The silence that time was even heavier, but all Blessard said was, "Copy."

Viggy trotted back into the cooler and dropped his penguin next to Theo's right foot, then looked at him expectantly.

Trying to keep calm, Theo ran his gaze over the shelving the handcuff chain had been looped around. It was welded metal, and cutting or dismantling that would take longer than waiting for Fire to arrive and snip the chain.

"Fire's on their way to the door."

At Blessard's words, Theo stood, grabbing the end of Viggy's leash. "I'll be right back."

"Don't." Her mouth shook, and the flashlight beam reflected off the tears gathering in her eyes.

"I have to leave you for just a second," he explained, guilt clawing at him at the misery on her face. "I'll be back as soon as I grab the tool we need."

"No," she said, her voice catching on the word. "Don't come back. Leave. I'll wait for the bomb squad. Don't sacrifice yourself for me."

In response, Theo took her face in both hands and kissed her hard. "No. That's the stupidest thing I've ever heard in my life. Be right back."

"But..." Her words sputtered out behind him as he left, tugging Viggy with him. There were a couple of figures shaped like firefighters in bunker gear silhouetted against the glass door. He lifted Viggy and sprinted for it, arriving just as they opened the door.

"Thanks." He thrust Viggy into the arms of one of the startled firefighters and grabbed the long-handled cutters. "Take Viggy and get back."

"Wait—what..." The fireman bobbled the dog, surprise keeping him from holding on. Viggy squirmed free, jumping out of the startled man's arms. He darted back into the diner, nearly knocking Theo down on his way back inside.

"Fuck!" Theo grabbed at the dog, but Viggy slipped out of reach and tore behind the counter. Frustrated, Theo watched the end of his tail disappear. He moved to follow the dog, tossing back over his shoulder a final "Go!" to the firemen.

Shoving open the door to the kitchen with his

shoulder, Theo almost tripped over Viggy as the dog slipped through the doorway with him.

"You decide *now* that you want to be around me?" he muttered, running through the kitchen toward the propped-open door of the walk-in cooler. Jules was staring fixedly at the box, tears running unchecked down her cheeks.

"Get out, Theo!" she cried. "It made a beeping sound. I think it's going to blow up. Please go."

As if to punctuate her words, a quiet tone sounded from the box. He turned toward it, not liking that noise. He was torn, not sure if he should see if he could diffuse the device or if he should just cut her loose so the three of them could run like hell.

He was no explosives expert. Although he'd been trained in the basics, it was mostly in identifying explosive components and learning the protocol. If he was told something was a bomb, then that meant he treated it like a bomb by evacuating and calling in the bomb squad. Disarming an explosive device was not his forte.

"Cut and run, then." He turned toward Jules. "Lean forward."

She obeyed, and he set the flashlight on the shelf next to where her hands were secured. He tried to maneuver the blunt head of the cutters so it could clip the chain, but the way Jules's hands were linked to the shelving made it awkward.

"Pull your hands to your left, as far as you can." This gave him another half inch of chain to work with. Sweat beaded on his face, even in the chill of the cooler. It stung his eyes and made it harder to see, especially in the dim and uneven light. He finally was able to ease the chain into the opening between the bolt cutter's jaws.

The box holding the bomb gave another beep, making Jules jump. Her movement jerked the chain out of position.

"Jules." He tried to keep his voice calm, although in his head, he was screaming. "Stay as still as possible."

"Sorry," she apologized in a small voice, moving her hands back to their original position. He lowered the bolt cutters again, working them around the chain until they were in position. "I'm really sorry if I get you killed, too."

"Not your fault." It was his. Once again, he'd been blind. Don, Sherry…who else was hiding their true desperation behind an amiable mask? He gritted his teeth as he squeezed the handles together. He'd missed the warning signs, and now Jules and Viggy could die.

The chain resisted, and Theo pressed harder, twisting the cutters from side to side until Jules gave a pained yelp.

"Sorry," he told her, wiping the sweat from the side of his face onto his shoulder. "I can't get a good angle."

"No, I'm sorry." Even in the bad lighting, her face looked too pale, almost green. "I'll stop whining. Try again."

Instead, he put down the bolt cutters and examined the chain. There was a small dent, but it wasn't even close to being severed. The cuff around Jules's right wrist had tightened even further, digging deeply into her flesh. A line of dark-red blood streaked the metal bracelet.

Theo swallowed a torrent of curse words. The cutters weren't working. The way Jules was chained to the shelving prevented him from getting a good angle, one which would allow him to put enough pressure on the chain to cut it.

"Plan B," he said, running a gentle finger over Jules's purpling wrist and turning away. He was just going to have to use his rudimentary explosives knowledge and disarm the bomb.

No problem.

"Plan B?" Jules sounded a little panicky, but Theo figured she'd earned it. So far, she'd been pretty calm for a person chained in a walk-in cooler with a beeping bomb. "What's plan B and how quickly can it get us out of here?"

"I'm just going to shut this thing down," he said, still trying to use his calm voice. As Hugh and Otto had both told him many times, however, comforting people was not part of his skill set.

"Okay." Her voice was higher-pitched than normal. "That sounds good. Shutting it down would be very good, especially if you can do that before it blows up."

"Yeah." He snorted, shocked that he could experience even a second of amusement, considering the situation. "That would be good."

Using the same pen as earlier, he lifted the flaps slowly, one at a time. There were so many ways to trigger an explosion. Even removing a cardboard tab inserted in the electrical switch could set it off. Once he'd managed to get the box open, he blew out a slightly shaky but thankfully silent breath.

It was a good-sized bomb, homemade by the look of it, and the blasting cap was obvious. This would be simple. All he'd need to do was disconnect the blasting cap, and there would be no explosion—at least until the bomb squad took it away and did a controlled blast.

He pulled his multipurpose tool out of his BDU

pocket and reached toward the box, but then paused, his
hands hovering. The position of the blasting cap bothered him. It was too obvious, too glaring—almost like
someone *wanted* him to find it.

There had to be a secondary one, one that would be
triggered if the current running through the first was cut
off. With the flashlight in one hand and the tool in his
other, he gingerly moved aside wires, peering into the
depths of the box to the piece of plywood at the base.

There! Almost hidden by the bundled explosives, a
second blasting cap was tucked in the shadows, deep
in the box. He kept searching, looking for a third, but
he couldn't find any more. If he could remove the
second one from the circuit—assuming there weren't
any motion sensors or other traps—then he might have
a chance of disarming it.

A bone-deep tremor vibrated through him. If he
screwed up again, if he made a mistake that cost Jules
and Viggy their lives, killed them just because they
were connected to Theo... The thought was unbearable. Glancing over his shoulder, he couldn't resist a
final look at Jules. As bruised and scared and mussed as
she was, Jules was still the most beautiful woman he'd
ever seen. Viggy sat next to her, his eyes on Theo, that
silly penguin at his feet. For them, for these two who,
for whatever misguided reasons, loved him and trusted
him, he'd do this. He'd fix it, fix what his mistakes and
inattention had caused.

Pulling out the wire cutters in his multipurpose tool,
he took a deep breath and reached in with surprisingly
steady hands. The beeping had accelerated, making his
heart pound in sync with its rapid rhythm. This was it.

He detached the hidden cap, carefully snipping it clear. As he squeezed the handles on the wire cutters, he held his breath, half expecting that disconnection to trigger an explosion.

Instead, the beeping stopped.

All remained silent. Letting out a harsh breath, Theo removed the hidden blasting cap from the box, placing it on a shelf as far from the explosives—and him—as he could reach. He disconnected the first cap he'd noticed, again waiting for the boom as his cutters sank into the insulated wire. The beeping had stopped, but Theo didn't know if he'd successfully disarmed the bomb.

"Did you do it?" Jules whispered, as if a too-loud voice might set off the explosives.

"Think so." He returned to crouch by her feet, picking up the bolt cutters again. "But we should get out of here anyway."

Jules huffed a half laugh. "I'm all for that plan."

Theo slid the tool next to her hip, reaching the handcuff chain from underneath. With this new angle, he was able to get a better grip with the cutters. Pulling the long handles together, he made the heavy blades bite down on the links until the metal parted with a snap.

With an inhaled gasp that sounded very close to a sob, Jules threw her arms around his neck and hugged him, hard. The remains of the handcuffs dug into his upper back, but Theo didn't mind. It reminded him that he was alive—and so was Jules. Something damp touched his arm, and he looked down to see Viggy trying to insert the bedraggled penguin into their embrace. Theo dropped a hand to the dog's head and rubbed his ears.

"Let's get out of here," Jules said, her voice muffled

against his chest. With a glance at the bakery box that held such deadly contents, Theo gave that plan his enthusiastic agreement.

"Agreed. Let's go."

CHAPTER 21

OF COURSE HE HAD COME FOR HER, HER CRANKY WHITE knight with his battered but not broken K9 partner in tow. She didn't know why she'd doubted it, when he'd been there every other time her life had been in danger—and even when it hadn't—over the crazy past few weeks.

He helped her to her feet, which had gone shaky from fear and cold. When Jules swayed, catching his shoulder to keep her balance, Theo frowned and bent as if to lift her in his arms.

"No," she said. He gave her an appraising look, and she knew any hint of weakness on her part would lead to him scooping her up and carrying her from the building. "I've been too much of a damsel in distress already today. I want to walk out of here."

Although he frowned, the lines on his forehead predicting an onset of stubbornness, he didn't push the issue. Instead, he stepped back, allowing her to take her first, admittedly shaky, steps out of the cooler. As soon as she got her legs under control, she moved quickly toward the back door, wanting to leave the place as fast as possible from the closest exit.

Behind her, Theo spoke, making her jump. She twisted her head toward him, but once she realized he was talking on his portable radio, she resumed her quick almost-run to the door.

"Let the bomb guys know I removed two blasting caps, but the explosives are still live. I have Jules, and we're exiting through the north side of the building."

The smooth release bar was under Jules's hands again, and she shuddered as she remembered her first escape attempt of the morning. This time, though, nothing was going to stop her. She shoved the bar down, letting her weight carry her forward into the new morning sun.

"Wait! Jules!"

She tried to turn, but all her momentum was carrying her forward, and she stumbled farther into the alley instead.

"What is it?" she started to ask, but her words trailed away as she saw the look on his face. Her gaze followed his, and her stomach cramped at the sight of Sherry stepping out from behind a dumpster only ten feet away.

She held a cell phone in one hand and a matte-black gun in the other—a gun pointed right at Jules for the second time that morning. "It didn't work," she said in a strangely conversational tone. "Gordon promised me it would work, but it didn't."

With horror, Jules realized the cell phone was some sort of remote-control device for setting off the bomb. If Theo hadn't disarmed it, they would all be in pieces.

Theo took a step toward Jules. "Sherry—"

"No!" She raised the gun another inch, keeping it aimed at Jules's chest. Looking grim, Theo stopped advancing on Sherry, his gaze shifting between Jules and the gun. She was having a hard time believing the whole situation was real. They'd been so close to safety, so close to being okay, but then Sherry had yanked the rug out from under them yet again. "I don't want to hear anything you have to say, Theo Bosco! If you hadn't been such a selfish prick, my dad would still be alive."

Flinching, as if her words had been one of the bullets from the gun, Theo went silent.

"You're going to pay now." Smiling, a vacant, eerie look in her eyes, Sherry slowly unzipped her rain jacket. "They heard you were in danger, so everyone came running. Otto, Hugh, your lieutenant, all the cops who have your back. Your *family*." She almost spit out the word. "Everyone's going to die. And it'll be your fault. Just like it was your fault my dad is dead."

Her jacket flapped open, revealing an odd vest strapped around her middle, wires linking cylindrical objects, each tucked in its own pocket. It looked like some kind of twisted fanny pack, but Jules knew right away what it was.

Sherry was wearing a bomb.

"Like it?" Slipping the gun into a pocket of her open jacket, Sherry turned slightly from side to side, as if modeling the explosives. "It was almost impossible to get Gordon to make it for me. He's developed a bit of a crush. Bailing him out of jail just made it worse. I finally convinced him by telling him it would be my plan B, just in case the other bomb failed. It is in a way. I meant for the first blast to bring everyone running to help, and then I would take all of your buddies out. This way is better, though. Now you know what your selfish actions have caused."

Jules sent a frantic glance at Theo. His face was an

expressionless mask, but she could almost see his mind
working, coming up with possible ways to save her.
The thought rang a discordant note. Why did he have
to keep saving her? Maybe it was Jules's turn to save
him this time. Viggy gave a low whine as he sat, his
attention locked on Sherry—and the bomb strapped to
her body. The sound made Sherry's gaze flicker from
Theo to the dog for a fraction of a second, and Jules
knew that was what she needed to do. She had to distract
Sherry long enough for Theo to act. Jules tried to come
up with a more specific plan, but her mind was racing,
her thoughts bouncing around like her brain was a tram-
poline. Still, she had to do *something*.

"It seems like you're the selfish one." Jules forced
out the shaky words. Despite her fear, she felt a tiny
ripple of pleasure at Sherry's startled expression.

"What?" she almost shrieked. "How can you say
that? I lost my dad because of him!"

"So you're going to kill all of these people, these good,
innocent cops, these *heroes*, to get back at Theo? For
something he couldn't have prevented?" The more she
talked, the less scared and more furious Jules got. "You're
going to take me away from my family, my brothers and
sister who depend on me? I'm the only parent they've
got!" By the time she finished, she was yelling.

"He needs to suffer!" There was no empathy, no guilt
in Sherry's expression. All that Jules could see was self-
righteous rage. "He needs to feel what I did!"

There were shouts at the end of the alley where the
entrance had been cordoned off. Otto and several officers Jules didn't recognize were running toward them,
until Sherry turned slightly toward the oncoming cops.

"Hold up!" Theo shouted, and the group skidded to a halt. "She's wearing a bomb!"

"Everyone back!" Otto shouted. "Back!"

"Showtime." Sherry smiled. It was her usual sweet and gentle smile, and that made it even more horrifying. Dramatically, she raised the hand holding the cell phone.

The rough—very rough—beginnings of a plan coalesced in Jules's mind. Although she didn't want to look away, she forced her gaze to focus over Sherry's shoulder. "Too bad that vest isn't going to work."

"What?" Sherry's smile faltered, her hand lowering slightly.

"Gordon gave you a dud." Forcing a mocking smile, Jules met Sherry's gaze. "The first bomb didn't go off. Why would you think this one will? Besides"—Jules nodded at something behind Sherry—"if Gordon thought the bomb was going to explode, would he be here right now?"

Sherry's entire body jerked in shock, and her hand holding the cell phone dropped to her side. She twisted around to look behind her. Jules started to launch herself forward. At that point, she wasn't sure what her plan entailed—maybe something fuzzy about tackling Sherry and muffling the blast with her body, but Theo's quiet command brought Jules to a stumbling halt.

"Viggy, hold."

In a flash of fawn and black, Viggy shot forward, latching his jaws around Sherry's right forearm. Yelping, she dropped the phone. As it skittered across the wet pavement, Theo rushed to grab it, and Viggy pulled Sherry to the ground.

"No!" Sherry yelled. "Viggy, stop! What are you doing? You're *our* dog!"

"Not anymore," Theo said, carefully placing the phone into his BDU pocket before heading for Sherry. "He's my partner now."

With a wordless scream of rage, Sherry twisted toward Viggy, snatching something from her pocket. *The gun!* Jules screamed in her head. She'd been so focused on the bomb that she'd forgotten about the gun.

"Don't shoot!" Theo shouted, sprinting toward Sherry and Viggy. It felt like the world slowed down as Jules realized Theo wasn't going to reach them in time. He was too far away.

The barrel was pointed at Viggy's vulnerable head as he kept his jaws closed around Sherry's arm. Jules lunged toward the pair, her gaze fixed on the handgun. She didn't think about getting shot or whether the bomb would detonate or anything except that Viggy was about to get shot, and she had to stop it. Her body plowed into Sherry's at the exact moment the gun fired with a cracking boom.

Just like after the barn exploded, everything went quiet. Dazed, Jules saw the gun spin away from them, skidding across the pavement. She ripped her gaze away from the gun just in time to see Sherry's fist swinging toward her face. There wasn't enough time to push away from Sherry or even to cover her face and protect herself. All she could do was watch as the fist got closer and closer. Cringing, she braced for the blow.

It never came. Opening her eyes, Jules saw that Theo was there, that he'd caught Sherry's arm before she could connect. His lips were moving, but Jules could hear only a roaring sound in her ears.

Viggy! The gun had gone off. Had Jules been too late to save him? Dreading to look, so terrified of what she'd see, she twisted her head to the side. Viggy was standing next to them, no bullet wound in sight, his tail wagging madly, his tongue lolling out in the happiest of doggy grins. A wave of utter relief crashed over Jules, and she burst into tears.

Suddenly the world snapped back into place, and Jules could hear again—Viggy barking excitedly and the distant sound of sirens and Theo snapping out orders to a silent Sherry. Theo hauled Jules to her feet and then reached for Sherry, who kicked out, catching Theo on the side of the leg. He staggered, stumbling into Jules and grabbing onto her arms to keep her from toppling over and bringing them both to the ground.

As they regained their balance, Sherry scrambled to her feet and ran toward the diner. Theo pivoted around to chase after her, but Viggy was there, eager to help, and Theo had to come to an abrupt halt to keep from plowing over the dog. By the time he'd disentangled himself from Viggy, Sherry had disappeared through the back door of the diner.

Theo spun around and sprinted back toward Jules, grabbing the end of Viggy's leash as he came. "Go! Go!"

It clicked then, clarity erasing the last traces of Jules's daze. Sherry was in the diner…with *two* bombs and nothing left to lose. Turning, Jules ran.

Within just a few strides, Theo caught up to her and grabbed her hand. She tried to speed up, but she was already sprinting as fast as she could go. The barriers marking the end of the alley and the beginning of the safe zone looked miles away, rather than just blocks.

"Go ahead!" Jules said between panting breaths. She'd never run so fast in her life, but she knew Theo's long legs could get him to safety much sooner if he wasn't keeping pace with her. "I'll be right behind you."

"I'm not leaving you." There was no give in his tone, no room for doubt, and Jules knew there was absolutely no chance of him leaving her side. Jules pushed her legs to move more quickly. Despite the terror and the uncertainty and the horribleness of everything that had happened, it helped having Theo and Viggy next to her, supporting her.

The orange-and-white barricades were visible up ahead, and she flew toward them, air sawing in and out of her lungs. Everything seemed too quiet. The only sounds were rough breathing and shoes slapping the pavement.

There was a *boom* that seemed to fill the entire space between her ears. The sound echoed through her body, so deep and loud that it took over everything. The early morning dimness suddenly turned incredibly bright, too bright, and the ground shook beneath them. Jules stumbled, almost going down to her knees. Theo used his grip on her hand to haul her upright, and they were running again. The barricades drew closer and closer, and then they were there, in front of her, and Jules had to stop abruptly so she didn't crash into them. A roaring cheer broke the silence as everyone waiting behind the barricades celebrated their little group's safe arrival.

Only then did she turn to look behind her. A tower of flame and black smoke had taken the place of the diner. As she watched, another explosion rocked the ground, and she flinched back, instinct making her cover her head with her arms. Debris rained down around the diner, the clatter and crashes barely audible over the roar of the fire. Shouts and curses and barking surrounded her, adding to the chaos, as a fresh plume of flame rose from the remains.

She'd just been in there. Theo and Viggy had just been in there.

The scene went a little hazy, and she swayed. Theo stepped in front of her, and she welcomed the sight of him. He was beautiful…and so *alive*. Ignoring the fire blackening the sky behind him, Jules gave him a wobbly smile. "I'm glad you're okay."

Although he didn't respond in words, his actions were clear enough. Wrapping his arms around her, he squeezed her tightly, lifting her feet off the ground and tucking his face against her neck. His heart was still beating fast. She could feel it where her chest was pressed against his, just like she felt his relieved exhale against the skin below her ear.

A hand dropped onto the back of her neck at the same time another one squeezed Theo's shoulder. Looking up, Jules saw that the hands belonged to Otto.

"Quit scaring us like that," Otto said.

"Bosco! You and Jules get over to Med to get checked out!" one of the cops ordered, an older man whose beaky nose and heavy eyebrows made Jules think of the eagle character on the Muppets.

Theo wrapped an arm around her shoulders and held her tightly against him as they walked toward an ambulance. It made moving a little awkward, but it was worth it to feel his warmth and strength. Different first responders darted around them, looking stressed but focused. There was a line of fire trucks at the barrier, the firefighters clustered around, waiting for the signal that it was safe to get closer. Steve, the firefighter who'd been so kind to Dee, lifted his hand in greeting. When she returned the wave, the cuff around her wrist gleamed.

"Ouch," Jules muttered. Now that the numbing adrenaline was wearing off, the throbbing in her wrists and hands was returning with a painful vengeance.

He glanced at the separated cuffs that still circled her wrists. "We'll get those off." As they reached the cluster of emergency vehicles just beyond the perimeter, Theo called out, "Hugh!"

Whirling around, Hugh crutched over to them quicker than Jules thought he could move. Dropping both crutches, he threw his arms around them, yanking them into a three-way hug. "Fuck! Don't ever scare me like that again."

There was a snort from Otto behind them. "You're sounding like our grandma again."

Theo thumped Hugh a few times on the back and then asked, "You still have your lock-picking skills?"

Surprise made Hugh draw away and then hop on his good leg to keep his balance. Otto offered the crutches he'd retrieved from the ground, and Hugh accepted with a grimace, fitting the padded portions under his arms. "Of course. Where do you want to break in? Can we do it tomorrow? I'm kind of done with drama today."

In answer, Theo ran a hand down Jules's arm so he could lift it and show the remains of the handcuffs. "Can't wait. Can you get these off?"

"Handcuffs are easy." Hugh leaned closer for a

better look, wincing in sympathy when he saw how they were digging into her wrists. "But why don't you just use a key?"

"I would," Theo answered, sounding crabby, "if I had a key to Rough Rider brand cuffs."

"Yo!" Otto shouted suddenly, making Jules jump and all the cops in the immediate area look in his direction. "Anyone have a Rough Rider handcuff key?"

The blank expressions on all the cops around them answered the question.

"Guess I'm picking them," Hugh sighed in mock-resignation, leaning on one crutch so he could dig in his pocket. "Come here, little sister."

Using one crutch and leaving the other one for Otto to retrieve—which he did with a long-suffering sigh, Hugh pulled Jules over to sit on the bumper of a fire truck. He waved away a couple of EMTs who were heading toward Jules with medical kits and purposeful strides. "You'll get her in a second. Let me get the shackles off first."

The Muppet eagle appeared next to them. "Bosco. A minute?" The question turned out to be more of an order, and he pulled a reluctant Theo out of earshot to talk. Theo kept shooting glances in Jules's direction, the eagle evidently not holding his attention.

"Oh! How's Norman Rounds?" The sight of the EMTs had reminded her, and the immediate mental image of his bloody, fallen body made bile rise in the back of her throat. "Is he...dead?"

"No," Hugh said. "He's in surgery now, but the doctors are pretty optimistic he'll pull through. He's a tough little bomb nut. What the hell happened in there?"

The idea of telling the story, of reliving every terrifying moment, made Jules start to shake. She opened her mouth to speak and then closed it again. If she tried to talk about Sherry or Norman or the gun or the bombs or Theo and Viggy almost getting killed, Jules knew the only thing that would come out would be howling sobs.

"Never mind," Hugh said hastily. He must've seen the signs of impending breakdown in her expression. "That can wait. Let me get these cuffs off."

Grateful for the reprieve, Jules held out a hand to Hugh.

"I thought you didn't like me," she said after swallowing several times. Her voice still sounded rusty. "And why do you carry a bobby pin around with you?"

"For my man bun," he said absently, working on the cuff around her right wrist. Jules glanced at his shaved head and frowned. "And it wasn't that I didn't like you. I just didn't trust you."

"Okay." Although that stung a little, Jules couldn't blame him. After all, she had committed multiple felonies. He was right not to trust her. "So what changed?"

"You brought my boy back to life." As the cuff clicked open, he met her eyes. "Don't screw him over. We're kind of related now, but that doesn't mean I can't make your life a living hell." He started fiddling with the lock on the second cuff.

"Kind of related?" she echoed, feeling dazed and wondering if this whole conversation was a product of her traumatized brain.

"Yep. You want Theo? Otto and I come with him. We're a package deal."

Next to them, Otto snorted a laugh. "Lucky you."

The idea warmed Jules, even as it terrified her. Not only was she opening her life to a cop, but, it appeared, to the entire K9 unit. Her attempts at staying away from law enforcement officers had failed dramatically. She didn't know if this would help keep her family safe or if it would bring their new lives crashing down.

"Yeah." Even she wasn't sure if her words were true—not yet. "Lucky me."

CHAPTER 22

THE SUN WAS JUST DROPPING BEHIND THE WESTERN mountain peaks when Theo came around the final curve of the rutted driveway and saw Jules on the porch steps. Dee and the two younger boys were running around the yard, playing some kind of game that seemed to be a mix of rugby, lacrosse, and freeze tag. They shouted hello to Theo and welcomed Viggy into their game.

Stopping a few feet from the bottom step, Theo paused, looking at Jules. The red-gold light of the sunset warmed her face and hair, and she smiled at him. It was as if she controlled something in him, and he *had* to smile back. Not that he fought it…at least anymore.

"Hi."

"Hey." Theo took the last few strides he needed before sitting next to her on the step. "How are you?"

"Okay, surprisingly," she said, leaning into him. "How about you?"

She still wasn't close enough for his liking. Theo wrapped an arm around her shoulders and pulled her in tight. "I've got another week of mandatory leave and a whole new round of critical incident debriefings, but I'll live." It felt good to say that. "Gordon Schwartz skipped bail. I don't think he'll come here, but stay alert. Call me if you notice something suspicious, have a bad feeling, notice anything off at all."

"I will," she promised, and then gave him a slow smile. "You could stay here, too, if you like. Keep a... personal eye on things."

He smiled back, feeling a surge of relief so intense it was almost painful. He'd almost lost her again.

Reaching up to the hand dangling over her shoulder, she caught his fingers in hers. "It's nice to have you here."

It was nice to be there, to feel the bite of fall in the air with Jules pressed close to his side, watching the kids and his K9 partner playing against the backdrop of the mountains. Theo realized that, for the first time in months, he was glad to be alive.

"Want to go see a movie tomorrow?" he asked, trying to play it off as casual even as his body tensed.

She stiffened, as well, turning to stare at him. "A date?"

"Yeah."

"A real date?"

"Uh..." He sent her a sideways look. "What's the other option? A fake date?"

Her laugh had a sharp edge to it. "I don't know."

"When I saw your SUV, and I knew you were in the diner..." He blew out a harsh breath as the remembered fear flooded through him. "I've never been so scared. Ever."

Her fingers tightened around his.

"If something had happened to you, I would've been so pissed at myself for all the time I wasted. I should've asked you out that first time I saw you at the diner." He stared at Viggy, who was dancing circles around the laughing kids, before meeting Jules's eyes. "I don't want to waste any more time. I love you. I want to be with you."

"I love you, too. And I want to be with you, more than anything. It's just..." She paused before words burst from her. "I can't tell you everything."

"You mean about your past." It was a statement, not a question.

"Yes." Shifting around so she faced forward, she leaned against him again. "I can't."

"Because of them." Again, it wasn't a question. He gestured with his free hand to the playing kids.

She was quiet for so long that he didn't think she was going to say anything, but then she admitted, "Yes."

It was his turn to be silent for a moment. "Okay."

"Really?" She swung around again to stare at him, and he smiled.

"I know you're a good person, Jules," he said. And he did. As much as it went against his nature not to ask questions, not to snoop and grill and do whatever it took to find out the truth, he believed she was doing what she felt was right. He didn't have to hear the details to know that was true. "Whatever happened, I'm sure you did the right thing."

"I did." Her body softened into his. "Thank you. I know you don't know the specifics, but it's still good to hear."

Sam came into view as he rode a beat-up bike around the final curve of the driveway. Although he slowed when he spotted them, he kept his bike pointed toward the porch. When he got close, he climbed off and walked the bike to the bottom of the steps. He stood there quietly for a minute, his eyes on Theo.

"I g-got the j-j-job," he said finally.

"So I heard." Theo tried to keep his voice gentle. It wasn't a natural thing for him, since he generally sounded a little gruff, but something about Sam made it easy to be kind. "Congratulations. Nan said you're a natural with the dogs."

Sam's smile was so quick, Theo would've missed it if he'd blinked at the wrong time. Next to him, he felt, more than heard, Jules's inhale. Theo guessed it was her happy reaction to her brother's rare smile.

"Of course he is," she said, almost able to cover the choked note in her voice. "Sam's awesome in all ways."

Although he rolled his eyes at his sister, he looked even more pleased. "Th-thank you," he said to Theo.

Theo waved off his thanks. "All I did was give you the number. You got the job, and it'll be up to you to keep it."

"I kn-know." He turned his head toward his younger siblings, who were calling for him to join them. "B-b-but th-thank you anyw-way."

"You're welcome." He watched as Sam propped his bike against the porch and then jogged over to join the other kids.

"Is it strange," Jules asked quietly, "that when you're sweet to my sister or brothers, it makes me want to drag you to my room and have my wild way with you?"

That startled a laugh out of him, one he cut off quickly. It still felt odd to be happy. "I don't know if it's strange, but you can drag me to your room anytime."

Snuggling closer, she gave a melodramatic sigh. "I suppose we should wait until the kids are sleeping."

"Probably a good idea." Now that she'd mentioned it, though, it was all he could think about.

They sat there quietly for a few moments. "Want to join them?" Jules asked, nodding toward the kids.

"In their game, you mean?" It hadn't even occurred to him. It'd been a long time since he'd played any sort of game.

"Sure." Standing, she grabbed both of his hands and dragged him to his feet. "Let's go. It'll be fun."

"Okay." He didn't think he could deny her anything. In this, he didn't think he wanted to. They walked toward the kids and Viggy. "What are the rules?"

She laughed, making him want to kiss her. "We kind of make them up as we go along." With that, she ran over to Dee, scooping her up and twirling her around, making her shriek with laughter.

"Heads up!" Ty threw the ball to him, and Theo caught it. Turning, he tossed it to Tio, who took off for the big evergreen that was apparently some kind of goal or home base or end zone. Everyone tore after him, and Theo joined them.

For Jules, for this family, for once in his life, he could do it. He could make up the rules as he went along.

EPILOGUE

THE PHONE VIBRATED UNDER HER PILLOW, AND JULES grabbed it and accepted the call before it could wake Theo. He shifted as she slid out of bed, and she glanced at him, smiling. It felt right to have him there next to her. She slipped out of the room and hurried downstairs, closing herself in the bathroom before she said a word.

"Hello?" Her voice shook. Only a few people had her number, and five of them were sleeping upstairs.

"Ms. Jackson." The sound of Mr. Espina's voice saying her name—her *new* name, the one he shouldn't even know—jarred her. Jules reached out and put a hand against the wall to steady herself.

"What are...how...?" She was having a hard time getting enough air needed to talk. Why was he calling? Did Courtney know where they were? Was he going to warn her that they needed to run? Her heart collapsed at the idea. She'd just gotten Theo; she didn't want to lose him. "Does she know?"

"No." Mr. Espina's answer made her muscles weaken in relief, and she sagged against the door. "Her investigator is following up a lead in Dallas."

Something about the way he said it made Jules certain he'd been the one to plant that false trail, and she let out a relieved huff of air. *God bless Mr. Espina.*

"You'll have a visitor tomorrow."

Jules blinked. That was not expected. "Who?"

"Grace Robinson."

That told her nothing. "Who is she?"

"She needs a place to stay."

Her brain racing, Jules tried to comprehend what he was telling her—and what he was not telling her. This Grace must be on the run, and Mr. Espina was sending her to Monroe, to Jules's house, to Jules's *family's* house. "Is she dangerous? Is someone after her? The kids—"

"She won't hurt any of you."

Jules noted that he didn't comment on whether the person after Grace Robinson would be a danger. "I don't think—"

"I'm calling in a favor," he interrupted.

Jules closed her eyes, leaning more heavily against the door. He'd kept her stepmother from calling the police, plus he was leading her private investigator away from them. He also knew how to find them. Really, she had no choice. "How long will she be staying?"

"As long as she needs to."

"Okay," she sighed, resigned. How was she going to explain to Theo that a strange woman would be living with them for an undetermined amount of time? "What time will she be arriving?"

There was no answer.

"Mr. Espina?"

He'd already ended the call.

SPECIAL BONUS!

Have you ever read a fabulous book and thought to yourself: I wish there was more?

Well, you're in luck! There were so many interesting characters and scenes to explore in *Run to Ground* that whole chapters found their way to the cutting room floor. Usually that material would never see the light of day, but we've polished it up and included it here for you...that little bit more to whet your appetite as you wait for book 2 in the Rocky Mountain K9 Unit series.

Here's how it works. Each bonus scene will be clearly marked with a page number. Simply flip back to that page to reorient yourself with what is happening at that point in the book. Then read the scene that was originally intended to come next. There's so much to love in these scenes, and we're so excited to be able to bring you this very special extended edition of *Run to Ground*.

You wanted more Katie Ruggle? Well, who said wishes didn't come true...

EXCERPT #1
Page 7

Juliet Young knew the exact moment she decided to commit a felony. It was when her sixteen-year-old, six-foot-two, two-hundred-pound jock of a brother cried.

"Oh, Sam…"

"J-J-Juju…" His stutter hadn't been this bad since he was thirteen. It killed her that they were talking on the phone and she couldn't hug him—not that he'd probably want to be hugged. "Puh-puh…" His inhale shook with tears. "Please!"

Resting her forehead on her kitchen table, she felt all the despair and hopelessness and frustration that had swamped her after talking with her lawyer consolidate into a hard ball of resolve. She sat up straight. "New plan, Sam-I-Am."

"Wh-wh-wh…" When he couldn't manage the word, he just went quiet, waiting for her to tell him.

Now that she'd decided to do it, to break her life-long law-abiding streak, Jules felt strong again. No wonder people became criminals. "The lawyer said that, with the FBI investigation and without my CPA license, it's unlikely I'll get custody. The money's almost gone, and I'll need a really good, really expensive attorney to even have a chance at winning y'all."

His intake of breath was audible. "I-I-I-I c-c-can't *stand* i-it anym-more, Ju."

"I know. That's why we're going with plan…heck, I don't even know what letter we're on anymore. Probably triple-Y or something."

His laugh was just a short huff of sound, but it still made Jules smile.

"I'm calling the mob."

EXCERPT #2
Page 17

She was only five minutes late when she leaned against the stegosaurus, gasping for air. If she'd known that going on the run was going to be so literal, she would've started jogging a while ago. More comfortable shoes wouldn't have hurt, either. Jules scowled down at her pumps. "Practical, my sweaty butt."

Once she was able to concentrate on something other than sucking in precious oxygen, she scanned the crowd for Dennis. The dinosaurs were scattered through the playground equipment, and the place was packed with the eight-and-under crowd. Once she'd dismissed the too-young-to-forge and the old-enough-to-forge-but-appeared-to-be-female individuals, she was left with two possibilities: a blond thirtysomething leaning against a tree, messing with his cell phone, and a slender, dark-haired man sitting on a bench, holding a baby in his lap.

Picking the more likely of the two, she started to make her way toward the guy with the cell phone, but the other man waved at her with the hand not securing the baby. Startled, she stopped and gave him an "Are you sure?" look, to which he responded with a firm nod. Either Dennis was the one with the baby, or this man was a client she didn't recognize. He didn't look familiar, and Jules was fairly sure she would've remembered his striking, vaguely Asian features and almost-colorless blue eyes.

"Dennis?" she asked when she got close enough to keep her voice low.

In response, he buckled the baby into a stroller that butted up against the side of the bench. "Ready to walk?"

Unsure of whether the question had been directed at her or the baby, Jules answered, "Sure." Her feet would've preferred some bench time, but the area was crowded with too many would-be eavesdroppers. She mentally told her feet to suck it up and quit whining.

The baby secured, Dennis pushed the stroller briskly along the asphalt path. "Beautiful day."

The back of Jules's blouse was soaking wet from perspiration. If her shirt hadn't been white, she would've left her stifling suit jacket in the car, but she figured that flashing her new-identity-maker would be inappropriate—or at least misleading. "Uh…sure."

They reached the turn where the path began to circle a swampy pond. "So, which Mr. Espina gave you my number—Luis or Mateo?"

"Um…Mateo." She was happy to let him lead the conversation. Now that she was here, Jules wasn't sure how to go about asking for illegal goods and services.

The baby tossed a plastic ring onto the path. Without losing a step, Dennis scooped up the discarded toy and tucked it into the diaper bag lodged in the back of the stroller. "How do you know my boss?"

Jules hesitated. Was this a test of her secret-keeping abilities? When Dennis just glanced at her, his expression mild, she mentally shrugged. There was no harm in his knowing. "I am—*was*—his brother's accountant."

His unexpected laugh made her jump. "I bet that was…challenging."

That, she knew not to answer directly. Instead, she hummed noncommittally. "Can you help me?"

"Depends."

An approaching jogger smiled into the stroller. "Beautiful baby," she said as she passed, her voice obnoxiously not at all breathless. Jules scowled, thinking of her one-block, panting sprint from the parking lot to the dinosaurs, before pulling her focus back to the man next to her.

"Depends on what?"

"What it is that you need."

Glancing around, Jules didn't see anyone within earshot, but she still leaned toward Dennis and lowered her voice. "New birth certificates and social security numbers for me and my four siblings, and a place to live a long ways away from here."

His eyebrows shot up as he stared at her. "Five of you?"

She nodded.

"That will be expensive."

Jules had been afraid of that. "I have some money." She could say that only thanks to the twenty thousand dollars Mr. Espina had handed to her like it'd been a dime. Every penny of her own had gone to her get-the-kids-away-from-the-witch fund, leaving her with an apartment only slightly bigger than a refrigerator box and minimal groceries. The lawyers had eaten all of her savings, and her clenching gut thought that Mr. Espina's gift probably wasn't enough for Dennis's services. "How much?"

"Ten apiece."

Feeling like he'd punched her in the midsection, she choked for breath. Her knees went wobbly, and she had to force them to stiffen enough to hold her. "Fifty..." She couldn't even finish saying the amount. It was too staggering, too...heartbreaking.

Once the initial shock had passed and her lungs started working again, she searched her brain for a solution. Every problem had a fix. It wasn't helpful to just despair that she didn't have the money.

"Can I do payments?" She was proud that her voice was only a little wobbly.

His expression was unreadable, but Jules took slight comfort in the fact that he hadn't immediately turned her down. She could figure out how she'd be able to make money while hiding after she solved the immediate problem.

"I don't do payment plans," he finally said, grinding a casual heel into her newly blossoming hope. "But we might be able to figure out a trade."

Trade? Even though Dennis was wheeling his baby around the park and looked about as un-lustful as any man possibly could, her brain immediately went *there*.

"What kind of trade?" Her voice was flat and thick with suspicion. There were a lot of things she'd do for her siblings, but that was not one of them. If that was Dennis's offer, she'd figure out another way to get what she needed to steal the kids.

"Not what you're thinking." Instead of sounding offended, amusement crept into his tone. "Not that you aren't pretty and all"—his wave indicating her form was dismissive—"but this little one takes all of my extra energy. Right now, a hookup just sounds exhausting."

"Okay." She believed he was being sincere, but he still hadn't named his price—his nonmonetary price, at least. "So what would I need to do?"

"Mr. Espina has me do *this*"—he tipped his head toward her in a gesture that Jules interpreted as the whole disappearance-assistance thing—"a lot. Sometimes, his clients need a temporary place to stay for a few weeks until I can arrange something more permanent. Once I set you up with a safe new home, I'd like to send the occasional traveler in your direction."

Jules considered this. It was much more reasonable than what her overactive imagination had been conjuring—so reasonable, in fact, that it made her suspicion flare even higher. "We'd just have to let someone live with us for a few weeks?"

"Exactly."

"No criminals or anyone dangerous?"

"No dangerous criminals."

Not missing his careful wording, she narrowed her eyes at his impassive face. It was true that, if all went to plan, she'd be a felon herself shortly, so it wasn't fair to judge others for their possibly justified crimes. He'd covered the "dangerous" part, and that was the most important. "How long would we need to keep the vacancy sign up?"

His shoulders raised in a shrug. "Indefinitely." He straightened the collar of his polo shirt, as if concerned that it had been mussed by the gesture. "I won't abuse the privilege, however. Only one visitor at a time, and no more than…let's say four a year."

Even if the person staying with them was obnoxious and left hair in the shower and empty milk cartons in the fridge, the strangers' invasions would be temporary and infrequent. If it meant her brothers' and sister's freedom, then she could put up with Attila the Hun as a houseguest for a while.

"This would cover the whole fee?"

With a strangled cough, Dennis said, "Half."

That still wasn't possible. "Three-quarters."

"Two-thirds, and I throw in a vehicle."

"Three-quarters." She could squeak by paying a third, but she'd rather have as much start-up cash as she could keep. "I have a car."

"Registered to your name?"

Feeling stupid, she tightened her lips. "Three-quarters, we get an SUV and you get my Camry." At least, this way, the five of them wouldn't be jammed into her Camry the entire way to…wherever they were headed.

Lifting his right hand off the stroller handle, he offered it to Jules. "Deal. This is what I'll need from you…"

EXCERPT #3
Page 55

Five Days Earlier

They'd been on the road for an hour before she broke the bad news.

"We can't stop until we reach the car-switch point in Georgia." When none of her siblings made any concerned sounds, she added, "It'll be another five hours." There was still no reaction. "I brought snacks and water, but no stopping means no bathroom breaks."

"We'll be fine," Ty responded for all of them.

"Dez?" Jules couldn't believe that everyone in the family had an iron bladder.

"I'm used to holding it when I have to go," Dez said, sounding distracted. A glance in the rearview showed that she and Ty were playing some kind of writing game, probably tic-tac-toe.

That was weird. "Why?"

"Why what?"

"Why are you used to holding it?"

Dez's round blue eyes met hers in the mirror for a second before Jules had to look back at the road. "It takes too long to use the bathroom in a pageant dress. I get to go before and after, but not during."

Filing that away as reason number five thousand and seven why kidnapping was, for certain families, a good thing, Jules said, "After we get to the car-swap spot, Dezzie, you can pee whenever you want to pee, okay?"

"Hey!" Ty yelped. "Let's not get crazy. You're not in the backseat with her."

Dez giggled.

"Will you miss doing the pageants, D?" Jules was suddenly hit by the realization that the kids' lifestyles were going to change dramatically. They'd be scrounging for the basics—food, utilities, clothing—and extras would be impossible, at least at first.

"No." Dez's voice was flat.

"Good." There was one concern erased. Unfortunately, a whole new batch swarmed in to take its place.

As she followed the directions to the location Dennis had referred to as simply "Billy's," the knot in her stomach, which had loosened a tiny bit when they'd crossed the Florida state line, drew tight again. The industrial area was just outside of Atlanta, and it was a maze of warehouses, each one looking more desolate than the one before. Jules was glad it was three in the afternoon, because she would hate to be wandering around there after dark.

"What's next, Sam?"

"L-left. At Hawth-th-thorne." He held his fingertip on their current line of direction. It was strange using written instructions instead of GPS. Jules kind of missed the robotic voice telling her when they were approaching a turn. With the old-fashioned way, they actually had to look for street signs.

"There!" Tio spotted it first. Despite their earlier unconcern about driving for six straight hours, Jules knew they were all very ready to be out of the car for a while. She turned onto Hawthorne Street.

"G-g-go three-quarters of a m-m-m..." Sam gave a huff and tried again. "M-*mile*. It'll b-be on the right."

"Got it." She glanced at the trip odometer so she could measure when three-quarters of a mile had passed. "Is there an address?"

"N-no."

Of course not. Why make it easy? "Does he describe the building at all?"

"Buh-rick w-w-warehouse."

She snorted, sending Sam a sideways look. "To distinguish it from all the other brick warehouses?"

Although he just shrugged, his mouth curled up in a reluctant smile.

"Are we close?" Ty asked, jiggling his knee up and down. Jules wasn't sure if he needed a bathroom or just to run off excess energy, then figured it was probably both.

"Two-tenths of a mile to go. Keep an eye out for it."

Despite her earlier sarcasm, Jules picked out the correct warehouse easily, as did the three spotters in the back. Tio had finished his book an hour earlier, and he was anxious to retrieve another from his backpack as soon as they could stop. His knee was bouncing as much as his twin's.

She pulled up to an oversized overhead door that looked like a semi could fit through it, and Sam jumped out. As he jogged over to the keypad, Ty opened his door as if to follow.

"Stay!" Jules snapped, her head whipping around in true *Exorcist* fashion. "Everyone else stays in the car until we're inside."

Although he groaned, Ty pulled his door closed again.

"It'll be ten more seconds." The overhead door started to rise, and Jules kept a sharp eye on Sam as he jogged back to the car. "I think you'll live."

No one appeared in the opening as the door continued to lift. Heart thudding in her throat, Jules eased the car forward as soon as there was room for it to fit. She tried to relax and trust that Dennis wouldn't have sent them into a dangerous situation. Even though she didn't know the man well—or at all, really—it seemed like killing off his boss's clients would be a poor business move. It would definitely cut down on word-of-mouth referrals.

Once the car was through the doorway, she stopped to allow her eyes to adjust to the dim interior. It looked like a mechanic shop merged with a beauty salon had decided to have a garage sale. Most of the space was taken up with standard equipment needed to work on cars, but there were racks of clothing against the far wall, as well as a table covered by several filled boxes. They were in too much shadow to make out the contents from Jules's spot in her Camry. A hairdresser's chair sat next to two shampooing sinks.

A bearded man in light-blue coveralls stepped out from behind a green Pathfinder and made his way over to her door. Taking a deep breath, she lowered her window and turned off the car. As he got closer, he also got bigger. His hair was brown and pulled back into a low ponytail, and his beard matched his hair except for a stripe of gray that ran through the middle.

"Julie Jackson?" he asked in a raspy drawl.

She almost didn't recognize her new alias, but she caught herself in time and nodded. Her siblings sat as still and quiet as statues.

"I'm Billy." Sticking out a grease-lined hand for her to shake, he grinned. It was wide, friendly, and made Jules's held breath leave her in a relieved rush. She accepted his hand and shook it.

"Nice to meet you." Once he'd withdrawn his hand, she opened the door a crack. Taking the hint, he stepped back so she could get out of the car. "Is there a bathroom here?"

"Everyone always asks for that first." Chuckling, Billy pointed to a pair of doors next to the clothing racks. "There're two. Have at 'em."

The three in the backseat scrambled out and rushed for the bathrooms. Ty made it there first, and Tio hung back so Dez had first crack at the other one. Although Sam climbed out of the car, he circled around the front to stand next to Jules instead of joining the stampede to the bathrooms.

"Man of the house, huh?" Billy slapped him on the upper arm. Jules eyed her brother with concern, but he didn't react to the contact except for tensing slightly. "Good for you, watching out for your sister. While you're waiting, you can pick out your new look." Looking comically like a game-show hostess, he gestured toward the wall of clothes.

"New look?" Jules headed toward the clothes and saw that the boxes covering the large table were filled with hair dye, cosmetics, wigs, glasses, and even fake facial hair, which made her laugh. "This is perfect for you." She held up a blond mustache for Sam to see.

He snorted. "Right."

"The guys will probably do fine going boot-camp style," Billy said, having followed them. "You and the little lady should probably change colors, as well as chop off some of that." He eyed Jules's light-brown hair, which fell to her lower back. "It's pretty distinctive."

"Sure," Jules said, even as she felt a slight pang at the thought. She hadn't had short hair since she was a chubby seventh grader. In eighth grade, she'd lost weight and grown out her hair, and she still associated cropped hair with the pudgy little girl she'd been.

"Great!" Billy clapped his hands together, connecting with a sharp sound that made Jules jump. "Let's get cracking."

EXCERPT #4
Page 70

Four Days Earlier

Jules had never been so tired. It made it worse that she was trying to minimize bathroom stops, so she couldn't suck down excessive amounts of coffee or Diet Coke to keep herself caffeinated. Her eyes kept moving to the dashboard clock, which only made time go more slowly. It was a few minutes before four a.m. central time, and she'd been driving for almost twenty hours.

The rest of the Pathfinder's occupants were sleeping, which filled Jules with an odd mixture of proud satisfaction and boredom. She was tempted to poke Sam, just so he'd wake up and she'd have someone to talk to.

"Bad sister," she muttered under her breath. "Let sleeping siblings lie."

It didn't help that Kansas was freaking *dull*. The other states hadn't been much better, but at least she'd had adrenaline and sunshine to help her through. Now that she was exhausted, having only the tunnel her headlights created on the mostly empty interstate made staying awake a form of torture.

"Eight more hours." She glanced at the clock again. "*Less* than eight hours. Seven hours and some minutes." "Some" sounded better than "fifty-eight." It probably wouldn't be exactly eleven a.m. when they arrived, but it helped to have a countdown.

"You ok-kay?"

Sam's voice was low, but it still made her jump. After the initial shock, she welcomed the buzz of adrenaline. It might give her an extra ten minutes of being fully awake. "Hey, Sam. Did my muttering wake you?"

She saw his shrug in her peripheral vision. "Not r-r-really sleeping, juh-ust in and out."

"Do you mind staying up and talking to me, then?" She sent him a grin. "I'm fading a little here. It'd really suck if I fell asleep and killed us all in the last hours of the drive."

"Sure."

When he went quiet, Jules smothered a smile. Apparently, he was going to do more listening than talking. She was fine with it, though. That was just Sam.

"I was worried about Tio at first," she said quietly after a snore from the backseat caught her attention. "He hates change so much, but he seems to be adjusting okay?" She raised the end of the sentence into a question, hoping Sam would share his opinion.

"T's f-fine," Sam said harshly, although Jules was pretty sure the rough edge of his words wasn't directed at Tio. "He knew w-we had to g-g-g…to leave. Sh-sh-she'd st-started l-l-l-looking at T-Ty."

Her stomach churned, and Jules breathed through her nose, worried for a few moments that she was going to have to pull the SUV over so she could throw up on the shoulder. Swallowing several times, she choked down the need to vomit.

Sam apparently mistook her silence for accusation. "I-I tr-tr-tried, J-Ju! I tr-tried to prot-t-tect th-th-th…" His voice got louder until he cut off his attempt at the final word with a frustrated exhale. In just the dim glow of the dashboard lights, she could see his fists had clenched around handfuls of his jeans just above the knees.

"Shh." Reaching over, she covered one of his tense hands with her own. "I know, Sam-I-Am. You went above and beyond for them, and they know it, too. That's done, though. Our life with her is over, and we get to start fresh."

His hand didn't relax beneath hers, but he didn't pull away.

"What's something you're looking forward to doing in our new Monroe, Colorado, life?" she asked, trying to lighten her voice to keep it from shaking.

His silence went on long enough that she figured he wasn't going to answer. Just as she opened her mouth to change the subject, he said, "L-learn to drive. C-Courtney wuh-ouldn't sign the p-perm-m-mission f-f-form."

Giving his fist a final squeeze, she returned her hand to the wheel. "We'll make sure you're enrolled in driver's ed at your new school. It's only the second week of classes, so I doubt you've missed much. Probably just the 'driving is a privilege' lectures." She sent him an amused glance. "Besides, you already know how to start a car, back it out of a space, and drive it across a parking lot."

"Everyth-thing e-except p-p-parking." A hint of a smile touched his mouth.

"Eh." Jules waved off that small detail. "You're probably still way ahead of the other students. None of them have actually driven a getaway car."

His laugh was husky and so, so precious.

EXCERPT #5
Page 84

Present Day

"You're taking Viggy home with you." Hugh held the end of the lead toward Theo.

He couldn't seem to bring himself to grab it. Instead, he glowered at Hugh, keeping his eyes off the dog half-hidden behind the other man's legs. Theo had just left Lieutenant Blessard's office, where he'd endured a half hour of getting his ass chewed, and he wasn't in the mood for playing nice with Hugh. It'd been an endlessly long day, and there was nothing left inside him to give to Viggy.

Hugh kept the leash end extended. "This isn't working. It's been two months, and neither of you has gotten better. In fact, I think you're both *worse*. From now on, where you go, Vig goes."

Having the dog with him constantly would mean there'd be no escape from the guilt. Theo's molars ground together as he considered his fellow cop, who was wearing his stubborn expression. Even though he was normally an easygoing guy, once Hugh dug in his heels, there was no budging him. With a grumbling exhale, Theo held out his hand.

"Good!" Hugh grinned as he slapped the end of the lead onto Theo's outstretched palm. "Knew you'd see the light."

Instead of answering, Theo just made another disgruntled sound as he forced himself to look at the dog.

Blessard had been right about one thing. The cowering animal attempting to hide behind Hugh bore little resemblance to the confident, talented Viggy he'd been when Don was alive.

People probably said something similar about him. He knew he'd changed dramatically since the day he'd learned Don had eaten his service weapon. He just didn't know how to return to his old self—or if that Theo had died along with Don.

"Why don't you swing by the old Garmitt place on your way home?" Hugh's suggestion pulled Theo from his morbid thoughts. "Otto saw some people going inside when he passed by there earlier this week. He would've checked it out himself, but he was headed to a call."

Theo grunted. He knew exactly who'd moved into that house—the new waitress, although he had no idea why she'd thought it was a good idea to live there. It had been sitting empty for as long as Theo had been in Monroe—over five years. A few months earlier, the gossip around town was that some guy from out of state had bought the place, and everyone assumed it would eventually be torn down and replaced by vacation condos. As far as Theo knew, the new owner hadn't done anything to fix up the place, nor had he made any move to demolish it. Theo was tempted to stop, to seize on the excuse to see the squirrelly waitress again, but that spark of interest was the reason he had to shut it down quickly.

"Be a police ambassador." With a grin, Hugh casually began to walk in the direction of Theo's aging Blazer. Viggy stayed close, not wanting to lose his hiding spot apparently, and Theo was towed along behind. "Stop by there. Welcome your new neighbors and find out what their story is at the same time."

Despite his foul mood, Theo couldn't restrain a huff of laughter. "You want me to get the gossip."

"Sure." Hugh's smile didn't falter at all. "Nothing wrong with being informed. Call me when you leave there."

"No." Opening the back hatch of his SUV, Theo tried to keep his expression severe. Damn Hugh for always cheering him up when he just wanted to wallow in his misery. "Viggy, load."

Hugh positioned his hip closer to the opening before giving the bumper a pat. "C'mon, Vig," he crooned in the voice he reserved for furry creatures. "Up you go."

As Theo watched, torn between frustration and pity, Viggy jumped into the rear compartment of the Blazer and immediately pressed his body against the back of the seat.

"He's such a mess."

"Yeah." When Theo glanced over, Hugh was looking at him instead of the dog. "He is. He'll get better, though."

With a skeptical snort, Theo slammed the hatch door with a little too much force.

EXCERPT #6
Page 92

Four Days Earlier

A new life was expensive. Jules had been living on

her own for five years, so she should've been aware of this, but trying to buy all the necessities for five people in a couple of hours was bringing her very close to a panic attack.

As she handed a ridiculous amount of money to the clerk at the sporting goods store, after spending an *insane* amount of money at the furniture store—only to find that everything couldn't be delivered until next week—she mentally thanked Mr. Espina for his contribution. They were bleeding money, but a week sleeping on bare wood floors would've been torture almost as severe as something Courtney could've dreamed up.

"We st-still n-n-need kitch-chen st-st-st…th-things." Sam's voice was tight, as if one more shopping stop was going to send Jules over the edge, making her shove them all back in the SUV and drive them back to Courtney.

"I know." Her smile was forced, but it was the best she could do. For all her years of being an adult, she'd scrimped and saved. Spending all this money in one go was almost painful, when her instinct was to squirrel it away. "I saw a thrift store a few doors down. Let's haul this stuff back to the SUV, and then we'll see what they have for dishes and pans and things."

All four of her siblings nodded solemnly and picked up the sleeping bags and air mattresses they'd just bought. Their quiet obedience made her think that Sam wasn't the only one worried about Jules changing her mind about keeping them.

As they crammed their purchases into the SUV, Jules felt the back of her neck prickling. She tried to resist the urge to look behind her, telling herself that it was just paranoia making her feel watched, but she had to turn. There were people scattered all around Monroe's quaint downtown, from the older man sweeping the sidewalk in front of the leather repair and tack shop to the couple leaving the diner. Her throat tightened when she noticed a squad car parked on the street. Jules squinted, trying to see if a cop was inside it, but the sun reflecting off the windshield hid any possible occupants.

The prickle of awareness turned into the burn of multiple malicious gazes, and a wave of dizziness hit Jules. She pressed a hand against the side of the SUV until her vision righted itself again.

"Y-you ok-k-kay, JuJu?"

"Sure." She needed to stop with the crazy. There was no way Courtney could have found them, not this soon. They were safe—for now. "Just starving. Are y'all hungry?"

Their enthusiastic, affirmative chorus sent a wave of guilt through her. If she was going to be their only parental figure, she needed to step up and do a better job of it. Feeding them was important. *Mothering Rule Number One: Don't starve the children, Jules.* Swallowing a punchy laugh, she closed the SUV hatch door and waved toward the diner. "Let's eat, then!"

The bell on the diner door sounded harsh and loud to Jules, and she tried to hide her flinch. A quick look around the crowded diner showed that no one was paying any attention to them, though, and she allowed her shoulders to drop from their current position around her ears.

"Sit anywhere!" a woman hollered from the far side of the dining area, where she was setting plates in front of a family with a couple of kids in booster seats and one in a high chair. "Anywhere you can find, at least."

A scan of the diner showed no empty tables, except for a couple of spots at the high counter facing the kitchen. The bell clanged again, and Jules turned to see more people file in behind them. Just as Jules resigned herself to waiting and watching her siblings' hungry expressions every time a tray of food passed by, a group of guys stood and shuffled out of a booth toward the back.

"There!" she whispered. From the corner of her eye, she saw the group of newcomers behind her shift in the direction of the vacated table.

"We're on it," Ty said, and he and Tio hurried toward the booth, sliding into the seat just before the other group reached it.

"Nice save." Jules slid into the booth, holding her hand toward Tio and then Ty for a discreet slap of congratulations. "Lunch is apparently a competitive sport in Monroe. Good to know."

"I'm glad we don't have to wait," Dez said from where she'd wedged herself between Sam and Jules. "I'm starving."

Glancing around the table, Jules frowned. "Y'all need to tell me things. If you need something, let me know. If you're hungry, speak up, and I'll feed you."

"Y-you've sp-p-pent a lot of m-money on us already," Sam said, glaring at the carousel of jams on the table.

Jules eyed his profile, trying to figure out the direction of his thoughts. "It's all stuff we need. Getting set up will be the most expensive part, and then things will get better. I'll get a job, too." She wasn't quite sure what job she'd be able to get, though. Although Dennis had provided her with a shiny new social security number, Jules didn't really want to test it out on a W-3 form. Also, she wouldn't be able to put down any references, or a job history, or her schooling, or anything. Who'd want to hire someone without a past?

"M-m-me too."

Jules, pulled out of her worried job-seeking thoughts, glanced at Sam, surprised. "You don't need to work. School's your job right now."

He set his jaw in the way he did when he'd decided on something. Once she saw his expression, Jules threw up her hands. Sam's stubborn streak rivaled her own.

"Fine. Get a job." She put on her most determined face. "But no more than ten hours a week."

After a long moment, he dipped his chin slightly.

"We'll work, too," Ty declared, and Jules turned her stern expression toward the twins.

"Not until you're sixteen."

Instead of responding, Ty and Tio looked at each other, speaking silently in that way they'd done since they'd been toddlers.

Jules narrowed her eyes at them. "No jobs for you."

After a moment, Ty met her gaze and smiled innocently. "Okay. We won't get jobs."

She didn't trust that for a minute. Before she could dig deeper into the twins' plan, though, Dez piped up. "I want to work, too."

"Dezzy, no." Jules resisted the urge to bang her head against the table. "You're a kid. Kids don't work. They play, and have fun, and go to school. I want that for you."

"I'll do something fun, then." Her thoughtful frown turned into a smile. "I'll walk people's dogs. That'll be fun."

Before Jules could respond, the server was at their table. Her curly red hair was poking out in all directions, and her heavily tanned face looked harassed as she handed them each a menu. "Sorry for the wait. It's a zoo in here today, and one of my servers ran off with one of the dishwashers a couple of days ago. Anyway, you don't care about that. Did you want anything to drink?"

A sudden idea popped into Jules's head. "I'm actually looking for a job."

The server gave her a sharp look. "Any experience waitressing?"

"No." The interest in the woman's face faded, and Jules cursed herself for not lying. She had a new life now. Why couldn't she have waitressed in her past? Quickly, though, she dismissed that idea. Her inexperience would've been obvious in her first five minutes of work. It was better to save the lies for those things not so easily proven false. "You wouldn't have to pay me, though. I could work for tips."

As the server eyed her speculatively, Jules held her breath. That would solve the social-security-number issue, as well as bring in some much-needed cash.

"Trial period only. You screw up, and you're out. Quietly. No tantrum. Got it?"

Resisting the urge to bounce on the seat in excitement, Jules tried to keep her voice calm. "Got it. When do you want me to start?"

"Tomorrow. Be here at five." She started to turn away.

"In the morning?" Jules's voice squeaked the tiniest bit. She'd never been a morning person.

"Yep." The server stopped and looked back over her shoulder. "That a problem?"

It was a small price to pay for a job that kept her off the map. "Nope. I'm Jules, by the way."

"Megan. Don't mess this up." Without another backward glance, she headed for the next table.

"I won't." Turning back to her siblings, she shared an excited grin with them. She couldn't resist a little wiggle of excitement, as well.

A job! She already had a job. Their brand-new life was looking up.

Read on for a sneak peek of the next book in the Rocky Mountain K9 Unit series from Katie Ruggle

ON THE CHASE

"I don't trust him."

Kaylee stared at her friend—her apparently *insane* friend. "How can you not trust him? Have you not seen his cheekbones? And those eyes? And pretty much his entire face? He looks like a freaking Disney prince. How can you not trust a Disney prince?"

"Pretty is as pretty does," Penny muttered, shoving dresses aside with a little too much force.

Kaylee snorted, reaching toward the rack despite the risk of losing a finger to Penny's violent sorting. She grabbed a dress and moved out of the closet so she could toss it on the growing pile on her bed. Not for the first time, Kaylee was grateful for her expansive walk-in closet. Not only did it hold her excessive amount of clothes and a truly extravagant number of shoes, but it also made it possible to give a wrathful Penny some space. The woman had pointy elbows and knew how to use them. "You're channeling your Grandma Nita again."

Yanking another dress off the rack, Penny used the hanger to point at Kaylee. "She'd totally agree with me on this. You're blinded by hormones and can't see that your prince is actually the villain—or at least the semi-villain. I deal with men like him every day. I know what I'm talking about."

Crossing her arms, Kaylee leaned her shoulder against the closet doorframe. "Do you think that maybe, just maybe, the guys you come into contact with at work are making you a little bitter and jaded? I mean, it's an emergency women's shelter. That's a pretty skewed sample of the male population."

"I'm not bitter and jaded." Penny paused before adding, "Not yet, at least. And I'm really good at spotting a toad in prince's clothing. It's my superpower."

Despite her best efforts at keeping Penny's gloom and doom from darkening her mood, doubt tugged at Kaylee. Trying to hide her sudden frown, she turned to stare at the mound of dresses on the bed, a rainbow of silky fabrics and wonderful possibilities.

The California sun streamed through the window, making the entire room glow and turning the white bedding silver around the edges. When she'd been searching for a condo two years ago, one of Kaylee's requirements had been space and light—a lot of it. After spending her childhood in a cramped Midwestern basement apartment, she couldn't get enough sunlight. Her condo was everything her home growing up had not been—warm and bright and clean. She'd spent too many years cold, poor, and helpless, and she wasn't going to go back to that...ever.

The scrape of a hanger against the rod brought her back to the present.

"It's been so long since I found a good guy," Kaylee said wistfully, keeping her gaze on the dresses. "They're out there, though, and I need to believe that Noah is one of them. After all, he invited me to his uncle Martin's house—the man who pretty much raised him. A toad wouldn't invite me home to meet his family, right? You just need to give him a chance."

Risking another glance at Penny, Kaylee hid a half smile. She knew that scowl. It meant her friend was seconds away from caving. "Please? Let me have my fairy tale for a few more dates? If he turns into a complete ass, then I'll even let you say 'I told you so' while we throw darts at his picture—the really pointy, dangerous darts that they've banned in the U.S. because too many kids lost their eyeballs. *Please?*"

"Fine," Penny grumbled. Kaylee had known that she wouldn't be able to resist. Besides peanut butter ice cream and motorcycles, Penny's favorite thing in the world was being right—and getting to crow about it. Now if Noah could keep acting like the perfect boyfriend he'd promised to be, then Penny would be proven wrong, and Kaylee's story could have a happy ending. "Here." Penny thrust a dress toward Kaylee.

"Oh, Penny...you're the best!" As soon as she accepted the hanger, Kaylee knew it was the one. The dress was simple and elegant and just perfect. Pressing it against herself, she did a little spin, her happiness bubbling out of her. The dress felt silky and sinfully good under her hand, and she couldn't help but remember all the thrift store hand-me-downs she'd worn growing up—all the thin coats and musty-smelling boots and scratchy blankets that never managed to be warm enough. The memory of that bone-deep cold was the main reason she'd fought so hard to be here in California, a place where winter never came.

Penny snorted a laugh. "What's with the dress-dancing? Are you trying to be an ethnically ambiguous Sleeping Beauty right now? Since that makes me the helpful rodent, I'm not loving this theme."

"No," Kaylee huffed, although she couldn't hold a straight face. "You're the twittery bird." Grinning, she dodged Penny's mock punch and twirled around the bedroom again. "I'm just happy. Everything is going right. I have a job I love, a home I love, a Penny I love, a dress I love, a new boyfriend I..."

Narrowing her eyes, Penny warned, "Don't say it."

Even Penny's death glare couldn't dampen Kaylee's spirits, and she laughed merrily. "A new boyfriend I could really, really come to like. How about that?"

Penny made a skeptical sound. "As long as you don't let that 'like' blind you to any creeper warning signs."

"I won't," Kaylee promised. The sunlight soaked into her skin, warming her, and she wiggled her toes in delight. It was going to be an amazing night. She could just feel it.

"You really are a Disney prince," she blurted.

Noah's eyebrows drew together even as he laughed and leaned closer so the other guests around the table couldn't hear their conversation. "What?"

"I mean, your hair alone is pretty much irrefutable evidence." Kaylee fought the urge to reach over and muss it a little. It was gold and perfect, just long enough to frame his handsome face. Sure, credit could be given to a talented and expensive stylist, but Kaylee was leaning more toward princely genes. "And you open doors and pull out chairs and—"

"That's manners, not proof that I'm animated royalty," Noah interrupted, his mouth still curled in amusement. "If I really were a prince, I would've picked you up tonight. That was very unprincely of me."

Kaylee waved off his apology as she leaned to the side, giving the server room to place a delicate cup holding her after-dinner coffee in front of her. After thanking her, Kaylee turned back to Noah. "You had a meeting, *and* you offered to send a car. I don't think that qualifies as being rude."

With a mock frown, he said, "An offer you turned down. I hate that you have to make the drive back alone."

As smitten as she was with Noah, she had to roll her eyes at that. "It's a thirty-minute drive. I'll survive." Kaylee didn't mention that the seed of doubt Penny had planted had prompted her to decline. It made her feel safer to have her own transportation, just in case. *Not that I'll need to escape*, she thought, taking in Noah's warm smile and amused blue eyes.

Noah's uncle Martin cleared his throat, drawing her attention to where he sat at the head of the table, framed by the wall of windows behind him. Darkness transformed the glass into a mirror, reflecting the enormous room back at them—as if it needed to look twice as big. The house was huge, set like an island on lush irrigated and landscaped acres. Kaylee couldn't even imagine how much the sprawling LA property was worth.

As expensive as it must have been, the decorating scheme was a little too ostentatious for Kaylee's taste, however. It felt as if everything had been chosen to impress visitors with the owner's wealth, rather than to create a home. Although Kaylee had a healthy appreciation for financial stability, she was happy just to be able to pay her mortgage and buy food and have enough left over for some really nice shoes. The pushy glamour of Noah's uncle's home left her cold.

"So, Kaylee," Martin said, jerking her out of her thoughts. She gave him a polite smile. "You work at St. Macartan's College?" Although he put a lilt at the end of the statement, it didn't sound like a question. From the look in his eyes, Kaylee was pretty sure he knew perfectly well where she worked—and a whole lot more about her. Before inviting her to their gazillion-dollar mansion, Martin had probably had her investigated to make sure she wouldn't steal the silverware.

"Yes," she said. "I'm in development."

"And how do you like that?"

"I love it." A warm glow of satisfaction filled her, as it always did when she thought about her job. "Scholarships made it possible for me to go to college." Scholarships and working her tail off, but Kaylee left off that part. It sounded too self-pitying. "Now I get to raise money so that other kids have that same opportunity."

"Sounds…noble." There was an off note to his tone that made Kaylee stiffen, even as she tried to define it. The expression on Martin's face was uncomfortably close to a sneer, with a wrinkled nose and curled upper lip that made him look like he was smelling something foul. She knew that look, had seen it thousands of times as she was growing up, but she wasn't sure why Martin was wearing it now. She braced herself, ready to defend her job or her background or her worthiness to even be in the same room as his nephew, but Martin changed the subject. "Where did you go to school?"

"University of Minnesota for my undergraduate degree, and St. Macartan's for my master's." There was a hint of challenge in her tone, but Martin didn't take her up on it. Instead, he just asked what her major had been.

The conversation continued, so polite on the surface that it made Kaylee nervous. To be honest, Martin freaked her out a little. He had that crocodile-in-disguise manner, his eyes flat and cool even as he smiled. As soon as Martin turned his attention to an older couple seated next to him, Kaylee gave a silent sigh of relief and leaned toward Noah. "Restroom?" Martin had flustered her, and she needed a minute and some privacy to remind herself that she wasn't that helpless, needy child any longer.

Noah tipped his head toward one of the doorways. "Turn left, then right; it's the third door on the right. Want me to take you?"

"Oh no." She stood, making patting motions with her hands as if to keep him in his seat. "I've got it. My sense of direction is excellent." With a teasing smile, she excused herself to the rest of the guests. It was probably her imagination, but she thought she felt Martin's sharp gaze on her back as she left the room.

Within a few minutes, she was hopelessly lost.

Kaylee made a low sound of frustration. She'd followed Noah's directions, turning left and then right, but there had only been two doors on the right in that hall. Deciding that he'd left out a third turn, she'd made her way down another hallway, which only brought her farther into a twisted maze.

"Rich people and their ginormous mansions," she muttered, deciding to just start checking rooms. There had to be a thousand bathrooms in this place, so she figured she'd eventually stumble over one. She tried several doors, most of which were locked, and the rest of which were definitely not bathrooms. As she reached for a doorknob, male voices caught her attention, and she turned toward the sound. As she rounded the corner, she saw two burly men enter a room at the very end of the hall.

"Excuse me," she called, hurrying as fast as she could on her impractical—yet very cute—shoes, but they'd already disappeared, closing the door behind them. When Kaylee reached it, she tried the knob…locked.

With a growl of impatience, she considered kicking the door, but refrained. Not only did she not know where a bathroom was, but she wasn't sure how to get back to the dining room. Annoyed with herself, she started trying doors again.

She yanked at one. The handle turned with the heavy click of an automatic lock. Kaylee frowned. Why did Martin have a room in his house that could only be opened from the outside? She pulled at it, curious. The door was heavy and resisted opening at first, but then it swung toward her. To her disappointment, it wasn't a bathroom. Instead, a flight of stairs descended to a concrete floor. She was about to allow the door to swing shut when she heard a sound.

"Hello?" she called, although her voice came out wispy. There was something about the blocky, utilitarian stairs and fluorescent lighting that gave the space an icky basement vibe. After spending her childhood in a musty lower-level apartment, she held a special abhorrence for basements.

"Help!" someone called in a hoarse voice. The hair rose on the back of her neck. "Please help us!"

The words were so unexpected, so out of place in the glamorous mansion, that it took a moment for the plea to register. Her heart rate sped up. "Who's there?" Forcing her feet forward, she descended a few steps. The door started to close, and remembering the automatic lock, she wedged her clutch purse against the jamb before releasing the door.

Her shoes sounded too loud on the steps. "Who's there? Are you hurt?"

"Down here!" The voice was rough and scratchy, the urgent tone enough to make her stomach clench. How had she gone from fairy tale to horror movie in just a few hallways? Her gaze darted toward the door, and she briefly considered running up the stairs and escaping, but she told herself firmly that she was being ridiculous. This was Martin Jovanovic's fancy-pants mansion, not a haunted house. She clomped down the remainder of the stairs with forced confidence. She was the girlfriend—well, almost-girlfriend—of the perfect man. She'd been invited to a California dream home. She belonged here, damn it. There wasn't any reason for her to feel intimidated.

Then she saw the blood.

Oddly, the first thing Kaylee felt was exasperation. Now Penny would get to say "I told you so," because her friend had been right...again. The mansion, the boyfriend, the food...everything had been too perfect, so it was time for reality to kick Kaylee in the face once again. Her gaze followed the dark-red trail across the floor until it reached the source of the blood...so much blood. Then her brain shut off as horror swamped her, rushing over her in a black wave as her lungs sucked in a huge breath, automatically preparing for a scream.

"Help," a man—although he was barely recognizable as human—gasped, startling Kaylee into swallowing her shriek and turning it into a harsh croak instead. "Please."

There were three of them, tied to chairs and facing one another in a rough triangle. Her gaze darted from one battered, blood-soaked form to the next, unable to comprehend what she was seeing. "I was just looking for a bathroom," she whispered.

A wheezing choke—was it a laugh?—came from the man whose face was so swollen that it was hard to pick out his features. A slitted, glittering eye peered at her from the wreckage. Her lungs flattened and refused to take in any air as Kaylee stared at his battered visage. Someone had done that to him, had tied him up and tortured him...someone who could be coming back at any moment. "Good thing for us. A hand?" He tilted his head toward the table that sat in the center of the small room. When she stayed frozen, he added, "If you could grab something sharp and cut us loose, we'd appreciate it."

His words were oddly polite, but they held an underlying plea that jerked Kaylee into motion. It was hard to think, to understand what was happening or what she needed to do, and she seized on his gently worded request. *Cut them free*, she mentally repeated. *Cut them free*.

Sucking in a much-needed breath, she rushed toward the table, her heels clattering against the concrete. Her body felt foreign and awkward, and her movements were jerky, as if she were a marionette with someone else controlling her strings. She stumbled to a halt next to the small folding table, and a small, near-hysterical portion of her brain noted how the cheap metal stand didn't go with the rest of Martin's decor. No wonder he hid it in the basement.

Stop. Don't freak out. Just breathe.

She forced herself to focus on the task at hand. As her brain registered what the items on the table were, what horrific things the knives and pliers and hammer and—*oh shit*—the *ice pick* had been used to do, she couldn't stop from returning her gaze to the first man's ravaged face. He tried to smile at her, but the result was macabre.

"It's okay, sweetheart," he said, but tension lay beneath his soothing tone. "Anything with a sharp edge will work. Let's get out of here, huh?"

His last sentence echoed in her mind, reminding her that the people who'd done this could walk in at any time. With a hunted glance at the stairs, she grabbed a small but wicked-looking knife from the table, forcing her brain to ignore how sticky the floor was beneath her shoes, or the purpose of the other tools lined up neatly, ready to be used again in an instant. She kept herself focused as she started cutting the zip ties securing the first man to his chair.

"You're an angel," he said as the knife sliced through the binding around his wrist. The zip tie popped open, revealing a bloody groove where it had been. Her gaze fixed on his wrist, on that evidence that he'd struggled against his bonds. She was unable to look away from the gory sight until he cleared his throat.

Kaylee jolted at the sound, fumbling and almost dropping the knife. Recovering her grip, she squeezed the handle tightly as she gave herself a mental smack. *Get it together, Kay*, she commanded, reaching for the tie on his other wrist. When she noticed how badly she was shaking, though, she stopped before she accidentally cut him.

"You've got this, angel," the man said, and his calm assurance helped. Taking a deep breath, she steadied her hand enough to slip the tip of the knife under the plastic tie. When she pulled up, it opened with a *pop*. His ankles were easier, and she cut his legs free in seconds before hastily backing up several steps. She almost felt like she'd opened the cage of a circus lion. Would he reward her help or just eat her?

"Thanks, angel." The man stood and immediately moved to the table. Although he stumbled, his legs wobbling beneath him, he managed to stay on his feet. Grabbing another knife—this one much scarier-looking than Kaylee's—he moved to the second man and cut his hands free. As he worked, she stared, wondering if she'd made a horrendous mistake. Two out of the three were free. What if they were dangerous criminals? What if they hurt her—or killed her? She was so worried about the return of the torturers, but what if the biggest threat was already in the room with her?

She pushed away the doubt. It was too late to worry about that now. If the men did try to hurt her, they looked to be in bad enough shape that she was pretty sure she could outrun them.

Kaylee forced her body into jerky motion. She headed toward the last guy, who was slumped to the side, only his bonds keeping him semi-upright. He was limp and still, his head lolling to the side as blood ran from his ear and across his cheek before it dripped steadily on the floor. Kaylee seized on the fact that he was still bleeding. Dead people didn't bleed, did they?

"Please be alive. Please be alive," she pleaded almost soundlessly. Kaylee sawed at the zip tie securing his hands until the plastic separated and released suddenly. His arms flopped to hang by his sides. Without the restraints holding him, he started to slide sideways, heading toward the floor.

With a squeak of alarm, Kaylee tried to catch him, but his deadweight—*no! His* unconscious *weight*—brought her to the floor with him. She put out a hand, trying to catch herself, but her palm slid across wet concrete. Her hip and then her head hit the floor painfully, and the man's limp body fell heavily across her legs, pinning her. For several seconds, she lay still, stunned.

Then the weight disappeared from her legs, jerking her back to reality. The first man was pulling his unconscious friend's arm over his shoulder. The second supported the unresponsive man's other side.

Her gaze landed on his face, and she flinched so violently that the back of her head bumped against the floor again. There was a gory mess where one of his eyes should have been. Bile rose in her throat, forcing her to swallow several times. Barely able to keep from vomiting, Kaylee ripped her gaze away from the empty, bloody socket.

"Up you go, Angel." The man with the swollen face offered the hand not holding on to his unconscious buddy. When she grabbed it, he pulled her up, almost lifting her to her feet, and she scrambled to get her wobbly legs to support her. "Let's get out before our *friends* come back, yeah?"

Kaylee couldn't speak. The best she could do was a jerky nod as she moved to follow the trio. The stairs were too narrow for three big guys to stay side by side, so they were forced to turn sideways. The unconscious man's boots struck the edges of the treads, and each thud made Kaylee flinch as she climbed the steps behind them. Every sound seemed thunderous, too loud to not be heard everywhere in the mansion, and each step they made, each inch farther that the men dragged their unconscious friend, felt horribly, painfully slow.

When they finally reached the door, all the air left Kaylee so quickly and completely that her head spun. After a quick glance into the hall, the men slipped through the doorway. Kaylee hurried up the final few steps, not wanting to be left behind. The thought of being trapped alone in the bloody basement made her stumble forward, rushing to flatten her hands against the opened door.

The man with the swollen face glanced at her as he

hitched the unconscious man higher. "Better not go back to the party like that."

Confused, Kaylee glanced down and saw that, on her hip, a white section of her color-block dress was now smeared with dark red. *Blood*. The salmon she'd eaten earlier threatened to climb back in her throat.

"You have a car here?" he asked.

She stared at him without seeing his face. All she could see was blood. It was only after he repeated the question that it finally penetrated. Kaylee nodded.

"Head that way." He jerked his head to the left. "Turn right at the T, and you'll get to some stairs. They'll take you to a back entrance."

"What about you?" Her voice was a husky imitation of its usual self. Her throat felt as rough and sore as if she'd actually been screaming the entire time, instead of just wanting to. "How are you getting out?"

His half grin contorted his abused face, twisting the cuts and bruises and making his eyes almost disappear. "We're going out the *other* back door. Good luck, Angel." He and the other man started making their painful-looking progress in the opposite direction, the unconscious guy slumped between them, his boots dragging across the polished hardwood floor.

The sight of them walking away, leaving her alone, sent a surge of panic through her. She had to bite the inside of her lower lip to keep from calling after them. They were strangers, but it had felt like they'd been on her side. Now she was on her own.

At the thought, the voice in her head screamed at her to get out of the nightmare house. As she moved out of the doorway, Kaylee stepped on something and stumbled slightly. She glanced down and saw her silver clutch. Her fuzzy brain wondered how it got on the floor, until she recalled that she'd used it to prop open the door. Automatically, she bent to grab it.

Once it was in her hands, she remembered that it held her phone. "I can call the police," she called in a carrying whisper to the retreating men.

They stopped abruptly. "Won't help," the one missing an eye said. His voice was raspy, too, and she wondered if he *had* been screaming. The thought made her shudder. "The Jovanovics have deep pockets and a wide reach. Just get out and get far away from these people."

It felt wrong, not calling for help, and Kaylee's fingers tightened around her clutch. Urgency was building in her, panic expanding like air inside a balloon, stretching her tighter and tighter. She needed to get out before she broke. Turning away from the men, she hurried in the opposite direction. It was hard to believe that Noah's family had the entire police force on their payroll, but she'd wait to contact them, just in case. Later, after the men had a chance to get out and she was safe, Kaylee would call. The thought of being out of this nightmare mansion, of being home, made her hurry her steps.

As she reached the end of the hall, she snuck a quick glance behind her. The men were nowhere to be seen. Sucking in a shaky breath, she turned right toward the stairs…and what she hoped was safety. She refused to think about how she'd gotten so terribly lost in the rabbit warren of a mansion just a short time earlier, or about how easy it would be to get turned around again. The thought of running through Martin's gilded house, frightened and trapped, made her throat close. There was a door right in front of her, but would it lead to escape or a continuation of her waking nightmare?

Turning the knob with shaking fingers, she didn't know whether to be grateful or scared that it wasn't locked. The door opened to a neatly kept yard, lit by an almost-full moon and discreet landscape lights. She was out. Relief flooded her, even as a hundred other emotions—fear and paranoia and horror—pounded through her veins. The cool night air felt good on her flushed cheeks, and Kaylee bent at the waist, trying to catch her breath and make her brain reboot. A revolving chain of images flashed in her mind—blood and knives and the one man's ravaged, empty eye socket. Her next inhale sounded like a sob, and she forced herself to stand up straight.

There was no time to fall apart. She was out of the house, but Kaylee definitely wasn't safe yet. Even though he'd been sitting innocently at the dining table with her and the rest of his guests all evening, Uncle Martin had to have given the order for those men to be tortured. After all, they were in his house. Her memory of his flat stare seemed even more menacing now, and she hurried to follow a flagstone path that led to the front of the house.

With every step, Kaylee's shocked brain was tuning back in to reality, her fear spiraling into panic. Surely they would've noticed her extended absence by now. What if the men's escape had been discovered? How fast would they put the two together?

Her breaths were getting quicker, louder, and she forced herself to slow. Hyperventilating until she passed out was not a good escape plan. In fact, it was a very *bad* escape plan. When the panicked haze had cleared slightly, she hurried along the path again. Her shoes were loud on the flagstones, and she shifted her weight to the balls of her feet.

The path ended at the entrance to what looked like a garage. Kaylee wasn't about to go through another unknown door leading to who-knew-what horrors, so she turned, stepping onto the grass and staying close to the exterior of the building.

Her heels sank into the soft, sprinkler-fed lawn, and she shifted to her toes again. A light flickered to life right above her, and she froze, feeling like she was a cat burglar caught by a police spotlight. Clenching her jaw against the need to scream, she looked away from the glare, not wanting to lose her night vision.

No one yelled or chased her or shot her or did any of the horrible things she was expecting. Instead, the night remained quiet except for the chirping and buzzing of nocturnal wild things.

Must be motion-activated, she decided, and her pent-up breath escaped in a whoosh. All the creatures around her went silent, and she hesitated again, hoping her relieved sigh hadn't been loud enough to catch someone's attention. A small walkway peeked from around a corner, taunting her with its normalcy.

She forced her feet forward, heading toward the small paved path. As she rounded the corner, Kaylee could see the lights from the front of the estate. She was hit by concurrent feelings of hope and fear, the need to get into a populated spot warring with the panic that someone knew, that she would be grabbed as soon as she stepped into the closest puddle of light—grabbed and brought to that horrible basement room. This time, she'd be the one tied to the chair, the one with the swollen face and empty eye socket and—

It was too much. Kaylee turned off her brain and jogged toward the front entrance, silently praying as hard as she could. The valet startled as Kaylee walked toward him. She'd lengthened her stride and was trying to project confidence, although she didn't know if she was succeeding.

"Can I...help you?" the valet asked, his voice squeaking a little in the middle, even though he looked many years past puberty.

"Yes, please." *Oh God, not the quivery voice!* Kaylee pinched her arm hard, trying to shove back the tears. All that did was make her want to cry harder. "Could you get my car? It's the Infiniti Q50. And hurry? Please?"

Instead of running off like a good valet, he visibly swallowed and took a step closer. "Are you okay?"

"Yes, I just...I need to leave." Her brain frantically grabbed for an excuse to explain why she was running out of Martin Jovanovic's mansion, shaking and near tears and covered in blood—*oh God, the blood*. How could she explain the blood? Quickly, she shoved her hands behind her back and hoped that the stains on her dress wouldn't be that noticeable in the poor light. "My boyfriend's been cheating on me, so I broke up with him, but he'll be following me, and I need to be gone before he makes it out here and tries to convince me that he's the perfect guy that I thought he was, so if you could hurry, that would be great, and then you won't have to watch a really uncomfortable scene with yelling and tears and drama, okay?"

The valet blinked rapidly before turning and jogging away. Kaylee hoped he was heading toward the parked cars and not just running away from the crazy girl. Now that she was alone with only night sounds and the fading footsteps of the valet, she could hear her heartbeat pattering in her ears. She was breathing too fast, each inhale catching on a tiny bit of a sob.

"Calm down," she muttered. "Calm down, calm down, calm do—"

Someone grabbed her arm and yanked her toward the house.

"No."

Hugh didn't think he'd ever seen Blessard so angry, not even when he'd discovered the Tight-Buns Tommy blow-up doll dressed in his uniform sitting at his desk. "But, LT, the Rack and Ruin MC will be passing through town in less than an hour. No question they'll be hauling coke from Denver to Dresden."

"I know this," Blessard snapped. "The question is, how do you know this? You're on mandatory medical leave. You have a goddamned bullet hole in your goddamned leg. Your duty weapon and your radio are locked in my desk. Want to tell me, Murdoch, how you still know every word that comes out of the dispatchers' mouths?"

"Guess I just have a sixth sense for when I'm needed?" From the way Blessard's face went from dark red to purple, Hugh figured that the lieutenant didn't care for his answer. "Forget how I heard about it. The

R and Rs are going to have twenty or so riders, plus support vehicles. Lexi's our only narcotic-detection dog, and there's not enough time to borrow a K9 from Denver. Even if they left now, they couldn't get here in less than an hour. Let us help, LT. My leg's fine. It's a waste having us sit at home, watching daytime television. Besides, there are only so many episodes of *Tattered Hearts* that I can stand without losing my mind."

His lieutenant's face showed no sympathy. "If you show up on scene, Officer Murdoch, I will arrest you." The corner of his mouth twitched. "And your little dog, too."

"Really, LT?" Frustration nipped at Hugh, making it hard to stay silent, even though he knew he'd lost the battle already. "*Wizard of Oz* jokes? Way to add insult to injury."

All hints of humor disappeared from Blessard's face. "Do not go to this call, Officer. You have three more weeks before we'll even consider letting you return to desk duty, and that's with a doctor's okay. Until then, if you even *think* about popping up at another call uninvited, I'm going to add another mandatory month to your leave. Got it?"

Blowing out a hard breath, Hugh resisted the urge to continue arguing. It was done. If he kept pushing, he knew he'd risk not only missing the next seven weeks of calls, but his job with the Monroe Police Department. "Fine."

"Now get out of my office."

As he drove away from the station, Hugh glanced at Lexi, who was riding shotgun. "Where are we headed?

Home?" He grimaced at the idea. "Nah. I'd just pace and then bitch because my leg is sore. Besides, *Tattered Hearts* is a rerun today." Lexi turned her head, her attention caught by something in the VFW's parking lot. "Good idea, Lex. Let's go bug Jules. If she's not working today, we'll just get food. It'll be a win-win."

He parked in front of the VFW and turned off the engine. Silence settled over the lot. The back of his neck prickled, and Hugh rubbed it, fighting the urge to turn and look out the back window of his pickup. He knew what he'd see if he did—absolutely nothing. Apparently, a side effect of getting shot in the leg was paranoia.

In the seat next to him, Lexi growled.

"Seriously? Are we having a mutual psychotic break, then?" he grumbled, although he followed his K9 partner's gaze across the VFW parking lot and saw exactly what he expected: *nothing*. Rolling down his window, he listened. The street was as still and quiet as it always was so early in the morning. All he could hear out his open window was the first twittering of dawn birdsong and the howling, ever-present wind.

Several businesses had already closed for the winter, and the buildings looked abandoned. The town emptied out every fall, occupants and tourists fleeing to ski towns or warm beaches to escape the cold and storms. Hugh couldn't blame them. As one of the few year-round police officers in Monroe, Colorado, he could attest that the place got pretty dull in the winter, when the few hard-core residents who remained got snowed in on a regular basis. With mountain passes bookending the town, the highway in either direction was closed more often than not.

The blackened ruin of the town diner a few buildings down from the VFW added to the post-apocalyptic feel. After an explosion destroyed it a few weeks earlier, the diner's owner had moved into the VFW temporarily so that the Monroe residents weren't forced to go without their morning eggs and coffee. She was planning to rebuild the diner, but the work wouldn't start until spring. The construction crews abandoned town before winter just as quickly as everyone else.

Hugh frowned at the front of the VFW. Things had gone to hell over the past month. He missed the diner. In fact, he missed a lot of things he'd taken for granted a month ago: sitting in his usual booth, going to work, being pain free.

After checking to make sure Lexi's window fan was on, he headed toward the VFW entrance. His scalp and the back of his neck began to prickle again, warning him that there were eyes on him. Slowing his stride, he surreptitiously glanced around, checking the surrounding buildings and the street.

No one was there.

Everything was silent, as if even the ever-present wind was holding its breath. The scuff of his boots against the pavement sounded too loud, and he stopped, this time not caring who saw him looking around. Nothing was moving, though. The entire town was still.

With a swallowed groan, he turned back toward the VFW. He'd been sensing these phantom stalkers for days now. Boredom and inactivity were obviously driving him insane. He'd only taken one more step toward the makeshift diner when Lexi started barking. Pivoting, he half jogged, half limped toward his truck. It was one thing to ignore his own instincts, but there was no way he was going to ignore Lexi's. His partner was never wrong.

At the truck, he hurried to attach her lead to her harness, clipping it to the ring he used when they were going to do a search. Lexi quivered with anticipation, already in drive and ready to go.

As soon as he stepped back and gave the command, she was bounding toward the building across the street. It was a historic brick building that had been a bank at one point. Now, it housed a laundromat—closed for the winter—on the first level and several offices above.

When Lexi led him to the alley behind the building, Hugh was relieved. Without a uniform or a badge, snooping around the front of the laundromat was likely to attract suspicion from passersby. His relief disappeared, however, when Lexi led him to a back door and promptly sat, looking at him expectantly, waiting for him to open the door so she could continue tracking.

The door was locked. Hugh pulled his phone from his pocket but then hesitated. Everyone else was dealing with the Rack and Ruin bust. He wasn't chasing a suspect or following a confirmed tip; he wasn't even on duty. All he had was his K9 partner tracking an unknown scent. If this caused officers to be pulled off the drug bust, he could be endangering lives. They needed all the help they could get with that motorcycle club.

Dropping his phone back in his pocket, he pulled out his lockpick set.

His uncle Gavin had taught him how to open his first lock when Hugh was eight. It was the bathroom door, so it wasn't the trickiest of locks, but they'd moved on to the front door dead bolt next. After that, Gavin had shown him the trick to opening school lockers, handcuffs, and car doors before he'd advanced to disabling alarm systems.

Uncle Gavin was currently serving a fifteen-year sentence at Colorado State Penitentiary for second-degree burglary. When Hugh was eleven, he'd been home when the cops had come for Gavin the first time. After the arrest, one of the officers had walked over to where a terrified Hugh had been watching on the front steps. The policeman had sat down next to Hugh, given him a rub-on tattoo of a badge, and explained the importance of leaving other people's stuff alone. When the cops had left with Gavin, Hugh had decided to become a police officer. After all, the front of the squad car seemed like a much better place to be than the back.

As Hugh casually glanced over his shoulder, checking to make sure the coast was clear, he gave silent thanks for Uncle Gavin's lessons. The dead bolt was a simple single-cylinder style, something he could've handled with a couple of bobby pins. With his professional torque and pick, it only took seconds for Hugh to gently press the keyhole pins into place and unlock the door.

After another quick look around, he turned the knob and slipped into a small, dim entry. Lexi brushed past his leg in her eagerness to get inside and immediately trotted up the stairs. Drawing his gun, Hugh followed, keeping his footsteps as quiet as possible.

At the top of the stairs, Lexi took a left. Hugh paused, looking at the three closed doors to the right. Someone could be hiding in one of those offices, and Hugh didn't want to turn his back until he checked them. His hand tightened on the leash as the impatient dog hauled against him in her hurry to follow the scent. An almost silent command brought her back to him, albeit reluctantly, and they headed down the hall to the right. Keeping an eye out for anything behind them, he listened as he walked softly toward the first closed door. All he heard was the click of Lexi's nails and the occasional creaks of the elderly wood floors under his weight.

The first knob resisted turning under his grip. Locked. He tried the second and the third. Both were locked as well. Only then did he allow Lexi to lead them down the hallway in the other direction. She surged forward eagerly and sat in front of the first door on the right.

This doorknob turned easily under his fingers. Pushing open the door, he stepped into the room in the same movement, gun up and ready, turning right and then pivoting to the left to check the entire space.

It was empty. The small area had been an office at some point, but now the only evidence of its former occupation was the cables that snaked out of the wall, the ends sprawled uselessly into dust and cobwebs. The dirty blinds were down, but the slats were at an angle, as if someone wanted to look outside without anyone being able to see in.

Lexi trotted to the window, sniffing along the baseboard. As he moved to follow, Hugh noticed the dust on the floor was smudged. There weren't any shoe prints that he could make out. Instead, it looked more like someone had knelt or sat next to the window. He walked to the spot where the dust had been rubbed away and looked around the room. There were other marks in the dust, including where his own boots had scuffed, but nothing as distinct as the area where he stood. Hugh crouched awkwardly, extending his injured leg out straight, and peered through the slats of the blinds.

He had a clear view of the VFW parking lot and the top of his pickup.

A door slammed. Shoving to his feet and ignoring the spike of pain in his thigh, Hugh ran out of the room. Lexi quickly took the lead as they tore through the hallway and down the stairs. Hugh shoved the door open, and he and Lexi tumbled out into the sunshine.

Squinting as his eyes struggled to adjust to the brightness after the dim, dusty interior of the building, Hugh swiveled his head back and forth, looking for whoever had just exited the building. There was no sign of anyone, no sound, not even a chirp of a bird. Lexi wasn't hauling on her leash. Instead, she made uncertain circles, facing one direction and then another. Hugh swore under his breath.

Whoever had been in that building, whoever'd been *watching* him, was long gone.

ABOUT THE AUTHOR

When she's not writing, KATIE RUGGLE rides horses, shoots guns, and trains her three dogs. A police academy graduate, Katie readily admits she's a forensics nerd. While she still misses her off-grid home in the Rocky Mountains, she now lives in a 150-year-old Minnesota farmhouse near her family.

ROCKY MOUNTAIN BOUNTY HUNTERS

Four bounty-hunter sisters track down bad guys, kick butt, take names, and solve the mystery of their family's downfall...claiming their own happily ever after along the way.

Coming soon from award-winning author Katie Ruggle!

SEARCH AND RESCUE

In the Rockies, lives depend on the
Search & Rescue brotherhood. But this far
off the map, secrets can be murder.

By Katie Ruggle

Hold Your Breath

Louise "Lou" Sparks is a hurricane—a
walking disaster. And with her, ice
diving captain Callum Cook has never
felt more alive...even if keeping her
safe may just kill him.

Fan the Flames

Firefighter and Motorcycle Club
member Ian Walsh rides the line
between the good guys and the bad.
But if a killer has his way, Ian will
take the fall for a murder he didn't
commit...and lose the woman he's
always loved.

Gone Too Deep

George Halloway is a mystery. Tall. Dark. Intense. But city girl Ellie Price will need him by her side if she wants to find her father...and live to tell the tale.

In Safe Hands

Deputy Sheriff Chris Jennings has always been a hero to agoraphobe Daisy Little, but one wrong move ended their future before it could begin. Now he'll do whatever it takes to keep her safe—even if that means turning against one of his own.

"Vivid and charming."

—**Charlaine Harris, #1 *New York Times* bestselling author of the Sookie Stackhouse series**

ROCKY MOUNTAIN K9 UNIT

These K9 officers and their trusty dogs will do anything to protect the women in their lives.

By Katie Ruggle

Run to Ground

K9 officer Theo Bosco lost his mentor, his K9 partner, and nearly his will to live. But when a ruthless killer targets a woman on the run, Theo and his new K9 companion will do whatever it takes to save the woman neither can live without.

On the Chase

Injured in the line of duty, K9 officer Hugh Murdoch's orders are simple: stay alive. But when a frightened woman bursts into his life, Hugh and his K9 companion have no choice but to risk everything to keep her safe.